Oh, Play That Thing

Roddy Doyle

Oh, Play That Thing

Volume Two of
THE LAST ROUNDUP

JONATHAN CAPE
LONDON

Published by Jonathan Cape 2004

2 4 6 8 10 9 7 5 3 1

First published in Great Britain in 2004 by Jonathan Cape
Random House, 20 Vauxhall Bridge Road, London SW1V 2SA

The Random House Group Limited Reg. No. 954009
www.randomhouse.co.uk

A CIP catalogue record for this book is available from the British Library

ISBN 0-224-07436-9 (Hardback)
ISBN 0-224-07443-1 (Trade Paperback)

Typeset by Palimpsest Book Production Ltd, Polmont, Stirlingshire
Printed and bound in Great Britain by Clays Ltd, St Ives plc

PERMISSIONS

'Macushla' by MacMurrough/Rowe © Copyright 1910 by Boosey & Co (London) Ltd.
Reproduced by permission of Boosey & Hawkes Music Publishers Ltd.

'Five Foot Two, Eyes of Blue (Has Anybody Seen My Girl)'. Words by Samuel
M Lewis and Joe Young/Music by Ray Henderson © 1925 Leo Fiest Inc and
Warock Corp. Redwood Music Ltd., London, NW1 8BD for the Commonwealth
of Nations, Germany, Austria, Switzerland, South Africa and Spain.

'Hobo, You Can't Ride This Train'. Words & Music by Shapiro & Bernstein © Copyright
1930 Shapiro, Bernstein & Co Limited. All Rights Reserved. International Copyright Secured.

'Irish Black Bottom'. Words & Music by Louis Armstrong & Percy Venable © Copyright 1925
Universal/ MCA Music Limited. All Rights Reserved. International Copyright Secured.

'Tight Like This'. Words & Music by Louis Armstrong & Langston Curl © Copyright 1923
Universal/MCA Music Limited. All Rights Reserved. International Copyright Secured.

'Sweethearts On Parade'. Words by Charles Newman and Music by Carmen
Lombardo © 1928, Edwin H Morris & Co Inc, USA. Reproduced by permission of
Francis Day & Hunter Ltd, London WC2H 0QY.

'When You're Smiling (The Whole World Smiles With You)'. Words and Music by Mark Fisher,
Joe Goodwin and Larry Shay © 1928, EMI Mills Music Inc, USA. Reproduced by permission
of B Feldman & Co Ltd, London WC2H 0QY.

'I Can't Give You Anything But Love'. Words by Dorothy Fields and Music by Jimmy McHugh ©
1928, EMI Mills Music Inc/ Cotton Club Publishing, USA. Reproduced by permission of Lawrence
Wright Music Co Ltd/ EMI Music Publishing Ltd, London WC2H 0QY.

'You Rascal You'. Words and Music by Sam Theard © 1931, EMI Mills Music Inc, USA.
Reproduced by permission of EMI Music Publishing Ltd, London WC2H 0QY.

'Russian Lullaby'. Words and Music by Irving Berlin © 1927, Irving Berlin Inc, USA.
Reproduced by permission of Francis Day & Hunter Ltd, London WC2H 0QY.

'St Louis Blues'. Words and Music by W C Handy © 1914, Handy Brothers Music Co. Inc
New York, NY. Reproduced by permission of Francis Day & Hunter Ltd, London WC2H 0QY.

'Shine'. Words by Cecil Mack and Lew Brown and Music by Ford T Dabney © 1924,
Shapiro Bernstein & Co Inc, USA. Reproduced by permission of EMI Music Publishing Ltd,
London WC2H 0QY.

'The Man Who Owns Broadway'. Words and Music by George M Cohan © 1909, E B Marks
Music Corp, USA. Reproduced by permission of B Feldman & Co Ltd, London WC2H 0QY.

Judgment Day by James T. Farrell. Reproduced by permission of Cleo Paturis.

This book is dedicated to
Stephen Byrne

One never knows, do one?

Fats Waller

PART ONE

1

I could bury myself in New York. I could see that from the boat as it went under the Statue of Liberty on a cold dawn that grew quickly behind me and shoved the fog off the slate-coloured water. That was Manhattan, already towering over me. It made tiny things of the people around me, all gawking at the manmade cliffs, and the ranks of even higher cliffs behind them, stretching forever into America and stopping their entry. I could see the terror in their eyes.

I could stare into the eyes without fear of recognition. They weren't Irish faces and it wasn't Irish muck on the hems of their greatcoats. Those coats had been dragged across Europe. They were families, three and four generations of them; the Irish travelled alone. There were the ancient women, their faces collapsed and vicious, clutching bags they'd carried across the continent, full of string and eggshells and stones from the walls of lost houses. And their husbands behind them, hidden by beards, their eyes still young and fighting. They guarded the cases and boxes at their feet. And their sons and daughters, grandsons and granddaughters, under embroidered scarves and black caps, and younger children still, and pregnant girls with scrawny boys standing and sitting beside them, all cowed by the approaching city cliffs. Even the youngest sensed that their excitement was unwanted and stayed silent, as the *Reliance* sent small waves against Bedloe's Island and the big stone American woman – *send these, the homeless, tempest-tost to me* – as their parents and grandparents shivered at the new world and tried to know if they were looking at its front or back. I was the only man alone, the only man not afraid of what was growing up in front of us. This was where a man could disappear, could die if he wanted to, and come back to quick, big life.

I had arrived.

But we turned from Manhattan and sailed, almost back into the night, towards the New Jersey shore. And the silence around me fell deeper as the island crept up in front of us. The last few square feet of the old, cruel world, the same name in all the languages on board as we were pulled closer and closer, *isola delle lagrime, Tränen Insel*, the isle of tears. Ellis Island.

Hundreds of shuffling feet trapped under the vaulted ceiling of the great hall, the air was full of the whispers of the millions who'd passed through, the cries of the thousands who'd been stopped and sent back. I listened for the tap of a famous leg, but I heard none. Old men tried to straighten long-crooked backs and mothers rubbed rough colour into the white cheeks of their children. Wild men ran fingers through long beards and regretted that they hadn't shaved before they'd disembarked. Jewish women caressed sons' ringlets and tried to push them under hats. Fragments of new language were tried, and passed from mouth to mouth.

—Yes, sir.

—No, sir.

—My cousin, he have a house.

—I am a farmer.

—Qu-eeeens.

The medical inspector stared into my eyes. I knew what he was looking for. I'd been told all about it, by a lame and wheezy anarchist who was making his seventh try at landing.

—They see the limp but never the brain, he'd said. —The fools. When they confront the fact that I am too dangerous for their country, then I will happily turn my back on it. But, until then, I commute between Southampton and their Ellis Island.

—If you could afford first or second class, I told him, —you wouldn't have to set foot on the island.

—You think I am not aware of this? he said. —I can afford it. But I *won't* afford it.

The inspector was looking for signs of trachoma in my eyes, and for madness behind them. He couldn't stare for long – no one could; he saw nothing that was going to send me back. To my left, another inspector drew a large L on a shoulder with a brand new piece of chalk. L was for lung. I knew the signs; I'd been seeing them all my life. The man with the brand new L had already given up. He collapsed and coughed out most of his remaining life. He had to be carried away. An E on the shoulder meant bad eyes, another L meant lameness. And behind those letters, other hidden letters, never chalked onto shoulders: J for too Jewish, C for Chinese, SE, too far south and east of Budapest. H was for heart, SC was for scalp, X was for mental.

And H was for handsome.

The guards stood back and I walked the few steps to the next desk. I let my heels clip the Spanish tiles. Two beautiful sisters held each other as they were pushed back. Without parents or children they were too likely to fall into bad hands waiting for them on the Manhattan or New Jersey wharfs. If they were lucky they'd be kept on the island until relatives were found to take them; less lucky, they'd be pawed, then let through; less lucky still, they'd be deported, sent back before they'd arrived.

I handed my passport and papers to the Immigration Bureau officer. He opened the passport and found the ten-dollar note I'd left in its centre. The note was gone before I saw it missing. I'd taken it from the wheezy anarchist; its loss didn't sting. Then came the catechism, the questions I couldn't get wrong.

—What is your name?

—Henry Drake.

—Where are you from?

—London.

—Why have you come to the United States?

—Opportunity.

So far, so easy.

But he stopped. He looked at me.

—Where are you travelling from, sir? he asked me.

It wasn't one of the questions.

—London, I said.

He seemed to be staring at the word as I spoke it.

—You are a born Englishman, sir?

He read my latest name.

—Mister Drake?

—Yes.

—Henry Drake.

—Yes.

—And where is Missis Drake, sir?

—She's in my dreams.

—So you're travelling alone, sir, is that right? You are an unmarried man.

—That's right.

—And how do you intend supporting yourself, sir?

3

We were back on track.

—By working very hard.

—Yes, and how, sir?

—I'm a salesman.

—And your speciality?

I shrugged.

—Everything, and anything.

—Alright. And do you have sufficient funds to sustain you until you commence selling everything?

—I do.

He handed me a sheet of paper.

—Could you read this for me, sir?

—We, the people of the United States, in order to form a more perfect union—

And as I strolled through the literacy test, I could feel Victor, my brother, beside me, his leg pressed against mine in the school desk, and Miss O'Shea at my shoulder, my teacher and wife, the mother of the daughter I suddenly missed, her wet fingers on my cheek.

—and secure the blessings of liberty to ourselves and our posterity, do ordain and establish this Constitution of—

He took the paper from my fingers. He picked up a rubber stamp and brought it down on top of a card. I read the stamp: ADMITTED.

—Welcome to America, he said.

It was America, not just the U.S.A. America was bigger than the states, bigger than the world. America was everything possible.

He handed me the passport and registration card, then held them back.

—But you'd want to work on your accent, sir. *Slán leat.**

That shook me, but only until I climbed the last few steps and walked out into my first American sunshine. And another accent hit me.

—Speakee American, bub?

—Fuck off.

—That answers my question, I guess, said the shark.

He was there to hijack the new Americans milling around and past me, train tickets pinned to their lapels, registration cards held in their teeth, their hands busy with cases and bags. He must have been good, this lad, to be allowed on the island, right under

* Goodbye.

4

the portico. I studied him closely, the movie suit, the hat, the hidden accent. I handed him my cardboard suitcase. It was empty. I didn't look back but I heard him weigh its hollowness and lob it into the water. I took out my passport, to send it the same way. Then I changed my mind. I turned back.

—Hey, I said. —Want to buy a passport?

He put his hands in his pockets and pulled out forty or fifty passports.

—Your turn to fuck off, bub, he said.

I waved, turned and skimmed the passport onto the river. I watched it gather water and sink.

I was a clean sheet.

It was the 16th of March, 1924, two years since I'd sailed out of Dublin.

I looked back at the last of Dublin and, soon enough, there was no land and the boat was just a thing on the sea. I stood on the deck, my back against the cold iron wall for all the rolling night and I watched trenchcoated men watching me, and other men watching them. I saw the swing that a gun gives to a coat, and the shine that fear gives to the eyes. I was still in Ireland, still a man on the run.

And Liverpool was worse. I'd thought the place would soak me up, but not a chance. At every corner, in every doorway. Distance didn't matter. They were always there before me. Ready for the chance to hit. I could never stop and know that I'd escaped.

I walked deeper into England. I found rooms in Blackburn, Bradford, Warrington. I found work and women but eventually, always, I had to move. A head turning, eyes staring, at everything but me; a face I'd last seen looking across Mary Street after I'd read my death sentence on a piece of paper.

I stayed out of the towns and went into the mountains. I stopped at farmhouses and did the work I'd learnt in Roscommon. The farmers admired my strength, but they weren't happy. My accent and unwillingness to use it made them nervous. They saw their wives and daughters glaring at me and knew that I was dangerous. I moved again, and again.

A man called Smith took me on just as his sheep were about to drop their lambs. He'd no daughter and his wife was dead; he could ignore the urge to look up whenever I walked past him. I

5

liked Smith. I liked the cold up there and I liked the work. I thought I'd stay there until my head was clear of gunmen.

I was on Smith's rented hillside one night in early March, all night dragging lambs and their mothers out of snow with hands so cold they could feel no wool. I pushed open the door and walked into his kitchen an hour after dawn and, this time, he did look up.

He looked, and looked away.

—There were people looking for you, he said.

—People?

—Men, he said. —From your country. In a motor car.

—Did they say anything?

—No. Only. Are you Henry Smart?

—Yes.

—Yes, he said. —It was you they were looking for. I told them I didn't know you.

—Thank you, I said. —I'll go.

—Yes, he said. —I'll give you your money.

He stood up and went further into the house, to where he had his money hidden. He came back with a five-pound note, a lot more than he owed me.

—Those men. They want to kill you, do they?

—Yes.

—Stay until you're ready to go.

—Thanks.

—I had three sons, he said.

—I'm sorry, I said. —The war?

—Yes, he said. —The war. Go when you think it's best.

I left when it was dark. I stayed well off the roads and climbed through drifts of snow. Sometimes I could feel the earth hard under my boots. Other times I climbed shifting mountains, like slow waves in a black storm. But the thought of the men in the car gave me the anger and heat to melt a path in front of me. They weren't going to stop me and they wouldn't make me kill them. I'd been the expendable fool for years, the man who'd hopped when his betters called. No more. I was going to get away from that, even if I had to be buried. And I'd do the fuckin' burying, not them.

The river threw rubbish at the slick plank walls – torn vegetables, pale and soaked, squashed fruit, dead fish. And some of the new Americans looked down at the soup and were weak, almost angry at the thought that their new home could afford such waste.

The ferry from the island emptied the people, their bags and boxes, onto the crowded slip – pimps, cousins, conmen, housekeepers looking for kitchen staff.

—Need somewhere to stay?

—No.

—Need a job? Good money?

—Got a sister?

I climbed in among sacks and children, and the train brought me, slowly, to the heart of Manhattan. Through steam and whirling smoke and breath that licked the carriage window, I watched thick cables lifting girders, and I saw men riding the girders, taking on the sky, specks of men, but men like me, rising over the smoke, taking the freedom of the air. I leaned into Manhattan, pushed my weight against the train's fat crawl.

And I pushed through the beams of solid sunlight that hung from windows high above me, in the great hall of Grand Central Terminal. I looked around and swam in the noise. It was a long walk to the steps and the clock right over me – 2.47p.m. – and I was out again, out into the crazy air, and 42nd Street.

No ocean, no edges, no return.

I climbed into the back of a waiting cab. The driver spoke over his shoulder.

—Where to?

—I want an American suit, I told him.

—Suit?

I had the rest of the anarchist's cash burning a hole in the pocket of my old one.

—American, I told him. —A good one.

—Man wants a good suit, I'll take that man to the man who'll give him his suit.

—And after the suit, I want Douglas Fairbanks.

—*The Thief of Baghdad*? he said. —It's the latest.

—Sounds like my kind of town.

—The Grand Opera House sound good?

—Does it show the pictures?

—Well, it certainly don't show opera. I might even park the jalopy and join you.

—Let's go, I said.

And we rode out into America. I looked out the window of

the covered car, up at the sheer walls, and the new walls going up as I watched, and I saw the tickertape falling – the rest of them thought it was snow – on the taxi, on the street, on everything, for me.

It was too early for stars but I knew that my voice, steered by the glass and concrete, would meet them as they came out later on. I opened the door and, right hand gripping the running board, I hung out over the street as the car turned onto Park Avenue.

—My name is Henry Smart!

2

ELECTRIC RAZORS –
BOUGHT
SOLD
AND EXCHANGED
GUARANTEED REPAIRS
ON ALL MAKES

I was an honest toiler, paid to carry the honest claims of small-time commerce through the streets and avenues of lower Manhattan.

STAR OPTICAL CO.
EXPERTS
GOOD RATES
333 PEARL ST

And I was value for money. Women's eyes went from my eyes and, as they wondered about the rest of the handsome man inside the sandwich, they read the words and were very often sold. Women had their perfect eyes tested, bought electric razors for dead fathers and infant sons.

I carried a world of ceaseless invention, well hidden behind the plain words on the boards. Vacuum cleaners, electric ice-boxes, teeth that didn't hurt. I promised a life of science and bang up-to-date ease. Ready-cut clothes, electric razors, music in every room. Spectacles for the working man, cigarettes for the working woman. I killed the day with words of my own. *There's a* CAMEL *just for you.* I wrote and rewrote, filed slogans for my future use, got ready for the break.

I'd meet other sandwich-board men. I'd read the dull, literal words that, much more than the heat and weight, were pushing them into the sidewalk.

MAX'S FOUNTAIN PENS
ALL MAKES
REPAIRED

I'd measure the length and breadth of the wooden pages and, always, I saw waste and opportunity.

But then, as night raced through the avenues and time became my own, I changed the sheets on the boards and carried my own promises.

CARLMOR
CAFETERIA
THE BEST SANDWICH IN
NEW YORK

A full belly, jangling change.

GOOD EATS
CHEAP
CHEAP
CHEAP

Hettie had never known business like it.

—What crowds, what mouths! Thank you I can. But cope, I can not!

I paid the rent in what was left of my boot leather. The suit was new but the boots had once belonged to a dead man buried in Roscommon. My boards dragged the tired and hungry stiffs to the Carlmor. And the first sight of Hettie's plenty terrified the ones who still had Europe in their guts. Drawn by my good looks and walking words, they pressed the brims of their hats to Hettie's window. Then they crept further in, sold by the smells that came out with the swinging door, the eats under the glass bells on the counter, the meatloaf and cinnamon toast, Hettie's famous Eskimo pie, won over by the prices that decorated the windows –

LARGE RIB STEAK
15c.
READ AND BELIEVE

and the sight of Hettie's magnificent, flour-patted arms.

I slept in a room behind the cafeteria. Sometimes Hettie slept with those floury arms around me, and sometimes not, depending on her mood and how drunk her husband was and where he'd fallen. She was fifty or the other side of it. She'd had her children, all grown to men and women. She wasn't sure how many, she said.

—Maybe seven.

—Boys, girls? I asked her as I sat at the counter.

Rudy Vallee whispered from the radio cabinet behind her. TIME TO EAT said the clock above her head, and 1.37, late night, very early morning. I'd just finished my dinner, bean soup, pot roast, two slices of bread and butter, apple pie and coffee – great value at 58c., and better yet because I wasn't going to pay for it.

—Who knows? she said. —Who cares? Boys girls, both. What's the ballyhoo?

She handled the language like the mince she choked with her long man's fingers, forcing it into the shapes demanded by the menu. She'd come from some place further away than Ireland but she wasn't telling me where.

—Don't know the American for it, she said.

She roomed and fed me in return for the customers I hauled to her counter and she lay down on the mattress because she liked me. She wrapped herself around me, and that was all.

—You don't want to get lost in an old chicken like me, she said.

—Yes, I do, I said.

—No no, she said.

And she held my head.

—Tell me the truth, my Henry, she said. —Am I older than your mama?

I thought about it.

—Yes, I said. —A lot older.

She laughed and pressed my face into the cotton that covered her stomach.

—Think of that, she roared.

*   *   *

I walked across and back across lower Manhattan, carrying the boards and the bottles hidden behind them. It was the fourth, and fifth, job I'd had since I'd arrived.

Beep Beep, the taxi driver who'd picked me up outside Grand Central, had taken me on to a rooming house run by a Dutchman, a sailor who hated the sea. The house was on Millionaires' Row, still called that long after the last fat cat had legged it. The room was clean, the sheets were clean. I woke the next morning, ate the food that was the topping on the rent and went looking for work. I followed the smell to the river, and found some of the docks I'd seen from the Ellis Island ferry. There was work there for thousands. I saw the men waiting for the nod. The shape-up, a toothless Connacht man beside me called it. He was too old to get into the crush.

—Will we make it, d'you think, young fella?

I said nothing.

I'd seen it before, although the clock boss here was two feet taller than the dwarf with the eyes who'd ruled the Custom House dock, in Dublin. He let his eyes wander from face to face, and stop. He held out a toothpick and the lucky man had a job – for the day. The toothpick went behind the chosen lad's ear and he marched off to work.

I turned away.

The familiarity of that routine – acceptance, rejection, daily pay and kickback – the Irish accents all around me, the red ears on the men dying for one of the clock boss's toothpicks, they all told me to stay far away from the water, or as far as four or five avenues could get me.

I turned back inland and a few blocks in I found my first start, with a blacksmith, a big man called Thompson. I pulled lengths of still-warm iron from a huge drum of water, arms, joints and panels of iron that Thompson and his three sons would assemble and burn into the fire escapes that clung to every wall I'd seen since I'd arrived. I liked the work, enjoyed the heat as I felt it hardening me. But there were too many sulking Irishmen coming in and out of the foundry, lugging the still-soft fire escapes. I left without collecting my three days' pay – a Corkman said he knew my face.

—I know your fuckin' clock, boy.

I walked until my ears felt very far from home, to East Harlem and another job. I read the newspapers to Puerto Rican cigar makers, in a loft on 109th Street. These men rolled tobacco leaves and learnt their English twelve hours a day and I, their *lector*, read the *Daily Worker*, the *Daily News* and the *Saturday Evening Post*, my head swimming in the gorgeous stink of the world's best tobacco. As they got to know me and my voice, they brought in books of their own, that their daughters got for them from the branch library – *Les Misérables*, *The Jungle* and *McTeague* – and they learnt to gasp and cry in English, and they lingered long after they were knee-deep in panatellas and listened until I got to the end of the book or chapter. I read in a fog of tobacco sweat, for more than a month. But I walked again. I left when one of those small men put a knife to my throat; I'd just closed *The Call of the Wild* with five pages to go. I had to pick it up and finish it while the blade leaned into my neck.

I walked downtown through the night and, early the next morning, the air from the East River tempting me to the docks, I was saved by an undertaker. He was struggling with a heavy roll of canvas and, curious and hungry, I stopped and helped him, up narrow steps and more steps, into a small room full of good dark furniture and a dead man. He thanked me, took off his stovepipe hat, wiped his head with a kerchief that shone like a mirror and offered me a job. So I started hefting for him. Mister Grass's caskets came with mourners, if wanted, lace curtains for the windows, and backdrops – landscapes on old canvas, badly painted chunks of home – a Sicilian village, the Tower of London, a river that passed for any of the thousands that had been left behind. The one I'd carried for him was the river. I thought it was the Liffey at the Strawberry Beds as I watched him hoist it behind the dead man on the table. But, no, he said, today it was the Danube.

—Five, six times out of ten it is the Volga.

—Is it ever the Shannon? I asked.

—One time, said Mister Grass. —The departed admired the tenor voice of John McCormack. But he himself was Polish.

He gave me a stovepipe hat and taught me how to say, 'I'm sorry for your troubles' in eleven different languages. I buried his share of the Lower East Side dead, with his brother and, now and again, his son.

—Grass & Son, he said as he showed me how to get a tie onto a dead man who wasn't co-operating. —My dream. But Grass and a Corner Boy is what I get. He will grow out of it, says the missis. He is thirty-four, thirty-five, I tell her. I will pray for him, she says. Pray for the corner, I say. Second and 11th.

One day, at Grass's mortuary, I found bottles of hooch inside one of the caskets. I held up one of the bottles and shook it. I knew the trick: if I saw bubbles the contents were on the reasonable side of bad. There were no bubbles in this bottle but I could still feel its possibilities. It was dangerous stuff, the property of hard men, its route from coffin to mouth already sewn up and guarded. But it was money and I needed some, so I walked up to the two men who came in later to stare into the coffins with & Son.

—Are you lads looking for help?

I took my beating, nothing to it, and got up off the floor. The hard men left. & Son followed them but he came straight back.

—Am I in? I said.

—Up to me, you're dead.

—So, what do I do, Pavel?

—That's Paul.

He sent me to Johnny No. (And I forgot all about the hard men.) I picked up the bottles from a tall blond kid, an alky-cooker who called himself Fast Eddie but whose real name, his sister told me, was Olaf. Fast Olaf lived with his sister and his dying mother, on the fourth floor of a five-storey Orchard Street tenement. I met him three or four times a week on the roof, under the shadow of the wooden water tower, in a forest of chimneys, pigeon coops and new radio antennae – *the air is our theatre* – more of them every time I went up there. Fast Olaf's gin stills and bathtubs were hidden under the pigeons on all the rooftops along his block. He handed over the hooch, bottled and brown-bagged, and I hid the bottles in the muslin pockets that were tacked to the insides of the sandwich boards, front and back. Then I'd go and meet his customers, shrinking, skinless men leaning into walls at street corners, and women, purple-eyed, crumbling on the steps of other people's buildings, all of them dying but always punctual. I'd hand over the horse sugar, and they'd produce the readies, and no one really watched or cared or tried to stop us. The hand of Prohibition never reached to the depths that these men and women had dropped to. They always paid something, cash – coins and the odd sodden note. Fast Olaf's booze was killing them and they were going out on the instalment plan. It was bad liquor, gin only because Fast Olaf

14

called it gin, until he added tea to the mix and it became malt whiskey. I'd even seen him pour some of Grass's embalming fluid into the bath. Dead homers and tiplets decorated the Orchard Street sidewalks. Paralysed by the fumes from Fast Olaf's stills, they took off but couldn't flap. But Fast Olaf knew his market. Even without Prohibition, his experiments would have been their drink of choice.

—Pre-war imported, I said as I handed over a brown-bag.

My client dropped small money onto my palm. He took the top from the bottle without opening the bag and drank big through the paper.

—You brighten the joint, he said as he walked away, when he was able to speak again.

Manhattan was the Big Bottle. There were thirty-two thousand dives and speakeasies on the island, Fast Olaf's sister told me.

—I been in all of them, daddio.

But Fast Olaf's clientele had always chosen the benches and weeds. Not for them the teacup and phoney Scotch label; they wanted his poison clean and honest. I brought the loot back to Fast Olaf, minus my 15 per cent. I watched him count the money, his face travelling across deserts of sums and figures.

—How'd he get to be called Fast? I asked his sister.

—He can fuck a girl in ten seconds, easy, she said.

—You've seen her?

—I *am* her. I'm only his half-sister, she added.

—That's fair enough, I said.

—Damn right. His daddy's not my daddy; that's fair game in this girl's town.

—He pays you?

—Because he wants to. Makes him feel like the big cheese, see. And that's okay. And, hey listen. I'm gonna tell him about that five per cent you was telling me about.

—Unless?

—You give me three.

—But this, I said.

I waved a hand over her. She was on her back, right under me, giving it the Henry Ford. Sewing machines, dozens of them, whirred and clacked in the rooms right under us; they invaded our work, sent lint up through the floorboards.

—This. This is free, right?

—Right.

15

—Okay, doll, I said. —You've got yourself a deal.

—You can put it in my mouth for three and a half.

—No no, I said. —This'll do fine.

—Fine is fine, she said. —But you got to have ambition in this life, you know.

—Next time, I said.

—This time is always the last time, daddio, she said. —My heinie is available too.

And she put a finger on mine.

—Go on, she said. —Don't be a sis.

And she stretched back off the bed – she was a long, long, good-looking girl – and, with her hair dusting the floor, she yelled at the wall.

—Shut the fuck up, Ma!

At her dying mother who was pounding her side of the wall with a shoe or mallet or the front of her head.

—Bring soup!

The tiny kitchen was no man's land between them. Her mother had the box-room with a view of the airshaft. I never saw her. Fast Olaf's half-sister had the bigger front room, with a view of lower Manhattan.

—How come? I said.

—Who pays the rent? she said. —And what's it to fucking you?

—Soup!

—Shut up!

The city of the good time, the Big Noise. I was there three months and I felt at home. And I felt that way because it was no man's home. It was too big, too fast; nothing stayed fixed. I knew the blocks, the corners, but that wasn't enough. This was the city that fell and rose every day, the city that was colonising the sky. A man with ambition just had to look up to meet his possibilities. I did it all the time. And I listened. To the clock that hung higher above Manhattan than the men on the girders. I could hear it clearly. I could feel its beat.

I had 18 per cent of Fast Olaf's gin money. Olaf was forking out for my adventures with his half a sister. It was still my honest boast: I'd never paid for a ride. I had plans. I had the measure of the town. Those who got on lived by the clock hanging over it. I listened to the clock. The city that dished out the time. It could be bought and spent, borrowed, stolen, wasted, fucked and killed. Time was money. Time was life. It was up to me.

16

I stood at the corner of Broadway and Fulton. In the stew of noise, heat and the smells that came from the market. The grinding wheels, the buzz and stink of crawling engines, the shouts of vendors and buyers – *Yiddische Morgenjournal! Yiddische Morgenjournal!* – German, Russian, East Side English, pidgin-everything, fighting through air trapped by the walls, and the quilts and sheets that hung dead across the street on pulley lines. My suit was wringing wet. My Clarence Darrow suspenders – lavender; I'd walked for days looking for a pair – were sawing through muscle and sinew, pulling me to the ground. I pushed my pearl-grey fedora to the back of my skull. I stood there in my sandwich –

HARVEY'S HATS
246 BEEKMAN STREET

I listened. I could hear the clock. I turned from Fulton and looked up Broadway. It was all there and it went on forever, the backbone of the whole world, in neat, expendable blocks. The clock was ticking, measuring out the din and commerce of the Fulton Street market, and all the other markets and stores and dives and emporiums and brothels and freak-shows and arcades and picture palaces and dens and nightclubs and churches and roadhouses and dance halls and banks – further and further, as far as I needed to see, over the hill that was the horizon, and further, all the way into America, right through the continent, slicing a path clean through it. Ticking away, beating just for me. I could feel it in my feet and bones. Counting down to my birth. It was up to me. Time was life. Time was money.

My time had come.

—No, said Johnny No-Can-Do.

—What?

—You heard me. No can do.

I'd expected the answer but not the face that came with it. His expression had none of the usual vaudeville, none of the grim fun that apologised for the big No that always strolled out when he opened his mouth. Even from behind the cigar smoke, it was clear as the early day outside: NO.

He looked down at his desk and the half-bits of paper and stains.

I picked up the boards.

ITSPEP
FOR
COLDS AND COUGHS

—Hey.

I looked at Johnny No.

—Up to me, I'd still say No. It's up to bigger people, see. Understand?

I carried the boards to his door.

—Understand?

—Yeah.

—Remember that.

Down four flights to Fulton Street. The heat and my disappointment pressed the straps in good and hard, into the ditches that now ran across my shoulders. A passing El shook the world and loosened the grime. I could see it; I could feel it sticking to me.

Beep Beep was right.

—You ain't arrived till you don't hear the El.

The words I was lugging were careful and dull.

GOOD FOR THE WHOLE
FAMILY

The things I could do with these boards, and more boards, a fleet of the things, carried by fine men like myself. The straps weren't cutting; they were pushing, pressing at me to get on with it.

—Fuck that, I said.

—Talking to me, friend?

Leon the Cob put a sack on top of the other sacks he was building into a wall at the edge of the path – the *sidewalk*. He was always there before me, selling corn, potatoes, cabbages, tomatoes, before the day got hold of them and turned them into mush. And his pickles, things I'd never seen or smelt until I reached New York – tubs of piccalilli, gherkins, pimentos – great names with a stink that took away all sound and heat when I held my face above them.

18

Leon marched over and tapped my front board with a cob he'd just ripped from the top sack.

—What about that Louise?

He was talking about Louise Brooks, the movie woman; the same words, same conclusion, every morning. Today, I got there before him.

—You fuck her good, I said.

—I'll do that, he said.

—She'll be grateful.

—Yes, she will.

He threw another sack onto the wall.

—And her sister, my friend, is yours.

—Thank you.

—Thank her.

My plan had been simple, and right: I was going to go out on my own. Lugging another man's boards, I was another stiff, a mick fresh off the boat. Lugging my own boards, I was a man of business, a young man on the go. And not lugging them either; *presenting* them.

But, No, the man had said.

And fair enough. The boards were his, and the business that came with them, and his 60 per cent of Olaf's 10 per cent of the booze money. I'd been hoping to buy the boards off him. But why set up some dope to take his business out from under him? So, fair enough. I couldn't blame Johnny No.

So what was I going to do?

The answer was easy, now that I was out on the street. I'd rob the boards and lose myself. I'd stay well clear of Johnny No; there were other streets, and lots of them. At the end of business today there'd be a new me sitting at Hettie's counter. The coming man in advertising, the new man in the new, new thing.

The boards were weightless; they were wings and I was the man to flap them. But there was still one thing: Johnny No's face. For a second back there in his office, for less than a second, less than the time it took to blink his yellow eyes, I'd seen Jack Dalton behind that desk, just after he'd let me read my own name on a piece of paper and sentenced me to death. (—I'm dead, I said.

—Yes.

—Because I'm a nuisance.

—Because you're a spy.

—Oh, I said. —Fine. Were any of them really spies, Jack?

—You killed plenty of them yourself, he said. —Of course they were.)

But this was New York, not Dublin, and the sky was all around me, new and beautiful, waiting to be packaged. It pressed at me and gently rocked the boards. *My* boards. Johnny No was Johnny No, a small-talking man with a small-time head. And Jack Dalton was dead. Caught in the middle of reprisal and counter-reprisal, one hundred and three bullets had been taken from his body and for years, while it suited him, the bullet that mattered was claimed by Dinny Archer. Johnny No was no Jack Dalton. Jack would have loved New York. Johnny No didn't even know it was outside his window.

—Bad news comes to town, said Leon.

I followed Leon's eyes, and watched as the man went into Jimmy the Priest's, a badly hidden flophouse further down the street, with four or five of his boys, through a doorway that was much too small for them.

—Louis Lepke, said Leon. —Stay clear of that man, my friend.

—I will, I said.

I took the boards off. Then I leaned over the pimentos and let them wipe me clean.

I lifted myself onto my elbows.

—Say that again.

—It'll cost you, she said.

—Name your price.

—A buck.

—Only if you put your heart into it.

—Done deal, daddio. Lie back and learn.

And Fast Olaf's half-sister lifted herself slowly and hung there over me.

—Day by day—

And slid slowly down.

—in ev-ery way—

Her mouth came down to my ear.

—I am getting better and better—

She was over me again.

—and better and better—

And down.

—and better and better and—

20

By the time I came she was sitting on a chair beside the bed examining her face in a mirror that threw the sun all around the room. She was fully clothed, all set for the great outdoors.

—Value for the dollar?

—I didn't pay for the ride, I said. —But yeah. You've got ambition.

—I got that, she said, to the mirror. —In spades.

I sat up.

—You believe it, I said. —Don't you? The day-by-day thing.

—Sure I believe it. In ev-ery way.

She got hold of an eyelash; I heard the tiny click of her fingernails as they captured it and pulled.

—It's the thing, she said.

She rubbed her fingertips and I watched the lash glide slowly to the floor.

—Wanna know more?

—Yeah.

—Wanna pay me?

—I'll wait.

—Waiting is dying.

She stood up.

—Be seeing you, daddio.

And she climbed out the window, onto the fire escape. I could still see her in the window long after her heels on the steps had died.

Fast Olaf was on the roof, baking his head in the sun. He was leaning over a bath of his ten-year-old malt, stirring it with what looked like a ladle.

—How's it going, Eddie?

He looked over his shoulder and stood up straight. It *was* a ladle, and there was a pigeon lying in it, legs up, head back. He walked the few steps to the side of the building, tipped the ladle, and the homer fell with a thump that I was too far up to hear.

I took the boards off my shoulders and put them, like cards, leaning into each other on the tarred roof.

—Grand day, I said.

Fast Olaf shrugged.

We loaded the latest bottles into the muslin pockets.

—Did you take out the feathers this time, Eddie?

Fast Olaf shrugged.

—The big ones, he said. —The fuck you care?

—Fair enough, I said. —I have an announcement. Are you listening?

—Yare.

—I'm going out on my own, I told him.

I made sure every word was heard and understood.

—The boards are mine now.

I pointed at them.

—They're mine now. Do you have a problem with that?

I watched him thinking.

—Someone else's problem, he said. —The fuck, I give a fuck?

—Good, I said. —Business as usual, yeah?

He scanned the sentence as it passed him.

—Yare.

—Fine.

It was a hectic time, dropping off Olaf's ardent spirits, collecting more, forcing the time to cold-call the businesses of the Lower East Side. I needed Olaf's business until I had a squad of men on the streets. I deducted my take – 23 per cent and rising; his half-sister was bleeding the poor fucker dry – and I did it while I ran.

I'd choose my street, I'd examine it door by door, in the blunt half-hour before first thing in the morning, just out of Hettie's bed, an hour after Hettie. She made her noise in the dark. Found the clothes – the stockings, apron. The shoes on the bare boards. The smell of her flour a map of her moves. Her echoes kept me company, prodded me out of the scratcher, into the small part of the day that made it down the airshaft to Hettie's window. It was always dark and the window had to be kept shut against the coal-gas outside, pressing at the glass.

But I was glad to be up, a half-step ahead of the world. I'd walk the street – a street a day – and compose as I went. Compose first, and call later. The cold call. I loved it. I delivered the goods before they were asked for.

—Mister Levine about?

LEVINE'S DRY GOODS –
WITH PRICES LIKE
LEVINE'S

I'd have the words ready, up on the boards in their black and artful glory. I'd walk into the shop – and let them read – take

22

off the boards – and let them read – lean them together – let them read.

YOU'D BE
WET
NOT TO BUY THEM
62 FRONT STREET

The boards were painted on Fast Olaf's roof. One of his clients was a sign painter, or had been before the booze gave his hands the yours-forever shakes. But, with a brown-bag safe in his left fist, he could hold a brush in his right and deliver lines and curls that brought purple tears to his eyes.

—I was the best, said Steady.

—Still are.

—Best in the business.

—Don't doubt you.

—That fuck, Picasso? He'd clean my fucking brushes.

I didn't even have to buy the bottle. Delivery was all he demanded.

—Mister Levine about? I said.

I took off the boards and made them kiss. They stood in front of the counter.

—Mister Levine?

—That's right, I said.

—There are three Mister Levines.

—Are you one of them?

—Nope.

—Well—

—Want to know what my wife was called before she gazed into my eyes here and took the plunge?

—Levine?

—That's right.

—Congratulations.

—She's a baby doll.

—I'm sure she is.

—I'm sure you're right.

—So, I said. —Your name's not Levine. But would you be, more or less, the fourth Mister Levine?

—Well, I guess the other three would have something to say about that.

He pointed at the ceiling.

23

—It's getting pretty crowded up there. But, between you and me—

The voice didn't drop. If anything, he raised it.

—Yes is the answer to that question. I'm first banana around here.

—Good, I said. —I'm talking to the right man.

—I guess you are, at that. But am I listening to the right man?

—Yes, you are.

He listened, and so did all the other bright guys who ran lower Manhattan's village commerce. They listened, and saw the boards, and more boards, then hoardings and neon, the whole sky lit by the stuff. They saw where I was going, in the dingy rooms and back offices, and they smelt it, the cold bracing air that expelled the dead heat of the day, and they heard it – the booming calls of construction men, the steam shovels, the jackhammer, the saw, the hook, the till – and they felt it on their fingertips – the money, the cloth, chrome, the skin – and they wanted to come with me.

—Beat it.

Most of them did.

THE SANDWICHES
THAT
BUILT AMERICA

—Mister Sauls?

—Beat it.

I put down the boards and let them kiss. I let him read the words.

—D'you like it? I asked him.

—Yare, I like it.

He stared at the message, his name above and the Beaver Street address below, the whole package standing there waiting for him.

He looked away, and stared at me. And spoke.

—But you wanna know something, Mister Sandwich Board Man? My customers, 90 per cents of them, can't read American. And the other 10 per cents, they can read but they know the truth. That my sandwiches are good sandwiches, and that's it. Good. No more. I don't tell lies. I give them sandwiches that fill them. They eat them because they're hungry. Nothing beside. So take your smart words there and beat it.

He stopped looking at me.

—Go on, scram.

But most of them came with me. Those first weeks, I was selling on the run, subletting the space on my boards.

HOME
OF THE
HAPPY HAIR –
LADY'S HAIR BOB – 25c

I walked for the barber in the morning and for Hettie in the evening, in the aching hours when all the other stiffs were done and heading home. But I wasn't a stiff any more, and I was loving it. I was stretching the day to new limits, forcing new seconds into every minute. The sun was following me, on the back of my neck all day. Not burning or hammering at my brain; it was trying to keep up, and failing. I'd feel the coolness of tomorrow's shadow on my neck, and I'd know that I was winning.

And Fast Olaf's half-sister wasn't far behind me.

She sat up on the bed in front of me.

—Watch me. I'm a wow.

And I watched.

She held her nipples.

—See these, daddio?

—I'm broke, I told her.

—No, she said. —I want to show you. A lesson, you know. See them?

She pulled them, let go, pulled them, and let go.

—They're getting bigger, she said.

—That's what usually happens.

—No, look. They're getting *bigger*.

I watched her as she worked. I could see it in her eyes, in the deep, beautiful spaces where they'd been a minute before. She sat at the far end of the bed, miles from me. I saw her lips. I could trace the words – *better and better* – while she ran the course of the sentence again and again – *in ev-ery way* – while the room got darker and her mother in the room beyond the kitchen stopped hammering. The room was night now. The machines below – they never stopped – were a part of the half-sister's chant – *in ev-ery way* – again and again and again. I sat there for hours and watched.

And, suddenly, she was with me.

—Pow.

She looked at me, and down.

—See?

She crawled over the bed and got up on her knees.

—See?

They were right there in front of me, and she was right: her nipples were bigger. They were longer, the length of a good-sized finger, tip to first knuckle. She held them and stared at me.

—Ev-ery thought entirely filling my mind becomes true and transforms itself into action. As the guy said. Think titties, *be* titties.

—Who's the guy?

—Me to know.

She held her nipples again.

—I love 'em. Don't you?

—Yep.

—Know why I'm doing it?

—For me.

She laughed. She threw her head back and laughed at the ceiling, and stopped.

—The market wants it, she said. —The flappers are the thing, see. All the girls out there want to be flappers. No tits, no hips. That's what the girls want. But that's not what the boys want, you know. And the boys are the market right now. Always and forever. The boys want tits, tits I can give them. Want to feel them?

—I told you. I'm broke.

—Broke broke, or broke kinda?

—Broke broke.

—Pity, she said. —I like you. But—

—Business is business.

—Too right, daddio. Even on my day off. Long hair too. The girls want it short, the boys like it long. But hair grows anyways, so it don't need imagination. Just time. Which I ain't got, if you're as broke as you say you are.

And she was gone. I heard her on the fire escape – *in ev-ery way* – and gone.

I needed more backs, more boards on the backs. I needed fine men, walking ads for the ads they carried. Not the sad-faced, unshaven guys who hid inside their boards and hauled them like

26

a punishment through the streets. I was sorry for them – I knew those faces – but they weren't getting on to my payroll. I wanted men who could sell by the spring in their stroll, by the way their hats sat on their heads.

—Bring your cap down to the river, I told the kid. —And throw it in. Then get yourself a good-looking hat.

—Like yours?

—Like mine.

—You pay for it?

—Yeah, I said. —I'll pay for it. Then we can see how you go about paying me back.

—That's a fedora, right.

—That's right.

—What's the colour on it?

I had the right man.

—Get your own colour.

He was already away, picking his hat; I could see it in the way he stared at mine. He was Beep Beep's sister's boy. Seventeen and bursting out of himself. He was tall, a bit shorter than me – I'd always be able to look down at him – and handsome in the way all the Yanks were after a few generations of American food and air.

We were at the corner of the Bowery and Bayard. I was keeping a distance between myself and Johnny No. I hadn't seen or heard from him, or & Son, or anyone else. It was a month since I'd walked off with his boards. A hot month, and this was another hot day. The kid took off his cap.

—This your office? he said.

I liked him, but I wasn't going to like him too much. I didn't need a little brother.

—He's got a mouth on him, Beep Beep had told me. —But there's a noodle there at the back of it. Grace needs the bacon and he'll bring it home to her. He's a good kid.

—So, I said. —Are you with me?

The kid threw his cap onto the roof of a passing Ford delivery truck.

—My head's starting to bake, he said. —A man needs a hat.

I gave him three bucks and a good man's handshake.

—See you here tomorrow, I told him. —Bring your hat and your shoulders.

—Swell.

His name was Joe, and it was the first time he'd sounded like a real kid. The job was his; he could loosen and grin. He wanted to call me something.

—Mister Glick, I said.

I was Henry Glick these days. *Glic,* clever, cunning, smart. An American name, invented to be remembered, and easily thrown away.

—Mister Glick, he said. —Thanks, Mister Glick.

Hettie stared out over my head.

—Can I help you, missy? she said.

—I *am* kinda peckish, said a woman behind me.

—I bet, said Hettie.

The woman sat beside me. She was twenty-three or four, but the age was an average. There was a lot of her that was older. The neck was a kid's but the cheeks were spoiled by thin dark streaks where the veins had given up. Her eyes were huge, but badly stained. She was a fine big thing but a year or two off being a slob.

—You're the guy she won't tell me about, she said.

—There's lots of those fellas.

—You're he.

I looked at her broad forehead, slowly from left to right, and down to her mouth. One of her front teeth was missing a tiny chip; it did her no harm. She stayed still for me, but her mouth was getting impatient.

And I spoke to her mouth.

—The skin you love to touch.

—What ya say?

I wandered her face again, not for as long this time.

—The skin, I said. —You love to touch.

She sat up.

—I don't get you, she said. —You talking about me?

—I'm talking about your skin.

—And you want to touch it. I heard you right.

—Not me, I said.

Hettie was putting together another sandwich. I could hear her knife sawing clean to the board.

—Not *just* me, I said.

She sneered, but there was curiosity clinging to the corners of her mouth.

28

—You're not the first guy ever gave me the glad eye, buster.

I hadn't expected the moment to be so neat. I put my hand into my pocket and felt for the package. *In ev-ery way.*

—Touch your face, I said.

—Get lost.

—Go on, I said. —Touch it.

Hettie had turned to watch us.

—Why? said the woman.

—I want you to feel it, I said.

She sneered, and lifted her hand. Her fingers touched her cheek. She seemed surprised when nothing happened.

—So? she said.

—What do you feel?

—Nothing, she said. —Just—

—Just your memory of what you used to feel whenever you felt that cheek. Am I right?

She touched her face again.

—I guess, she said, before she let her fingers drop back to her hip. She sat up, shook herself, sneered at me again.

—Men will always want to look at you, I told her. —You're a beautiful woman.

The sneer warmed, became a question.

—You see yourself in the mirror, in the window there when you came in, and, it's confirmed. Always. You're beautiful. You see it in the eyes of men you pass, who sit beside you and talk to you. You see it now in my eyes. Right bang in front of you.

She waited.

—But you used to *feel* it.

She didn't know it, but she nodded.

—You used to feel it when you touched your skin. You used to feel it all the time.

She smiled.

—And you know that men felt it too. When men put their fingers to your skin you could see it in their eyes. It wasn't a broad they were feeling up. It was beauty. You could see it in their eyes, their gentleness. Adoration. Everything in life they'd ever wanted. And it was all *you* ever wanted.

She stared at me as my fingers touched her cheek.

—It'll come back, I told her.

Her eyes grew dark. She blinked.

—It *will* come back. That touch, that feel. You know they say

29

it; beauty is only skin-deep. You've heard it all your life. They used to say it to you, didn't they? Your girlfriends said it when they saw the guys giving *you* the eye. Your mother used to say it.

—Not me, said Hettie.

She was Hettie's daughter; I didn't blink, I didn't swerve.

—Other mothers said it, I told them, my eyes stuck to the daughter's. —Other mothers said it. To stop their crying. Beauty's only skin-deep, Daisy. Beauty's only skin-deep, Hazel. But they got it wrong. We know that.

She leaned forward; only my words would catch her.

—Beauty isn't the skin, I said.

And I touched her face.

—It's there, under the skin.

I took my hand away.

—What's your name?

—She's Mildred, said Hettie.

—It's still there, Mildred. Just under the skin.

I took the soap from my pocket and put it on the counter, not too loudly. I wanted it there but not announced.

—The skin becomes a shell, I said. —Life does it. Wind, smoke, the sun. Just a few years' living. Laminosis. The hardening of the skin. Happens to us all, but men get away with it.

They waited for me.

—But the beauty is still there, I said. —Right beneath the skin. Only, you don't feel it any more. The skin gets harder and deeper.

I counted to three.

—But doesn't have to be that way.

I sat up straight, pushed myself away from the counter, and now the soap was sitting there, wrapped in brown paper. I picked it up and handed it to her.

She went to grab, but stopped.

—What is it?

—Soap.

—You saying I need a wash?

—No, I'm not.

I held the soap in front of her. She gazed, and took it.

—Thanks, I said. —What you have in your hand is, essentially, soap. But it's more than that.

—Now there's a surprise, said Hettie.

—Hang on, I said. —It's more, but not much more. Not much, but vitally more. It cleanses, but it also softens, which is beyond

30

all other brands. It softens the skin. It adds nothing. It takes nothing. It simply revitalises what has been dormant. What's already yours.

She looked from the soap, to me. Her eyes fought her mouth for control of her face.

—That feeling you miss so much, Mildred, is right beneath your skin.

I pointed at the small block in her fist.

—And *that* will give it back to you. Simply wash with that bar, once a day, preferably in the morning. The skin is at its most receptive but, between ourselves, whenever you like is grand. And that feeling will rise through your skin, back to where you know it should be. Right there, at your fingertips. At the world's fingertips.

I let myself rest against the counter again.

—Results in days. Guaranteed.

She eventually spoke.

—I ain't so sure about the world's fingertips.

—It's an option, I said. —You decide.

And, suddenly, her eyes were sharp and mean again.

—How much?

—Dollar, ninety-nine.

—For soap?

—If it was just soap I wouldn't be selling it. Who's going to pay two bucks for a bar of soap?

I made no move to take it back.

—What's it called?

—It has no name. It's not a gimmick. It isn't Lifebuoy or Listerine. It's the real thing. It makes no claims. It simply does what it's supposed to do. It's up to yourself.

She looked at Hettie.

—See me two bucks, Mama, will ya.

—No chance, said Hettie.

—Ah, go on.

—I give, you go?

—Yes, dearest Mama.

Hettie took exactly two dollars from under her apron and put them on the counter.

—So, go.

Mildred put her hand on top of the cash. She looked at me, and lifted the hand. She slid off the stool.

—I'll go when I get my change, she said.

I took the penny – the only one in my pocket – and held it

31

between my fingers. She took it. Her nails were broken but not destroyed. Now she held the soap.

—This doesn't work, I'm back.

—It'll work, I said. —And you'll be back. It's great stuff but it doesn't last forever.

She stopped out on the street, looked in at us over the price cards, and smiled.

—That is the way, said Hettie.

She looked away.

—That is how to remember her. Smiling.

Then Mildred was gone.

—I'm cruel, you think? said Hettie.

—No, I said. —I don't.

—It hurts too much. It is easier to remember.

She tapped the plate.

—She forgot her sandwich.

I'd forgotten my own. I looked at it now and didn't want it. I wanted to get out on to the streets. I'd just sold a repackaged cake of soap to a hophead with no money. I'd passed my own test; there was no fuckin' stopping me. But I took a bite from the sandwich. I nodded my satisfaction.

—You have more of that soap for me? said Hettie.

—You don't need it, Hettie.

—My money is not good if I want something with it?

I hadn't picked up the two dollars on the counter. I took another brown-papered packet from my pocket – the paper from off one of Olaf's bottles – and I put it beside the money. Then I picked up the money.

—This'll do.

—It will work if I don't pay for it?

—You paid, I told her.

—It will work?

—Yes.

She took a dollar from under her apron and placed it in front of me.

—I don't want it, Hettie, I said, and I stood up to go.

—Take, she said. —Take it. I don't pay, it don't work. I buy expensive soap, don't work if it ain't expensive.

I had to take it. If I didn't, I was robbing her. *The skin you love to touch.* It was the words I'd sold them. I was never going to be the man who sold soap. The words, not the product – the story, the spell. And sex appeal too, the Big It. The present tense, and happy ending. The *skin*, uncovered and waiting; the intimacy and hugeness of *you*; the thrill of *touch*, the held hand, the sin, excitement; and *love* in the middle, fat with sugar and immortality. *The skin you love to touch.* It was the words, and the clear, honest eyes of the man who'd spoken to them, and terrified and rescued them.

I'd been looking at the words all day and night since I'd landed on Manhattan. *Pleasure Ahead.* In crackling neon and paint. *I Found the Way to Happiness.* On every wall, in every window. In the air, in the pools of water on early-morning streets. *Keep That Schoolgirl Complexion.* In stagnant puddles that the sun never got to. They were everywhere. Blinking on and off ceilings all night, following me all day. *Critical Eyes Are Sizing You Up.* I knew what they were doing – *Right Now* – the men who'd come up with the slogans. *Let me carry your Cross for Ireland, Lord.* I knew how to unsettle and soothe with words. I knew how to bully and push. *Shun all policemen and spies!* And inspire, provoke and terrify. I was still only twenty-two, but I'd been inspiring and provoking with words and more than words long before most of the New York ad men knew what they were for. It was soap now instead of freedom, cash they were after instead of votes and safe houses, but it was the same thing, the same approach and tactics. Sell the words, sell the goods and the life. Sell the need, and the salvation. Smile with the consumer, suffer with her. *Little Dry Sobs through the Bedroom Door.* Terrify the man – *Dandruff!* – then save him – *End Dandruff.* Create the hole, then offer to fill it. *Let me carry your Cross for Ireland, Lord.* I am your best friend. *Blow Some My Way.*

I was late arriving. I wouldn't be joining the club – the ad men and consumption engineers, the princes of ballyhoo. And I didn't care. This was the land of the itch. The ad men and their clients had it salved and numbed, ready for slicing. They were hacking away goodo, and had been for years. America was huge – *mass* – and it was shrinking – *market*. But there'd always be more. The ad men had the walls and airwaves, the water and the air. I had the sandwich boards. They were after the woman with the dollar. I'd go after the woman with less. They had the land behind the doorbell. I had the streets, the alleys and tenements, the land behind the doors with no bell. I had everywhere else.

★   ★   ★

His face was already in mine; his breath drenched me.

—You got something that's mine.

—Mister Vaux, I said.

—That's a funny thing, he said.

The grip on my arm was solid. The yellow eyes held mine and wouldn't let go; there was no talking to them.

—Funny, he said. —You remember my name but I don't remember fucking yours.

The cigar was lit but the smoke didn't get in our way.

—What's else, he said. —I don't even want to know your fucking name. What I do want is this.

He slapped the front board with his left hand, and held me up with his right. The crowds parted, flowed past us. I'd been lazy; I'd underestimated Johnny No. He'd kill me now, here – the corner of 7th and Avenue A – safely away, I'd thought, from Fulton Street. He was in complete control. He wasn't angry and he wasn't going to waste time.

I decided.

—D'you want it back?

That surprised him, a bit. I could see it now; he was used to men apologising.

—Yare.

—Fair enough. If you let go of—

He slapped me. He let go of my arm and whacked me hard. My fedora went to the ground but I didn't follow it. I was held by someone behind me.

He slapped me again.

—I don't think I'm going to do that, he said. —Let people see me, people I do business with. Carrying my own boards. Important people. I think not, pally. You're a smart guy. You got the message already. Am I right?

—You're right.

—I guessed, he said. —I'm going this way, you're going that way. The boards will be at my place of business when I get back. And I'll never see you again.

And he slapped me again, two hands – the world was dots and heat.

—I don't see you again, he said. —You hearing that?

—Yes, Mister Vaux.

—Forget my name, he said. —You don't need it no more.

I could hear him moving away before I could see him clearly,

34

or the guy who'd been holding me up. I wasn't sure I was standing.

I felt his breath again, and his morning eggs.

—I know what you been doing, he said. —That sound like a warning?

—Yeah.

—Yare, he said. —You got that one fucking right. What's my name?

—I can't remember.

—You keep on can't remembering and you will live a whole lot fucking longer. See this?

He was standing in front of my hat.

—I'm not going to stand on your fucking hat. I want to. It's a good hat, I'm jealous. You don't fucking deserve it. But. I'm not going to. Because, you go on a long journey, you need a good hat. We will not meet again. Be fucking missing. That sound like another warning to you?

He was gone before I gave him his answer. & Son was waiting for him at the corner. They were gone. I picked up my hat and turned towards Fulton Street.

I left the boards outside his office. The door was locked. *J. W. Vaux*. Nothing else. I tore off the sheets of paper, front –

HOLY SMOKE!
STERN'S CIGAR STORE –
107 AVENUE A –

– and back.

BUY YOURSELF A
CIGAR
MR STERN HAS
THEM ALL

It wasn't one of my better ones. The client had liked the front but he'd vetoed the back.

STERN CIGARS
FOR
SERIOUS PEOPLE

—I don't get it, he'd said.

35

—It's the play on the name, I told him. —Stern.

—What, I'm stupid? he said. —You think I'm serious because I have the name to match?

—No.

I was learning fast. Never disagree with the client.

—It is a clever slogan but, I told him. —It'll draw the custom.

—It's an insult to my family, is what it is, he said. —It's an insult to my father. And my mother. It's an insult to me. It's my store. Who's here first thing every morning to open up? You?

—Mister Stern, I said. —I'm sorry.

—Yare, well.

—We'll change it.

—Yare. I should be in it. I'm the store.

—Yes, I said. —How about this? Give yourself a cigar.

—What, give? I don't want to give. I want them to buy.

—Buy yourself a cigar.

—Not bad. What about me?

—Mister Stern has them all.

—You got that right.

—Or, *Danny* Stern has them all. It's less formal.

—This a party we're selling or cigars?

—Mister Stern has them all.

—You got that right. You name them, they're here. They ain't here, they don't exist.

—That's great, that. We could use that.

—What? You want to walk around with my conversation on your back?

I left the boards against Johnny No's door and went back down to the street.

—What about that Louise? said a man I hadn't seen in weeks.

—You fuck her good.

—She'll be thanking old Leon in the morning.

I pointed at Johnny No's building.

—If he asks, tell him you saw me bringing the boards up.

—He won't ask.

—D'you ever see him with other people?

—Nope, said Leon. —But that don't mean they ain't there.

I pushed my fedora away from my eyes.

—They're always there, certain guys, said Leon. —You don't have to see them, is all.

I knew what he meant. I was back in Dublin.

I could still feel No's fingers on my arms, his slaps on my face. I could have decked the cunt with half a thump, I could have creased him. But it wasn't how I wanted it to be.

I'd given him his boards, done what he'd told me to do. No big sacrifice; I had boards of my own now. I had Beep Beep's Joe and two other kids wandering for me. So, were we all square? He'd told me to make sure we never met again. Would that be enough? My guess was, Yes.

My hunch was, No.

But I wasn't leaving. I'd only arrived.

I opened my eyes.

And there she was.

The air was thick and well-fed. The day outside was winding down; the once-sharp horns and shouts were soaked in sweat. And the vicious band of light on the floor beside me would soon slice its way up the wall and go.

I'd been asleep for hours. I'd no memory of lying back.

She was sitting on the side of the bed. And she was looking at the photograph. She knew I was looking at her. The picture was in one hand, my wallet in the other. She was caught, but that wasn't how she saw it. Her eyes made no budge from the frayed and fading picture of my wedding day.

But she spoke.

—The dress is a wow.

—It was a great day.

The 12th of September, 1919. A gunman on the run married a ruined schoolteacher. A happy man and happy woman, both made shy by the sun thumping into their faces. The two of them sitting on a bench in front of the whitewashed wall of the bride's mother's house.

—How long ago?

—Five years.

—You lived some since then, daddio.

I didn't answer.

—Like the tommy, said Fast Olaf's half-sister; she was talking about the Thompson sub-machine-gun on the groom's lap.

—No wedding should be without one, I say.

She put a finger on the photograph.

—She the one gave you the marks on your forehead?

37

—I'm still your teacher, Henry Smart.

I didn't answer.

—What's her name?

—I don't know.

Now she looked at me, and she held it up.

—This the real thing? she said.

—Yes.

—You got yourself hitched.

—Yeah.

—That's the wife?

—Yeah.

—And you don't know her name?

—No.

—That the thing, where you come from? Not knowing the name.

—No, I said. —I don't think so.

—You forget it?

—I never knew it.

I sat up.

—I don't know yours either.

—We ain't married, daddy. She dead?

—No, I said. —Not as far as I know. Give it to me.

—Who's the fat sport?

—I know *his* name, I said. —Ivan.

He stood behind me, one hand covering his holster, the other feeling his cousin, the bridesmaid. Ivan the Terrible – *Ireland's an island, Captain, a dollop of muck* – probably Ivan Reynolds T.D. by now.

—Give it to me, I said.

—Please.

—Please.

She dropped it to the bed. It took its time. The air, full of the day it had been feeding on, held the photo before it slid onto the blanket.

—So, how come?

—What?

—You here, she wherever.

—It's complicated, I said. —The wallet as well, please.

—Nothing in it, daddio.

—I knew that before I came here. But that's not the point.

—What is the point?

38

—Willing to pay for it?

—No.

—Then.

She looked out the window for a while. She never had to squint. Then she spoke.

—Miss her?

—Yes.

The wallet was the point, not the contents. I was a man with a wallet. The fact that it was empty didn't matter. (My money, when I had any, was in a calfskin belt that hugged my waist and added no seen weight or bulge. And when I lay back on the half-sister's mattress, the belt was under Hettie's.) The client saw me take out the leather billfold, saw me throw it open, saw me handle his money, casually, respectfully, and saw me slide it between the layers of soft leather without counting it first. He saw a man who was familiar with money, who made plenty but wasn't excited or corrupted by it. An intelligent, handsome man who was looking after business, his own and his client's, a calm man with quiet flair, and a man they could trust.

And what they saw was what they got. I *could* be trusted. I was doing it by the book. Their book. They paid; I delivered. Few of the clients tried to deny that there were more customers falling through their doors since my squad of good-shouldered boys had started parading the streets that clung to their own street.

I closed my wallet – always thin, never a dollar sticking out a grubby tongue – and I smiled at the fourth Mister Levine. He smiled back and answered my question.

—Yes, he said. —I'd say I'm happy.

He lifted his eyes very slightly, showing me the ceiling.

—We're all happy. We're busy and that's the way we like it here. There was a stretch there, Saturday, when all the Mister Levines and their wives and my own baby doll had to man the floor, there were that many customers suddenly needing good fabric for the coming winter.

He wiped his brow. It was another hot one.

—Normally they don't turn their minds to cotton until the first morning they wake up cold. So, yes, Mister Glick. We're all happy here at Levine's.

He smiled again.

—And, he said. —I have another reason to be happy.

The smile became a grin.

—There's another little Levine on the way. Although, of course, his name won't be Levine.

—Congratulations, I said.

—Thank you, Mister Glick.

—Levine and Nephew, I said. —It has a ring to it.

—It does, at that.

The wallet was one thing. And the shoulders were another. Honesty and shoulders. My boards told no lies and the shoulders that held them were broad and day-long straight. They were shoulders for carrying commandments, for humping the world – reliable, upright, dust- and dandruff-free. I had six young lads on my books now, all good, strapping kids, two of them older than me. All of them bright and on the go. My boys were several cuts above the rest. They carried the boards like well-cut suits of armour.

And the market approved. Even Mister Stern admitted that he'd noticed.

—Women, he said. —All kinds of women. Dames, janes, women kind of women. Cuties. All kinds.

—And they're buying cigars?

—Some of them.

—Are they smoking them?

—What you think? I follow them?

The women didn't smoke the cigars; very few of them did. But they admired the bearing of the boys who carried Stern's poetry and address. They stopped and watched and sometimes even followed – I'd seen them do it – and hoped that a Stern cigar would work any sort of magic on their own men – husbands, fiancés, strangers. The fact that the boys between the boards weren't smoking didn't matter. The message was in the shoulders. The women gave the men these unexpected gifts and watched them as they smoked, and they imagined they saw happy results – better men walked out of the smoke. Women carried a Stern cigar in their pocketbooks and bags, or hidden beneath silk or sacking, around their necks or strapped to their waists, behind their ears or as fat hairpins. At night, they lit them at open windows and waved their incense across airshafts to men who sat alone at tables. Or they went out to dark, dry halls at strange hours of the morning and blew the magic smoke under locked apartment doors.

40

And Stern thought it was all about tobacco.

—I sell good cigars, is all.

But he paid me every Friday.

And it wasn't just cigars. Happy families were wrapped in Levine's cloth, Hettie's clients were fuller, Palumbo's ice stayed solid through the dog days.

It was the shoulders that did it. The mouth and nose were at the front, no good to eyes following the boards. A good back was just that, a back. But shoulders were front and back; they advertised the man from every angle. And my boys wore well-dressed shoulders, because women were the market. Even the dykes preferred boys with shoulders to girls with none. Men's clothes, automobiles, office furniture, cigars – women were still the market. I knew it, and the big shots on Madison Avenue knew it. *For the Modern American Girl.* The only surprise – and it did surprise me – was that the women didn't know. And neither did most of the clients. But I knew. And the ad men knew. They sold their dreams to women. They frightened – *Domestic Hands!* – then flattered them – *You modern mothers have set your babies free!* They gave the women the words and pictures, on every corner and page. But I went further: I gave them the words made flesh.

She was drifting in front of my face again.

—Every one of our thoughts becomes a reality.

She opened her eyes.

—Say it.

I repeated the words, exactly as she wanted them.

—You got a way with other people's words. The trick is—. Listening or looking?

—Listening.

—You can look too, daddio. The trick is to say the words often enough, and you'll start to believe them. Believe me?

—Yeah.

—No. You don't. Every one of our thoughts becomes a reality. Believe me yet? Cross your heart?

—No.

The blanket slid off her shoulders. She pointed at my lap.

—Look, she said. —My thought is becoming reality right in front of my eyes. But that's an easy one, I guess.

I kissed her shoulder.

—See those orange wrappers beside the pot? she said.

I turned my head and looked at the chamber pot, to the left of the window.

—Yeah, I said.

—Know why they're there?

Her breath was scalding my ear.

—I wipe my ass with them. Say it.

—Every one of our thoughts becomes a reality.

—Fast learning, daddio. It's saying the thing, all the time. Not just remembering. Here's another. Listening?

—Yeah.

—Sure?

—Yes.

—Goodie. We are what we make ourselves and not what circumstances make us. You believe that, daddio?

—Yeah.

—So, say it.

—We are what we make ourselves and not what circumstances make us.

—And ain't you the living proof? What circumstances we got here, daddio? Me, you, the bed. We're not going to let these circumstances bully us into doing something we don't want to do. Are we?

—No.

—No. Because we are what we make ourselves. Ain't that the case?

—Yes.

—Yes. I shouldn't say *ain't*. It's *not* the thing. But guys like the way I say it. Now, where was I? Oh, yare. Circumstances. Got any circumstances in your wallet today, daddy?

—No.

—Now ain't that a wad of lettuce. A dollar or two could've tipped the scale. So, back to school, I guess. Because there's the thing, you know. I can make me what I am. And you can make you what you are. But, sometimes – most times actually, not together. And not now. For me to make myself me, I need some of your circumstances. And for you to make yourself you, you need me to flip over. And that just ain't what I am right now.

A finger touched my nose.

—This stuff has a name, she said. —Want to know it?

—Yeah.

—Autosuggestion.

She leaned at me a tiny bit more and spoke straight at my left eye. All I could see was a mouth, and wet teeth.

—Autosuggestion. Sounds good, don't you think?

—Yeah.

—Yes. Want to know what it means?

—Yes, please.

—Polite. I'm going to tell you. Listening?

—Yeah.

—Implanting an idea in oneself by oneself. It's the up-to-date thing. We all know how to do it. Don't we?

—Yeah.

—Yes, we do. We have will and we have imagination. In there, daddio.

And a finger touched my temple. A cool, wonderful finger. It stayed as a cold point on my skin after she'd stopped touching me.

—And the thing is. Most people think the will's the thing. Strength, domination. Control. All that guy bullsh. Don't get me wrong. I like it, you know. Us dolls could do with more of it. But. Here's the thing. The will ain't the thing. The will *is not* the thing. Want to know what is the thing?

—The other one.

—What is that?

—Imagination.

—Pow. It's masturbation, daddio. Like that word?

—Not really.

—Me neither. Don't do much for me. The word. But that's what it is. You masturbate, you use your will when you do it? Got an answer for me?

—No.

—Right. Imagination's the thing. Close your eyes, daddio.

I did. I felt her breath melting my ear.

—Your eyes are shut and you ain't even touching me. But your imagination is fucking my brains out. Want to know what my imagination is doing?

—Yeah.

—Ain't telling.

And her finger was on my temple again.

—The madman at home, she said. —That's all the imagination is. Mad doll in my case. Bet her tits are even better than mine, too. That's a thought, ain't it?

43

—Yes.

—Yes. I think so. You've just got to make that mad guy do what you want him to do. Piece of cake. You're up to it already.

—Can I open my eyes?

—Nopie. The next bit. Listening?

—Yes.

—Your imagination gives you your hard-on. What else you need to deliver the goods?

—You?

—Ah ah. You a right-handed daddio?

—Yeah.

—That's all you need. You just grab that thing and pump him, and not too often, I guess. You're cooking. But it's the handwork's the thing. Repetition. That's the key. Saying it, again and again. Up and down. Every day, in ever-y way, I am getting, better, and better. Until you don't have to believe it any more.

I heard a creak. She was getting off the bed.

—Lesson over.

I opened my eyes. It was night, and cold.

—So, she said. —Remember the deal, daddio.

—I'll remember.

—You better, she said. —One good turn. That one there was good, I guess.

—I was disappointed with the ending.

—How come? she said. —Expect it to end in a fuck?

—That would've been nice.

—Oh, come on, daddio. You know me better than that. You wanted education, and you got it. In spades. Better than the book. You want me, it's a different proposition. You knew that. I know you did. I prey on weakness. You know that. I'm being straight with you. Always.

She was dressed now, at the open window.

—Look at me, daddio.

I looked across, through the few feet of darkness, to her outline, in front of the echoes of light that popped and died in the night behind her.

—See much?

—No.

—Remember what I looked like a while ago?

—Yes.

—Make the most of it.

44

I heard her heels on the fire escape. She spoke again.

—It's a land of gold, daddio. Only, the gold ain't in the streets. It's in your head. Believe that?

—Yes.

—Well, so do I. You owe me.

I called after her.

—What's your name?

—You'll know when you see it in lights, daddio.

She was gone.

And so was I.

I didn't want a desk or the walls and door that would map me and make me easily found, by Johnny No or & Son, or names from further back, names that could translate Glick to *glic*, to clever, to Smart. I'd live without the sign on the door. I'd wait. My office was the street, whatever street I was on. Beep Beep's Joe had my boards now. He was the best of my bunch. And he watched it all – writing the copy, roping the mark, judging the shoulders of the young lads wanting work. Soon, he'd come up and announce that he was going out on his own. He'd plunge right in. He'd even take some of my clients with him.

And Joe was suddenly in front of me, boardless, out of breath; this was on the hot edge of a new morning. Joe tried to speak but there was an El passing over us. We waited as shadow and light fought around our heads, and then I could listen. He looked scared, excited, already on top of it.

—Hooper's been hit, Mister Glick.

Hooper was one of my new kids. Yezierski was his real name; he was Hooper because he was tall and won basketball games all by himself.

—Hit? I said, the retired hitman. —Where?

—Baxter and Bayard.

I ran the wrong way.

I ran towards Baxter and Bayard, as cleanly as the crowds and barrows would let me. There was a sudden ache in my chest, yelling at me to turn and walk away and further away, and keep walking. But I ran. I got out to the centre of the street and ran against the traffic. Horns honked, horses sneered – *my blue heaven* – an organ-grinder's monkey laughed as I passed him and the organ. But I pumped air to my legs and raced, full-steam, into a war.

But Hooper hadn't been hit. He stood against a lamppost and

held his right shoulder. His hat was beside him on the ground. He was paler than his usual pale. He was in pain but still between the boards, working.

TWEED'S ELECTRICAL –
LET OUR RADIOS
SERENADE
YOU
AND
ONLY
YOU

—What happened?
—Got jumped, Mister Glick, said Hooper.
He was fine.
—How many? I asked.
—Five, six.
—Did you know them?
—No, Mister Glick. They was just a gang, is all.
—Jewish, Italians, anything? Irish?
—They didn't say nothing, Mister Glick. They didn't look like nothing. Just kids. But they wasn't Jewish, I don't think. They didn't have no books with them. I think it's broke.
He took his hand from his shoulder. I could see the lump; his collarbone had been smashed.
—They had a baseball bat, he said.
—Did they frisk you?
—No, Mister Glick. Whacked me hard, is all.
—And they didn't say anything? Warn you or anything?
He looked at Joe before he spoke.
—No, Mister Glick.
But I didn't see it.
—No, Mister Glick.
Until months later.
—They didn't say nothing, not evens to each other. Just whacked me on the shoulders, is all. A couple of times, then some more. Then they beat it.
He shuddered.
—They couldn't reach your head, I said.
He tried to smile.
—They *was* a pot of shrimps, at that.

46

—Good man, I said. —We'll get you fixed up.

—Thanks, Mister Glick.

—No problem.

I picked up his hat and beat the dust off it. I put it back on his head.

—Don't worry about anything, I said. —Look after Hooper, Joe.

I left Joe to deal with Hooper, to get him to a doctor, the hospital, to slip him a folding bonus and another for his mammy. That gave me time to think, as I ran; it was something I was good at. And I could watch out for eyes watching me – something else I was good at, although that extra New York level, the roofs, made it a harder job of work. I ran on the melting street – the asphalt tried to grab me. But it wasn't the asphalt. There was old water under me; I could feel its pull for the first time since I'd left Dublin.

I stopped; I had to.

I could feel the water, but it was different here. It wasn't flowing, rushing, the water of escape. I was on top of still water. Stagnant, ancient, evil. I could feel it, warm, oily, creeping to my feet. I tried to move. The shouts and screams of the city's throats and engines drowned the cries of the dead that were held by that water below. I suddenly knew that they were there. There were no black faces walking past me, and none driving the trucks and automobiles that fought for passage between the barrows – I'd never noticed the absence – but they were below me, and not far below, their bloody, soil-blacked fingernails inches from my feet, hanged men, mutilated rebel slaves, trapped forever in water that went nowhere. And more dead men below them, red men, screaming to be heard, screaming their defeat and rage.

I pulled my feet away. I stood on fingers that were finally cracking the surface. I ran. I ran a path through the traffic and dust. I was on dry land again, nowhere but the present.

It was fine.

I already had to look behind my back, to the sides and in the air. And now the ground was after me. The place was older than Dublin.

But it was fine. I was running on new streets. My legs were still a young fella's. I'd only stopped for a second, a breather. I was running and looking again.

Hooper had been jumped. By kids, the same kind as himself. But they hadn't taken or demanded anything. I'd been a kid once

47

and I'd hopped on other kids, but always for money, food, anything to sell. It was no different here. Hunger was hunger. Fear was fear. These kids were fighting for their place on the couple of streets that were the world; growing up, grabbing the chance, shoving up to the big guys, the Yiddish Gomorra or the Italian gangs, or the Polish or the Irish, terrified behind the strut, praying behind their sneers. Street kids measured everything. A kid here could earn a buck for poisoning a horse or a nickel for sharpening hairpins, to be stuck into the scabs who kept their mothers and sisters out of the sweatshops. They could steal anything – a pickle, a shirt, a Buick – and find a taker while they were still running. They could make serious bucks by waiting for dark and making Jewish lightning or Italian or Irish or German lightning – setting fire to the stores, stables, news-stands of those who thought they didn't need protection. There was a kid on this street, and the next one and the next, for every job.

So, was Hooper's broken collarbone a message back to me? From Johnny No? From someone else, other men I hadn't met? Or others that I'd met before? I'd never held a baseball bat – I hadn't seen the game being played – but I knew that a well-aimed swing could kill. I'd known the weight of my father's wooden leg. Fast Olaf patrolled his roofs with a baseball bat under his arm. I'd seen him send a pigeon clean across Orchard Street, seen it sail right past the visiting nurse's head as she took a shortcut across the roofs. They could have killed Hooper.

So, why?

I searched the sidewalks, and the ledges above; I looked on the stoops, in the doorways that I passed. No one staring back, or deliberately not looking. I swerved back onto the sidewalk, so I could work the hinge, look behind without too much of the twist that would have given it away. No one coming after me, halting suddenly, turning away.

Maybe Hooper had known them. It wasn't unlikely. Tall, good-looking, successful – he was memorable. And these were his streets. That was the thing of it: the streets were divided and subdivided, conquered and lost, reclaimed by grown mobs and kids and their sons and grandfathers, a constant multi-floored battle that went on forever; it was impossible to map or explain. The baseball bat was something between those kids and Hooper. It had been brewing when I was cycling across Ireland, when Hooper's parents were walking across Europe. It had nothing to do with me.

48

But I didn't believe that. I was sure of only one thing as I ran back past the organ-grinder's monkey: that bat had been aimed at me. I glanced around me: nothing. But the dead water was with me all the way.

I ran all day. But I wasn't on the lam. Fuck Johnny No or whoever's stool pigeon was glaring at my back; I wasn't running away. I ran past the store pullers, the thick men in derbys who patrolled the sidewalk.

—*Guten* suits today.

—Not interested today.

—Come on, pal. There's a sheeny suit inside, waiting for you.

—I'm a busy man.

—Get ya coming back, schmuck.

I brought my clients the business but I had to bring them excitement too, the possibilities that came with the willingness to spend, to invest in themselves and me. There were sixteen dry-goods stores on a stretch of Orchard Street that took me three minutes to gallop. I had boys already toting boards for five, and I was putting the convincers on another four. These were village men; I was dragging them out of their territories. I had to deliver a little fever with their bigger profits.

I ran up the dark, airless stairs, all colours smothered by decades of coal smoke. Past the buzzing sweatshop, sawing away the hours and days of the women locked inside. I could feel the machines in my feet as I broke through the wall of lint, up. Up, past Fast Olaf's home, and his half-sister's. I listened for sound from inside – I listened as I climbed – but I heard nothing that was definitely hers, just the noises that belonged to every tenement everywhere. A song, a cough, dying, laughter. *Every day, in ev-ery way.* I sang it as I rose – *better and better and better.*

Mildred had come back for more soap, her eyes clear of hard life, her sneer a loose, uncertain thing.

—Got any more of that soap?

I had a cake of the stuff, waiting in my pocket.

—I got the cush here, she said.

And she opened her hand like a kid who'd been clutching a treasure. There were two dollars there on her palm, folded over again and again, to the shape of a very small box. She smiled, but she was worried.

I put my hand to my pocket and kept it there for exactly one New York second. She stared at the pocket.

—Need a job? I said.

And she nodded.

Up the stairs, climbing away from the sewing machines. Past the room where Bummy Mandelbaum was making lead dimes and quarters. There were sacks of potatoes on the landing outside. Bummy put each brand new coin between two halves of a spud; in a day or two, the dime was shining and nothing like lead. He restitched the sacks and sold the spuds to the neighbourhood eateries. Bummy was slowly poisoning the population of the Lower East Side, and everyone knew and admired him for it. They even paid for their lead-spiced meals with quarters they knew came fresh from Bummy's tiny hands.

Up, past Bummy's. One last flight, through the hottest, deadest part of the house. To my favourite part of my new city, the floor with no ceiling, the roof. The roof of Manhattan. Where everything belonged to those who wanted it.

Mildred held the package in her hand. She fought the urge to dash – she had the goods. I saw the fight, admired the strength that kept her planted.

—What kinda job?

—Sales.

—Me?

—You.

—Gee whiz, she said, and blushed, angry at her readiness to be the sucker.

She looked at the soap in her hand.

—How much?

—Twenty a week, and commission.

She liked the word.

—Commission, she said. —That's a cut, right?

—Right.

The red word on the board had been Steady's idea.

He took the paint from a hole in his coat, a little tin with a red lid. His right hand did a crazy dance on its way to prise off the lid. I watched the sweat forming on his temples. Two black-painted fingernails tried to shift the lid.

—Been years, he said.

He grunted. The lid lifted and hung to the side on a thread of dry paint. We looked in.

—Enough, said Steady. —Got my milk?

He put the tin on the ground. And I handed him Fast Olaf's brown-bag. He pulled out the cork with no big effort and threw it onto the air over Orchard Street. He put the bag to his mouth and pulled back his head. He took the bottle from his mouth, put it down, then picked up the tin. His hand was calm now, fit for shaving and surgery. He dipped his brush, and painted the word, without stencil or pencilled outline, just like that, in wild, wild red. The O was done in one clean sprint. The N was quicker, perfectly judged. He sang, very quietly – *My country 'tis of thee* – the L was alive and gorgeous, done while I still gazed at the N – *Land of grape juice and tea*. And the Y made me laugh, done in two cocky strokes.

He put the tin back on the ground and picked up another brush. It went into the black can, a big graceless giant beside the red.

I had to say something.

—Is that all?

—Trust me, he said, and painted the last word.

YOU

He threw the brush to the ground and picked up the brown-bag.

LET OUR RADIOS
SERENADE
YOU
AND
ONLY
YOU

Around us, the homers were suddenly restless. Fast Olaf was approaching. Under washing lines, over the low wall that divided this property from the one next door. He didn't look at us. He unlatched a wire-mesh gate and, and telling himself to bend his head – I saw his lips move – he went into the coop.

Steady took the bottle from his mouth.

—That the kid makes this stuff?

—That's him.

—He's a fucking genius.

51

He looked at me, then nodded at the board.

—I know what you're thinking. You want more. You want to run off and buy more red, and more shades of it.

It was more than he'd ever said before.

—A mistake, he said. —It's perfect there. Fucking perfect. It draws the eye. Demands attention. It makes no sense. *Only*. The fuck is that about? You read it all. Ah. Pulling power. More of the red, yeah nice, but less power.

—What about other colours?

He was looking at Fast Olaf as he stirred the bath of liquor with his baseball bat.

—Nope.

He waved at the board; he seemed to be dismissing it – he wanted to fling it off the roof.

—Not for this medium, he said. —Posters now, that'd be different. Or magazines. But there's no room for swank on these things. Resist the temptation.

He leaned out and touched the red, and looked at his fingertip.

—Ready for business, he said.

He looked at his finger shaking, tapping away at nothing.

—Just thought I'd try it, he said. —The good old red.

He looked away from his hand, let it drop to his side.

—Got thinking, he said. —Surprised me. Haven't thought in years.

Again, he gazed at Olaf. He seemed to have forgotten that I was there. Then –

—Colour, he said. —It's the sex appeal of the advertising business. And know how I know?

—How?

—I told them, the fucks.

—I thought you were a sign painter.

—Didn't tell you what signs. The sex appeal of the business. Don't remember what sex fucking is. But red there.

He nodded at the board.

—That's sex. Even I see that.

He took up the brown-bag and pulled back his head.

—Do you actually need that stuff? I asked.

He stopped the bag's journey but didn't straighten up.

—Don't get sentimental on me, he said.

I was on my way up, to Fast Olaf's roof, to meet Steady again, to admire his latest magic. Out, through a gap made for smaller

52

men than me. Out into the sun, to the roof and the glare and heat that always washed me, a barber's towel that soaked the pain from my face and shoulders. The chimneys cut the world into sharp, expensive tiles. A man's hat, a pigeon's wing, a drifting sheet, their shadows were black, more solid than the real things that shimmered in the sun. A world waiting to be made and remade.

—Marketing consultant, I told Mildred. —How's that sound? We were in the back of Beep Beep's taxi.

—Sounds good to me, he said over his shoulder.

—I wasn't talking to you, I said.

—When you want my opinion, you'll ask for it.

—That's it.

—You're the bird that's paying.

—That's right.

I spoke to her again.

—Happy with that, Mildred? Marketing consultant.

—I'll say, she said. —You sure got the words. Consultant. Never been one of them before.

The title pleased her. She was doing a great job and enjoying it. She shrugged.

—It's a bit like acting, I guess.

—Have you acted before?

—All my life, she said.

Mildred was the excitement. Colour was the sex appeal of the advertising business. Steady had told me that. The red on the board, and the shoulders that carried it. That was what sent women off buying drapes and cigars they hadn't known they needed. But the clients, the winchells who forked out for the business, they needed the pull of sex too; they needed to feel the slow, caressing possibility of *it*. And it wasn't red or shoulders with these guys; it was sex itself – the safe promise of sex. A woman was what those guys needed – they were all men – what they needed in front of their eyes. Dressed in red, sure, shoulders on her, fine – but a real live woman. No symbols, no parts, but the fact right there in front of them, safe on the other side of the counter.

And that was where Mildred came in. Other women bought and went. But Mildred lingered and usually didn't buy.

—You Mister Stern?

—Yare.

—Love the sandwich board.

—Yare? So?

—Made me just want to come on in and buy all the cigars in your store.

The lines were mine; the delivery was out-and-out Mildred.

—Then just stay there a while, I told her. —Let him look at you. Let him want to touch that skin you're after finding.

—That what a consultant does?

—Yeah.

—Then I'll do it.

—And don't complicate things, I told her. —Don't actually take it anywhere, if you know what I mean. Just linger a bit. Look a bit overwhelmed and giddy, and go.

—Listen, buster, said Mildred. —Talk to me like that again and you can find yourself a new consultant. I know what you want me to do. And I'll do it. Overwhelmed, giddy, I'll give them to you. And I know why. And I know something else, big words. What you want me to do don't make me a consultant.

She slapped my leg.

—Call me a consultant, fine. But you ain't looking at a numskull here.

The soap had released more than her skin. Mildred was making up for lost time, and she was running right beside me.

—Words, words, words. You need more than that, even if one or two of them is red.

She wrote **$5** on a piece of paper, then ran a quick **/** through it. Under that, she wrote **$4**.

—That'll do the trick, she said. —Add a buck to the price, then change your mind. Sex and a whole dollar back. Beats sex.

Most of the boards now featured red slashes across old black prices. The storekeepers giggled at the happy lie. Except the few.

—What? said Mister Stern. —I don't know what a cigar costs? I'm an idiot?

And that was why Mildred was in the taxi with me. And why Fast Olaf's half-sister had joined the list of my handsome employees.

—Oh, this and that, the half-one said when I'd asked her what she did for her money. —Sometimes, a hat-check girl. Sometimes, checking other stuff and things.

—How much does a hat-check girl make?

—Depends on the hat, daddio.

—Want to make a double sawbuck and commission?

—Commish? she said. —Some of the famous 10 per cent.

—More like five, and the nights will still be your own.

—Lead me to it.

So, while me and Mildred travelled in Beep Beep's cab, Fast Olaf's half-sister was bellying up to Levine's counter and the other Front Street counters, looking like money very well spent to the tired men on the working side.

—Just stay there a—

—Yare yare, the half-sister interrupted. —Show them the blow-job mouth, then turn and walk away. Second nature to me, daddio.

She was fuckin' dangerous.

Mildred looked out at the streets, the walls, windows. We were heading uptown, under the Second Avenue El. Up to the numbered streets, the streets too young and wobbly for names. Through the passage of white light and dark, cut by the El's tracks and girders.

Two more of my boys had been hopped on, their shoulders smashed by baseball bats. The streets of the Lower East Side were dragging at my blood. It was old water under there and I didn't want to find it.

But I wasn't running away. And I wasn't giving up on the streets I'd conquered in the summer months. I was expanding; that was what I was doing. I wanted America, not just a few village streets on a tiny island tucked into its east coast. It was too easy to be fooled by the numbers, the seven hundred souls on every acre, the clatter and screeching, the constant growth. It was all villages, *shtetls*, crossroads, parish pumps.

Hettie never strayed beyond her street.

—What's to see? she said. —More faces from home.

She went to the door. It was creeping up to midnight. She looked out over the menu cards. She lifted her left arm and pointed a finger.

—Walk this way, Poland.

She dropped her arm; the flour she'd left continued to point, until it scattered when she raised her right arm.

—This way, Mother Russia.

She turned.

—I stay at home. Where I've always been.

She walked towards me.

—It takes me thirty years to know this. I never left home.

55

She kissed me.

—And now it is the way I like. How is my Mildred?

Mildred took one side and I took the other.

—What're we looking for, big words?

—Possibilities, I said.

—Oh yare? What they look like?

But she knew.

Hettie was wrong. It *was* a new world, and newer the further uptown we went. Taller, wider, sparkling. I looked out, I leaned into the real Manhattan. Beep Beep got us out from under the El, and the sky was up there, corralled by sheer walls. He took us on to Broadway. The crowds were here, the pushcart pedlars – pretzels, cookies, roasted chickpeas – the open-mouthed visitors, the pickpockets, phonies and fakers, the cops and robbers, the pitchmen and barkers outside the burlesques and flea circuses, bargain stores and dance halls.

—This way for a good time, folks!

All pushing and roaring for their share of attention and profit. And all changing as I looked; there was room here for ambitious elbows. I could hear the hiss of neon and accents that were American and nothing else, hiding no old geography or muck. *He is the man who owns Broadway, that's what the daily papers say.* Beep Beep took us off Broadway, and we kept our eyes peeled as he fussed across the island.

—See anything? I said.

—See lots, said Mildred. —See too much.

—What d'you mean?

—I got a feeling.

She scanned the walls and sidewalks.

—We're too late, she said. —It's all gone.

—But that's it, I said. —It's here, going and gone. It's always changing. Do you see anything not moving? Anything built and staying that way?

Lights, billboards on top of billboards – *Graduate to Camels* – out-climbing the construction, climbing right out of the city. *It beats – As it sweeps.* And down here – *As it cleans* – not a sandwich board in sight. In the scramble to hang the words from the sky, they'd forgotten about the ground.

—It's never too late here, Mildred, I said. —See anything missing?

—Nope.

—Keep looking.

Steady was alone on the roof. There was no sign at all of Fast Olaf. And Steady was dead. He was face-down in Fast Olaf's gin bath, inside the coop, and the pigeons were upset. They flapped and crashed in a box of feathers and blood, caught in the chicken wire, on the white-stained floor of the coop, and floating dead and dying beside Steady. There were ringed claws clinging to the mesh, single wings caught tight by the wire. And the noise, Jesus. It was life being torn from meat, fighting the last and only terror. But Steady's fight was over. His back was the back of a dead man.

I moved closer to the coop – the screams, the panic, grew even louder – and I found the hook that held the wire gate to its shaking timber frame.

I looked around me. No one that I could see, no shadow growing from stricter shadows. I looked back at Steady. My eyes walked his coat from collar to gin-soaked hem. No new small holes, no blood creeping from the holes. I looked around again. I listened. An El, and further west, another.

Go now. Now. Just go. Now.

I grabbed the hook again. I shoved my hand into feathers and crazy air.

Go. Now. Now.

I lifted the hook and pulled the gate from the timber. The chicken-wire and wood came part of the way. I pulled again, got both hands to the job. The nails slid from the frame, with shrieks I couldn't hear. I threw the gate over my head.

I stood back quickly. Fat birds darted from the coop. I shook what was left of the walls. I beat them with my open hands. More birds fell from the cage or flew, and fell and tried to fly. They limped, or rolled. One bird pecked at the tar, slowly buried its beak in black chunks and strands.

Slowly – fuckin' hell – the coop emptied. Some of the birds refused to leave or weren't able to, but the insanity was gone, spread across the roof and sky.

Again, I looked around.

Go. For fuck sake, go.

I stepped into the coop, just one foot. The baked smell of shit and death swam around my head. Feathers floated on nothing; the place was airless now. It was worse than any cell I'd ever been locked into.

Go.

Another step, I was properly in. Trapped. I looked behind me. Still nothing. Less birds now. Three or four suffering silently, puffing their breasts, trying to outstrip their pain. I listened. Transport and construction, the sounds that thumped out time. No foot-clicks, breath held, finger slowly pulling metal. I was alone with Steady and the pigeons. I was sure of it, and scared.

The old bath stood on its four clawed feet. Steady's weight had thrown some of the hooch to the floor; I could feel it in my short, slow steps. The hooch in the bath was absolutely still. No twitching wing or foot to make a ripple. Everything floating was dead.

Closer now, I studied his back again. No bullet holes or blood. I looked at his neck, the back of his head. No marks, no livid stains across his thin, soaked hair. I bent down further. No bruises, no thumb-marks – no hands had grabbed and forced his face into the bath. Years of dirt, a mole, life's creases. Nothing recent, nothing violent.

Go.

The man had drowned.

Go.

I listened.

I plucked the pigeons from the hooch and dropped them to the floor. Five of them, heavy with the gin they'd soaked. I examined the gin. There was blood in the mix, but not much. Enough to drain the life from a homer but not a man, not even a small man like Steady, who hadn't eaten solid food in years.

This man had drowned.

Now. Go. He drowned. Go.

I grabbed the shoulders, didn't let myself think too much. I took two fists of saturated cloth and stepped back, slid back a few steps so the hooch wouldn't drench me. I pulled the far shoulder first. He was dead-heavy, the heaviest thing I'd ever hefted. I thought about stopping and taking off my jacket, rolling up my soaking sleeves. I thought about just stopping. The man had drowned. I knew that. But I'd liked the man. I pulled again.

It was the coop that saved me.

Fast Olaf couldn't manage a clean swing; the roof was too low, the walls closed in. The bat hit my back, below my hat and neck. It hadn't the clout to kill or cripple. But I didn't know that. I'd seen nothing, heard nothing. It was instant pain, bad pain. Unexplained, explosive.

I dropped away, let go of Steady's shoulders. I rolled. Over feathers, pigeons, shit. I saw the legs. I knew the trousers.

—Eddie!

I saw him try another swing. He tried to beat the roof, to push it back with the bat. I rolled and got to my knees. And feet.

The butt hit my chin. Slid, and caught my ear. It hurt. Things swam. All sounds were gone. But I could see. Could see Fast Olaf out there. I blinked, saw him clearly. He didn't look stupid now. He looked mean and almost happy. He'd turned the bat; its working end was staring at me. He stabbed.

And missed. I fell against the wire. It held me up. He stabbed again, and hit – my shoulder, not my face. Relief drowned the pain. And I could hear again.

—Eddie!

—Fuck you!

I couldn't blame him. His birds were dead and dying – he was inhaling their absence and feathers. His hooch was contaminated, probably past saving.

—Listen to me, I shouted as my shoulder took another stab. Christ, it hurt. He was chipping away at me.

And maybe there was more. I'd never seen him coo at those birds, or seen him fondly count them. Maybe it was him who'd killed Steady, and he'd been waiting for me. Somewhere on the roof; he knew where to hide. He was following orders, meeting a deadline. I didn't know, and I needed to. I didn't want to kill him.

—Eddie!

I was in a corner. Trapped by the bath and Olaf.

—Who did this? I shouted.

It worked. I knew by the questions that bumped behind his eyes; he hadn't come onto the roof with a plan. He'd seen what he'd seen and swung his bat.

—The fuck?

—Did you do this? I said.

He looked guilty for an Olaf-second, then growled and pointed the bat at me.

—The fuck I kill my own boids for? That aren't even my boids.

It was only now that he noticed Steady.

—The fuck's that?

—Steady, I told him. —He was dead when I got here. Just before you.

He gave me his suspicious look.

—Before, he said. —How long before?

—A minute. Maybe two. You should have seen it.

—I do see it. Fuck!

But he didn't. He didn't see it at all. He was confused. I wasn't trapped any more. He wanted sympathy, not revenge. His mouth hung open as he looked around.

—He's gonna kill me.

—Who?

—The guy.

—What guy?

—Just, the guy.

I watched him pick up dead birds. He leaned the bat against the chicken-wire. He held one in both hands, and let it go, and watched it drop and thump the ground.

—They all like this? he said.

—More or less, I said. —The ones that haven't flown away. They might come back, I suppose.

He shook his head slowly.

—Fuckin' kill me.

—Does the guy own them? I asked.

—What?

—The birds.

—Fuck the boids. But yare. *He* don't own them. The next guy owns them.

—The next guy?

—The big-shot.

He looked at the bath again.

—Who's the egg in the fucking merchandise?

— Steady.

—That his name?

—Yep.

—Who is he?

—You know, I said. —The guy who's been painting the signs up here.

—What happened?

—I don't know, I said. —Give us a hand. You take the legs.

He grabbed Steady's sockless ankles and started to pull, before I'd taken hold of Steady's shoulders.

—Hang on, I said, as Steady floated from me.

I got my hands under Steady's arms and, together, we lifted

60

and slid him over the rim, to the floor. Fast Olaf let him drop, but I gripped wet cloth and landed him gently. The hooch ran from his coat and from under his coat, like water from a tap. And it was clear – no stain, no red.

—He dead? said Fast Olaf.

I put my foot against Steady's left shoulder. Then I leaned across and grabbed the coat at his other side, and pulled. My foot held him firm as his right side rose. I got my foot from under him as he dropped over on his back. More gin ran from his clothes and joined the slush. I could feel the hooch inside my boots, already getting warm.

He looked like a man who had roared as his life ran out. The dead eyes still held fury; the mouth was twisted, not yet slack and gone.

—What d'you reckon, Eddie?

—Dead, he said.

—I think you're right, I said. —How, but?

He didn't answer.

(And he hadn't answered my first question either, but I'd been too thick to notice. *Dead*, he'd said. He'd been talking about himself; he'd been talking about the two of us.)

I looked down again at Steady. No bruises on his face, or slap marks. I put a finger behind an ear, pulled it gently towards me, and looked behind for hints. Nothing hidden by either ear.

I stood up.

—Know what? I said. —He drowned.

—Drowned? said Fast Olaf. —There's no fucking water for drowned.

—In the hooch, I said.

I looked into the bath and saw something. I dipped my hand, arm, elbow, grabbed and pulled it out. The ladle. I gave it a shake.

—Where would this normally be, Eddie?

—What?

—This.

—There.

He pointed to the corner behind me. I looked, and saw a four-inch nail hammered into the wooden corner stake. There was a hole in the handle of the ladle. I put the ladle up on the nail and let it dangle.

—Like that?

—Yare.

—He fell in, I said.

Fast Olaf was staring at the ladle.

—The fuck how?

—He gave in to temptation, I said. —He was your best customer, Eddie.

Olaf looked down at Steady; every breath was a brand new lesson.

—He had you down as the best alky-cooker in town.

Fast Olaf looked at me.

—Yare?

—Yeah.

—The fuck I care?

—It's a compliment, Eddie. Look. It's simple. He saw the hooch.

I pointed at the bath.

—He saw the ladle. You weren't here. He took the ladle. You with me?

—Yare.

—He leaned down to help himself. He slipped, or tripped. He was probably soused already. And he fell in.

—How'd he drown?

—Feel his coat. It's saturated. It probably weighs twice as much as he does. And he was rat-arsed. He couldn't get out. He couldn't lift his head.

I was beginning to believe it myself.

—He got tired.

—He was helping himself to the merchandise?

—Yep.

—The fuck.

I looked at Fast Olaf's face.

—Don't kick him, Eddie, I said. —He'll feel nothing. Don't do it.

I waited until Fast Olaf was looking lost and safe again. Then I got out of the coop, and the open sky was over me. I stayed out of the shade and walked to the crates that had been Steady's easel. There was the brush, resting on the low wall, the ledge that divided the properties. Resting. Put there deliberately, position chosen, not dropped or thrown. There was a small red tin, closed, beside the brush. Everything in proper order, left there by a man who'd taken a break. And the boards –

62

MOSTEL
THE TAXIDERMIST
YOUR PET
CAN
LIVE
FOREV

No black line racing away from the last letter. No spilt paint or hidden message. The man had taken a break. No one guarding the bath, except the birds; it was too much temptation for him.

I looked at the coop. Fast Olaf was bending over the bath. I could smell the hooch from here. I could smell it in my clothes, but that was a separate, more urgent tang. I could smell the hooch in the bath. I could taste it in my breath. And I remembered, now when I really didn't want to: I'd always been able to smell it.

And so had Steady. All the long days he'd been up here, painting my signs. Alone. And he'd never given in to the exact same temptation. I could smell it – no sweeter, no stronger. No more tempting than it had been four hours earlier, or a week or two weeks or a month earlier.

Go.

Fast Olaf was taking pigeons from the bath. And he was crying.

3

I walked.

The map was beautifully drawn, probably to scale. There were wide streets and various thinnesses, swerves and knuckles; each street was named, even those that weren't along our route. Time and hope had gone into it. I couldn't let the man down.

—I'll be there, I said.

I tapped my finger on the **x**, on the corner of Houston and the Bowery. And I slid the map across the counter.

—You might need this yourself.

—I might, at that, he said. —I don't get out much.

He sighed, and smiled. Then he bunched up the map and put it in his mouth.

—Evidence, he managed to say, and his eyes guided me to the ceiling.

I walked.

He was at ease in the night, away from the tall shelves and bolts of cloth. The hat, a black derby, almost silver, was on good terms with his head, and a cigarette parked on his bottom lip.

—Mister Glick, he said.

I could feel the water under us; I wanted to move. But I let him take the first step.

—Who's looking after the shop?

—The Levines, he said. —Couldn't agree which of them should take over, so all three disagreed to do it.

—What about your wife?

—Oh, she's fine. She's the only one knows where I'll be. I didn't tell her brothers. Tell them nothing. That's my modus operandi. But my wife. She isn't a Levine these days. She's foursquare with me. I need a night out. Sometimes we go to one of the theatres on Second Avenue, she and I. I enjoy it but I don't

64

understand a word. Ever seen *Hedda Gabler* performed in Yiddish, Mister Glick?

—Missed it.

—Or *Twelfth Night* or *Hamlet* by that Shakespeare? My grandparents came over from the old country. There was no Yiddish in the house; my pop was an American. So, know how I follow it? I hold my wife's hand. It's the nerves in her hand or something; I can read what's happening, pretty exactly, I'd estimate. So, there's that. Which I like. And then there's a couple of times a week I go out for an hour. I stroll over to Auster's there, on Cannon and Stanton. For an egg-cream or two. I stand outside and talk the talk with the other gents there. I like the egg-creams but they ain't a night out. My wife knows this, and she knows I won't get slopped or come home smelling of scent.

We were heading uptown, at a fairish clip.

—Where? I asked.

—I got a name from a gent came in to buy silk for the missis. So he said. Should have seen his kisser when I asked him if he wanted it delivered. We knock at a door and tell them Joe sent us. All there is to it, according to the gent buying the silk.

He liked me, he wanted my company; I could tell by the way we stepped together. But there was more than that going on. I looked behind me. Nothing sudden, no one diving. I could still feel water; I could feel it pulling.

I walked.

Corners, streets.

He surveyed the bare wall around the lone, black door. We were the only people on this street off a real street. No lights lit the puddles. I looked around.

—It's got a name, he said. —Did I tell you that? Although you'd never know it from this side of the door. Which is the point, I guess.

He knocked on the door. There was no bell, no brass knocker.

—Max's Little Estonia, he said. —According to the gent buying the silk.

No bell, but there was a judas window; I heard its screech before I saw it. I remembered the last time I'd been stared at from a judas, before I'd walked out of Kilmainham Gaol. This was a fairer version. The window trap was bigger; I could see most of a face – black eyes, a mouth that hung over the painted iron of the trap.

—Yare? said the mouth.

—Joe sent us, said my friend.

—That a fact? said the mouth.

The door opened out like a jail door and it was darker in there than on our street side. My friend went in, past the mouth. I followed him.

My first speakeasy.

I'd delivered Olaf's goods to back doors but I'd never carried them inside. As far as the door: that was the deal. Inside was where I'd meet old faces and grudges; I wasn't the only retired gunman in New York. I didn't want to run or hide, but strolling the daytime streets, every corner propped up by a cop, each a rednecked reminder of home, and carrying Exhibit A on my memorable back; it wasn't the ideal way to stay out of harm's way. It would be temporary, until I became an onside man of business. I delivered, and legged it.

This was before I realised that I could carry a barrel around all day, and no one was going to stop or even notice me. The copper on the corner was on a weekly retainer to make sure that no one stopped me, and his boss and *his* boss and their political bosses were all in for their cut of the action. It was all a done thing, down to every step and drop, all of it arranged long before I'd arrived. I was just the new guy who'd do what the old guy had done – I never knew what had happened to the old guy but it was nothing dramatic, nothing with gunsmoke or screeching wheels. It was simple business expansion. More kegs, shoulders, speakeasies.

There were two hundred and seventy dry agents in Manhattan but most of them were lazy or affordable. There hadn't been a raid in over a year, and most of those had been well rehearsed, part of the cabaret. On Manhattan Island, it was business as usual. It was more business than usual. There wasn't a sober pigeon in the city. Good tenants were evicted to make room for new speakeasies. And there was a constant flow of booze from else-where, from Canada and further. There'd never been a night out like it.

And the citizens loved bellying up to a bar, on the chance that the belly beside them belonged to a real live hoodlum. Because the hoodlums were in there. They'd turned from real live crime to this more sedate law-breaking. A room, a few stools, a couple of teacups, maybe a piano and a lad willing to play it – and easy, cosy profit. Manufacture, distribution, retail, ambience – the right guys chose the drapes, they supplied the sawdust that soaked up the spillage and tears. Their teamsters hefted the grain across the states. Old men were paid to sweep up each night's sawdust, and boys were paid to squeeze the juice from the dust – it could be done – back into old bottles. The guys had carved the city amongst themselves, invisible borders that were seen and respected. A time of peace and plenty. The shoot-outs and screeching drive-aways were for the visitors. The odd expendable body, the hat lying close by, one knee always bent. A photo, a reminder – business as usual, if called for. Only the saps and the mad died, the ones too stupid to see or too bright to conform. And even they were in on it. They always brought their hats, they died with style – their chalked outlines on the sidewalk were a hard but elegant message. And they drew the thirsty crowds.

Corners, streets.

Sharp corners.

An old face, a new one. A gun, a knife.

Down black steps to noise behind a door. No one behind me. We'd been let in and left alone. My friend pulled back the drape. The door opened – light, the quiet voices of people enjoying the place, a piano playing a ragtime thing. A guy standing at the door. No real meanness in the face, no real interest either. He'd show us the door if we acted up, but he wasn't there to stop us. This place survived on regularity. There was nothing here to be giddy about, none of the ballyhoo.

The bar ran the length of one long wall. Dark shining wood with a foot rail, and nicely rounded dents where elbows had grazed for years. It was dark, but hiding nothing. All the corners plainly there, no cloths hiding the tables or anything under them. No lull or increase as we walked to the bar – no whispers, glaring eyes. A place used to coming and going. Sawdust under my feet. The drapes and wood panels, the painted ceiling – little fat angels, with overflowing glasses of beer – they told the story: the place had never been raided. And the two cops drinking in the corner told the same story. Just a bar. No cover charge or floor show – and it was a player-piano, no longer playing, no one interested in walking over to crank it back to life. No flappers or raggles, no right guys passing death eyes over the not-so-right guys. Just men like ourselves, a few women, backs leaning into the bar, a few more at the tables, chatting, laughing quietly, sending smoke to the angels. More a night in than a night out. Five years ago, this place would have been on the street. It was heaven, and a disappointment.

A barman in front of us. A wiry guy in a blue bow-tie and boiled shirt, sleeves rolled up as far as he could get them. He rubbed the counter, stopped rubbing and waited.

I looked at the high shelves behind him.

—Is there Vat 69 in that keg that says Vat 69?

—Could be.

—Sounds good, said my friend.

—Could be.

—Any whiskey? I asked.

—Sure.

—Irish?

—Could be.

—I'll have one of them and he'll have the Vat 69.

—Rocks?

—Yes, said my friend.

—Rocks is extra, said the barman.

—Extra is fine.

—Then that's fine, said the barman.

He turned and took two white china teacups from the lower shelf. He held one under the Vat 69 keg, and then the other one. He turned again and brought the cups.

—Who's for the Vat 69?

—That's him.

He put the first cup in front of my friend, then he parked the second cup in front of me.

—And a cup of the Fenian tears for you.

I listened to his voice, to anything still held in the air. No accent that I could hear, no malice or sarcasm. I'd been stupid, asking for Irish when I knew it would be pure Lower East Side; I'd been very stupid.

—What about the rocks? said my friend.

—We're all out of rocks.

I still couldn't hear a past in his voice; he left us to ourselves.

—Well, said the fourth Mister Levine.

He picked up his cup.

—What's your name? I asked him.

He looked at me like I'd pinched him.

—Well, he said. —Which one?

68

—I'm Henry, I told him. —What are you?

—Why, I'm Henry too. As a matter of fact.

And he hoisted his cup. I hoisted mine. We brought them together and tapped.

—Here's to, he said.

—Fair enough.

We looked at each other and sipped. It went down, and stayed. My tongue and throat wouldn't blister. So far, so good.

—Could be worse.

—And that's as much as we can expect, I guess.

He took a step backwards, away from the counter. He put his hands in his pockets and took a good, long look around.

—Suits me, he said. —And you?

—Fine.

—Not disappointed? he said. —You weren't expecting more razzmatazz?

—No, I said. —But, to be honest.

He joined me again at the bar.

—Please. Go on.

—Well, I said. —I thought *you* might be.

—Be?

—Disappointed.

—No, he said. —Not at all.

He brought the cup to his mouth and drank again, a less tentative sip. He looked into the cup.

—No, he said. —I'm quite happy. Good company, bad booze. It's as much as a man can ask for. You thought I was out for a taste of high-hat living?

—I wondered.

—No, he said. —This does me.

He brought the cup to his mouth again.

—And women? I said.

—No, he said. —Don't get me wrong. I know a mammal when I see one. And there's that to be said about dry goods. The sweeties keep walking in the door. And they make my day. Especially in the winter months when we keep the door shut. I hear that ding and I look, and it's a looker or it ain't a looker. And if it ain't, she'll still want cotton. And there's this much to be said.

He sipped again.

—Jewish girls, he said. —They make my heart sing. They pretend they're not girls, but they're girls till they're eighty. They're girls when they're six feet under. Dolls from start to end. It's a secret but it's the truth.

He looked into the cup.

—There's something in there, at that. So.

He smiled.

—I want to look at women, I get up in the morning. I want to shtup one, I stay in bed that extra ten minutes. Did I say that?

He looked into the cup again.

—My oh my.

And he sipped again.

—I'm a happily married man, is what I'm saying. With an eye for a Jewish ankle. And I'm no bigot; I'll take any ankle walks my way. What about you, Henry? Are you a married man?

—No.

I wanted to show him the photograph; I knew I could talk all night. But I didn't want him to see Henry Smart. There was a machine-gun in my lap in the picture; there were bandoleers crossing my chest. There was Ivan Reynolds, and a whitewashed cottage wall. My whole life and times. I was here because I didn't exist. But, God, I wanted to look at the picture, to hold it to my face.

—Footloose and fancy free, he said.

—Something like that.

—Want to know if I envy you?

—You don't.

—Not even a bit. Believe me?

—No.

—You're right not to. I do envy you. Cup's empty. Now, how did that happen?

The barman was there again, wiping the counter.

——Same again?

—Try a different keg this time, I said.

—Same again, it is.

I emptied my own cup – it got no easier, it got no worse – and put it on the counter. The barman took the cups to the same squat keg. He quarter-filled both and brought them back.

—The Irish for you, the usual for your friend.

He went away. We left the cups alone.

—But you're right, Henry, said the other Henry. —I don't envy you. And, by God, I do.

He picked up his cup and sipped.

—I've got my future, he said when he'd recovered. —I've chosen

70

my direction. And I have my best girl right beside me. Might I be crude for a minute here, Henry?

—Fire away.

—I have to bend double when I think of that girl upstairs when I'm downstairs in the store. Her, wandering through all that Levine furniture up there. All that rosewood and varnish. The pants weren't invented to hide my happiness.

—Sounds good.

—Oh, it is. By crikey. The things that girl does. I won't quote chapter and verse. You know the score.

I said nothing, but kind of nodded.

—It's what I said about Jewish women, Henry. They're *girls*.

He drank again.

—I love her so.

—But, I said.

—No, he said. —No but. In that regard, no. I landed on my feet there. Although, granted, I could do without the brothers. And, aha now. That brings me to the point—

—What about their wives? I asked, before he got there.

—They undress me with their eyes.

—Do you undress them?

—With my eyes?

—Yes.

—No. But, the point. Do I envy you? Yes, I'm afraid I do. You got any direction you want. You got your business there, you're doing fine. But. You can grow, you can move. Me? I got dry goods. I share dry goods. With three dry men. I got ambition, they got haemorrhoids. But.

He drank, and emptied his cup.

—You're free to fly. I see that when we talk, when you come into the store. It kills me. We're not in competition but it's what I want. The freedom. To grab the opportunity. You see it, I see it. You grab it, I mind the store. What age are you, Henry?

I gave him the truth.

—Twenty-three.

It was my birthday. The 8th of October, 1924.

—I'm twenty-nine, he said. —You're passing me by. You're only twenty-three?

He was looking straight at me, examining my face.

—Yep.

—I'd have put you at older.

71

The barman was there.

—Same again?

—Fill 'em up, said the other Henry.

The barman took the cups.

—Now, said the other Henry. —The point. Let me talk a while here, Henry. Will you bear with me?

—Sure.

—I thank you for that. So. I'm in the store. I got ideas there. More stores, better stores. The usual. Baloney, if you don't act on them. And I want to. But how? Because, frankly.

He whispered.

—The store is not mine. Strictly speaking. Legally speaking. I am an employee. So. This is where you come in. I think. If I'm not mistaken. And I might be.

The barman brought the cups, left us alone.

—So, said the other Henry, after he'd picked up his cup and put it down again. —So. Into the store one day, not so long ago, walks a young lady.

He stopped and looked at me.

I looked straight back at him.

—The bell does that ding, he said. —I look up. And there's the young lady. And she comes on over to the counter. I'm on my own there. And she's. She is be-yoodiful. And kind of breathless. Lips open, heaving nicely in the chest area. And what an area. In a red dress, of a cloth I wasn't selling. Her coat open there. And she stops at the counter. Well, actual fact.

He picked up his cup and helped himself to a mouthful. He was enjoying the story, but nervous.

—She more or less walked straight into the counter. She knew exactly when to stop. She wasn't even looking at it. Me. That's what she was looking at. And she's right there. Like she wanted nothing else but to saw through that counter with her hips. And. You Levine? she says. In a manner of speaking, I say, but, no. She looks disappointed but she's still hugging the counter there. And I don't want to disappoint her, so. I'm the man you might be looking for, if it's the man in charge you're hoping to meet, I say. So. She takes a breath. Never knew there could be so much to that particular exercise. No man could carry it off, I reckon. Her chest there. I'm not being salacious here, Henry?

—No, I said. —Fire away.

—Let's just say, this was a performance. And I thought no less of her for it. So. I just want to congratulate you, she says. And why? I say. Well, she says, I just loved your sandwich board. Made me want to come in here and buy up all your stock here. *All* your stock. Her exact words, and she sucked each one on the way out.

He stopped and lifted his cup, and looked at me as the cup hid his face. I copied him. We stared at each other across the teacups. The fumes began to pull at our eyes. I put the cup back on the counter. So did he.

—So, he said. —That's the situation, as I recall it. There we are. She and me. The counter taking care of us, if you get my drift. And here, I say to myself, here is the work of Mister Glick. I didn't know you as Henry at the time.

—Yep, I said.

—So, you *can* arrange it?

—Arrange what?

His mouth opened; his thoughts swerved around the question. I saw anger and fear behind the affable confusion.

—She said – he started, and stopped.

I decided to trust him.

—Look, I said. —I'll tell you what she does and then you tell me what she said and we'll see if they match. First, though. Did she tell you that she works for me?

—No, she did not.

—You guessed it.

—Yes, I did. She gushed about your product and I said to myself, here's a girl that don't gush for nothing. And here's a man that knows how to choose the girls to gush.

He was relaxing a bit.

—Well, there you have it, I said. —That's her job. She gushes about the boards. And the clients decide to spend some more. They're all men, like yourself. Ambitious, but hemmed in. So I thought I'd dangle some of the investment possibilities in front of them. And it's been working. I can't keep up with demand, to be honest with you. Her name's Mildred.

—Oh.

—What?

—May I ask a question?

—Fire away, I said.

—What is the extent of the service you provide?

I looked at him.

—The boards, I said.

—That it?

He looked disappointed, and relieved, like he'd stepped over a big decision.

—What did Mildred tell you? I asked.

—I don't want to rat on a girl. Especially that girl.

—It's too late to stop.

—I know, he said. —I know. She came back once or twice.

—Once or twice?

—Four times. She was a welcome sight. And we got to talking. Mildred, though; she didn't give me that one.

—What did she call herself?

—Miss Boulez, he said.

—Boulez?

—Yes, he said. —And, well, on visit number three, I told her I was Henry and, well, she told me she was Shy.

—Shy?

—That's right. Shy Boulez. Has a ring to it, don't you think? It wasn't Mildred.

—So, he continued. —We got to talking. And. She said she'd get rid of them for me.

—The Levines?

A gun, a knife.

—Yes.

—Kill them?

—Yep. Not those words, exactly. Not quite so bluntly put. But, yes. We can get them prunes out of your hair, daddio. They were her words.

—Fuckin' hell.

He coughed.

—So, you don't offer that particular service?

—No.

—So, who does?

—Probably Miss Boulez.

—Alone?

—Probably.

—My God, he said. —To think.

He hung on to the counter. I'd never seen a happier man.

I walked.

Through the night. Bad eyes on my back. The corners were

sharp. A gun, a knife. A brick dropped from a roof. I kept going. *In ev-ery way.* I turned – east. A shadow – gone. A skid, car, a cough. Ahead, and west. East, ahead, west again. Waiting for me. Old faces kept me company.

—I felt sorry for the guy. He's a sweetie.

—So we're – *you're* going to drill his wife's brothers because you think he's a sweetie?

—Not for nothing, daddy. I said it would cost him.

It was cold. She sat on the bed; she was wearing her coat.

—What made you think I'd do it?

—Seen the wedding picture, remember.

—Forget the fuckin' picture. Who have you been talking to?

—No one, she said.

—Who have you been talking to?

—No one.

She didn't look at me.

—Honest.

—Listen, I said. —I've killed men before.

—See? I knew.

—Shut up, I said. —D'you want to know why I killed them?

—Tell.

He fought like a lion with an Irishman's heart.

—The idea was put into my head.

—How many?

—I came here to get away from killing.

—Could be a fire.

—No.

She was looking straight at me now.

—I know other guys, she said.

I lifted the window and climbed onto the fire escape. I could still hear her when I got to the sidewalk.

—Just a little fire. You owe me, daddio.

Old faces kept me company. *Critical Eyes Are Sizing You Up.* There was nothing new about this place.

I walked.

Corners. Streets. A gun, a knife. East, west, straight ahead. *I don't see you again. You hearing that?* A shadow. *Be fucking missing.*

I stopped. I listened. Kept my hands out of my pockets. Walked a big square, took corners, passed corners, dared what lay ahead. Didn't run, didn't try to hide. *Better and better.*

I saw him.

Joe. The corner.

The hat. Fedora, like my own.

Gone.

A wind swayed in from New Jersey. It pushed into my face. A surprise at every corner. The rot from the river, the fat smell from National Biscuits; no man would shoot me in the fog of baking figs. Runkle Brothers' chocolate factory, and I walked into the stink that was Owney Madden's secret brewery. *And better.* A Chelsea slaughterhouse killed everything. It held me up, beat away the lies of the chocolate and malt. The wind was punching; I fought for my hat. *He is the man who owns Broadway.* I pushed across the avenues. Sixth, Seventh. No one could creep up in this wind. *Let me carry your Cross for Ireland, Lord.*

And there he was.

& Son.

The undertaker's boy. He stood there. Away from the wall. Didn't move, just watched me watching him. Hand in coat. I saw him; he watched me. I didn't stop. I didn't look back.

—What about my Mildred? said Hettie.

I'd just told her I was going. America was a big place.

—What about her? I said.

—She will go with you?

—I don't know.

—You will ask her?

—She mightn't—

—Ask.

—Okay. Why, though?

—She needs fresh air. Henry. Ask.

Joe again.

Gone. Behind the corner.

Hooper. The boards still on him. Gone.

★   ★   ★

—Say! You proposing or something?

—No.

—Only, I wouldn't say no.

—Business, Mildred.

—Well, gee, I reckon getting hitched to you would be a good business move. And fun with it.

—Fine, but are you coming with me?

—Where?

—Anywhere. Somewhere new. Really new.

I owed Hettie, and I liked Mildred. Knee to knee, we'd discover America.

—Like Florida? she said.

—Now you're talking. Or Texas. They won't know what hit them. The two of us, Mildred.

—When?

—Tonight. Tomorrow.

—Gee, Henry, you're sweeping me off my feet. Sure you don't want to marry me?

More men, corners.

No shadows now, no doubts.

Two men. Side by side, a solid wall standing while I passed.

A gun, a knife.

& Son, and another.

I began to feel angry. I began to change my mind. I'd get a gun and stay. I wasn't running from these cunts. *I don't see you again.* I weighed them as I passed. I counted them, filed faces. They came no nearer.

—Don't know, Mister Glick.

—No idea?

Joe shrugged. I wanted to grab his fuckin' neck. He looked straight back at me.

—None at all?

—Fast Eddie, he said. —He could get you a piece, I bet.

He shrugged again and looked away, and forced his eyes back to mine. I stared at him. I watched him sweat on this November day.

—Tell me, I said.

—What?

He knew I'd changed the subject.

—Just tell me, Joe.

He held my stare.

I don't see you again.

—Swear to God, Mister Glick. There's nothing to tell.

He held my stare, until he was half asleep in front of me.

—How come you've never been hit, Joe?

I walked away.

—Don't know, Mister Glick, he shouted. —My turn next, I bet.

I looked back. He smiled, and waved.

The coop was empty. The baths were full. The air trapped the stink with a cold hard hand.

Two boys were suddenly there. Caps and knickers, rolling shoulders; brothers.

—Where's Eddie?

—Private property, bub. Slip off it.

The air fattened their skinny voices. Small lads, trained to box, but wild – I saw it in the eyes and in the knives that sliced the fumes at my nose.

—Be a sport and beat it.

—Be a sport and stay.

—Ain't seen Olaf in days and days and days.

—Does that worry you? I asked.

—Happens time to time, said the half-sister.

She stood at the apartment door, and she wasn't letting me in.

—You owe me, daddy. Remember.

—No.

—Don't matter if you do or do not. You still do.

—Why?

—Lop-eared daddio. Autosuggestion. Taught you all about it. Remember?

—Yeah.

—Yare. So now's the time.

I turned; the hall was empty – no one on the stairs.

—Holy smoke. What has you so jumpy?
She touched my nose.
—You *are* like a rabbit.
—What do I owe you?
—You'll be surprised.
—I don't want to be surprised.
—Oh yes, you do.

She held my hand. Black coat, grey fur lying on her neck. Heels
tapped the time. She said nothing. Men on corners stood back,
the guys and coppers; they let her lead me past them. *The skin
you love to touch.* She didn't look at me.
　　So now's the time.
She didn't have to look. She had me in her hand. Nowhere
else I could go.
　　in ev-ery way
　　let me carry your cross
　　I don't see you again
　　you hearing that
　　so
　　now's the time
　　the soap of beautiful women
　　I am the man who owns
　　broadway
　　her
　　heels
　　tapped
　　the
　　time
　　beats
　　am I right
　　as it sweeps
　　for Ireland
　　as it cleans
　　for smokers like yourself
　　am I right
　　daddio
She was talking. Her mouth there, red and beautiful.
—Know where we are, daddio?
She was looking at me now.

79

—Know where we are?

Smiling. Frowning.

—Answering?

I got the word.

—Where?

Under the El. Didn't know which line.

—Death Avenue, daddio.

The street darkened by the tracks and the rusting scaffold that held it in the sky. And darker because of the dying year and walls that came too close to the tracks.

Now's the time.

Right now.

Shadows moving – slouching, darting. Under the El. Bodies on the sidewalk. Bums and hoboes too far gone for the Bowery. *I has a crippled sister, I works hard to support.* A hand reached for her foot; she sailed over it. *But when we knocks off Saturday, till Monday I can sport.* She walked me through it, a stench beyond despair. Right down the middle. Men, women got out of her way.

I could feel it, the approaching train. The tracks above began to vibrate, and girders; right over us now, the light, the dark and falling sparks. I could feel it rattle me, shake her grip on my hand, pound the human ruins around us. But I couldn't hear it.

I couldn't hear it.

Beep Beep had said it.

—You ain't arrived till you don't hear the El.

And now I couldn't. I could hear the traffic, her heels, voices – *My sister goes out washing* – and her voice – *This a-way, daddy* – horses, brakes as she stepped us onto the street, but not the train that hammered the world down onto our heads.

I'd arrived.

—Death Avenue, she said.

This was my town.

—Don't worry you?

—No.

—Big brave daddio.

—Where are we going?

—Right here.

I was going nowhere.

I was thinking now, looking. *Front Wheel and Axle Alignment.* A garage to the right. No one in it. No car at the open door. Coming and going, a door to the left, quick men disappearing. Old, frayed posters shaken by the departing El – *Clear Heads Choose* – long-dead offers.

Men everywhere.

Fuck them.

Waiting. Not hoboes, not lost. There for me.

She was bringing me.

By the hand.

To a door.

Another bare black door.

I could think. I could run. Simple as that. Nothing to it.

Where?

I could think.

Every corner was guarded. I could run – only as far as they wanted me to run. I was caught. But I was thinking.

She lifted her free hand and tapped the door.

I wasn't running.

Her glove killed the knock. She let go of my hand. Now. She pulled slowly at each finger. Now. The glove kept coming. I could run, dash under the El and run, tap tap, get out from under the line and run, get in among the people hard and lost enough to be wandering this patch.

Now.

They knew my hand was free. They knew I'd run. They'd see me all the way. They knew I was pushing to a decision.

They were inside.

Three, four times her knuckles kissed the paint. There'd be black flakes clinging to them. Her hands were long.

They were waiting. Behind the arches, pillars, in cars that crept behind me. I looked. Two guys half a block away. Standing still among hundreds.

I'd go in.

—'Bout time, she said, as we heard a lock being pulled.

There'd be less of them inside.

I watched the door opening.

She had my hand.

—I got him here.

I ran a finger over her knuckles; I felt grains of old paint.

She led me.

Into darkness.

—Is this him?

81

That surprised me. The voice male, but not a hard man's. And the question.

I couldn't see. The door closed as I entered. It brushed my elbow but no one followed it.

—This is he, she said.

I still couldn't see. I held her hand, read her movements. She was talking to one man. No turning, to include others. Her feet stayed still.

—Got some heat in the place today? she said.

—Yes.

Yes. Not *yare* or *yeah.*

—Goodie, she said. —That'll take the sting out of it.

A man who said *yes* could still point a gun. I held her hand and watched; I could see the side of her face. I followed her eyes, and met the man.

He was alone.

In a narrow hall.

He was alone.

Three, four closed doors. A stairs behind him. Empty, as far up as I could see.

A small man, no one behind his back. An empty corridor further behind. Not small, but shockingly thin. In a suit that added nothing to him. He peered at me through lenses that put his eyes inches ahead of his face.

—Hello, he said.

—This is Brotman, she said.

—Max, he said.

I was still alive.

—What's the story? I said.

—What do you mean?

—Why am I here?

—You did not tell him? he asked Olaf's half-sister.

—Didn't have the time.

—Come now, he said. —You can't expect this gentleman to—

—Stow it, Max, she said. —Remember that honesty-of-the-moment spiel you ladled out last week?

—Yes, I do.

—Well, there, see. I didn't tell him. To save the moment, you know.

I saw Brotman looking at me.

—I'm afraid I do not know your name, he said.

82

—Rudolph, she said. —Like Valentino. Right, daddio?

I didn't answer her.

—Want me to tell him, Max? she said.

—Please.

—You're gonna fuck me, Rudolph.

And I watched the man's huge eyes close, and open.

—That sound like hardship, daddio?

I didn't answer.

—Answering?

—No.

I listened.

Footsteps, high above us – gone. Someone singing somewhere, outside.

—I should explain, said Brotman.

I said nothing.

—Go to it, Max, said the half-sister.

—I am a publisher, Mister—

I said nothing.

—I am a publisher.

He coughed.

—Smut, I said.

—Too right, daddy, she said. —The big dirt.

—No, said Brotman. —No, no.

But he smiled at her.

—Do you believe in free speech? he asked me.

—Sweet, she said. —Must be fifty and still thinks he can get something for nothing.

This time I answered; I couldn't help it.

—It's a good idea, I said. —But I don't believe in anything.

—Pow.

Shut up, shut up – but I couldn't.

—I can hope and wish, I told him. —But I never believe.

He nodded.

—You are not American.

I said nothing.

—But, please, he said. —Let me show you some books.

He turned and took some steps, into the corridor. He stopped and turned back to us.

—Please.

I saw his hand and a white cuff, inviting us to follow. Her hand held mine again.

83

—Let's check out the merchandise, Rudolph.

—What's going on? I said.

—Trust me, she said.

Brotman walked past the first door, to the second in the corridor, and stopped. It was darker here. I heard him open the door, heard a step; there was light and he walked into the room.

A room full of books, and nothing else. Walls and pillars of books. I looked around for Granny Nash. I could smell the old witch in these new books. And brown cardboard boxes. Some empty, lying around. Some taped and piled near the door.

—Please, he said. —Come in. Come in.

The room seemed to contract as we went further in. He picked a book off a pile and handed it to me.

—By one of your countrymen, I think, said Brotman.

I read the title.

Ulysses. James Joyce.

—Are you familiar with the work? he asked.

—No.

—There are those who are determined to copper-fasten that situation. They do not want that book read. By anyone. Except, perhaps, themselves. You *are* Irish?

I said nothing.

He took back the book before I had time to open it.

—And this one.

I now held *The Fortunes and Misfortunes of the Famous Moll Flanders.*

—You know it?

—No.

—But you have heard of *Robinson Crusoe.*

—Yes.

—Perhaps you have read it.

—No.

He pointed at the book.

—The same author. Published first in 1722, and they still try to keep it from our eyes.

The title was gold, on good black leather. I opened it. Under the title and the name of the chap who'd written it, there was a drawing of a fine-looking bird, her dress hanging off her, showing two top-notch tits and a long half-mile of leg. There was a lad in garters and a three-cornered hat holding her arm, a club held

84

high in his free hand, his eyes glued to Moll's chest. She looked frightened, but not all that frightened.

—Maybe it's the pictures they want to keep from our eyes, I said.

—No, said Brotman. —No.

—Recognise her? said the half-sister.

I did: she was standing beside me.

—You're Moll.

—The original, she said, and touched the page.

—What about Shy Boulez?

—My nom de cunt. Which hit you first? The clock or the tits?

—Both at the same time.

—Liar.

The black certainties were shoved aside; those guys outside were gone.

—Even better pics inside, she said. —Want to see them?

But Brotman took the book and put a lighter one into my hand. *The State and Revolution.* V.I. Lenin.

I gave it a flick; no pictures. But I knew who Lenin was. I looked at Brotman. I pointed at Moll in his hand and lifted the book in mine.

—What's this got to do with that? I said.

—Freedom of expression, he said. —I am not a Bolshevik but I think that I am entitled to know what its greatest exponent has to say. That is my fight.

He waved at all the books.

—My cause.

He smiled, and waved again.

—Please.

I picked up books, flicked and put them down. *Fanny Hill, The Merry Order of St Bridget, Revolution and Counter-Revolution.* They watched me. They stood there as I browsed. *La Ronde, Oscar Wilde Three Times Tried, White Meat, The Secret Places of the Human Body, Ireland and the Irish Question.* Marx and Engels. I didn't pick that one up; I didn't even stop.

There were hard men outside again.

Broadway Virgins, Pavement Lady, Ireland and the Irish Question. Nita offers the treasure of her beauty. *Ireland and the Irish Question.* A California girl's love madness is awakened by a vagabond artist. At the north-western corner of Europe lies the land whose history will occupy us. *Untrodden Fields of*

85

Anthropology. Her money-mad father dangles her in front of wealthy directors. *Birth Control: A Practical Guide for the Married.*

Ireland and the Irish Question.

I stopped strolling.

I listened.

—So, I said. —What's the story?

—What is the story?

—What's going on?

—I distribute and publish these titles, said Brotman. —Much of the great literature of the age. Many of the classics. The most challenging political theory and polemics. The groundbreaking works of anthropology and sexology.

—And good old dirt, said Olaf's half-sister. —He's a smut-monger, daddio. But he's right, you know.

I listened for noise behind the boxes, slow steps in the hall. And Brotman watched me. This, too, was a man who had to listen.

She had my hand again.

—Max there is a pioneer, she said. —And he's grinding out a living.

It was her turn to pick up a book. She let go of my hand and opened it. She pointed to the bottom of the title page.

—See that?

She read.

—Privately printed. Know why that's there?

—Why?

—Keeps some of the heat off *and* sells more copies. How's that for moxie?

—Are all of these books banned? I said.

—Just like the booze, she said. —Ain't that the truth, Max?

—In a manner of speaking, yes, said Brotman.

—Bootlegging and booklegging, daddio, she said. —Same business, see.

If that was true, there were hard men near and listening. Hitmen and smut-hounds – they were all behind those boxes.

And she had my hand again.

—Freedom, daddio. Freedom to drink and to read. Freedom to think different and dirty. Will you do it, daddy? He'll pay you handsome. You with us?

I remembered how to talk and listen to shifts and shushes that crept around the talk. I held *her* hand now. I felt and read

86

it, like the fourth Mister Levine at the Yiddish theatre – I *heard* it.

I picked up *Moll Flanders* again.

—This was written in 1722?

—Published, he said.

—Get down off your fuckin' horse, I said. —1722, you said.

She squeezed my fingers.

—Yes, said Brotman.

He'd stepped away from me.

One neat step.

She eased her grip, petted my thumb.

—Moll here wasn't around in 1722. So, why is she in the book?

—Don't be a mugwump, daddio, she said.

Her fingers grabbed my index finger.

—Freedom and profit, she said. —I'm the profit, I guess. Max has a name for the dirty ones. Don't you, Max?

She let go of the finger, held it again.

Brotman coughed.

—Furtive tomes in tasty bindings, he said. —I must make a living to survive.

A whistle from outside, train a station away, foot on the roof, maybe not our roof.

—You want to draw me for a book? I said.

—You and me, both, she said. —And not draw.

—I need a selection, said Brotman.

He stepped forward.

One neat step.

—A variety. Of poses, if you will. For various publications that I have in mind.

—What publications?

—As I said. A variety.

Another neat step.

—One or two works of erotology.

—How to do it, she said.

—A sexological study.

—How others do it.

—Religious ceremony, sexual mores. Being written by an eminent professor of anthropology. At Harvard.

—Still a smutbird, she said.

The feet on the roof were gone.

—Some illustrations for new classic editions.

—Your chance to dress up, daddio.

—What about *Ireland and the Irish Question*?

—Excuse me?

—D'you need pictures for *Ireland and the Irish Question*?

—No, said Brotman. —No.

He took another step.

—Fifteen to twenty illustrations in total. Twenty-five, twenty-six, at a push.

He was right in front of me. She stroked my wrist.

—Photographs, he said.

—The thing, daddio.

—My illustrators work from photographs. And, of course, the serious works of sexology require photographic accompaniment.

—That's pictures in American. Do it, daddy. Say *Oui*.

I got to wear the three-cornered hat.

—Grab the threads.

I held onto the huge dress that she'd let drop to her waist – good, tough velvet – and I heard the zip and thump of Brotman's flash as she pretended to pull away. Two flashes later, she took the hat and put it on her own head; she lifted the dress as she backed into me.

—Two hundred and twelve pages later, she said.

Zip, and flash.

—Bodies never lie, daddio.

Through three books at least, two literary classics and a how-to. The smell of the flash was trapped and dangerous. *Get out when you smell the cordite.* She led me from cardboard tree to couch, to and onto every prop in the studio, the last room in the long corridor.

We were right under the camera now. On my back on the floor, she had me in her mouth. Her knees held my arms; her fine, long hands pinned my knees to the floorboards.

Zip, flash – into my eyes – I was blinded and coming and the room was full of shoes. She was sitting hard on me, there were men standing on my feet and hands.

—Well, well.

I knew the voice.

The weight of bodies on the floorboards; patent leather sent sparks around my face. I tried to get up – I still couldn't see –

88

but she was strong, and the feet on my wrists and ankles pressed until I stopped. I closed my eyes; I couldn't wipe them. I'd slipped from her mouth but she still held me down. She hadn't budged. She'd done her bit.

—Good job, said the voice.

I knew him.

I could see again. The half-sister's gee was an inch from my chin, aimed at me like a sawed-off. The room was full of hard men; spats, leather, trouser cuffs.

—Good job.

Johnny No said it again.

And it wasn't the half-sister who answered.

—Nothing to it.

Mildred.

There were feet on my wrists.

And a scream.

Olaf's half-sister was off me and at the other side of the room. Thrown there. She was crying now, curled to as small a ball as a fine girl could manage. Her hair a shield.

I couldn't see Mildred. I looked to the door, got kicked – a slice to the side of my face.

There were men at each of my corners. Standing on my ankles and wrists. & Son was one I knew, and I'd seen the other three. They'd been following me for weeks.

—Want to know why you ain't been dead for quite a spell? said Johnny No.

He was standing beside the camera.

He tapped my cheek with his shoe.

—Why?

—I'll tell yis. I wanted to see if there was a limit to a block-head's fucking stoopidity. And guess what?

He kicked me.

—There ain't. You'd've kept on being stoopid for fucking ever.

He kicked me again. I watched him draw back his foot – I turned my head, he sliced my neck. Now his foot was on the side of my face. I could feel stone and glass in the sole.

—I could of got you any time. But Mildred says to wait. Something about a gat in a wedding picture her mama told her about. Here's a guy to be careful with, she says. So what? I think. But, I agree. But then a little fucking boid tells me you're tomcatting with a certain piece of ass that is un-fucking-touchable. So now's the time,

I say, and Mildred here don't argue with me. And she brings me here, and what do I find? I find the guy I told to get the fuck out of town so long ago I wasn't even shaving. Only, that's not all I find. He's with the broad. I was hoping, no. But, there they are. On the fucking floor. And, not only is he polishing his cock in the certain broad's kisser, but he wants fucking photographs.

Someone lit a cigarette.

—Do you know who that is who was sitting on your face not two minutes ago there? said Johnny No.

—No, I said.

It was true enough, and I thought the answer might save her.

—Well, said Johnny No. —I do, see. And it fucking scares me.

He held his trousers away from his knees and brought his face right down to mine. His eyes got bigger, yellower, his lips more cracked; the cigar was red and quickly hot.

—She belongs to a gent called Owney Madden. Have you, by any fucking chance, heard of Owney Madden?

—Yeah.

—Yare. You have and you are dead.

He stood up again.

—'Fact, he said. —Way I figure it, everyone here in this room is dead. Know who owns this room?

—Owney Madden.

And he kicked me, twice, took pieces of my face.

—You knew that?

—No, I said. —I only guessed now.

I could feel blood on my neck. I couldn't move.

—What are we going to do? said Johnny No.

It was a real question.

—Do you know Owney Madden? he said.

—No.

—Owney Madden is a little banty rooster from fucking hell. He is the fucking Devil. And you are so fucking stoopid, you might come up with an answer. How do we get out of this fucking thing?

—Well, I said. —Why don't we forget we saw anything and just go.

—Go where?

—Home.

—Jesus, Mildred, he said. —When you said he was a numb-skull you didn't come fucking close.

—Yare, said Mildred. —Sorry, Johnny.

—That's okay, lady.

His face was right over mine.

—You took something belonged to me. You remember this, by any chance?

—Yes.

—You took the boards that belonged to me. Right?

—Right.

—Wrong. The boards did not belong to me. They belonged to a man that's bigger than me. That is why I was sore with you. Nothing belongs to me. Nothing will ever belong to me. Or fucking you. The boards you took, who did they belong to?

—Owney Madden.

—Wrong. But not very wrong. They belonged to a man that is like Owney Madden. Everything belongs to a man like Owney Madden. Every fucking thing. Even the fucking air.

He bent down to me again. He had a club made of wrapped newspaper, the *New York World*. There was a length of lead pipe inside that package; I could smell it.

He placed the end of the club on my chest.

—It's not a bat, I said.

—The fuck you talking about?

—You whacked the others with a baseball bat.

—Yare? Well, you ain't fucking American. So you ain't getting that particular treatment. And, also, you want to open a cheap guy's head and don't want to see his brains on your fucking hands, you use what I got in my fucking hands here. The lesson is nearly over.

He pressed on the club. I tried hard not to gasp.

—You're lying on this floor, in this part of town, you belong to Owney Madden. I drag you downtown, and I throw you on a floor down there, who do you belong to?

—I don't know.

—Well, I do, see. Mildred knows. All of us here know. You've heard of Louis Lepke?

—Yes, Mister Vaux.

—He remembers my name. Fuck you.

I'd heard of Louis Lepke. I'd seen him. Leon the Cob had pointed him to me, as he went into Jimmy the Priest's, on Fulton Street.

—Bad news comes to town, Leon had said. —Stay clear of that man, my friend.

And I thought I had. I'd seen him, and his boys, waiting on stoops, leaning on Ford Coupés. I'd never gone close.

—The boards you took belong to Mister Lepke, said Johnny No.

—I gave them back.

—You forget my name again? You got yourself some more boards. And *they* belonged to Mister Lepke. You didn't know that, did you?

I didn't answer.

—No, said Johnny No. —And the shrimps you got to tote them for you. Those kids belong to Mister Lepke. They know that. Now. But you didn't know that, did you?

—No.

—And neither does Mister Lepke. He don't have to. He's got me and other persons like me to look after his business interests. He is king of all he fucking surveys, until he crosses the street where somebody else is the fucking king. Everybody knows this. Everybody knows where Louis Lepke is king and isn't king. Except fucking you.

He stood up straight and lifted the club over his head. He looked down at me – I watched yellow eyes, teeth – the cigar was gone – fury pumping weight and power into his arms.

I stretched, went nowhere. I couldn't even shut my eyes.

I stared up at him.

I heard the half-sister crying.

I heard one of Mildred's heels.

I heard Johnny No's teeth.

I heard the club brush the ceiling.

I watched the club come back, down.

But something happened. He chickened out, his grip strayed – he was talking to me again.

—The hooch inside the boards. Who do you think the hooch belonged to? Eddie Anderson?

—Fast Eddie?

—Dead Eddie. The poor fuck. Your fucking fault. You decide to skim off the top. Did you think you was fleecing Eddie? Are you that stoopid? Stoopider than fucking Eddie? Even he began to figure out he was in trouble. So he begins to baptise the hooch. Which is fine. Until there's no hooch in the fucking bottle, only fucking water. Then it is not fine. Then I find out. Then I deal with the situation before Mister Lepke finds out he has a situation. And

92

poor fucking Eddie learns how to fly. And all this time you think you are the fucking smart guy.

He prodded me with the club.

—Who owned the boids?

I heard a sigh; someone in the room was getting bored.

—Mister Lepke, I said.

—No. Mister Lepke has no interest in boids. He lets them fly for free off his roofs. But, no. Those particular boids that ended up dead belonged to someone else. The same someone that owns this room.

—Owney Madden.

—That's right. Eddie was looking after them for Owney Madden. Because Mister Lepke said so. As a favour to his friend, Mister Madden. Eddie knows about boids. Owney Madden knows about Eddie. Asks Mister Lepke if it's okay for Eddie to breed him some good ones, whatever it takes to make a boid a good fucking boid. To fly fucking fast and come back. So, Mister Lepke says, Certainly. And that's dandy. But, somehow or fucking other, all those boids that belong to Mister Madden end up not being able to fly any more. Not even fucking slow. And who's in the middle of the dead boids?

—I didn't do it.

—Do I fucking care? said Johnny No. —*I* fucking did it. Lesson over.

He was up. The club brushed the ceiling again, paint dust nicked my face. The club began to sing. I watched, I heard it—

The room exploded, and my head went with it.

But I was alive. I could see – I could smell a spent gun, my hands and feet were mine again. I couldn't hear anything, except the explosion, rolling in my ears – and the scream I'd heard before it.

I looked around.

Olaf's half-sister was standing there and the smoke was coming from the gun in her hand. Left, right – no floored bodies, the door was shut, no one crawling towards it. I blinked the ceiling from my eyes, I shook my head, tried to free the scream.

The scream. I looked. Mildred. Behind Johnny No. Standing, heels apart a foot or so. I couldn't see her face.

Olaf's half-sister was pointing the gun at Johnny No. The club over his head was starting to look funny. I still couldn't hear but the hard men could because their hands were in the air and they were listening to Olaf's half-sister.

I sat up; I could do it. I looked at her lips as I shook blood to my hands. She looked at me, barked an order I couldn't hear but understood. I hopped to it, leaned on the poor hands, got up, no bother.

And I could hear.

And I could see Mildred. She was scared and angry, trying for just scared. She looked at me.

—At me! the half-sister roared.

And Mildred locked her eyes back on the half-sister's.

—Clothes.

The half-sister was talking to me now. I did it in a dead man's heartbeat, got back into the suit, the toe-capped boots – laced and all. I took my fedora off & Son's head and kicked the legs from under him.

—Don't, she said. —My threads.

—I'll hold the gun for you.

—Do what I said.

I gathered clothes that kept trying to slide through my grip. But I captured them, and her coat.

—Open the door.

She answered before I asked.

—There's guys outside, a naked doll with a gun will live a couple seconds longer than a doll in her party dress.

—Fair enough.

The hall was dark – I looked – and empty. A shape against the opposite door. Brotman.

Olaf's half-sister flicked the gun barrel; they all followed her command. Johnny No, & Son, Mildred, the other lads, huddled in a corner, hands up high, on the blind side of the open door.

I stepped out into the hall.

She followed and shut the door.

No steps, no mad rush to catch us.

She fired into the door.

We ran.

4

We ran.

The warehouse wall was cold and sharp against my back. The gun barrel was pressed into my neck, the heat of its use burning, taunting – Get out when you smell the cordite – daring me to move, cough, blink. And five, six more guns staring at me, ranks of hard men waiting for their turn. I couldn't move my eyes, judge numbers; I couldn't talk. The barrel pressed deeper into my neck, deeper, inviting me to budge and die.

I heard the match, then smelled it. I couldn't see flame, or smoke. Then the photograph was in front of my eyes; I saw it burn and curl. It broke into weightless, black chunks and drifted up in the rising air, away from me. The wedding dress, the brooch, the glowing hair – the creases at the photograph's edges, the tears and folds and stains, the records of the years hidden in a fugitive's wallet; I watched the thin flame turn them all to nothing.

Then he shot me.

I could go home, I thought. It was 1924, nearly '25. The new Irish state was up and three years old; all fighting would be over. The triggermen were dead or politicians, or somewhere here, like me. It would be safe there now. I missed Miss O'Shea like a sudden wound, and Saoirse, the daughter I'd held only once, when she was five months old.

—I have a daughter, I told Olaf's half-sister.

—In New York? she said.

—No, I said. —Further.

—Know her name?

95

—Yeah, I said. —Freedom.

—Jeez, she said. —That's a tall order.

I couldn't think of what she'd look like now; no picture came to me. And the only picture I had of her mother was in my wallet, in New York, with three hundred and thirty bucks, under Hettie's mattress. Her eyes had been blue, but all babies' eyes were blue – Hettie had told me that. And a quick, gummy grin that had made me weak. Every movement under the cheeks, in the fingers that grabbed my beard – I could remember them all; I could feel them. I'd been on the run when I saw her. I'd become an old tramp and wandered for months, pushed out of the towns by men who were searching to kill me. But she'd seen her da behind the dirt and hair, the young lad in there, in the eyes looking out at her. She'd seen me, and I wanted to see her now.

—I'm going home, I told Fast Olaf's half-sister.

—Me too, she said. —Come on.

We stumbled in the black dark I'd forgotten existed outside cities.

—Where are we? I said. —D'you know?

—Haven't known since we went over the Hudson.

Six, maybe seven days ago.

It was a clear, cold night. There were more stars up there than ever came out over Ireland. The sky was alive with triumph and malice. I stopped looking, but one sharp light kept stabbing at the corner of my eye and wouldn't go away.

—Hang on, I said.

Then I yelled at the sky and my dead brother.

—Fuck off!

—Feel better?

—No.

—Come on, daddio. Step lively.

I slept black for half a day and woke with my hands on frost; it lay white and fine on top of the quilt. The window was shut but early winter had made it in. I was alone in the bed. The room felt long empty, like she'd never been in it. I hadn't a dime. Or a coat. Or, I realised when I took on the day and slid out of the scratcher, a fedora. She'd taken my fuckin' hat.

Then I saw it. The fedora. Through the diner window. And it suited her as much as it had suited me. She was sitting at a table

96

by the window and there were two women with her, their heads in under the brim, as if sheltering from rain. I was outside, off the sidewalk, standing on the ice-hardened muck of the street. It wasn't snowing now but it was cold and there wasn't much heat in a pair of braces. But it was good to see her.

I watched.

All three faces were looking at the table. Fast Olaf's half-sister looked up now and again, and the other two followed, and stared and nodded. Then back down they'd go, gawking at something. The women were young and older, daughter and the mammy. Country women. Leaner than the Irish brand but not much different. A bit harder around the mouth and eyes, and maybe straighter-backed. Faded flowers in the dresses. Hats that went on for town and came off back home. These girls didn't look like they sang or danced on Sunday night but they sat there, gobs hanging open, wild in love with the half-sister.

I pulled open the door and went in. The heat and coffee set me swaying; I hadn't eaten in days.

Two neat black hats and my fedora.

I went to the counter, just recently wiped shiny.

—What's yours? said the fat girl who stood behind the counter with the cloth.

—Coffee. Please.

—Coming up, she said, and lumbered off before I realised she'd left the coffee steaming at my elbow. It put the heat back into my hands, and I listened to Fast Olaf's half-sister.

—That sound right to you? she said.

The other two women nodded, looked at one another, and nodded more vigorously. The half-sister was looking into her cup.

—Nothing else in there this morning, she said.

She put the cup down.

—One of you ladies got a hand I can hold?

Again, they looked at one another.

—Which? said the mother.

—Left, right, don't matter much, said the half-sister.

—Which of *us*? said the daughter.

The half-sister shrugged.

—Don't know, she said. —Yet. Could be both of you, could be neither. Depends on the life force you got. And you both got it. In spades, I'd say.

I couldn't see faces but I knew they were smiling, anxiously.

—I can't predict if the life force don't want me to predict. Sometimes it keeps itself to itself. And sometimes it burns the skin right off my fingertips, just about. So. Who?

An older fist crept across the table and opened onto the half-sister's open hand. She touched the palm with the fingers of her other hand.

—Wow.

—Is it something good? said the daughter.

—Don't know yet, said the half-sister. —It *is* something, though.

She closed her eyes, and opened them.

—Children.

She was right on the button. Mother and daughter jumped in their seats.

—Am I close? said Olaf's half-sister.

—Grandchildren? said the mother.

—Not sure, said the half-sister. —But wow.

She looked from the open hand to their faces, one to the other.

—Don't know who they are but I *do* feel children. And lots of them.

The mother took her hand back and clapped it to the other, one happy, at-last peal. The daughter leaned forward.

—When?

She pushed an open hand across the table. Her mother caught the cup sent tumbling by the elbow.

Olaf's half-sister touched the hand.

—Something here.

She looked up.

—Soon.

—*How* soon?

—Quite soon.

She looked down again, and let her finger wait at the pad below the daughter's thumb.

—They're in there.

—Oh, my! said the mother.

The fat girl behind the counter was looking at it all.

—Want to read mine?

—Be right with you, toots, said the half-sister.

Mother and daughter tried to find the room to hug each other.

—Are you sure? said the mother.

—It's what I'm seeing, said the half-sister. —Good news, I hope.

—Oh, yes.

—Goody.

They were too excited now to stay any longer. They stood up, got their legs out from under the table.

—Thank you so much, said the mother.

—Pleasure, said Olaf's half-sister.

The mother was climbing into her coat. Then she remembered, and stopped. One arm in one sleeve, she opened her bag and dug in.

—Please, she said. —We must—

—Nope, said the half-sister. —It's on the house.

—But.

The daughter was suddenly terrified; her children would fade from the lines in her hand.

—But, she said. —You must take something.

—Thanks, said the half-sister. —But nope. It's a gift I got, it's a gift I give to you. Now shoo on home and get down to some knitting.

—Why? I asked her as she parked beside me at the counter and the mountain wind whipped at the door as mother and daughter dashed outside.

—Why whatee?

—Why my hat?

—Psychology, daddio. It'll make them talk.

—Grand, I said. —But I want it back. And why didn't you take the money?

We were broke. At least, I was.

We were two weeks on the lam and two days here, Mister and Missis Dalton, in Sweet Afton, with a room in the Trout Hotel that looked onto one of the town's two crossed streets. Not far from big mountains and the Hudson river. The train passed through twice a day, and stopped just once. Hens patrolled the crossroads.

—They'll come flocking, said the half-sister, quietly. —Wait and see. I'm a miracle, you know. I take their money, I'm less of a miracle. I might even be a grifter. Specially if the skinny one don't consider herself pregnant in the next day or two. Now, let's see what's to see.

She looked down at the fat girl's wet hand.

—Wow, she said. —You like your men dark and dangerous, honey?

—Like, nice dangerous?

—What other kind is there?

And she was right. They came with curls of hair, with little knitted pants, a sock – relics of little dead ones – and sometimes clothes for babies not yet born or conceived. They came for news of birth and money, land deals and the afterlife. They came with new-baked pies, buckets of apples and, sometimes, often, the folding odds. On the steps of the Trout Hotel, in and outside the diner, Billy's Happy Lunch, they waited for Fast Olaf's half-sister. I left her to it; I'd seen that shite in Ireland.

I broke the ice in the water pitcher every morning before I washed, tapped through it with my bare elbow. She'd be gone before me. The ice was thin where she'd broken it an hour before. I didn't see much of her in the day, the odd glimpse, her head, still under my hat, in the diner window, her leg as she climbed into a car. And we didn't talk much in the night. We pawed and ate each other till the walls sweated and we lay back under the blankets and coat and listened to our moisture on the wall turn to ice and slowly rip the wallpaper.

—Busy these days, daddio?

—Not really.

—Don't I know it, she said. —Want to get busy?

—There's not a lot to be busy about here.

—Where's your spunk, daddy? We're partners, right?

That was news.

—Are we? I said.

—Oh, come on, daddio. Sure, we are. We're stuck here together, until it's safe to toodle back. We got here together. We're in the sack here together. I got things you want, you got things I can use. Sounds as near to partnership as I'll ever need or want. Till it's safe to go back. Till it's safe for *me* to go back. They won't be looking for me. Not for long, anyways. You now. You're a different story, I guess.

—I'm going home, I told her.

—Yare. But you're the guy. They'll remember you. They're still looking, I'd guess. They'll stop but they'll remember. Good-looking guy, Irish. Too good looking for his own good, you know. They hate you. If all those guys was girls, I'd be on the list. They'd want to change my identity with a hammer. The dolls do hate me, but they ain't the guys. That Mildred is my only worry. But with a bit of that Irish luck you got there, she's floating at the bottom of the East River, and serve her right too. So, I'm going to drift back into Dodge one of these days and no one'll notice except what I want them to notice. There's a new doll in town. You, though, daddy, are a different little story. They'll be looking everywhere for you. They won't stray out this far, I don't think, but you can't go any nearer. We're stuck here, daddy. So we might as well be partners. So, what do you say?

—Okay, I said.

—Pow.

—We should celebrate.

—I don't think so, daddy, she said.

We were a month out of New York.

—Cos I'm the partner who's been doing all the partnering.

She put a small wad of folding cash into my hand. I couldn't see it, but it had the feel that only clean money had.

—We can't go back without the boodle, she said.

The money was gone, back to wherever she hid it. The bed didn't creak; she didn't seem to budge.

—So get partnering, she said. —Shouldn't take too long; they're out there for the taking. Find water, pull teeth.

She'd told me; I'd told her.

Just after we'd run, before we knew we'd got away. Under her coat, under the sniggering stars.

—Dead, she'd said when I asked her about her father. —But still breathing. I'll bet. Somewhere.

—What d'you mean? I asked.

—Well, the Pop went to work one fine day and never came home. Never went to work, neither. Just walked away. Wearing a pair of shoes he'd cut and stitched for himself. Left Mama with nothing but a pair of shoes that he hadn't made because the ones he made were too expensive.

—Do you remember him?

—Yare. I was six but I remember him alright.

There was nothing for a while. I put my hand on her hair.

—He was nice, she said. —He sang, you know.

She took my hand off her hair.

—Legally dead, she said. —That's what the Pop is. His uncle or something in Europe died and left some boodle that amounted to twenty bucks, just about, to the Pop. Mama couldn't get it

101

because the Pop wasn't dead. But he wasn't alive neither, if you get the drift. So she stomps off to the courthouse and has him declared legally dead. And I don't blame her. He'd been gone two years. Then she went and married again, and I do blame her for that one. What about you, daddio?

And I told her. About my father, and the water that ran under Dublin, and Dolly Oblong and Alfie Gandon; I spoke all the rest of the night. My mother, Granny Nash, my brother Victor, the other fucker above us – she blew him a kiss and we watched it hit and fizzle – I gave her the lot. My father's escape into the dark, his death, my fight for Irish freedom, and Miss O'Shea.

—And she's in whatever Sing Sing is called over there?

—She was, the last time I saw her.

—Wow, she said. —What a gal.

—Yeah.

—She'd get us out of this little situation, I'd say.

—Yeah.

—Wow.

So, she knew that water could find me; I'd told her about my underground escapes. But I didn't get the teeth thing.

—The market, she said.

—What market?

—You haven't noticed?

—No.

—Look at the teeth next time you're out there, daddy.

—They're bad?

—They're bad everywhere. But look at the faces, daddy. They're hurting.

—I never pulled a tooth in my life.

—Doesn't matter. Long as you pull the right one.

And that was it for a while. I wandered what there was of the town and out, into the county. And I remembered something: if a fine man stood in the same spot long enough, he'd be offered a job. So I'd stand and look at a pile of uncut lumber. I'd hear a screen door being grabbed by the wind, and a woman's voice, offering to let me cut it. I'd go at the cords of poplar and elm – names because the women told them to me – and I'd cut them down to stove length. I'd fill the freezing air with grey and red wood dust. I'd bring the scent of spring to the raw red noses of the women. The heat would work its way from my saw hand, to my feet, in under my new cap. My fedora was still on the half-sister and there wasn't another one to buy in town. The women paid me, quicker than the men. My growing pile of wood, the strong dust in the cold-dead yard; it made guilt scratch at the men, and they always took the saw back and got working. That, and the sight of their women standing stock-still in the sawdust storms or pushing their faces into kitchen window glass.

—Missis'll feed yah, then you'd best be gone to where you're going.

And they'd guard me till I was on the road and facing the rest of the world. It kept me going, the wandering and work. But I was still nervous. We weren't far enough away. I'd been on the run before; it never stopped, even under the ground.

Back in Sweet Afton, I'd stare at an empty wagon, a full truck, and I'd be invited to fill or empty it. The snow threatened and gusted, and stayed long enough to soak up blood marks on the sidewalk outside the slaughterhouse. I left my jacket hanging on a post. I froze but I wasn't going to get dirt on my duds, or the blood-soaked snowflakes that the wind swept up and tossed around me.

I carried sacks of onions and crates.

—Careful with those bibles, son. I don't want them spilling or breaking.

I'd carried crates like these through Dublin – *Bibles – No CommercialValue* – past G-men and spies. Boxes of new oiled rifles and ammunition; I'd carried them for Ireland and Michael Collins. This time it was bottles of hooch in the boxes, and I carried them for Mister Norris. There were no spies that I could smell, but the crates made me nervous. I'd learnt my lesson: where there were bottles, there were guys looking after them. So I crossed the street, over the hardened muck and horse-shit, whenever I saw crates in the back of a truck outside Norris's emporium, the Temple of Economy. I crossed and kept going and refused to see Missis Norris looking at me, her good-looking head between the two Rs in her husband's window name, the beginnings of ice creeping across the glass. I'd walk on, past the stores, across the lane that was Pigtail Alley, its few shacks and laundry, over the train tracks that cut the town, through the big meat stink of the slaughter-house, past the big open doors of the foundry, the shaking door of the diner. I saw the bare store windows, the peeling paint; Norris's was the only front that roared ambition. I was tempted to start again, to cold-call, get going with the colour and words. But I didn't. Not yet. I was careful. I was wise.

It wasn't well-digging weather but country people were always thinking a season or two ahead. No real city man would have thought of planting seeds or letting eggs hatch. So, once the half-sister let word out and around that her husband was a dentist and diviner, I was in quick demand. I found myself a forked stick, although I didn't need it. I stripped the bark off it till it glowed white and dangerous as I walked it around the farmhouses and cabins, held out in front of me, twitching, and I cracked ice with my boots. I began to enjoy myself. It was all an act, a piece of open-air vaudeville. I'd been feeling water racing all around and under me since I'd run from Manhattan; water inviting me to dive and duck, pulling, dragging at me, demanding that I jump. The county sat on water.

—They don't need new wells, I told her.

—You don't think they know that? she said. —They want the show, daddio. It's a long winter and we're miles from Broadway.

So that was what I gave them. The twitching stick, the even pace around the yard. *Steady, boys, and step together.* I marked the spots for the spring, when the ground would be soft enough to open. I made a mound of stones, like a baby's grave, and let the women feed me before they handed over the cash. It was two bucks a well, real money in a farm family's winter. The farmers held back with the cash, unwilling to cough up for a hill of stones right beside the old well.

—You'll be gone come spring, mister.

I said nothing. I let the wives and daughters prise the creased banknotes from the pockets and fingers, from under the floor-boards. The women were cute with the cash. I'd seen it in Roscommon, and everywhere. They had to be; there was never enough. But they knew what they were paying for now, and it wasn't new water. It was the elegant, wandering man they were paying for, and they had him for the day.

She was right, a long time before I understood it: we were a team. (And long before I knew it, we weren't.) We were the gypsies, and we were welcome in a time of quiet plenty. Children and stock were thriving; cattle stood full and upright. Fruit trees were young, raring to deliver again when the year turned. Government was far away. They wondered and looked, admired and feared us.

She was the barker. She announced their need, told them what they lacked and wanted. She worked on the women; the men came natural. They gawked as she passed. Loving her, hating her, wanting her, and more and more because they knew it wasn't going to happen. And then, sweet Jesus, it did happen – they came home from a day in the woods, hunting meat or making moonshine, or from under a truck or from mending the fences, finger-killing winter work, and she'd be there, in their own homes, the piece they'd seen on Main or Liberty, her coat off now and that ass on their own chair, her elbows on their table. And they could invite themselves right in and feast on her while she sat right there talking quietly to the missis, woman talk. They sat and watched, and raised no Cain when the missis passed the seed money to the cute little carpetbagger. There wasn't a bark or objection from those men; they were happily robbed. And the missises didn't know what hit them later in the dark, and never made the connection between the thrusts and loving paws of their eager husbands and the visit of that strange young lady who read their hands and told them some of what they had to know. She was fucking both of them, husband and wife, while she sat on the bed back at the Trout Hotel, prop. Gideon MacCarlton. But, before she left them to themselves, she let them know that I'd be dropping by to sort out their teeth and water, and I'd arrive a day or some days later and fuck them all over again.

Sweet Afton and county had never had a winter like it.

Our landlord noticed but couldn't explain.

—No one's complaining, MacCarlton told the half-sister; he never spoke to me. —That's what's different.

She leaned on his counter, shaving cents off the rent.

—Don't, please, misunderstand, said Mister MacCarlton. — We have a fine town here. Fine people. But, well, it's winter.

—Noticed.

—I'm right sure you did, Missis Dalton, he said. —But, well, complaining comes with the season. It's only natural. It *is* cold out there.

—In here, too.

—Not what you're used to, Missis Dalton, he said.

He held her eyes for a second.

—You were saying, she said.

—Yes. It is cold. It is a hard season up here, away from fancy living. The old bones do creak.

—Not yours, I bet.

—Mine aren't that elderly, I guess, he said, and he looked over her shoulder at me; he was brave enough to flirt in front of me – because she demanded it.

I left them to it.

The Happy Lunch was always full now. People stood outside on the sidewalks, leaned against jalopies and carts – their jackets frozen to the paintwork. They walked hard miles into town, came out of their way and time to buy nothing that couldn't wait. I knew what was happening. They were waiting for us, me and the half-sister. They had to see us. And, once they did, they turned to one another. They walked into town, these people, but they ran home. They prayed for the dark, for the livestock and kids to be fed and bedded. And sometimes, often, they didn't wait; they couldn't. Elderly couples fucked in weak daylight, and standing up, for the first time in lives that started during the Civil War – the American one. It took me a while to cop on but she was on to it from the beginning. She made an industry of it.

And soon – we'd tumbled into the new year, January, February – we had money worth counting. I bought myself a coat and we had a coal fire in a better room, over the hotel kitchen, a room drenched in heat and fat smells.

—These patsies sure seem to have taken to us, said the half-sister.

This was true, and it wasn't. The town itself hadn't really noticed yet. Sweet Afton was home to the young and the professional classes, and a very small Niggertown across the tracks and creek. The professional men had running water, boilers, insulation. The half-sister never got to their wives' soft palms. And the young lads who worked in the bagging plant, the slaughterhouse and foundry knew a sweetie when she walked herself past the double doors; they loved to hoot as they watched her arse turn the town's one real corner. But they weren't desperate for her magic. A good gawk kept till later, and they were too young to be sentimental. It annoyed her a bit, but she understood.

—They ain't the market, I guess.

The farmers and their ladies were that. This was a small town, not a small city. It could survive without the foundry. It could do without the bagging plant. The bags and galvanised iron would come from elsewhere, anywhere, and the men and women who worked there would move on to bigger places, Nobleboro, Gloversville, Albany, and further, to Boston or New York. The town might miss them and cry a bit as the train pulled out, but the town could hang on and even thrive without them. But the town couldn't do without its county. If the families didn't come in on Saturdays, the town died. If they didn't break their ploughs and need them mended, if they didn't need axle grease, piece goods, wire for their fences, schooling for their children, Sweet Afton was fucked. It was a farmer's town. The townies sneered and the farmers let them because they knew that it was they who called the real shots. There were hundreds of them out there, surrounding the town. If the farmers went down, if depression, flood or locusts took them, the town went with them. They knew it and the town knew it.

Which is why the fourth tooth I ever pulled belonged to Norris.

He pressed the gun barrel into my neck. The heat of its recent use burned and taunted me – Get out when you smell the cordite.

The half-sister was out on her rounds, and this particular Friday the wind had its dogskin coat on; it was fuckin' freezing. Aaron Hardwick looked out the window at nothing. It was dark and by staring at the glass he could gawk at the half-sister where she sat at the table Aaron himself had made in 1897. She'd just quietly told the missis, Cora, that she could see five grandchildren and a new coat in the lines that fought for space on the palm of Cora's right hand. She knew that Aaron was giving her the eye. The other eye was glass. The real one, blue, was lost when some barbed wire, new bought from Norris, had jumped back at him as he cut it, seven years before. Aaron was smitten, had been since the first time he'd laid the good eye on her.

—His words, daddy, not mine.

She stood up, and slid into her coat.

—You can't walk back to town, said Aaron as he gazed out at the weather he couldn't see. —We can't let you do that.

And Cora Hardwick cheerfully agreed; Aaron would drive her into town. He was one of the bigger farmers, comfortable, well respected; he had a flatbed truck that went and stopped when he wanted it to. So, in went the half-sister, tight beside Aaron. Aaron took them over the humps and holes that were most of the road to Sweet Afton, and talked all the way, and faster as she leaned across him and wiped the windscreen with her sleeve.

—How come *you* never whimper, daddio? she asked me, later, three seconds before I did.

He spoke about the farm, the truck, his eye.

—That son of a bitch sold me wire that had a weakness in it, he told her.

—The glass one's kinda cute, Farmer Hardwick, she told him.

—Nice of you to say that, young ma'am, said Aaron, —but it itches like by crikey. Not the glass, understand. The hole behind it. Too old to get used to it, I guess. It pesters me all times of the day. And night. To the extent that tears have rolled out of this empty socket, and I never did cry when the eye sat there. You explain that, ma'am?

—Nopie.

He rolled on and on. He told her about his great-grandaddy who had come over from Scotland, about his own hatred for all men who made moonshine, made or imbibed or profited by it, about his three children and their whereabouts, one at home, one married into a farm, south a spell from Rome, the New York one, and the last child, not the youngest, just the hardest to talk about, dead from the army, in Belgium over there, seven years gone now and it didn't hurt any less.

—Like the eye, she said, and he agreed.

Then he told her, as the truck hit Main Street, that some folks in this town, naming no names, were about too big for their boots, that Cora surely appreciated her visits, that the truck had never let him down, and that he loved her, the half-sister; as a matter of fact he'd loved her since he'd first laid the good eye on her, and that his tooth was aching so bad it was knocking the top of his block clean off.

—Know what? she said. —Those tears you were talking about? They're from your son. Messages from beyond.

And she saw them now for herself. Aaron's tears. They rolled out from under the glass, and sent the eye off course; the pupil turned in on Aaron. Big baby tears, so fat and heavy they fell off Aaron before they reached his beard.

He stopped the truck outside the hotel and cried. I saw the truck windows draw curtains of steam as I looked out from our window. Behind the steam, Aaron cried and cried. She put a finger to a tear and brought it to her mouth.

—Sweet, she said – she told me all – when she'd sucked the tip and put her hand on his shoulder.

108

He took the eye out and tried to dry it on his sleeve. It dropped to his lap. She picked it up. She blew on it. She dried it, turned it slowly in her fingers, dabbed it with the hem of her dress. She kissed the pupil, brought it to Aaron's socket and popped it right back in.

—Sweet Jesus, said Aaron.

He gulped, looked at his lap, gulped again.

—Thank you, ma'am, he said. —Thank you.

He wiped his cheek. There were no more tears.

—I guess I won't be complaining about that itch again. Already starting to love it. Thank you.

He gulped again.

—Thank you.

—Know what I think? she said.

She'd done her homework; she'd been listening to Cora.

She took his hand and straightened out the fingers. She'd never seen lines quite like them, scars and welts, fifty-more years of farm living. The lines themselves meant nothing to her – lifelines, heartlines – she couldn't read them; there was nothing there to read. But the market demanded, so she sent her finger strolling along, pretending to explore and understand.

—I think you lost your eye the exact same time that your boy got killed.

—I'm ahead of you there, young ma'am, he said, and smiled. —Thought the same thing myself not three minutes ago. And, got to say, it's a huge weight off of my soul.

—How's the tooth?

—Still there.

—Not better?

—Far from.

—See, she said. —The tooth ain't part of the deal. That's just a regular ache, nothing special about it. And I know the sport's going to get rid of it for you.

I watched her climb out of the truck. The whole town watched. Then she stood in the street and shook her hair, parked my hat and turned. She gave Aaron a wave and trotted up both steps, into the hotel.

Aaron drove home to Cora. She saw the tiny lipstick heart in the pupil of his glass eye and she fell into his arms. He drilled her on the kitchen table, on the stairs and up against the dresser. The fourth time Aaron came she was aiming his langer at a picture of Teddy Roosevelt, and he knocked the man clean off the wall.

109

She told the half-sister. The day after.

—Pow, said the half-sister.

—Just fancy, said Cora.

The half-sister told me about it, that night.

—Reckon I did a good day's work there, she said.

—A good deed?

—No harm if it's a profit-maker, she said. —And it is. Think I'm getting soft?

—Any softer you'll float away.

—Don't bank on it, daddy. But it is kinda nice, spreading a little happiness. And there now, talking of which.

And I began to wonder if there wasn't real magic there. It wasn't the palms or coffee grounds, but I wondered if she could really read, without the usual props of the con. She could feel those knots of unhappiness; and it was easy enough, then, to untie them. And I wondered if some of that magic didn't come from me, from rubbing up to me. It was coming back, the feeling – the glow. I was, remember, the miracle baby. I'd made women feel special, not that long ago, as they gazed down at me in my padded zinc crib. I could still see and feel their eyes years after they walked away, with light in eyes that had been dead for years – dead babies in unmarked holes, poverty, age, sickness, damp, husbands buried in the Empire's muck. One look at me had given them second thoughts, had brought back forgotten songs and the happy ache between their legs. And, long after my naming –

(My father got up, the chair fell back.

—His name's Henry, d'you hear me!

He came over to the crib. I heard the charging tap tap. He looked down at me. I saw an angry blur, shimmering fury.

—Henry! Henry! Shut up, Henry!

I screamed back up at him. I shoved my terror up into his face. And he stopped. He stopped shouting at me. He picked me up.

—There there.

I looked for a nipple in his coat. My lips met dust and blood. I tasted awful secrets. There was another Henry, the first and real Henry, up there in the sky, a little star waiting for his mammy.

They picked me up, fed me when they could or thought of it – but they never called me Henry. I was the shadow, the impostor. The boy, the lad, himself, he, the child. I screamed as I stretched; my glow became a crust.)

Those women still sang and walked like they were looking forward to the next day. I remembered seeing them later, when I took over the streets of Dublin. I always knew the ones who'd queued up to see me.

Fast Olaf's half-sister was doing the same thing now, glowing for Sweet Afton.

—Talking of which, she said.

It was only when Aaron and Cora Hardwick were crawling up to bed, at three in the dark morning, that Aaron's toothache came back to scream at him. But he didn't give it much care as he followed his wife's hard but well loved arse up the stairs and he leaned ahead to catch up with it. He shoved the ache aside, with his tongue. He could do that, for now. Because he knew the man who'd get rid of it for him.

And I made a bollix of it.

—You look the part, daddio, she said, as she settled the white coat onto my shoulders.

I had the coat and the pliers, presents from the half-sister. I had an air about me, authority, intelligence. Men had killed because I'd told them to, and Aaron Hardwick sat well back and opened his mouth, even before I asked him. Out in the yard, away from floors and good furniture. A sack around his neck for a bib, the old chaff blowing around us.

He opened his mouth.

She'd told me that the poor man had a rotten tooth but now I saw the truth: all of them were fuckin' rotten. And it was too late to run. So I looked for the tooth that looked the blackest. I reversed the pliers and tapped my choice with the handle.

—That it, pal?

—Sweet Jesus!

Then I did it. I pushed back his head and slammed my open hand to his forehead, shoved it back before he could object or even properly know. And I sent the pliers straight at the tooth. I had it, and pulled. And shoved his head back. And pulled. I kneeled on his lap, and shoved his head, and gave the pliers a good twist as I felt the root surrender. And I had it, out and high in the air; a shot of blood followed my hand, over my shoulder, and thunked the frozen dirt.

I got up and let him fall.

111

The root was an inch long. Huge and rough, like something ancient suddenly dipped in blood. And the blood itself was quickly old, although the man himself was still bleeding, badly, trying to hold it back with an open palm; it rolled through his fingers.

He stood up. Cora came down the steps, ready to help, looking for a way to get through his massiveness. He howled. But I had the tooth, the proof. I had it in the pliers, and my white coat was spotless. I stood there, job done, and the man howled again and groaned. He held his head, grabbed it in his huge hands. I saw him open his eye. He took long, slow, clinging breaths. I was ready to fight him. He took his hand from his mouth, and he looked at me. His glass eye had stayed put through his pain. It was a good one, store-bought in Saratoga Springs. In his current state, in the dying light, it looked exactly like the real one.

—Thank you, he said.

I was delighted, and surprised to be. I pocketed the pliers and held the lapels of the white coat.

—Pain gone? I asked.

—No, sir, he said. —New pain.

He tried to smile.

—Kind gets better, he said. —You could say I recognise it.

And we turned to go into the house. Cora was already in there, fussing at the stove. The half-sister was standing at the window. I was through the door when he howled again.

He sat down on the step.

—Oh, sweet Jesus! Oh, Lord!

So I had to do it again; there was nothing else to do. He sat on the chair and let his head drop back.

Two more teeth and the pain was finally dead, lying out in the yard while we all put away a pot of coffee and watched the day outside close down. I could see Theodore Roosevelt, inside the cracked glass, and I could still see Cora's needlework – *What Will Ye Be Doing When Jesus Comes?* – on the wall beside the wood stove. But I couldn't read it now. No one lit the kerosene lamp.

Aaron sighed before he spoke.

—Well, sir. This day has left memorable far behind.

The teeth had come clean out, no shards or roots left there; I was getting the hang of the business. But he wasn't going to chew anything harder than air again, not on that right side. He was almost unconscious, already snoring. But excitement and relief

112

kept poking at him. He was in love with his wife, in love with the half-one, and probably a bit in love with me.

He snorted; he'd woken again.

—I'm happy, he said.

And the next day, a Saturday, Aaron and Cora went into town, same as every Saturday. Aaron parked the truck as near to the Temple of Economy as he could get. There was nothing to keep him outside, no one leaning against their vehicle that he wanted to stop and chew the fat with, although he was feeling quite affable that day. It was cold in the truck and he was too giddy to sit still for long. So he went in with Cora. He stayed behind long enough to admire the sway in her arse, then caught up with her. They came to the door, and he stepped aside to give his space to Cora. She smiled and walked into the store, past Norris himself, who always walked the floor on Saturdays, the day that really mattered. And Aaron followed Cora.

—Afternoon, Cora, said Norris

Then he saw Aaron's swollen face.

—My God, Aaron, he said. —What happened there?

—Had a tooth pulled, said Aaron.

—Hope you hit the cad that done the pulling, said Norris.

—On the contrary, said Aaron. —I thanked him from the bottom of my heart and paid him two dollars.

Norris couldn't resist it.

—He pull your leg while he was at it? he asked.

And he laughed. He threw his head back and roared. Then he looked at Aaron, and knew. He cut the laugh but it was too late.

—Cora, said Aaron. —Let's drive on now, to Johnsville.

Johnsville was the next town, a half-hour west of Sweet Afton.

Cora stopped short of the counter and handsome Missis Norris who was waiting there. She turned and walked past Norris, back into the day. Happy to do it; she'd never been fond of the Norrises. She walked to the truck and Aaron was right behind her. I watched them from the hotel window. There was no obvious anger or upset in their pace. But there was something up with Norris; I could see that. He tried to get alongside Aaron but there wasn't room and Aaron wasn't giving any.

I looked over at the Happy Lunch. No half-sister at the window, and she wasn't on the street. She wasn't there just then, but she reported it all to me later, all the words that led to the knock on our door.

113

—Hold on there, Aaron, said Norris.

Aaron didn't answer or acknowledge the man. He got to his side of the truck. He opened the door.

—Now, Aaron, said Norris. —I didn't mean nothing. You know that.

Aaron put the door of the truck between himself and Norris. Aaron was one of the county's important farmers, a man whose son had died for his country, and he was about to drive away and take his business elsewhere, and maybe all other business with it. Norris was staring at bankruptcy.

He grabbed the door.

—Aaron. I apologise.

—I hear you, said Aaron.

He took the handle and pulled the door, and Norris came with it. There was a lot of Norris. He was only slightly smaller and softer than Aaron.

—Aaron, said Norris. —Think about it.

He put a foot on Aaron's running board.

—A dollar spent out of town never returns, he said.

—You coming with us or you going to get your hand off of this door? said Aaron.

He was enjoying himself; he must have been. Cora certainly was. She told the half-sister, a few days later. Cora, too, had always blamed Norris for Aaron's missing eye, but for seven years she'd been quiet about it. And she didn't much like Missis Norris. That woman had herself a peg and two above other folks. She was too good for the piece goods she sold to other women, to make their Mother Hubbard dresses. She went to Albany for her dresses, and she liked to let them know it. And she looked down on others because they came into town instead of starting off there, as if that little town was some big important city, and because they weren't married to the owner of the Temple of Economy. Cora could see her now, her handsome head between the Rs.

Norris had started shouting. I couldn't hear words but I felt them in the window glass as I pressed my forehead against it. I waited for the two men to grab each other and roll. But it didn't happen. Norris was shouting big agreement with everything that Aaron said. Yes, Mister Dalton was the best dentist this town had seen. And, yes, if he had need of a dentist, Mister Dalton was the man he'd call for. As a matter of fact, Norris shouted, he thought he detected a twinge there, at the back of his mouth.

He prodded a tooth with his tongue.

—Yes, he roared. —Something's brewing in there.

Aaron was loving this. All those nights awake, he had always imagined himself beating Norris. He'd never dreamt that he'd watch the man inflict the beating on himself. But that was what was happening. Norris stood away from the truck. He clutched his jaw, and roared. He roared at his wife in the window: he wanted Dalton the dentist: now.

I was lying back on the bed when the knock came.

—Come in.

She searched the room and found me.

—My husband, Mister Norris, needs you, she said.

—In what capacity? I asked her.

She actually smiled.

—Dental, she said.

—Lead the way.

I grabbed the white coat and followed three steps behind her. She knew I was back there and she led me down the stairs, past MacCarlton.

—Missis Norris. And Mister Dalton.

Onto the street. She walked quickly away; this wasn't for me any more. Her husband was about to be humiliated, already had been, so she had been too. Still, she did look over her shoulder before she stepped back into the Temple of Economy.

Norris was sitting outside, off the boardwalk. A straight chair had been brought out for him. Aaron stood behind him. Norris stared at me as I approached. He'd noticed me before, of course; he'd employed me, a day here and there. He couldn't remember ever talking to me. But here I was, strolling right up to him. I hadn't buttoned the white coat. The wind took and lifted it. Farmers and their sons got out of my way. Norris must have noticed that one side of the coat was a white wing behind me and the other sat plumb against the side, and he must have guessed. The effort at contempt fell off his face. He shook his head; I saw it. He sat up. There was a clear path now, straight from me to Norris. No voice or engine cut the air. The world was dangling right over his head. I held his eyes all the way, the last ten yards, right up to the poor cunt's knees.

—What can I do for you? I said.

He couldn't believe it. He caught his jaw before it dropped.

—Tooth. Tooth, tooth. Toothache. Got a toothache.

115

—That's right, Mister Dalton, said Aaron. —And I was sure happy to recommend you.

—Thanks very much, I said. —I just hope I can live up to your recommendation.

—You will, said Aaron.

—So, I said, and I looked down at Norris's upturned stare. — I'd better have a gawk.

Norris opened his mouth; he was no sissy. It was a big mouth and the light was still fair, so I had a good view of the man's teeth. They looked fine. Better than fine. They were his best feature.

—Ah yes, I said.

And the town nodded. Something had to go. That was what I was there for.

I stood back.

—Here we go.

I took the pliers out of my white pocket. I'd washed them that morning in a rain barrel behind the Trout Hotel. Norris backed further into the chair, and I saw it in his eyes: recognition. Norris knew his own pliers. He knew the feel and heft of all his merchandise, prided himself in his ability to find anything quickly, to know where every item was shelved or stored. Norris knew his store. He sold four types of pliers. He was able to recommend them, happy to use the cheapest one himself. Norris loved his work. He believed in it.

And he believed now that he was looking at a pair of his own pliers, and he had no recollection of selling them to me.

And that was what did it.

He opened his mouth and I got it done quickly. The tooth came clean, and I held it up, gripped in the pliers. I looked at Aaron looking at it. I didn't look at Norris. She told me about it later. The half-sister. She'd arrived in time for the show.

By the time I looked at Norris he was going in the door of the Temple of Economy. I shook the tooth and threw it over my shoulder. Then I gave it proper thought and went after it, before someone else picked it up. I got to it just before Aaron. I winked at him.

—Evidence, I said, for only him.

The wink didn't come back. He was a good, intelligent man.

I put the tooth in my white pocket and hoped to Christ that Norris wouldn't come back, demanding to see it: it was a fine, solid tooth. And now, there was another merchant sitting where Norris had been, mouth open, demanding to be humiliated in

116

front of his customers. I was on a roll. I bent right down and whipped out a black one.

I extracted a lot of teeth that late afternoon and they all went into my pocket. I brought them back to the Trout and threw them on the bed.

She counted them.

—Twenty-six. That *is* a wad, at two bucks a pop.

They were all of them blood-caked, most of them rotten, brown and yellow, ruined by years of sugar and tobacco. She picked one up and showed it to me.

—Bet this is the one came out of Mister Norris.

—That's it.

—Sweet.

She put it to her lips and held it there for a second or two.

—You didn't see his face after, did you, daddy? she said.

—No, I said.

—Should've looked.

—I did, but he was gone.

—Know what he did? she said.

—What?

—The big nothing. Just licked his lips, like the cat that got the cream. Stood up and walked away. The guy has style and you're in trouble, daddy.

—Why?

—Don't know, she said. —But you are. Why would he look so satisfied?

—Because I took his pain away.

—You gave him the pain, daddio. You're in the big T and so am I.

She kissed me.

—But I've wriggled out of trouble before.

I heard the match, then smelled it. Then the photograph was in front of my eyes; I saw it burn and curl. It broke into weightless chunks and drifted up in the rising air. The wedding dress, the glowing hair – I watched the thin flame turn them all to nothing.

—Hey.

It was hard as a stone on the back of my head.

117

It was Norris.

I turned and got back up on the boardwalk.

—How's the mouth? I said.

His answer came in the look that pushed right up to mine.

—Didn't pay you for your service, he said.

This was two days after I'd taken the man's tooth out of his head. Bright, cold and early, Monday morning.

—How much?

—Two bucks, I said. —Does that sound fair?

—Yep, he said. —You look to me like a two-bucks kind of merchant. You'll get it.

He turned away and walked back into the store. Missis Norris wasn't in the window. One of the kids he had working for him, a pip called Karlie Belden, came running after me, clinging to a five dollar bill.

—He said to keep the difference.

—No, I said, and I slipped him the three dollars change. — You keep it.

I walked out of the town and spent the day hunting a well over ground that was fat with water, for a handsome woman who'd found her husband hanging in the barn the previous winter. I walked the plot till dark and let her feed me and show me her teeth.

I walked back to beat the night. I knew the ruts and noise by now but dark was dark out there; five late minutes and you were stepping into emptiness.

But I made it. The bed was still settling under me when a woman's knuckles tapped the door.

—Come in.

She looked at me, and put the three dollars on the bed, between my feet. Then she walked the four steps back to the hall. She took the door with her and it clicked at the same time I heard her toes on the stairs.

I thought about it for a while. I'd keep the money; I needed it. I was going home the long way – and the job couldn't be done without a good, full pocket. And I knew an invitation when I saw one, even when its arse was going out the door. I was pleased with myself.

I slept.

★   ★   ★

118

She held her palm over the flame.

—Mind over matter, folks, she said. —See?

They watched the flame bend to eat her hand. The eight people at Aaron's home-made table. The fedora shadowed her face, her eyes. Two, three seconds, four. They all looked at Fast Olaf's half-sister. Then Aaron took her wrist and she let him bring her hand to safety.

—Not much in that, said a farmer's wife beside Cora.

—Whatee?

—Your hand on top of that candle, said the wife. —You only let it there a spell.

—I'm with you, toots, said the half-sister.

Aaron still held her hand.

—But that ain't what I willed, she said. —The old hand over the flame trick? That one, any flim-flam artist can do. See the way Farmer Hardwick grabbed my wrist there?

—Yare.

—That was the trick, toots. I willed it. Except it's no trick. It's the real thing.

She put her hand on Aaron's lap.

—It's love, toots.

I wasn't there. She told me some; I made up the rest. She was recruiting, converting; she was racing against certainty, and winning. She came back to the Trout room most nights – I missed a few myself. She pushed at me with a ferocity that left me sore and full of myself. She pulled me to her and tried to take me whole. But, really, she was putting the distance between us, the gap she hoped would be safe. She looked and saw a man on the run, who'd been on the run for years. She was making the right move. My days were numbered and she made the most of them.

Her strength was her unshakeability. She believed, absolutely, in nothing. But herself. Her head, her body. Her temple. Her tits, her face, her mind, breath, cunt, eyes, future, legs, her teeth, her choices, her wrists. The world was what she saw and came to her, and what she could make come to her. *Every day, in ev-ery way.* She believed in the power of her arse. She slapped it and got me to slap it. She loved the smack and sting, the proof that it was hers. She knew what it could do. One well-aimed swing could bring you fortune, fame, a bed for the night. She believed. She believed in the thing, the now, what she saw and felt, now; no putting off or waiting. The future would be better, only if you

119

had the now. It applied to everything, nipples, money, health, but only if you had them. Nipples got you bigger nipples, money made you more, health gave you everything, now. She believed this, and she was making a religion of it. All other faiths dangled transcendence, the transcendence of the dirty world as probable, possible, or sure-fire certainty; transcendence as a promise or threat.

—Who fucking wants it? she said.

She grabbed me hard.

—Want to transcend that, daddio? she said.

—No, I said. —I don't think so.

—Not even for eternity?

—No.

—Straight swap. This, here, now, for the everlasting. What say?

—No.

—Last offer.

—No.

She let go of me.

—Disappointed?

—A bit.

—But even what you had there was better than eternity. Rightee?

—Right.

—I think so too.

And she was gone, holding pricks or looking like she wanted to, all over the county. The Church of the Here and Now – I gave her the name. I was out there with her, the handsome priest, the living example, but I never understood. I just thought we were fleecing the place. I knew *I* was. I never really got it.

—Am I temptation? she asked me once.

I should have listened properly.

—You fuckin' are, I said.

—No, she said. —Am I *temptation*? Am I here to tempt you and other daddios from the path of righteousness?

—No.

—I'm with you, daddy, she said. —I'm just a doll, right?

—Right.

—Who might or might not want to do some of the doll things with you, right?

—Right.

—But, either way, a doll.

—Yeah.

120

—Not bad, not evil, just sumptuous and voluptuous and sensational and gorgeous and other sexy doll stuff.

—And a bit dangerous.

—Danger's sexy, daddio. Should I bite you?

—Yes, please.

—See. Danger is it.

And she bit me. And she bit others when I wasn't looking.

She bit Norris. She must have. She'd liked that look she'd seen right after I'd pulled his tooth. She'd admired it, the decision knocking aside the pain. Here was a man who knew how to root out pleasure. He saw what only he saw. Then the half-sister saw it too, and she was ready.

She already had Aaron and the farmers. So did I – I had their teeth and women – and I thought that that was that. It was the rebel in me, the world made simple; it was us against them. The farmers were Us and Norris was Them. We'd won.

But she didn't see it that way. She wanted all. Some time in that winter, she met her real power. Maybe as she brought excitement and joy to women just by looking at their palms. Maybe as she pointed men at their wives and made them see beauty. Some time in there, she saw it.

I don't think she planned what happened. She just knew it was coming; she'd seen Norris's face. She warned me, but I was too thick to hear.

It was the liquor that did me. Norris sold it and Norris bought. It was good, local stuff, squeezed from the produce of the valley. It went in and out the same back door, sometimes delivered by William Gantry, the sheriff. I'd heard the clink of bottle glass, and I'd kept the eyes open for the smart guys, every time I passed the Temple and Norris's wife. I listened and looked, for out-of-town accents and city stripes, un-nailed shoe leather on the boardwalk, for new cars that weren't black, for the low pocket that carried a gun. But I caught nothing. This was a local economy, blessed by the sheriff, controlled by Norris, totted by his missis.

I should have known, of course. I *did* know. There was no such thing as a local economy. It didn't happen in the Manhattan villages, and Sweet Afton was no different because it was far away and a real village.

They were there.

Months before we got there, weeks before we ran, days before we walked into town and took it over, Norris had contacted the men we were running from. The crop had been good that year; the barns were full and overflowing. Come winter, there'd be more hooch than he could move; a man with half a working nose could have walked through the county and straight up to every hidden still. It was the smell that infuriated Aaron, the stink of greed and wastefulness. It was the same smell that alerted Norris. There were farmers coming in, bringing with them the stink of their stills, picking up tools they couldn't afford, touching bolts of cloth that weren't for them, already spending the money they thought they'd be getting from him. And he wanted to give it to them. They'd spend it all again. Money made more; Norris knew that. But if they all arrived at once, the arse would fall out of the market; there'd be too much hooch to sell. So he told the missis to get her coat; they were going to Albany.

They drove there in their $1,200 Studebaker. She did the driving, and he watched her, hands on the wheel, her feet on the pedals. This was one of his great pleasures, watching his wife control the car. This was what the money was for; he loved life. And he loved his wife. She was bringing him to Albany – they might have passed us on the road. Her wrists, her ankles, her nose there, slightly upturned, driving this luxurious vehicle. To the hotel they'd spend the night in. The fine meal, the wine in china teacups, the good, deep bed, the sex they both sat up and begged for. They were going there, anticipating, silently excited. Because they could afford it. Because there was cash in his wallet, a wad in her pocketbook, and plenty more, if Norris played the cards right when he got to Albany.

And he did. He met his man while Missis Norris shopped and got her hair done up the way he liked it. He met a man who knew people who'd take the merchandise from Norris. Norris heard the price per bottle: it was fair, maybe even more than that. Payment up-front, they'd come and collect – they'd even bring back the empties. It could be a long-term thing, if Norris wanted. Norris smiled but said nothing yet to that. A late spring, a wet summer, early frost – he'd seen them all; he knew their impact. Plenty was never guaranteed.

When Missis Norris got back from the salon, Norris was waiting in the lobby, to admire her going by. He followed her up, exactly four minutes later. They drove back the next day, in the late morning, to Sweet Afton – they might have passed us on the road; we were on it. There was still enough warmth in the air to make dust; Norris loved to see it behind him. He drove this time; she rubbed his leg. And when the farmers came to town to rehearse their spending, Norris smiled – even after I took his tooth. He smiled, stood back and let them at it. They were happy; he was happy.

The guys came to town. They loaded up, and they went. They were Albany guys, upstate men. They left the good duds at home; they knew how shit can spoil a cuff. They came back a week later, collected, and went. Every week they came. The valley had as much as they could handle. They were taking it further than Albany; it had always been the plan. They came the day before I took Norris's tooth, and they came six days after. And in between those two Fridays, Norris took an interest in me. He'd seen me before, looked at by his missis. And he'd seen me look at her. He liked that. A man looked at his wife; Norris was a lucky man to have her, to know that she'd be sidling over to his side of the bed in a few short hours. He wasn't jealous or, if he was, he welcomed it. It put the iron in him. And she knew it, so she kept looking. She liked the results. They were mad about each other. I was a big guy who'd done a bit of lugging for him, and had gone off doing something else, probably something with more prospects. Good luck to me; I'd pitch up at his Temple and spend my cash money. It was good.

But then I'd pulled his tooth and, even before I pulled, as I leaned down towards his mouth and he recognised the pliers, it had changed.

The half-sister warned me. She'd seen the face. Calm, thinking outrage. When he'd come after me, to pay me the two bucks, it was my voice he wanted to hear, the confirmation that I came from far away. He listened, and knew: I'd be no loss.

He put the guys on to me. She said.

—Oh daddy.

She held the door as she shut it, tried to stop the click in the lock.

—What?

—Clothes on, daddy. You're in a hurry.

It was Friday morning, not yet bright. I'd been asleep.

—What?

—They're here, she said.

—Who?

—Come on. Get your duds on.

123

—Lepke?

—Come on.

I was out of bed, into my trousers.

—What'll we do? I said.

—You'll have to get out of town. And it'll be hard.

I sat on the bed as I laced my boots. I was ready, but lost.

—Are they downstairs?

—Not yet.

—How did they find us? Any idea?

—He.

—Who?

—You had his tooth in your pocket, daddio.

—Oh fuck.

—Yessee. They come every Friday, to collect their Scotch and whatnot.

—I knew it.

—No, daddio. You didn't. You've been lazy.

She was right.

—Where'll we go?

We were dead here. A hotel room was the perfect place of execution. I'd known and done a few. One way in and out, a gunshot easily lost, someone else's mess.

—Not *we* this time, daddy.

—What?

—They're not interested in me.

I stayed sitting.

—How come?

—I didn't pull his tooth. You did. Saw you myself, and so did he.

I looked at her, hard. She looked hard back.

—What's going on?

—I told you, she said.

She opened her coat, let it fall on the chair behind her.

—I saw his face. I told you. I knew he'd do it.

She was making me stupid.

—Do what?

—Revenge, daddy. He's got nothing against me. Just little you. 'Fact, he wants me to stick around.

—Why?

—Usual reason.

She was looking out the window now.

124

—There's two of them.

She looked the other way, followed the street east out of town.

—Least, that's as many as I saw.

I was standing now, ready to go. On the run again, but it didn't fit. I didn't want to go. I grabbed her arm.

—Ouchy.

—How come you know?

—He told me.

—Told you what?

—What's going to happen.

—You've been fucking him.

—You bet.

I'd never catch up.

—Why?

She smiled. There was no contempt, or sarcasm.

—He's a small-town wow. Which is as good as it gets in a small town.

—Did you tell him we're not married?

—That would have spoiled it.

—So he thinks you're dumping me.

— Drives him wild. And her.

—For fuck sake.

—She loves to think I rate him so high, I'm going to let my husband get himself perforated. She loves me for it.

She smiled again, and shrugged. She held up her hand, and raised the little finger.

—See that, daddy?

—Yeah.

—See the town wrapped around it?

I smiled this time.

—Yeah.

—Time to go, daddy.

—How?

—Listen. Hear it?

—No.

—Listen.

I heard it.

—Is it coming or going?

—Both of.

The train. A rattler, carrying lumber to Albany, same time every morning.

125

—Toodle-oo.

—Good luck.

—They'll be watching the station, she said.

—Thanks. Money.

—Your pocket.

—All planned, yeah?

—You weren't listening, daddio.

—I know.

I opened the door.

—Want to stay? she said.

I stood there.

—This ass here. For a bullet in your head. Want to risk it?

—Yeah.

—Go on, she said. —They come here, I'll have to tell them you're hopping the train.

I was gone. Saw no one, nothing I hadn't been seeing for months. But the water was roaring, pulling at me, pulling me off the street. Out to the trees; I wasn't good on names – big bastards; leafless branches swinging high over. Through them, to the tracks.

It came around the bend from the railroad yard, smoke behind it like winter breath. It crawled, and wouldn't go faster. I hid in the trees and scoped it. Flatbed cars, half a mile of them. Logs chained to every truck, no boxcars, and nowhere to hide. The engine passed. I waited, ran. Got down on my gut at the track, and waited. A clacking wheel went past my face. I rolled. My back hit the track; I was under, and grabbed.

I rode the rods out of Sweet Afton. The train rattled, pulled my bones apart. I watched the steel wheels push the ties into the ground, saw the spikes lift out of the wood, and sink again as the wheel crawled over and pushed down on the next tie. I watched the tracks fall apart and come together, fall apart and come together. I held on for hours. I slept – and woke. Still there, still crawling. Blood in my mouth, my hands were gone. I held on.

Because she'd told me to.

And she'd kept my fuckin' hat.

PART TWO

5

At last.

Dead eyes. Washed blue, red veins turned to grey. Old man's bristle; cracked, dry lips – all grey. Dried skin, dirt in the corners of the mouth. I turned away.

I got to know hard work again. I handled boxes in one of the packing houses. I came home each night with hands raw and screaming from the brine that seeped into the box wood, came home with men exactly like me, proud, silent and flaked; we tried to keep a straight path through the tiredness. These men were Polish, mostly, some Lithuanians, Slovaks, and others willing to work for less than the ones who'd been there longer. They spoke the English they were getting from their kids.
—Son of a beech.
—Boy, is hot.
—I'll say.
And I followed them back, and they followed me, every morning, through the Halsted Street gate, past the hundreds who stood there, waiting for us to die or strike; over the crossings, miles of tracks, a crazy mess of switches, alert for rolling trucks and engines, the air around us wet with slaughter, a stink that caught the throat and tongue, rich and sometimes sickening; nearer, into the big howl, the cries, the river of that day's pigs and cattle, the drovers among them, on horseback – there was money in this business – to the packing house, six days a week, seven o'clock till seven, and sometimes, when the trains came fast and full, it was dark at both ends of the working day.

I was like the men I walked beside, dinner pails brushing against our overalls, like hair across a drum, the same dinner every day, a poor-boy sandwich, onions, cheese, lard, cut big by Mrs Grobnik. I was humping boxes and huge hams sewn into oiled paper across the cellar floor, through a quarter-inch of icy water; bending and pushing, grabbing and stacking, counting the minutes without thinking about them, hating it, but knowing it was work, ignoring pain, the world outside the work, the bellows and howls from the pens at the other end of the plant; smiling grimly at going-home time as the whistle rose in pitch and volume, standing straight, turning away from stacks, machinery, carcasses, as the whistle's order began to dip and quickly fade; walking home, past men like us, and women, clocking in, swapping jokes learnt years before.

—How those pigs today?

—Boy, they bleed.

—Catch the squeal?

—Too fast to catch.

And home, together and alone. Through the streets of quick-built frame houses, all two storeys – none of the high tenements – all colours already fading, smothered, eaten by the smoke that dropped from the packing-house chimneys. Over bridges that leaned across the gullies and stinking creeks that had cut grass prairie not so long ago. The water looked like settling lava – I'd seen mice and chickens running on it. Across dead country that was nothing yet, bare spaces that would soon be gone. Through square miles of new-built, falling houses. Home, to wives and kids, husbands and kids, mothers, fathers, aunts; along sidewalks, where there were any, rotten planks five and six feet above the unpaved road.

I was there, in the swing, like these men and women. But I didn't go home. I didn't have one. I had a room. I lay and woke there, with six other men. I walked slowly through this patch of Back o' the Yards, to Mrs Grobnik's house. Up two steps, through the boarded-up porch that slept five men.

—Mees-ter Smarhht.

I was Henry Smart. I was back again, and working hard.

—Mees-ter Smarhht.

—Mrs Grobnik.

—Hard day?

—The usual, Mrs Grobnik.

—Yes, hard. Eat in, eat out tonight, Mees-ter Smarhht?

—Out, Mrs Grobnik.

—Again, out! Out! When in? Nev-errr.

She had a niece she wanted me to look at, a girl fresh in from Akron.

—Nice girl, big bones. For you.

She wouldn't believe I wasn't Polish.

—Smarhht-nik, yes?

—No, I told her, again. —Just Smart.

It was a ritual by now, daily ambush on the stairs, every time a step gave out the creak that only she could hear.

—Smarhht-ka, yes?

—No.

I'd never made it past her door. I'd skipped every step, one a day, for weeks, till I'd hopped them all, but still she heard. And now she grabbed my shoulders. I'd carried her up the first flight before I felt her nails through my shirt.

—Ah now, Missis Grobnik.

—Poh-lish!

—No, I said. —American.

—And father? she screamed.

—American.

—But mother!

—American.

—So grandfather!

—Don't know.

—A-hah!

—Irish. I think.

I'd stopped on the landing, so she could get down off my back, to the black patch on the once-green lino.

—Irish, she laughed. —Hear him, Mees-ter Grobnik?

He was around somewhere, the husband, although I'd never seen him. I'd hear her call him, screaming questions that he never answered. But he was there – a stiff door being shoved into place, a trunk moved in the attic, the tied dog's excitement as he approached.

I shut the door on her cheerful whine.

There were men asleep and lying on mattresses. I nodded at those that looked. I took the basin, brought it to the yard, filled it, brought it back, and placed it on the room's one chair. I dropped my face into the water and left it there, till I knew the day was gone. I got my head up, filled my lungs, felt the cold on

131

my skin like it was new. Then I dealt with the rest of the dirt, knocked it off, went at it with a hard brush, watched by lads who didn't really get it – it was three, four days to Saturday night. I put on the suit, polished the boots. I was the only man in the room with spare clothes, and they knew well not to touch them. No tiredness now, no lost years or fear. I was ready to ramble.

—Out!

—Yes, Missis Grobnik.

—Out!

I stepped out, every night. I walked. I covered the city, street by street, acre by acre. I sniffed and took in the town-wide stinks – meat, metal, big wind from wide spaces, and the smells that marked the districts, neighbourhoods, the old countries. I leaned on brick corners, knew when not to rest against other bricks. I got to know the Loop, crossed every street and alley. I looked for the eyes of ownership, the weight of guns. I knew when I was measured or could walk unnoticed. I was careful.

But it was good. There was room here. I strayed across the river, north, and west, and south. I walked and crossed the names and numbers. Huron, Erie, Ontario. West 31st, 32nd. Harrison, Jefferson, Polk. I copped the speakeasies as I strolled past, the sudden fumes, the snatch of song as a door opened somewhere. I spotted the gang hotels, the men and cars parked outside, the cop shops and brothels, all there, all in place, all avoidable. Crossing the street was enough, turning a corner was an old place left behind. I listened for talk and gunshots. The shots were there, some nights, and charging cars and more shots, but always far away. No one ran for cover. Business as usual; let them at it. It was the big city. Things could be distant here.

The neighbourhoods were easy. Big chunks of built-up prairie that a man could stay lost in, if he was quick and very quietly flamboyant. No good fedora – not since Sweet Afton – no Darrow suspenders, not even here, the home of Clarence Darrow. I could walk past and through – there was space for a man – without stepping aside or begging pardon. The Irish patches weren't as Irish, the Italians weren't as Mediterranean – there was room for America here. I wasn't stupid or senti-mental. There were plenty of fuckers, hot for murder and profit; but there was room for big elbows here. A man could turn and walk away, and walk as fast and as slow and as far as he wanted. I roamed the night. I got back for the two hours' sleep, all I wanted, on the mattress I shared with a chap on the night shift, a Slovak I'd only met once.

I was ready for Mrs Grobnik's call before she opened her mouth.

—Riy-isssse, shiy-nnnne!

She was at the bottom of the stairs, waking the stiffs of the house.

—In, Mees-ter Smarhht?

—In, Missis Grobnik.

—Away-ke?

—Yes, Missis Grobnik.

—Hon-gry?

—Yeah.

—You betcha. Out all night.

Out all night, and I was always heading south.

I'd stay away for days, sometimes the week and another day or two, but I always went back south. And, to get there, I went east, and north, to State Street. And, when I wandered that way, I took my Clarence Darrows and I let them twang. Here a man could wear lilac as he walked into the blues, past the pig-ear-sandwich truck, around the sidewalk dice game. Through new smells and meat goods – *Chitterlings, Spare Ribs, Neck Bones* – past pool halls and stores – *Plaids, Stripes, Checks.* I strolled the Stroll, past newsies flogging the *Defender,* and the open door of the Greater Lily Baptist Church, next door to the fight club. And I felt the freedom I'd really never known before. Because there was no past now waiting to jump. I had to be careful but there was nothing behind my back; it was all ahead. The place was wild, and as new as I was.

I waited for Dora.

At last. I wasn't Irish any more. The first time I heard it, before I was properly listening, I knew for absolute sure. It took me by the ears and spat on my forehead, baptised me. There was a whole band of men on the bandstand, and a little woman at the piano, all thumping and blowing their lives away. Two horns, a trombone, tuba, banjo, drums, filling the world with their glorious torment. There were two trumpets blowing but the spit on my forehead came from only one man's. I looked at him through the human steam – it was too hot there for sweat – and I knew it.

133

I was a Yank.

At last.

It was like nothing I'd heard before, nothing like the American songs that Piano Annie had played on my spine in Dublin, before I'd had to run. This was free and wordless and the man with the trumpet was driving it forward without ever looking back. It was furious, happy and lethal; it killed all other music. It was new, like me.

—You got a name, honey?

There was a gorgeous thing beside me, checking out the fabric of my suit. The suit was old – three years since I'd bought it – but the collar was hours-old new.

—I've got several, I told her.

—That supposed to impress me?

—No, I said. —When I'm impressing you, you won't have to ask.

—Now ain't you a man.

—And ain't you a woman.

I was recovering. I was Henry Smart and there was a woman here who was interested in getting to know me. I looked at her properly.

She wasn't black. She wasn't white. She was new too, invented seconds before and plonked in front of me. Just for me, the new American.

But the trumpet was butting at me; I had to look. She wasn't put off or put out. I could feel her breath, and it was new too, made of things I hadn't tasted. It was stroking my neck.

—Who's that? I said.

I nodded at the stage.

—You don't know him? she said.

—No.

—He the man all you white folks come down here to see.

—Who is he?

She told me. I learnt all his names that night. Dipper. Gate. Gatemouth. Dippermouth. Daddy. Pops. Little Louie. Laughing Louie. Louis Armstrong. The names danced among the crazy lights that jumped from the mirror ball above the dance floor. He was dancing now as he played, as if his legs were tied to the notes that jumped from the bell of his horn. His steps were crazy but he was in control. He was puppet and master, god and disciple, a one-man band in perfect step with the other players surrounding him. His lips were bleeding – I saw drops fall like notes to his patent leather shoes – but he was the happiest man on earth.

—Any man worth a damn need more than one name, said the woman. —Ain't that the truth?

—I've had a few, I told her.

—Well now, drop one on me.

—Henry.

—More.

—S.

—And?

—Smart.

—Henry S. Smart?

—Hello.

—What's with the S?

—So.

—Henry So Smart?

—You're looking at him.

—Well, my oh my.

I was Henry Smart again – no more running and hiding.

—What's your own name, baby? I asked her.

I could say *baby* now; I was American.

—What day is it? she said.

—It might be Monday, I said. —I'm not sure.

—Then I might be Dora, she said. —I'm not sure.

The band stopped suddenly and the man with the trumpet yelled.

—Oh, play that thing!

Then the band was off again, all back on crazy tracks, heading for the same place by routes that were all their own. And the man wiped blood from his lips with the back of his big hand; he put the horn back to his mouth, hopped tracks and never crashed.

There was a beautiful woman close beside me but I couldn't take my eyes off Louis Armstrong.

—Ain't he the blowin'est? she said.

I looked at her now. She really was something.

—Want to try the Bunny Hug, Henry S.?

—Sounds good.

—Is good.

And I danced with her. I was dancing with a woman for the first time in my life. She was wrapped around me, even though we hadn't touched. Then my hands found her back and hers found mine. And we danced right out of the music, to the back edge of the dance floor, but we kept ourselves trapped in the rhythm, and danced right back in again, under the lights and trumpet drops. And we stood there as the music stopped, gut to magnificent gut. Her elbows rested on my hips and she tapped my arse with her sequined pocketbook.

—Well. Now.

—What do they call you on Tuesdays? I asked her.

—Why?

—I'd like to know your name when I wake up beside you.

I hadn't spoken in months; it was great.

—Oh now, she said. —Where's your ambition, Henry S.? I'll be Ethel on Wednesday.

—Fair enough, I said. —Ethel it is.

She grabbed a handful of my shirt and we walked out under a canopy that stretched forever in front of us, and out, into light, hot rain, to State Street and the rest of the new world.

I asked her a question.

—Is this going to cost me?

—Nothing but a whole lot of sweat, said Dora.

Jesus, though, it was good to be wet and alive. Less than a week in Chicago and I was holding down a job, a room and the makings of a night of serious riding. I was clean and clean-shaven, going nowhere far. I was on solid ground, strolling through air full of the caressing rain that couldn't kill the rich stink of the new-dead cattle and pigs, and the live ones in the stockyards that knew their hours were numbered; I could hear them from miles away – the music couldn't kill them. There was money in this air and music coming from every open door, and Armstrong's music followed us all the way, shoving and pulling, rubbing our shoulders.

Oh, play that thing.

No old villages here. This was a city. Manhattan was an island; I'd walked it side to side. There was no walking this one. Chicago had room. It was a great port, a thousand miles from the sea, surrounded by all of America. All trains led to Chicago but I'd spent two years, more, getting here. And here I was, alive again, young again, new.

We crossed a hopping street. We didn't talk as we turned off State, one more Bronzeville block to Dora's house and a room three flights up.

There was no one else there.

136

—Way I like it.

She kicked off her shoes. They landed where she wanted them.

Oh, play that thing.

We hit the mattress – the room had five; hers was the only one on a bed, on castors that took us all over the floor. By the time we slid out onto the floor, Tuesday was well spent.

—Well my, she said.

I was probably out of a brand new job; I didn't know, and I didn't care.

She sat up and grabbed a blanket from the bed. There was a red curtain hanging to our left, making two rooms of the one; the kitchen – a sink and stove – was behind it.

—Well, Mister Henry S., she said as she covered us. —Long time since you did that trick with a lady.

—What makes you think that? I said.

—Oh now, she said. —I can tell. You went at it for near two days, boy.

—You were with me all the way, baby.

Bayay-bee.

—Ain't just the hours, said Dora. —It the way you fill them. Fucked for two days but you came in seven seconds flat.

She was right. It had been a long time since I'd buried myself in a woman's hair, since I'd rubbed my hand on someone else's skin. And her skin; she was gorgeous, away from the club's mirror ball and the music that had made all women gorgeous. It was good to be alive. I was relaxing for the first real time since I'd left Ireland. I could lie back and feel only the tiredness. I was looking at her window, taking in the sounds from the street below us and streets beyond, sounds that travelled miles to die at our feet.

—I've been here five days, I told her. —And there hasn't been one second when I haven't heard music.

—Music being born every minute in this city, she said. —I love it.

—Are you not from here?

—No one from Chicago, Henry S., she said. —No coloured, anyway.

—Where are you from?

—Where from? Where the darkies beat their feet on the Mississippi mud. That where from.

—Is that from a song or something?

—That right. A song or something. Ain't no darkies in Chicago, even if the white boys still sing about them and call it jazz. You been here five days. Where was you six days ago?

—Between places, I said.

—Cheap answer. Ain't no need for it. You mysterious without it.

—Mysterious?

—Sure. You like that? Being mysterious.

—Yeah, I said. —It's grand.

—Grand.

—Yeah. How am I mysterious?

—Oh boy, she said. —We going to talk about you all the day?

—No, I said. —But give us five minutes.

—Well, she said. —I gave you two of my names. Remember them?

—Dora and Ethel.

—That right. So how come you was calling me Annie and Miss O'Shea? What shit you got going on there? You fucking your old schoolmarm last night?

—Well. Yeah, I said. —Now and again.

She didn't object.

—You Irish, right?

—Yeah.

—And your schoolmarm in Ireland a coloured woman?

—No, I said. —But she's beautiful and a woman. And it was dark.

—How come you was at that club on a Monday night?

—It was just Monday, I said.

—Notice something?

—Like what?

—Like you was just about the only ofay in the joint. Monday night is coloured night.

—Ofay?

—White.

—Oh. I noticed that, alright.

—And it not scare you?

—No.

—Surrounded by all those coloured women and their angry men wanting to kill you for looking at them?

—No.

—I believe you, Henry S.

—Grand.

My only real friends had been women; I could always talk to

women. I missed Piano Annie. I missed old Missis O'Shea. I even missed the old witch, Granny Nash. She'd always known what I was up to; she probably still did. And, Christ, I missed Miss O'Shea. I turned every corner expecting to see her, even though there were thousands of miles between us, as far as I could know, and it was five years, more, since I'd seen her and longer still since I'd been able to hold her. I'd heard nothing of her; I didn't know if she was free or still in jail, fighting her war or rearing our growing daughter, missing me or doing what I'd been doing for years, running away.

And I wondered now if Hettie had ever found the wallet. Or if someone else had found it. If the photo was still there, waiting, with the money. Was it there? I weighed the thought. No. It was gone and spent, and thrown aside, away.

I stared at Dora. She was beautiful.

—What colour are you? I asked.

She took her hand from my back and passed it across my eyes.

—I just been fucking a blind man, she said.

—I'm serious, I said. —What colour are you?

—Well, from where you are, I'm a nigger.

—No.

—Yes. A negro, if you want. A negress. A darkie. A shine. They're all nigger. You're here because I'm a fine-looking negress. That's what you see.

—You're a fine-looking woman.

—And any woman will do if you get to call her Annie or Miss O'Shea.

Her hand was on my back again, in a circle between my shoulder blades. Round and slowly around, no push, no anger, no hard point being made. My latest teacher, presenting me with nothing but the facts.

—Now, if you was a Negro sitting there, I'd be a high-yaller bitch. I'd be one bright yellow feather in your cap, black boy.

—Why?

—Because I ain't as much of a nigger as you are, that's why. I'm the nearest thing to white you'll ever get to weigh in your hands.

—So what?

—So what? How long you been here?

—Three or four years.

—Three or four years. And you can say, So what. You *are* blind.

—I've been busy, I told her.

—Busy! she said. —Boy, you been asleep! You got no right to be here that time and not notice a thing or two. No right.

She slapped my shoulder.

—You Irish and you telling me you don't know the difference between black and white? You don't know the rules? You people wrote most of the goddam rules. What day we meet?

—Monday, I said.

—That right, she said. —Monday. Because I wouldn't be there Tuesday, Wednesday, Thursday, Friday, Saturday or Sunday. And if you say, Why not, I'll tear your balls off and throw them down to the street.

—Because you're coloured, I said.

It was feeble but the best I could manage. She was terrifying and marvellous.

—That right, she said. —I'm coloured. No coloured let in that door any other day of the week. Monday our night. Even on State Street. Our street.

—It's a shame, I said.

—A crying goddam shame, she said. —Five, six more days to Monday. What am I going to do?

—You could pass for white, I said.

—You know more than you pretend, she said. —I don't want to pass for white.

—We could always stay in, I said.

—About all we can do, she said. —'Less we want to get ourselves troubled. You want to know why I ain't interested in being a white woman no more?

—Fire away, I said.

She stared at me.

—It ain't because I can never be one, she said. —That ain't it. I spent all my life being less than white. Thinking I was better than most because I had some white man's blood, and knowing all the time that I was just a nigger bitch. Get my hair straighted, put bleach on my face, I was still a nigger bitch. And not enough of a nigger neither. Not white enough, not black enough. Just a jaundice-coloured bitch, didn't matter a goddam how many men was after my tail. I hated my own self and walked through those nigger bitches thinking I was better than them because my ass wasn't as black as their black asses.

She said nothing for a while. She hummed something that I couldn't catch. Then she looked at me and spoke.

140

—Took a long time to get out of that white man's trap. Want to know who did it for me?

—Who?

—Dipper.

—Armstrong?

—That right.

She hummed again, and looked at me.

—Be what you be. That what he said. And that the way he plays.

She rubbed the blanket like it was a cat on her lap.

—Want to meet him?

—Yeah.

—You never know, she said. —Maybe he can cure you being Irish.

—He already has, I said.

—No, brother, she said. —Ain't that easy.

He was dressed only in big white towels, one around his waist, the other wrapped around his neck. He'd been off the stage ten minutes but the sweat was still flowing onto his neck and down his chest and arms. He wiped his forehead with the handkerchief he'd had with him onstage. Off the stage, he was a small man but his smile and his face were huge, and everything and everyone surrounded him. The dressing room was crowded with sharp-dressed white men and women, but I could see none of the other musicians.

Dora had just introduced me to him. She was white tonight – this once, for me – the only way to get us together through the big, leather-padded doors. The white boys in charge of the door knew her; they knew her when she was black too, but that didn't matter. Tonight she was white, and she was with a white man. She was inside the rules.

He was sitting deep in a broken chair, but he stood up to meet me. He stood in front of me and held out his hand. Then he saw something, and the hand went further, and gently grabbed one of my lapels. He felt its threads with the fingers that had helped him to his impossible notes – a long line of them that had sliced the roof a few minutes earlier. I could feel the heat of his fingers close to my face. He was standing right against me. I could smell his work and genius.

—That's a mighty sharp vine, Pops, he said.

More than three years after I'd bought it, the suit was still an eye-catcher; my first American suit, my own wear and tear hadn't worn down the fabric.

—It one of Mister Piper's? he asked.

—Don't know him, I said.

—Mister Scotty Piper, he said. —Fine, fine tailor.

—It's not one of his.

He looked down at the trousers.

—And the nice wide pants, he said.

—I saw them coming, I told him.

He smiled.

I was remembering how, giving it the old Henry.

—I got there before the rest, I said. —But, you know yourself, it's the shoulders. The difference between a good suit and a bad one.

—Well, that the truth, he said.

He laughed and slapped my shoulders. He looked at me carefully. Then he looked at Dora.

—He features somebody I know, he said.

He looked at me again. He looked up at my face.

—We met before, Pops?

—No, I said.

—No, he said. —But it's a problem. You ofays all look the same to me.

That got laughs; I didn't mind.

—An ofay that can carry a coloured suit, he said. —We got to talk, Pops.

He picked up his trousers, then turned to me again.

—Hang around.

Dora shoved me with her hip.

I was in.

It was the same night that Sacco and Vanzetti were finally strapped to the chair and cooked; I saw it on the front pages the day after. But I was happy that night. I'd been to see *The General* at the Paradise, my first film since New York. I sat through it twice, laughed twice as hard at Buster Keaton, and forgot that my girl wasn't at my side. She was sitting above me, in the gods, up in nigger heaven. She was black that afternoon. And now my hand was still wet with Louis Armstrong's sweat. He'd held my hand; he'd seen the man I used to be. A man who carried a good

142

suit through checkpoints and locked doors. Louis Armstrong had looked at me and seen someone he wanted, a man he needed to know, a man who'd stroll right on with him. He'd seen Henry Smart.

It was months before we spoke again but it didn't matter. I waited and, sometimes, I knew.

I waited now for Dora.

Sometimes she got off her streetcar three blocks before her stop, and sometimes she didn't. She sat in the car and looked ahead or down at her book as I stood and watched her pass. She looked older, coming home from work. And, sometimes, maybe once a week, she stepped off and there I was, sometimes. Sometimes, she went straight past me and, sometimes, I jumped on the car and left her there.

She was white enough to work in the Loop but she'd given that up. She worked for a family now, in Oak Park.

—Clean some, cook some. Do what the bitch should do her own self.

Doing the black woman's work. It paid less than the Loop dress shop had, and the hours were longer, but she wasn't pretending now. No more hair straighteners or powders, no more care with the accent.

—Don't play it up neither. I just be Dora.

—So you're happier.

—Don't be so dumb, Henry S.

I took care; I even noticed – but I still didn't get it. I'd spent three years trying not to be Irish, but I didn't understand. I thought I did, but I was never close enough.

—You think they live here cos they want to? she asked me once, when she met me off the trolley, before she got too angry to talk to me. —There's a line, Henry S., and you don't see it cos you don't have to. But *we* do.

—I only said I liked it, I told her.

But she'd gone. I watched her stride away, under a string of rabbits that hung from a telegraph pole, across the pavement, to a window above a butcher's door. Her anger made the rabbits swing. The red in her head-rag caught the yellow streetlight, threw it back.

That was all I'd said: I liked the place. I saw the alleys. I saw the kids – the rickets and glaucoma. I saw what the houses were, the old rotten homes of the rich, worse, more packed, than the one I slept in; as bad, sometimes, as the one I'd been born in. And I'd seen few black men working in the packing houses. And fewer in the push of men at the gates every morning, hoping for their turn and the nod. And none in the Loop going in and out the front doors, none that weren't moving off the streets, getting quickly to where they were going.

I wasn't a sap.

—I only said I liked it here.

I ran after her.

—You fuckin' like it.

—Go away, fool.

But I kept up, got beside her, made men and women step out of our way.

—What you doing?

It wasn't fair; I knew that. I was drawing attention, dragging it to her, just to prove her wrong. To prove that we could stand here and talk, that we could do it as long as we wanted.

Past the Palace-de-Luxe Beauty Shop, and no one in the window took much notice. I looked back, and I was right – three lye-soaked heads waiting for the next sight to see – we were already gone. The loan bank, the bargain store, the storefront church – no hard eyes or mutters. Past the poolroom and barber shop and the hard men who always stood outside. They stared, more frankly than white men ever did, but it wasn't me they were looking at. They were gawking at a good-looking woman.

The Stroll was lighting up.

—You wait, she said.

I wasn't getting in. If she brought a white man home, she was working – she told me this. If she brought him home more than twice, or he started arriving by himself, using what looked like his own key, started nodding at folks, patting the heads of kids on the steps – the *stoop*, she was attracting bad attention. I hadn't been back to her room. And the room wasn't hers. She shared the rent with four other girls. They'd been on a round-trip excursion to Memphis the first night she'd parked herself in front of me. They left on Friday night, got back on Monday morning, partied all the way and back—

—A dance on wheels, she said.

—Ever do it yourself?

—No reason to, she said.

—back in time for the charge to work. But they'd missed the

144

train, all four of them, and rolled back into town a whole week late.

While she changed, took off the servant's head-rag and threw it in a corner with the years she didn't want, I waited on the corner of 35th and State, the district's big corner, and listened to a tailgate band, on the back of a flatbed truck parked right against the pavement. There was a piano player I'd seen and heard before. Albert Ammons. He was up there with a trombone player and a drummer, and a guitarist, sharing the stool with Mister Ammons, all on the back of the truck, under a banner advertising the same trip that had sent Dora's flat-mates south, the Illinois Central round-trip excursion to Memphis. There was a barker too, in a sharp suit and polished derby, sitting on the fireplug, waving tickets, and often selling, to anyone who stopped to hear the band.

—I got them here, folks! Got them right here!

He stayed away from me.

—Tickets here to Paradise! All way home to the land of cotton *and* change in your pocket!

It was good music. Men grabbed home-bound women, made a dance floor right outside the loan bank.

—If you can't do it a long time, do it twice!

It was the rough sound of home, played for city floors and pavements; it was good-time music for homesick slickers.

—Oh, shake your wicked knees!

There were four couples dancing now, flinging and flung, moving just enough, watched and clapped by dozens more, six or seven couples now, and Mister Ammons thumping out the steps and shouting as the barker shouted. This was what I'd meant; this was what I liked. The back-home music of Manhattan's Lower East Side had been miserable; even the reels were meant to draw the tears. But these men here were beating out the blues, and laughing as they worked. The steps hadn't come north with the dancers; they were made up, there, on the sidewalk, and abandoned when the barker decided that enough was enough. There was no one left buying. They could come back in an hour, the next day, next week, and the steps would be brand-new different.

The dancers sensed it, knew it in the shift in tempo.

—Oh, shake, shake, shake your fat fanny!

Their dance was nearly over. The guitar man climbed over the side of the truck, and the dancers turned and grabbed each other;

145

they left the ground, inches below, a whirr of hats and elbows. The streetlight couldn't hold them clear.

Oh, play that thing.

The barker had the last word before he hopped onto the running board.

—These fine, high-powered maestros be playing their fine, high-powered stomps and boogie-blues, in the fine, high-powered choo-choo train, all the way to Memphis, Tennessee. The Shimmy, the Black Bottom, the Charleston. All can be dooed in the Coloured Only car. All night, all the way. Every number a gassuh.

The trombone player jumped from the back of the truck, holding the instrument high. He waved back, and walked away. The truck moved out in the opposite direction, to join the State Street crawl. Mister Ammons was still belting away, although the other men held onto the sides of the truck. And, as they crept over the intersection and moved more freely south, his piano was joined and swallowed by other pianos and horns and drums that took over the street, the streets, same time, every night.

Oh, play that thing.

This was living like I'd never seen it. This wasn't drowning the sorrow, the great escape, happy or unhappy. It was life itself, the thing and the point of it. No excuses: it was why these men and women lived.

Dora took her time, but standing on that corner was a very good night out. I soaked in the sounds, the victory and joy. The packing house was far away. I wasn't going to stay there. The pay was bad, the work was bad, and they'd be getting worse as autumn – *fall* – surrendered to my first Chicago winter. I'd had enough of Packingtown. I hadn't moved west to live with Lithuanians and Poles. They were grand, but impenetrable. Big decent, grunting people. They ate too much, too fast; they prayed too much, too often – they were too like the fuckin' Irish. I was safe there, but that was all.

I'd be safe here too, but alive again. I didn't know what I'd do, but I knew I'd be doing it here. I didn't know why – it was stupid, sentimental; I could see that. And dangerous. But not tonight, it wasn't. I was ready again, excited. I believed.

Her hand was on my arm, fingers quickly tucked in to my chest.

Her anger had been thrown in the corner, gone the way of her head-rag. She was glowing, happy, younger than she was, already dancing to the tunes and steps that were fighting it out around us. It was officially night time now, play time, and we could be together. We'd be looked at. She was gorgeous and I wasn't far off it. Henry Smart again, because she'd looked at me. I'd come out of hiding. And here was a woman who'd got there before me; she'd stopped hiding too.

—We were made for each other, I said.

—No, she said. —We were not.

—Where'll we go?

—Well, now, she said. —You a white man on a coloured street that ain't your street. That the problem? No, sir. A coloured lady on her own coloured street. She the problem.

She moved, and took me with her.

—But tonight, Henry S., we got the answer to that problem.

Through men on their way home, and women on their way out, past pimps and preachers, a one-legged man with a begging cup – war or stockyards, I couldn't tell; past two black cops – I hadn't seen black cops before. We passed restaurants, cabarets, and loud speakeasies. We passed because we couldn't go there. She could enter some, or I could. But we couldn't enter together.

We strolled at a clip; she knew where we were going. They were all there, on or just off State Street: the Dreamland, the Sunset, the Plantation, the Elite Café, the De Luxe. All fighting, grabbing as we passed. But they weren't for us tonight.

We stopped a block short of the Panama Café. She let go of my arm. I knew the trick by now.

We could walk into the Panama Café.

The words had made me jump when she'd first whispered them. I went for the gun I didn't have.

—A black and what?

—Tan.

—Black and Tan?

—Yes, Henry S. What the matter?

—What the fuck is a black and tan?

—Where your blood go, Henry? You gone all pale.

I told her all about the Black and Tans. (The headlights caught the corners of our eyes, then sprayed across our shoulders and made black shadows of the way ahead. We heard the boot nails scratch wood as the Tans abandoned the tenders to chase us. They were right behind us now. We could feel their pace in the ground. They were fit, angry men, an army of them on our backs.

We ran out of the power of their headlights. But a flare zipped above us, and crackled. And there we were, caught in bright red, running across a hopeless field, far from the next stone wall. And the firing started.)

The sweepings of England's jails, Jack Dalton had called the Black and Tans, back when they landed and declared war on every man and woman in Ireland, with the secret blessing of their government. They burnt towns. They took people from houses and shot them. They shot livestock. They murdered priests and mayors.

—Sound like the Klan, said Dora.

—What clan?

—Go on. You finish first.

They burnt the creameries. They stole wedding rings. They declared all Irish people Shinners and made terrorists of them all. They were veterans who'd been unable to get work in England and Scotland after the war. And they'd been promised good money, ten shillings a day, to sort out Ireland. They were foreign and savage, and their presence in the country was proof that we were winning. And, all the time, we were the puppet masters. We knew how to make them set fire to the right creamery, how to draw them to the right house. We controlled them. We pulled the trigger and they went off.

(I felt the bullet in Miss O'Shea's arm; it shook mine. We kept running. She didn't slow down. She didn't even moan. The blood slid down between our hands.)

—That was a war? said Dora.

—Yeah. I suppose it was.

—Didn't hear about that one.

—It was only small.

—You win?

That was a hard one.

—Yes and no.

(We were still in the middle of nowhere. I felt another bullet. They were killing her slowly.)

—She die?

—No.

(She dashed ahead of me, knocked forward by the shot. She squeezed my hand, let go. I grabbed it back. I wanted her pain. I wanted it all. I'd carry her the rest of the way. I ran ahead. I turned to lift her as she caught up and, as I raised my arm to hoist her to my shoulder, the bullet slid in.)

148

—That the scar I like?

—One of them, yeah.

(I was falling hard. I couldn't see anything, I didn't know anything. When I was able to see again and think, when I looked and saw the ground jumping below me, she was carrying me.)

—Good for she, said Dora.

—Yeah.

—Where she now?

—Don't know.

—Alive?

—I'd say so.

—Care?

—Yeah.

It was a while before she spoke.

—Well, Henry S., I'm willing to carry you on my back but I don't think I'll be needing to. Less'n you misbehave. Black an' tan is just a club. Where you and me can dance.

The Panama Café was a black and tan, and a black and tan was a club where white men and black women – and black men and white women, although I never saw it – had licence to dance, together.

She went first. We could both go in, but not together. Once in, we could dance together; we could dance, but not sit together. There were no written rules, nothing to point at; they had to be learnt and remembered. It was all about money, of course; the whites stayed away if the mingling stepped too close to permanence. It was tricky and stupid but it was better than the nothing that other establishments offered.

I watched her walk past the doormen. Their eyes followed as she walked under the canopy. In the same dress she wore the night I first saw her, the silver sequined thing she always threw on when we stepped out together.

—How many dresses you reckon I got? she said. —How many dresses the women have in Ireland?

I shrugged.

—Streets paved with gold over there?

—Nope.

—I guess not, or all those nice Irish people be right back over there. Where nobody poor and the girls throw out the dresses they wear but once. Might go there myself.

—You've made your point.

149

—I made one of my points. I also wear this dress nights I step out by my own self, or with some man else.

She was in, through the black leather-padded doors that opened out to the street as she approached.

It was my turn. I strolled right up to the doormen, white. A black man couldn't have stopped a white man from entering. They nodded, stepped back – *tap tap* – and let me pass. They knew me by now. They saw the same suit every time I came their way, the cap, the boots beneath the cuffs. I was one of their own; they could wink and cheer me on.

—I got the heebies, said one.

—I got the jeebies, I said back.

They were Armstrong's lines, and they'd become famous since he'd first shouted them the year before.

—Is he frying tonight? I asked.

—Word is.

—But you don't know for sure.

—No one knows for sure, sport.

—Fair enough.

—Word is, he was in the Sunset last night. Maybe our turn tonight.

—Okay.

I slipped them both a dollar, no show, no high-hat. I had the money, but didn't flaunt it. They liked that; one of their own. They let me open the door myself.

—See you on the way out, lads.

But I didn't.

I left my cap with the hat-check girl; it was a hats-off kind of place. The girl, a light-skinned doll who seemed new to the job, didn't seem sure what to do. I leaned across and took the ticket from her hand, left a nickel in its place, and walked straight into the music and the heat that always came with it.

I worked all day for the dollars and nickels I handed around as I moved through this new world and made myself memorable, a man to know, a man to step aside for. But I was handing out far more than I earned lugging beef and hog-meat. I was spending more boodle than I'd ever had before.

I looked for Dora.

So, where did it come from?

I robbed it.

She was, as always, easy to locate. I looked where everyone else was looking, and there she was, dancing with another guy, doing what she called the Bunny Hug. I could tell her heart wasn't in it; the bunny was a dead one and the guy would be dragging its corpse around for another few minutes. But only she knew, and I knew. She was killing the time till I arrived. A coloured girl couldn't sit by herself and wouldn't be let stand alone for long. She'd be shooed along to a tableful of college boys or the hard guys bellying the bar. I could watch now and feel sorry for the sap. He was trying for the tough but elegant look, the spats, the stripes; he was almost there, not quite. He was too pink to impress, even a woman as pink as himself. He was carrying weight, too soft at the neck and ears, and sweating through the stripes – which didn't mean he wasn't tough. The white clients, the would-be guys and dolls, liked these tough guys leaning on the bar or mingling with them. The presence of gangsters made them feel safe on this knife-carrying side of town, especially in the black and tans, where the street sometimes followed them onto the dance floor. I looked again at the guy in the stripes. He was carrying a gun; it was sitting fat there in his jacket pocket, right side. But the gun and his wop credentials didn't matter. He was no match for Dora. I let them at it.

The tough guys had made me halt, the first time I'd noticed them. It was New York all over again. It was Dublin. They'd got there before me. But she'd seen me scope them, and guessed.

—They ain't Irish, Henry S., she said. —The Irish don't come down here.

—Never?

—Ever. They Eye-talians. They like to dance and they like to dance to hot music.

And she was right. The crooks were there for the night out, killing time between heists. So I left them at it and watched the band tap away the remaining seconds of their dance.

I'd seen them before, together or in different set-ups. They went wherever the work was. We could go to another place later and find two or three of these same men on the stage, along with others we'd never seen before. The leader one night sat well back another night. I'd seen some of these men in the orchestra at the Vendome, the picture house up the street, and I'd seen the trombone player on the back of a truck, minutes before, with Mister Ammons. He'd had time to change or shake himself; he was sharp as the other men up there, no sign of the street on his threads.

The gold drape behind him shimmered, as if there was a huge gorgeous woman rolling behind it, being tickled by the notes and beat. I knew the drummer; I knew his name. Baby Dodds. He beat the rim of his bass drum, and did a dance of his own, without moving his arse from the stool. Then, chorus over, he was moving among the drums again, herding the others, the great jazz drover, taking them with him without even trying.

Two hi-hat taps put a stop to the tune and, as partners stopped and people upped or sat, I got on to the floor and took Dora from the pink lad. I had to be quick. The band didn't wait; the applause was too polite. They were out there again, thumping and skipping through *Sweet and Low Down*.

—How's it goin'? I said to the pink lad with the gun, and we left him there, as the dancers filled the floor and quickly swallowed him.

Each dance was a new one, even when it had a name. I was a late starter, but I was climbing over the lost time. I held one of Dora's hands and jumped back twice. I pulled her to me, and jumped to meet her. We rubbed close for a second – we were free to while we danced – and jumped away and rolled around, and back around. I sent out a leg, just missed a fat girl whose chap had let her slip. Dora swung me aside, and planted a kick where I'd just been. My turn again – my toe just grazed her final sequin. Then, hard gut to just soft and right, we stared and promised each other a hiding. *Sweet and Low Down* was like a quick creep up the stairs; that was how these men were playing it, shoes off, before the light came on and caught us. Then, there, in the final bars and seconds, we invented the dance to go with it. We crept across the floor, my hand on her back, hers on mine, finger to my lip, mine to hers; we crept up to the bed. She bit my finger, I grabbed her arse. We hopped over the creak in the stairs, and the audience – there was no one else dancing – knew what we'd done, and laughed and gave us more floor, and more danger. I looked, and saw: the players were looking down at myself and Dora, staring at our feet. Baby Dodds was leaning over his kit, making sure he matched us. The banjo player stopped for a second, to pull his chair nearer the lip of the stage. The notes and beat were ours; we were playing the song. We crept backwards, looking over our shoulders, our faces an inch apart. We didn't kiss; we wouldn't get away with that. We pretended to trip, and caught ourselves. The horn player made his trumpet laugh – *waw, waw,*

waw, waaah. One last dash – she opened the door; I slammed it. She jumped; I caught all of her. Two perfect taps on the hi-hat; we were done.

It was stupid, but the sex beneath was well worth the sweat.

There were other couples across the floor, ready to dance up the stairs, waiting for the band to let them go. We stood aside; it wasn't worth doing any more. The band jumped right back into *Sweet and Low Down* and the floor was full of creeping couples, fingers bitten much too early, arses grabbed that should have been left alone. The band relied on itself again; the music was polite.

—I could use a tall drink, she said.

We could do that together, drink, if we stood and didn't share the cup.

She followed me to the bar. It was no big distance but the bodies were piled against it and pushing. Gin could be got outside, or at the kitchen door, for two paper dollars a pint, but me and Dora preferred our drink with a small bit of style. I held back, to catch the bartender, a stride piano tickler on his nights off. I'd met him once, in the Loop, recognised him from the Panama and stopped him for a chat. I'd terrified him. I didn't know how or why back then, six or seven weeks ago, didn't know that I could have earned him a kicking, far from home and talking to a white man. But I was learning.

—You don't sweat much, Henry S.

—Neither do you.

—Expected of me, she said. —But you? All you white boys sweat. Where is it?

—I sweat, I told her. —But I manage it.

—Well, how?

The barman saw me. He looked over thirsty faces, two-deep and angry, for the sign from me. I tapped my nose, then hit my temple – a drink for a woman and a drink for a man.

—I sweat when it suits me, I told her. —If the foreman's walking my way, I'll sweat like a bastard. In the company of a woman, in my Sunday best, I sweat a good bit less.

—You saying you turn it on and off?

—Yeah. More or less.

—Hell.

—True as God, baby. There's nothing to it, once you get the hang of it.

I'd learnt how to talk again. I handed over the folding cush, showed the barman the palm of one hand, to let him know the change was his. And I took the cups from him, over the heads of men who'd been waiting a long time to be served. Her cup was taller, thinner; her tea was pink. Mine was the usual.

—If there ain't nothing to it, she said, —you can teach me.

—You don't sweat.

—I sweat the stuff other bitches use to mask their sweat. Teach me, anyway.

—Fair enough, I said. —Listening?

—Both ears.

—Every day, in ever-y way, I am getting better and—

There was a face in mine. It was the pinkish tough guy's and he was looking pinker.

—Yeah, he said.

He nodded. Licked his bottom lip.

—A smart guy.

—Can I buy you a drink? I said.

—More smart guy.

I was stuck. I agreed with the man – I'd been stupid – but spoken agreement would have meant a smack in the mouth and consequences, and so would disagreement. I looked back at him and let him take it further.

—Know what?

Again, no answer was the order.

—That shine behind the bar. Employed here to serve the clientele. He's dead. And know who's to blame?

I said nothing.

—You. Know why? Because he served you and you ain't no client.

His hand was in his pocket. I was ready to break it. I was sweating now, not from choice.

—Yeah, he said.

He licked the bottom lip again.

I could tell: he'd nothing else to say. He was spent or he was building up to shoot me. But Dora was between us, tits on his gun arm. She was talking to him too, but I couldn't hear words – there was some kind of riot going on behind, around us. He had to take his hand from his pocket; he had to step back to get out from under Dora. He didn't want to – he was confused and delighted; she was a silver wall between us.

I turned, and saw him.

Louis Armstrong.

His mother had died – Dora told me; she'd come up from New Orleans and died. He'd been gone, and he was back. He put the trumpet to his mouth; the crowd went wild. He took it down. He did it again; he put the horn to his mouth. His eyes stopped looking – the pupils went up into his head, and he played. The drape behind him rolled and shook, and stopped. Nobody danced. Nobody sat. Nobody drank or took a breath.

It was the blues, his grief crying out of the bell. But it was no lament. It was the cry of a terrified child, left all alone, forever. No notes, no breaks, but all one howl that rushed at her dead body; it was angry and lost and – *What about meee!* – it turned, and turned, and returned to the body, and washed, and dressed her. His mother, mine – *she skips and she laughs, her black eyes shine happy* – he sent his mother home.

All by himself. He was alone there, somewhere of his own. The other men stood back, afraid to be too close to the death we were there to witness, and the aching, shattering sound that was coming from the man. It didn't soften; there was no fond look back, no shared prayer.

But it stopped. The trumpet was still at his lips, the eyes were still clenched shut. For the first and only time in my life, I lived in absolute silence.

—That it?

A kid at the bar, whose mother was at home waiting up for him. I laughed, like I hadn't laughed in years. The whole joint laughed, threw it at the ceiling. A pinkish hand held my shoulder.

—You're alright, smart guy.

And the eyes up there on the stage were open again, and so was the mouth. The trumpet was at his side, held like a bat.

—Good evening, ev-ery-bo-dy.

There were a few claps that tripped over each other; we'd just laughed at his mother's funeral.

—That it? he said.

He was smiling now.

—My name's Mister Arm-strong. We going to play *Saint James Infirmary. Saint James Infirmary*, and ah—

The trumpet went to the mouth. The arm brought it up without seeming to bend. He turned to the band, Baby Dodds hit the rim of the big drum and the trumpet walked them into a dirty piece of blues that cleared the floor, then filled it again with the

155

brave ones. The eyes were closed; the sweat rolled right over them. I watched him wipe his face while the trombone took a turn. That was the difference between the music when he was there, and the music when he wasn't. When he wasn't in on it, there were no turns, no solos; the players galloped along without them. It was tight, it was great, but it was anonymous. When he was there, they stepped out of the circle and had a go; names were made, sounds were invented. The trombone now rode every woman in the house and stepped back for a rest and a wash. And Armstrong put the horn to his mouth and played it like it hurt.

I looked for Dora and saw her with the pink lad. He was on his toes, pushing into her, trying to. Her hands were under his elbows, keeping his hands in the air. Any faster, she'd have been trying to get away. But, as it was, as I heard and saw, she was giving him the ride of his life. And the trumpet kept them at it. There were no dance choices out there; it was fuck or get off the floor.

I had to watch the face as he blew those notes and shaped them, let them go and followed. It was music made for riding, but he was working hard and having none of the fun. I couldn't get my eyes off him. But I had to. Dora was out there, on the floor with the pink lad, doing what the trumpet was telling her to do. But before I could decide how I felt, what to do, where to bury the cunt that was tiptoeing after her with his langer head-butting her gut, the music became something else. The banjo was there, the trombone dipped and rose; it was dancing time again.

The floor was full.

I knew the tune; I knew all the names – *Chicago Breakdown*.

I made my move.

I put my hand on his shoulder.

—Mind if I cut in, pal?

He looked back at me, and stopped.

—It's smart guy, he said. —I hear right? You want to take over here?

—Yeah.

—Be my guest, smart guy.

He held my arm.

—You're a hard-boiled egg, right?

He squeezed until I leaned down and my ear was close enough to his mouth.

—Keep that pussy good and wet for me, smart guy.

156

He squeezed again, let go, and patted my arm.

—I'll be watching yeh.

I grabbed Dora's hands.

—I'm all danced out, Henry S., she said.

—What were you doing there? I asked.

—Saving your hide, boy.

She looked over my shoulder, and started to dance.

—Who is he?

—Don't know his big name. Just the little one at the front. Carmine.

—Have you seen him before?

—Yes, I have.

—Here?

—Yes, Henry S. He might even own the establishment. You never can tell with these Eye-talian types.

—Christ.

—Do not profane in my presence, Henry S. We safe, I think. If we sensible. He made his point.

—And what's that?

—You being stupid again. The point ain't me. It you. So when Dipper finish this number, we finish dancing and you go.

—But—

—Listen to me. This number finish, you go.

Armstrong was bringing the song to its end. He stopped, and the clarinet was taking it to bed.

—Go, she said.

—Where—?

—No more. Get out. It me too, you know. You in trouble, I in trouble. Go on.

She was angry, and scared. And so was I. I didn't want to leave her, and I didn't want to step out there. The word from Carmine and the doormen, my pals, would have me dead and unmissed. *Alfie Gandon says Hello.* He was pink, his feet were small but, I saw now – too late – the fucker was lethal.

But Dora was right. She knew the rules, the do's and all the don'ts. She'd had a word with Carmine as she hauled him round the tiles. I was safe, as long as I did what was expected. There was no messing here; I saw that in her face. I was choosing life or death.

I turned, and walked away. I'd keep walking.

But he sang.

157

—ALL YOU HEARD FOR YEARS IN IRELAND—
WAS THE WEARING OF THE GREEN—
The voice was huge, dark, and hilarious and terrifying. It was bigger than the fuckin' trumpet.
—AND AH WAS BORN IN IRELAND —heh ha
SO IMAGINE HOW I FEEL—
It shook me, nearly took the fuckin' jacket off my back.
I hadn't heard him sing before.
—NOW IRELAND'S GONE BLACK BOTTOM CRAZY—
The power of the thing was shoving me to the door, forget the fuckin' cap, straight out onto the street.
—SEE THEM DAN – YOU OUGHT TO SEE THEM DANCE—
But I had to look, to see that it was actually him.
—FOLKS SUPPOSE TO BE REAL LAZY—
I turned.
—EVEN DANCE – I MEAN THEY DANCE—
He was looking straight at me.
—I HANDING YOU NO BLARNEY—
And the mouth was looking at me.
—WHEN I SAY THEY GO—
THEY REALLY GO—
I saw the words.
—AND THEY PUT IT OVER WITH A WOW—
Black bullets.
—ALL OVER IRELAND—
Coming straight at me.
I saw Dora, in a corner of my eye. I saw her silent shout; the fury, terror.
—YOU CAN SEE THE PEOPLE DANCE—
I moved away from Dora. I made my way to the bandstand.
—COS IRELAND'S GONE BLACK BOTTOM CRAZY—
I saw Pink Carmine.
Fuck him.
—NOW-OW-OW—
I'd been called.

I walked behind him, through the hidden guts of the club, the place below the stage, like the innards of a cruise ship manned by black men and women, chefs, waiters, ironers, men stoking

158

the furnace, through clouds of steam that were too big and wet for inside. Pink Carmine came as far as the furnace, sucking up to Armstrong all the way. Louis brought the business. They all wanted Louis.

—Want a steak before you go, Louis?

—Put it back on the cow, Gate. Had one before I got here.

And we left him behind. We were with Louis. I made sure Dora was with me.

—We're fine.

Someone pushed open the door in front of us; I watched the steam sail out and die. The cold air hit us and we were out in the alley. The door behind clunked shut.

It was raining hard. Dora was furious and wouldn't talk. We'd escaped; Armstrong had saved us. I tried to tell her that, but I let her go. I watched her break the light on the puddles as she went right through them. The music swallowed her heels, and I tumbled into the car beside Armstrong.

—They got rain like that in Ireland, Pops?

—No, I said. —It never rains in Ireland.

—Yeah, he said. —I heard that. It all desert.

He looked at me.

—Which of us getting out again?

—Why?

—The crank.

—Oh yeah.

I opened the door and slid back out into the rain.

—Get back in, Pops. Automobile's old but ain't *that* old. We can start her inside here.

He had me rattled, but I got back in, and he got us started. The windows shook. The water charged down the windscreen.

—No wipers, no?

—Wipers was extra. You drive?

—No, I said.

—No now, no ever?

—Ever.

—Got to learn. Hold the wheel. That half the job.

The rain came in on us and we nearly went over an Irish-looking cop who was stepping around a puddle, but by the end of that night, across and back across the city, in and out of the Loop, south, down State Street—

—Stop when you see the cotton, Pops.

159

I was driving the years-old Bearcat, Louis's Pneumonia Special, and he was sitting where I'd been. I didn't know where we were; I'd been lost for hours. The rain was still hammering down, and it was slightly drier under the roof than it was outside. To see where I was pointing the car, I had to stick my head out the window every couple of seconds.

He spoke.

—I describe the job, you tell me if it's yours. Sound right?

—Fire away.

—You stay beside me. Day, night, time in between. That the job.

—Is that it?

—I explain more as we go along. Sound right?

—Fair enough.

—Fair ee-nuff.

His hand was in front of me. I took, and shook it.

—Bad smell in this automobile, he said when he took his hand back. —Ain't me and it ain't the automobile.

—That leaves me.

—'Less there's someone we didn't invite sitting right behind us.

He was good at this; I looked behind.

—Guess it's you, he said. —Meat, Pops. You smell of the stock-yards.

—That's where I work.

—Work-ed. Can't be having that smell, O'Pops. We the people who *eat* the meat. We don't be smelling like it.

—It can't be the suit, I told him. —I never wear it to work.

—It *you*, Pops.

He looked at my feet on the pedals.

—That right, he said. —Lift the right, slowly, slowly, good and holy. The boots, he said. —They have to go.

—No, I said.

We were somewhere near Back o' the Yards; I wasn't sure. We argued all the way.

—It in the boots, he said. —That cow blood in the laces. Got to go.

—I'll get new laces.

—Nay nay, he said. —*Boots* stink, Pops. Right and left. Right into the leather, the only part of the cow should be on your feet. We'll buy you some nice shoes.

—No.

160

He slipped one of his own off and held it in front of my face.

—See? So sharp, they dangerous.

—No.

—Sharp as a wedding, Pops. The patent leather. See the pussy while you dancing.

—It'll keep till later.

He laughed.

—I like that.

He put the shoe back on and knocked his head on the dash when I took the right he told me to. I couldn't tell street from car lights; they looked the same through the wash that rolled down the window.

—Now see here, he said. —Got myself a bump 'account of your stinky old sha-boots. Why you attached? They made from your grandmama's hide or something?

—They've come a long way with me, I told him. —Where are we?

—Still Chicago, he said. —I start worrying we start driving through the corn.

The boots had belonged to my wife's dead uncle. They were all I had left of her. The wedding photograph was in New York, under Hettie's bed, or gone. There was nothing else. I'd worn them the last time I spoke to her.

(—Look for me!

—I will!

—Look for me!)

—Here's what, O'Pops. Keep the boots, we get you a nice pair of shoes. Wear the shoes, keep the boots for old times' sake, over the fire, under the bed. Build a museum.

—I'll go halfway, I said.

—Which half?

He pulled the window open.

—See why they call this place Back o' the Yards. Man, it the back of my ass. Have your boot smell, too. So, which half?

—I'll keep the boots for old times' sake.

—You going to go barefoot?

—New boots.

—You a cripple?

—No.

—Polio done got into you since I saw you dancing couple hours ago?

161

—No.

I knew where I was now. Even with the rain adding an inch to the windshield, I knew the streets, the slopes, the darkness. I stopped on the road below Mrs Grobnik's house, in seven inches of brown, roaring water, four feet under the sidewalk.

I looked at him.

—I don't have to explain to you the difference between having a pair of boots and not having a pair of fuckin' boots.

—We going to swap the we-was-po' stories?

—No. I'm getting out of the car, into this fuckin' weather. Am I better off with boots or shoes?

—Boots.

—If I have to leave town quickly and it might be a long time before I stop. Am I better off with boots or shoes?

—Boots.

—I get into a fight with a hard man. Boots or shoes?

—Gun.

—You get my point.

—I bleeding.

I opened the door and watched the water running past, halfway up the car wheels.

—Need more than boots to keep your toes dry out there.

—Back in a minute.

—Why we here?

—Your idea. To collect my things.

—What things you got?

—A toothbrush and a spare collar.

—That it?

—That's all I'll take with me.

—Toothbrush belong to your grandmama too?

—No.

—Bristles made from a sweetheart's cunt hairs?

—Not all of them.

—Got a sweet thing up that bank?

—No.

—Waste of time.

—I'll be back in a minute.

—I be safe here?

—I don't know.

—Might be gone when you get back.

—Fair enough.

162

—Oh, fair ee-nuff.

I dropped slowly into the water and climbed the mud to the house.

I heard him behind me.

—That a good set of boots you got there, suh!

—Mees-ter Smarhht! In?

She stepped out of the dark, in front of her porch. She was soaking, half her normal size.

—Yes, Mrs Grobnik.

I got past her, into the house.

—I hear auto-mobeee-le.

—It's not a night to be out, Mrs Grobnik.

—I hear, I look.

Up the stairs.

—You are in auto-mobeee-le, Mees-ter Smarhht.

I got to the door and tried to open it quietly.

—Good-night, Mrs Grobnik.

I shut the door. I listened. I heard her go down to the hall – I thought I did. I groped in the dark, found my spare collar, my toothbrush, my Listerine toothpaste – *The Dentifrice of the Rich* – I didn't have to hide it; the lads in the room wouldn't have known what to do with it, and it was too well squeezed to sell. My razor was in my inside pocket – there was nowhere else to keep it – and the shaving brush, brand new and stolen, was in there with it. My money was stitched into the mattress, but not my mattress.

—Hop it.

I shoved the big kid off the mattress, hoisted it and found my needlework. (The needle was stuck in the window frame, outside.)

—Hey!

—Sorry, son, but I'm in a hurry.

—Hey!

—Shut up, for fuck sake. You'll have it back in a minute.

The kid only rented eight hours' worth of mattress a day. A huge, hard-drinking Lithuanian slept on it all day, after nights of cracking heads and mugging poor stiffs who wandered his way in the dark. It was the safest mattress in Back o' the Yards. He'd been minding two hundred and twelve dollars for me. I had it now, and I slipped it into the pocket I'd stitched inside my trousers, behind the right-side pocket.

I was packed.

I gave the big kid a dime when he came jumping at me. The

other six lads were awake now, hitting out at each other. I held him back by the scruff of his long underwear and put the coin in his mouth. He knew the taste and stopped struggling.

—Spend it wisely, son, and sorry for waking you.

I made it over legs and heads, over to the door. I opened, and closed it.

—Meester Smarhht.

—I'm off out again, Mrs Grobnik.

—Out!

She grabbed my leg.

—In! Niy-ice girl, for you.

I opened the door and threw her in. As I hit the front door I could hear her sorting out the lads.

—Dow-wwn! Slee-eep!

He watched me slide down the slope, into the shallow river that was the road. The rain had stopped and the water level had already dropped. I got into the car. It was full of a smoke I didn't know.

—What's the brand?

—The brand. Yeah, yeah. My bones are at me, Pops. I'm tired of the ocean. Give her the gas.

I dumped the brush, paste and collar on his lap and got the car going.

—Left foot down on that nice pedal, Pops. Your toe up off the throttle. That the one. Make her sing.

There were stones under the mud, so the wheels dug in, and we moved without too much protest from the engine.

—Where to?

—Back to.

—Where?

—Where we was.

It was a street off the northern end of State Street and, by the time we got back there, I'd been driving all my life and Louis had my collar on back to front.

—Come on, Pops. Follow Father Armstrong.

We walked up, side by side. He was a small man – wide but small. To the big front door, and the doorman, white. I guessed what was happening, why I was there, and I held the door for Louis.

—Don't overdo it, Pops, he said when we got into the lift.

There was a black kid at the controls. We could talk in front of him.

164

—What d'you mean? I said.

—We together, that the tale. I hold the door, you hold the door. I drive, you drive. You not my manservant. I certainly not your boy; nay nay. You with me?

I wasn't, but I would be.

I sat in a warm room with carpets on the walls while Louis went into another room. I heard the bedsprings cheering him on and smelt the smoke that had filled the car. And I heard a little voice.

—It tight like this, Louie.

(The next time I heard that voice, it wasn't the real thing at all, but me, copying the woman I never saw and heard just once.)

Louis came out of the room, putting on his jacket, my tooth-brush standing up in the breast pocket, and he marched to the apartment door.

—Well well, Pops, he said as we waited for the lift – the *elevator* – to come up and collect us. —Enjoying yourself?

—Yeah.

—I believe you are. I have a old lady and a sweetheart that ain't my old lady and that nice chick back there ain't neither of them. And it weren't her pad and it weren't her own bed.

We stepped into the elevator.

—But it certainly her pussy and it purred like a Cadillac. Ah, yes. Lucked up there, Pops. She's one swell order of pork chops.

The elevator creaked and dropped.

—On the white folks' bed too; hey hey.

He winked at the black kid and slipped him a folding one. We went past the doorman. Louis stopped and let me go first.

—Time for home, he said.

—Where's home?

—Don't know yet, O'Pops.

He held the note forever. The red light went on over the studio door, to tell him and the other men that recording time was running out. But they kept it up, continued to play. And they did it again. Three minutes and sixteen seconds, once and twice, three times.

I stood in a corner, away from the band. I thought I'd fall over trying to keep Louis's endless note up there. Earl Hines sat at, in, the piano. Louis's trumpet soared and looped, and Hines' piano took it by the hand and brought it to the end and, as that end arrived, the world was moving again and I was able to breathe.

They stood and sat in a rough row, Fred Robinson, Mancy Cara, Jimmy Strong, Zutty Singleton – trombone, lazy banjo, clarinet, drums and bottles. There were three bottles, emptied to varied emptinesses, the contents still warm and inside Zutty. Missis Searcy's tea-stained gin. Robinson sat on the top rung of a ladder, to free his sound from the floor. Cara's shoes were at the door, well away from Cara – his feet on the studio floor were too heavy with them on, so he was sitting there now, tapping out a slow, barefoot rhythm.

—Can't afford no socks *and* eats, eh Mancy?

—No. Forgot them, is all.

Zutty Singleton sat at the drums and bottles, his tapping feet on top of a pillow; his drums were on a platform made of piled rugs, a big Mohawk rug the top one, put there to kill the vibrations. And then there was Louis, placed further back from the others – two more steps and he was out the studio door – because of the power of his noise. And they all sent the *West End Blues* into a horn as tall and as wide as a small man. The six men who that hot day – the 28th of June, 1928 – made up Louis's Hot Five.

—Why five?

—I goes without saying, said Louis.

It was true and getting truer. Louis Armstrong went without saying. The World's Greatest Trumpeter, star of the Hot Fives and Sevens records that were taking the hearts and feet of the world – *Snappy Dance Hits on Okeh Records by Exclusive Okeh Colored Artists.* (Was Piano Annie playing them yet?) The first black man to talk on the radio, the sound that made America quiver, the smile that made America feel tolerant, the nigger in a tux, the man who discovered music every new time he put the horn to his lip, the growl that scared no one, the clown, the actor, the singer, the music – Louis Armstrong was twenty-seven, a year older than me.

And I was watching him, listening to him invent the best music yet.

West End Blues was over. The third, and final, take. That was the way it was; they had three takes, and the best of the three went out into the world.

The studio was like all the prison cells I'd been in, but worse; I missed the damp of Kilmainham and Dublin Castle. The heat was bad, but it was the sound that made this place a torture. The

166

soundproofing was sawdust in the walls, and heavy, solid, black drapes. The room was dead. The men couldn't hear each other's instruments. They shouted to be heard in a space as big as an orange crate. I could feel my feet when I'd walked in but I couldn't hear a step.

But the music of the last three takes still filled the air; each speck was a clear note. And there was the dangerous aroma of the shuzzit Louis had insisted the men all smoke before they got down to recording.

There'd been none for me.

—We need you keen, O'Pops.

—I'm not fussed.

—Fair ee-nuff.

It was over. Zutty tapped his cymbals – bottles and cymbals; drums weren't properly heard in those early studios – and that was beautiful that.

They smiled and stretched, said nothing, waited.

The door to my left opened – there was no one behind the double-paned partition now; the engineer's bald head was gone – and a man in a very loose suit looked in at us.

—That was great, guys, he said. —The third take sent me. It's the one.

—I don't think so, Mister Wickemeyer, said Louis.

—Sounded fine to me, Pops, said Wickemeyer.

—I'd like another take, said Louis. —Fine can always be better.

—Come on now, Pops—

—You heard the man.

That was me talking and it was the first thing I'd said since I'd come in and taken my corner.

Wickemeyer looked at me. So did the other men; they didn't know me. (They never would.)

—Who are you?

There was no aggression in the voice, or the pale face. He didn't wait for me to answer.

—You with Louis?

—That right, said Louis.

—I'm with Mister Armstrong, I said. —He'd like another take and I'm inclined to agree with him.

Wickemeyer took a watch from his waistcoat pocket.

—I got the Greer Brothers Xylophone Orchestra coming in after you, he told Louis.

—How many brothers? I said.

—Two.

—I'll talk to them.

He looked at me and he looked at the watch.

—Okay, he said. —It's not as late as I thought.

—Fine.

He was gone.

There were no smiles; there was no triumph. The other lads didn't really know what was going on; it was all me and Louis – it was Louis. Fred Robinson climbed back up the ladder, his trombone over his head like a spear. Singleton checked his bottles. The bald engineer was back behind the glass, and Wickemeyer was standing beside him, leaning into the window.

He nodded.

And Louis put the horn to his lip and blew the opening cadenza for the fourth, and fifth, sixth, seventh time, before he was happy with it. He blew, and it was all new again, the most difficult music anyone had ever played, easy and surprising all over again. And, as the other five men joined him, still playing, still inventing, he looked my way and winked.

I was there, in that corner, in that studio. The most famous trumpet solo in jazz history was played by Louis Armstrong but it was brought to you by Henry Smart.

I was Louis Armstrong's white man.

And that was it, for months. I stayed right beside Louis Armstrong. I stuck to him, and it began to make sense. I knew why I was there.

I thought I did.

We smiled at each other, across the small space between us in one of the hundreds of hotel rooms. This one was two blocks from the house that soon wouldn't be his home. He stood at the open window; he let the wind come in and take the smoke. He leaned way out and pointed.

—My right-handed wife down there, he said, over his shoulder.

He changed hands.

—And the left-handed wife up there.

I hadn't met either.

—And soon, he said, as he shut the window. —I'm predicting here, understand? Soon the right-handed is going to be no-handed and the left-handed going to be the right-handed. Keepin' up, Smoked?

I was the smoked Irishman.

—No, I said.

He picked up the bottle from the table, beside his typewriter.

—Lean over here, man, and bring that nice glass with you.

I listened to my glass filling.

—What you reckon we drinking? he said.

—God knows, I said.

—I doubt. This hooch didn't come out the Lord's bathtub. What we drink to this time, Smoked?

—The works, I said.

—Yeah, he said. —I like that.

He hoisted his glass over his head. Big drops fell onto his shoulders and head, and onto the hotel carpet. He fell back into his chair and laughed.

—And to you, O'Pops. We drink to you.

We smashed our glasses together and we didn't care about the mess.

6

I was the sharpest ofay in Chicago, the best dressed Irishman anywhere.

—This not sissified business, Pops, he said in Scotty Piper's changing room.

—Shut up, Louis.

—Long as you know, he said. —I'm buying but I ain't your sugar daddy.

—Shut up.

—Fair ee-nuff. Long as you know.

Mister Piper had laid out three suits, and I was taking all of them. Big suits a smaller man would have been lost in. And shirts, with collars, and without.

—Nothing too colour, Louis instructed Mister Piper. —This here some serious white man.

—Noticed, said Mister Piper.

—Meeting serious white men, said Louis.

He chose; I vetted.

—I wouldn't be caught dead in that.

—That the idea, Pops. Not getting yourself caught dead. Take them away, sir. Man here wish to stay alive.

Mister Piper went off with the shirts and came back with some more – milder, paler, plainer, but still too fuckin' wild.

—Look it, I said. —Between ourselves.

I was speaking to Louis and Mister Piper.

—I'm a good-looking man.

They looked at each other. I held up one of the shirts, the red one.

—If I walk into a room full of other people wearing this shirt, what d'you think will get noticed first? Me or the shirt?

—I hear you, Pops, said Louis.

—No offence now, I said. —But if I wear this thing, they won't see a handsome man, looking after business. They'll see a fuckin' clown.

Louis picked up the shirts and handed them to Piper.

—Something dull, Mister Piper. Something won't get noticed in a room full of white folks.

—Don't think my colour scale run to that dull. Why don't you bring him to a Hebe tailor, give him some nice white threads?

—This the ofay with the difference, said Louis. —This the man that stand out.

—But you heard the man, Mister Armstrong, said Piper. —He think he stand out already.

—Fine, fine, fine, said Louis. —You the best tailor in Chicago. Why we here. How that sound?

—Be right back, said Piper. —With some of the best dull shirts you ever seen.

—We be waiting.

The new fedora, as pearl grey and as perfect as the old one, was my idea. He'd picked up a velour thing but he put it back down when he saw the fedora kiss my head.

—Nothing I can teach you about hats, Pops. That there get you noticed.

(He was right.)

—Lil, my old lady that was and, 'fact, still is, she taught me how to wear a hat, he told me.

He wasn't divorced yet but he kept well away from Lil. She was a tough bird. I knew that three seconds after she slapped me.

—When I came up from down in Galilee, said Louis, —I used to sit the hat right on top. The country boy.

He took my new hat and showed me.

—But Lil showed me how to park it the Chicago way, like you walking into the wind.

He took the hat off and studied it.

—Our heads the same size, Pops, near 'bout. Maybe I get one that match.

—That'd be sissified, Louis.

—I hear you, Pops.

She slapped me again. She had to jump to reach my head, but she did it and it stung. The silence around us was louder than the slap. A black woman had just hit a white man. It was a slap

171

that had to be followed. We both knew that. But she didn't give a fuck. She was tiny, lovely and mad.

—Get out of my way, she said.

I was in front of Louis's dressing room door. Mister Armstrong wasn't receiving visitors. That was what I'd told the little woman who'd decided to walk around me, just before she'd changed her mind and slapped me.

—I am no visitor, she said. —I am Missis Louis Armstrong.

That was big news. (This was a few days before he bought me the fedora.) I thought the woman in the dressing room with him was Missis Louis Armstrong. (It would be months before I caught up with him; he was running away from more than Lil.) And now she'd slapped me, twice across the face, and it didn't matter who she was and who was in there with him, because we were out here and a black woman had just slapped a white man and something had to be done.

I picked her up.

—Say!

Two of the club flunkies were filling the narrow corridor, rolling towards us. These were black, downstairs guys who would hammer her, one of their own, when they got her outside. They'd beat her to the street – it was what they'd have to do. I picked her up and turned, so my back was between them and her. She kicked and fought. I spoke quietly over my shoulder.

—I'll deal with this cunt, lads.

It was the only thing that would stop them, the words that would let them know that she'd be getting what was coming. And they couldn't take her off a white man.

I was learning.

I took her out to the alley. (For a city so young, it had a lot of alleys.) I put her down and held her. The fight was out of her; she'd had time to think a bit.

—Who is he with?

I didn't answer.

—He's still my husband, she said.

She looked at the ground, and up again – she made herself – and she looked at me good and hard, and down again, but not before I'd seen the shame and hatred.

—Henry Smart, I said.

I held out my hand. She took it. I could feel them in my palm, the nut-hard fingertips of a piano player. And I recognised her.

172

She'd been playing with Louis, the first time I heard him, when I met Dora. (I hadn't seen Dora in months.) This was Lil Hardin. She'd played with Joe Oliver, I found out later, when Louis first came to Chicago. That was how they'd met. Lil Hardin Armstrong.

She looked up.

—Who are you? You're new. Are you Louis's manager?

—No, I said. —I'm only a friend.

Her face became a sneer before she'd the time to hide it.

—I made that man what he is, she said. —Did he tell you that, you being his friend and all?

—No, he didn't.

—The World's Greatest Trumpet Player. I was calling him that before he knew the truth of it. And I made others call him that too. Before I believed it. He used to hide himself away behind Joe Oliver. Mister Second Fiddle. But then he met me. He's with that Alpha, isn't he?

That was her name, the woman I'd thought was his wife.

I said nothing.

She looked lost now, and still smaller.

—I know what happened, she said.

She would have talked to anyone.

—He heard the boys calling him Henpeck. That was what they called him. Because I was doing those things for him and he was letting me do them and they didn't believe that Little Louie was the greatest trumpet player in the world, or in the city, even though they heard the evidence every night. He was just Joe Oliver's boy and they liked him that way. Couldn't even dress himself, like he needed to. I told him to lose some of his weight. Little Louie! I got him the right food. I made Lou-is Armstrong out of him and now he wants to forget it. He's with that Alpha Smith. Isn't he?

—Yes, I said.

—If I sat on the bed, he told me later, —after it was made up, why, Lil would go into fits. Weren't ever no home, Pops. Fine and all as it was. And poor Clarence.

—Who's Clarence?

—My adopted son, he said proudly, and smiled. —Pretty hard keeping up?

—Yeah.

—Yes sir, Clarence my boy since I was a boy. Been calling me Papa since he was a little shaver in dresses. They call him feeble-

173

minded. 'Count of a accident; fell off a porch. My porch, down home in New Orleans.

He swept his hand across his trouser legs, brushed them.

—Porch was one storey high from the ground. Landed directly on his head. Doctors said the fall set him back four years behind the average. Called it feeble-minded. He ain't slow, Pops, not with me. But he different. He nervous. Made my blood boil to hear Lil holler at him.

We were in a taxi, going somewhere that was making him nervous.

—And her mother, Pops, my my. Won't call her a mama. She nobody's mama. But she a *mother*. Lil and that lady have some bad tempers.

He slapped his hands on his legs.

—And then I met Alpha.

He looked at me.

—I ever tell you about Daisy? The very first Missis Armstrong?

He laughed.

—Another time, Pops. But, hey, I weren't the only one tomcatting in and out of that marriage. Lil had herself a sweet man.

—She said she made you, I told him.

—That fair, he said. —She put my name up in lights, first one to. And she showed me how to carry a hat. I ain't denying nothing. But listen here, Pops. On whose big mouth be the chops that blow the horn?

—Fair enough.

—Fair ee-nuff. I have my horn to keep me warm.

The taxi stopped outside the hotel.

—Stick to me, O'Pops.

The voice was always a growl; it took hard reading. But I was learning. There was serious business ahead. He was nervous, staying in charge.

He paid, and my new boots creaked as we climbed out of the cab.

—Know why we travelling by cab these days? said Louis.

—Why?

—Had to sell my nice automobile to pay for those big ol' squeaky boots you have to have.

He wasn't joking. He was broke. His last folding dollar was driving away in the taxi.

I followed him to the hotel steps. He lifted his coat at the shoulders and let it settle again. And he shifted his hat a quarter-inch.

—How'm I looking, Smoked? he said.

—Sharp.

—Sharp as a Norwegian, he said. —Forty-dollar velour hat, marimba grey overcoat, shoes that can't lose. But still a nigger. Stick to me.

Up the steps, to a revolving door. I could see the guys, placed at perfect random on the street, on the steps, at the twirling door, inside. I very carefully didn't look at them. Behind papers, watching the world, yawning, playing with toothpicks, leaning against cars, in good suits with pockets reinforced for gun-weight – a few of them at first, but they were everywhere, dozens of them and dozens more I hadn't seen and wouldn't. Not one of them looked away or pretended to be busy. These guys weren't under-cover; they were the Outfit and not interested in hiding. This was the city where a squad car was yours for the hailing, if you knew who was who, a Cadillac with a bell on it. These boys were sharper than the New York boys, slicker. Pink Carmine wasn't among them – I didn't see him – but I wondered what I was doing, strolling squeakily into the middle of this gang. I'd gone thou-sands of miles and five years to avoid men like these ones, and here I was, following Louis. Into the Lexington Hotel.

He hit the revolving glass and we sailed in; I packed myself beside him. I kept my hat on.

—Mister Capone is in the building, said Louis. —He bring some of his friends.

—Jesus, I said. —What's he like?

—Nice little cute fat boy, said Louis. —Just like me.

No one stopped us; no one stepped into our path. It was a hotel, even if there was a guy dressed in spats and a tommy gun leaning his back against the piano, a white grand that could have housed three South Side families.

—These guys are all Italian, right? I said.

—Relax, O'Pops. You're long way from home. Fair ee-nuff?

—Fair enough.

—Cha cha.

The lobby was huge, deep and high, cut by marble stairs that swung away to left and right. A bellhop stopped when he saw the face under Louis's hat.

—Hiyah, Lou-ee.

Louis beamed, and whispered at the hop's back.

—Mis-ter Armstrong is well.

He stood his ground for a minute. As I got to know him I

175

noticed that he always did this when he entered a public place, where he was likely to be the only black man: he stood. It was a challenge, a yell – and no one knew.

—The chappie on the stairs, he said. —One-Lung Aiello.

—Why One-Lung? I asked.

—He got two, far as I know. He took one from another nice man. Brought it on a platter – like in the Bible – to Mister Capone's little brother, Francis.

—Why?

—No answer ever explain it. Though Francis was dead by the time Mister One-Lung brought him the plate. I love Chicago, Smoked. It's complicated. I like that. The nice man at the piano. Don't look, but see him?

—Yeah.

—Polack Joe.

—But he's not Polish.

—Right, said Louis. —And he don't even know his name is Polack Joe.

—How come?

—Something to do with his wife.

—Who isn't Polish either.

—Right the second time.

—But the lad who fucked her behind his back was.

—Wrong, Pops. Hungarian.

—So how come Polack Joe?

—Sound better than Hungarian Joe. Easier to say behind your hand. Didn't bring my atlas today, but Poland beside Hungary, I guess. Close enough. Like Polack Joe's wife and her nice Hungarian friend. And Polack Joe is a angry man. He knows Missis Joe has been some place, he just don't know where. Thinks his name is Big Joe. I'm ready.

—Lead the way.

—No, Pops, said Louis. —This time you do. Earn the boots.

Not one guest had come or gone, checked in or signed out, while we'd chatted in the lobby. The bellhop hadn't hopped. The place was awash with silent hoods.

—Where to? I said.

—Yonder. He'll be sitting down and he'll be eating peanuts. Walk straight up to his face. Like you know him and don't like him a whole lot of much. After you, Smoked.

We took a route to the right, through some of the quiet lads

– I looked at them but not for long, enough to let them know that I was fine, no one to annoy or interest them – a confident man, not too confident, handsome, at ease on the rug, packing nothing, going somewhere but in no mad hurry – into the darkness of the Geronimo Room.

A crack from my left boot brought a hand up to a sagging pocket, but it was fine. The hand went back down; the eyes moved away from mine. I walked in, through the double doors, and straight up to the only man in the place sitting down.

And Louis passed me.

—Mister Glaser, he said, as he sat into the leather chair at the other side of the low marble table.

This was Joe Glaser. Manager of the Sunset Café, at 35th and Calumet, where the name of Louis Armstrong had been well and truly made; this was the man who first billed Louis as the World's Greatest Trumpet Player – Lil's words, Glaser's lights – before the world beyond jazz had started listening. Glaser was young but didn't look it. The smile he gave Louis was a fixed thing; it gave him the freedom to glare. His hair was pulled back by more oil than I'd seen on a head before. There were stories doing the rounds: the man was a rapist, a baby fucker, the daddy of kids he wouldn't own up to. He was in on the rackets, and well in with Capone. The Sunset was a black and tan; the music was black but the clientele was black and white – six hundred on a good night, and they'd all been good since Glaser had taken over. I'd been to the Sunset but I hadn't seen Glaser. He scared me. There was something about him, something about the way he watched Louis and the world to his right and left, the eyes that glared and hid: the stories about him were true, and there were more things in his past and present that would never become stories. He was dangerous, and the floor around him was covered in peanut shells. They were right under my boots.

And now he saw me, or let me know that he'd seen me.

—Mister Glaser, said Louis. —Like you to meet Mister Smart.

He leaned out across the table and took my hand, and held it – and didn't let go. He sat back, slightly, and made me follow him, slightly. And now it was me leaning over the marble table, into the smoke that rose from the cigar he'd parked on the ashtray at its centre.

He spoke to Louis.

—Why am I shaking this guy's hand, Louis?

—Because your mama taught you manners, Mister Glaser.

—I don't think so, said Glaser.

He wouldn't let go.

I was in a room full of the hard men, my only friend a smiling black man. And what looked like the hardest man of the lot wouldn't let go of my hand. He was talking to Louis and he was looking straight at me. Glaser held on, and I made no effort to take my hand back. I leaned out over the table. It was up to Louis.

It was why I was there. I learnt as we went along.

I looked straight back at the fucker.

—My my, said Louis. —I never get used to the ways of white folks. That just about the longest shake of a hand I have ever seen.

I could see, and feel it: Glaser felt like an eejit long before I did. It was his play, but it had gone on much too long. He wasn't in command now; he never had been. Louis was in command, and always had been – because I was with him.

Louis crossed his legs and took out his Camels.

Joe Glaser wanted to manage Louis a long time before he became his manager, somewhere in 1935, years after I met him. He knew the music; he knew when it worked, and didn't, when to sack and hire. When he'd heard Louis, he knew what he'd heard; and he knew that the lights hanging over the street weren't messing – *The World's Greatest Trumpet Player.* The trumpet was filling the joint but Glaser knew more: it could fill the whole world. The Sunset was a black and tan, and Glaser had seen what Louis's music did to white shoulders, feet and faces. He'd seen what happened, and he saw what was going to happen. He was going to be there at the start. The white start. The only start that mattered. The last ten years didn't matter or even happen. Glaser was the man who was going to discover Louis Armstrong. He was going to take Louis across the line.

—He puts those peanut shells all around him, Louis had told me. —For protection, see.

This was back in the taxi, before we'd hit the Lexington.

—Puts them there on the floor to warn him, in case he take a little nap or look the other way when you hotfooting up to him.

He tapped my knee.

—Now, Pops, we go in, you stand on them shells good and hard.

And I did it. I walked right in and did it. I undermined the fucker. I stood on his fuckin' shells and shot the hard eyes back

178

at him, the blue eyes that had killed and could again. And then he was ready for Louis, on a platter.

Louis liked him; I didn't – we were a perfect team.

—Mister Glaser not one of those types look up at a blue note but down at a brown skin.

This, again, was back in the taxi.

—Might be good for me. We see. Stick to me, Smoked.

Glaser thought I'd got there before him. So, at that point, did I. But I'd learn.

He let go of my hand. I stood up straight without acknowledging effort. Then I sat beside Louis, like he'd told me to, beside him but not too close.

—You sit there, bask in my glory. How that sound?

—Grand.

—Grand; ah yes. And keep those peepers in back of your head wide and very open.

—Fine.

—What colour those eyes back there?

—Never seen them, I said.

—Alpha like the two you got there up front, he said. —That colour called blue, right?

—Right.

—See? Who say I don't understand white folks?

There was a glass bookcase behind Glaser that let me see most of the bar. I could see pictures on the far wall, Washington, Lincoln, and Big Bill Thompson, friend of the gangsters and, often, Mayor of Chicago; I'd see the shadows moving across them. And the carpet was like summer grass; every step was a crackle. I could do my job, and concentrate on the conversation.

—So, said Louis.

—So, said Glaser.

—So.

—So, Louis, said Glaser. —Pops, I wanted to talk to you, away from the club.

—And here we be.

—Here we are – be. I'll be frank.

—Now you confusing me, Pops.

They laughed.

—Was doing allreet up to the name change, said Louis. —But, Pops. I think I know – I have me an inkling what you throwing my way. You want be my manager. I'm warm?

—You're hot.

—You said it, Pops. Why?

—Why?

—Why?

—Well, you've no one looking after you right now, said Glaser. He stared at me, quickly. I was ready, and stared back.

—And, Pops, he said. —You should have.

—You.

—Me. I know the business, Louis. I have the ins. I know the outs.

—Rehearsed that part, said Louis, an hour later, as we moved away from the hotel. —The ins and outs. No improvisation there; nay nay.

—You're the best, Louis, said Glaser. —But your approach is all wrong. You need ambition. Lil was good for you, Pops.

He stopped for a reaction, but Louis said nothing.

—But I know, said Glaser. —She's history. And, don't get me wrong, Pops, Alpha's a doll.

—She good for me too.

—Right. You got there before me. But, Pops, look. Who the fuck is this guy here?

—Mister Smart, said Louis. —A friend of mine.

Louis patted my leg. I heard carpet crackle, and stop.

—Asked him to slouch along, said Louis. —Second opinion. We go back.

—New Orleans?

—Further than that, Pops, said Louis. —Way back. Bible back. I'm here and listening, Mister Glaser.

—Okay, said Glaser. —But I'm not comfortable with this. Can he – can you wait outside?

—No, I said. —I'm with Mister Armstrong.

He was sweating a bit, like there was more going on than a business proposal.

—Oh, fuck it, said Glaser.

He pushed his hair back further, over the top of his head.

—Where was I?

—Lil and history.

—What? Yeah. Yeah. The clubs are too small. The South Side's too small. You need to break out. I'm thinking big for you, Pops. Really big. The most famous Negro in the world.

Glaser let that one hang.

—My my.

Then he impressed me.

—You don't know me, Louis, said Glaser. —But you know two things about me. I have a terrible temper and I always keep my word. Let's give it a go, Pops.

He put out his hand, but Louis didn't take it. He was the bravest man I ever knew.

—Let me think about this and that, Pops, said Louis.

And then he took the hand and shook it. He let go of the hand and stood up.

—I believe him, said Louis, as we walked away, past the hard men. —I like Mister Glaser. He Jewish. Jewish people been good to me.

—So why don't you go with him? I said.

I waited for the answer I wanted to hear.

—Why, Smoked, he said. —I'm already the most famous Negro in the world.

I was learning.

I was the smoked Irishman.

—Where now? I said.

—*How* now first, Pops, said Louis.

He stopped walking, and looked lost for the first time since I'd met him.

—We broke, he said.

—How broke?

—Pick me up, I won't be jangling.

—I'll pay, I said.

—Pay what?

—The taxi.

—We *black* broke, Pops.

It was the only time he ever did it: he looked at the ground in front of me, head drooped slightly, the black man in front of the white man. I knew the stance; I'd been getting to know it. It shocked me there, from him, the hatred and helplessness, the big please in the shoulders. I didn't need it. I didn't want it.

—So, why not go back to Glaser? I said.

He felt the slap and stood up straight, out of the act.

—Not ready for slavery, he said.

—Good man.

His life was chaotic. Lil had minded him well. She'd made sure he'd had just enough cash, never enough to lose, and a clean hanky, clubs to play, people to listen. (His life was chaos but he was never, ever late.) But there was no one now to do that. Alpha Smith was no man's manager. I hadn't shared the same room with her much, but she was – they knew no race – a wagon. He hopped as she whinged, and he threw money at the howl. But she wasn't to blame. He could never stay still; even stoned, he rolled. He sat at his typewriter and pecked out his letters and stories, sang and recited, gagged, coughed and walloped the table; that was Louis's silence. He knew exactly what he was, but not how to make the world see. His horn was the song of freedom but his life was a crazy jail. He needed control, but he hadn't worked it out. I was the start but he wasn't sure how.

He turned out his pockets and flapped them.

—Can't fly, John Henry.

—We'll walk.

—How's that go?

I showed him.

—Seen that before, he said, and followed me till I was following him. It wasn't side-by-side territory; he couldn't be seen too close to a white man, away from the people who knew him. So we walked out of it, into other zones that Louis had never been to. I'd pass him by, and drop the words; he'd pass me, drop his. By the time we got to Prairie Avenue and the streetlamps were leaking their yellow smudges on the pavement right in front of us, Louis was ounces lighter and about to earn a steady income.

—Be happier doing this in a coloured neighbourhood, he whispered as I shoved him through the window.

—Nothing to rob in a coloured neighbourhood, I told him as I followed his arse indoors.

—You wrong there, Pops, he said. —What's here?

I could smell them.

—Books.

—We stealing books?

—No. Maybe a few.

We were ankle-deep in a rug. Louis held his hand out, discovered an armchair, and sat down. The leather gave out as he sank into it. We held our breath till he stopped.

—Ain't been sat in in fifty years, he whispered. —What we going to take, Pops? Nothing in here small enough.

He was right. The library was the size of a train station, but it had the closed, dead air of a room that was rarely entered. Packed with big, forgotten money that had been spent years before.

—Listen, I said.

I could see him now. We stayed still for minutes and got to know the house.

It wasn't a good idea. The place was too big, too important and famous, held together by a large staff that lived on the premises. Misery, creaking, insomnia – there was no time of the night when they'd all be asleep. But there wasn't a sound that came at us, not a creak or bedspring or ice-box door, no sigh slipped in under the door.

—Who live here?

I knew the answer.

—Missis Field.

—Who?

—The shop's widow.

He was quick.

—Marshall Field. *That* shop?

—Yeah.

I heard him laughing.

—Why didn't we just break into the *shop*?

The shop was Marshall Field's, department store to the heartland. Field had built the house, in 1876, and Missis Field had been widowing there for more than twenty years. A maid called Lillie had told me that.

—First house in the city with electric lights, she'd told me as I helped with her bags off the trolley car.

I rode the trolleys, reading the city.

—It must have lit up like a Christmas tree, I said.

—I wasn't alive back then, she said. —I sure wish I had've been.

—Sure, I said. —Bye.

I got back up on the trolley step. I didn't mess; I didn't string them along. I just let them do what they really wanted to do, talk. I never walked them home. I never swapped names or promises. They always spoke first. They always walked home happy, to a room that would never be theirs. (Ailing, fading women found long-forgotten spring in their steps. Unhappy women caught themselves smiling.)

—They'd expect us to do that, I whispered now to Louis. — Rob the shop. But the shop is guarded. And there's more money in this place. And look at us. We're here.

But it wasn't a good idea. Smaller houses made more sense. The hired help, the Doras and Ethels, went home at night. The cash was badly hidden in the kitchen, in cups and under chopping boards, and the goods were always new, the latest thing, safe and easily shifted.

But here we were, in one of the most famous homes in Chicago. I'd thought that the shock would do Louis good; I was bringing him over another line.

And I was right. He was taking to it.

He stood up.

—We take us a picture or two?

—No, I said. —They'd want them back.

There was big art on the walls on this stretch of Prairie Avenue, between 16th and 22nd, names that I later heard and knew. Renoir, Monet, Pissarro, Degas. Nice stuff but too hot to carry on the trolley.

—Cutlery, I said.

—Knives, forks.

—Yep.

—Spoons.

—You're with me.

—Nice silver.

—At least.

We listened some more, sorted the outside from the inside. Nothing. I could see books clearly now, fewer than I'd expected. Leather-bound, same-sized, untouched, in squat shelves that didn't rise higher than my chest. I'd been in better libraries.

I could see a different shelf, more promising, nearer one of the windows.

—Let's go where the spoons is, O'Pops.

—Hang on, I said.

I went to the shelf. Books of different sizes, standing, leaning rows. I didn't know why; I needed to smell one. I felt the dust on the spines, a looseness in the leather – books that had been cracked open and read. I chose one, slid it out. I felt the paper – the pages had been cut with scissors. Lightweight – a novel or poetry. Good dust rose to me. I put the book to my nose.

—Chicago, I said, very quietly. —Prairie Avenue.

I took it to the window.

—Now the time for reading, Pops?

—Hang on.

I took the heavy curtain away from the window, enough to let me read the title. It was the same window we'd come through.

—Oh fuck.

I dropped the book.

He was right beside me.

—We going?

—*Castle Rackrent*, I said.

—You said Marshall Field's.

—The fuckin' book.

I kicked it away. It hit a chair leg, and then the wall – two bullets, different guns. (I fell against more books, and my head hit the wall. For a while, the Auxies had lost me – I'd gone under the books. I could tell by the way they dragged me out – they were going to murder me. They pulled my feet, climbed in at me over the books. One slid past my eyes: *Castle Rackrent*.

—Which one of them did you kill!

—Which one?

—In cold fa'king blood!

—Get his shoes off.

—Get his own fa'king shoes off.

—Get your shoes off, c'nt.

The boot went straight down. Pain so fast and pure and shocking, I didn't know which foot. I roared. More books dropped to the floor.)

—We going? said Louis.

He was ready to jump; he was holding the curtain.

—No, I said. —It's grand.

Go!

—Book *that* bad?

—I'll tell you later. Come on.

Now. Go.

—Right behind you, Pops.

Go.

The door to the hall opened for me, no problem, no complaint. We waited. No pipes, no snores. The hall was vast, empty, with light enough to get us to our next door. Open for us – no sweat. The kitchen, warm; a cat crept past us. It didn't rub against our legs; it didn't sneak away to tell. It sat down there and watched.

The knives and forks fell quietly for us as we lowered them into the straw bags I'd last seen Lillie carry. It was the house's second-best silver; the best stuff had a telltale M.F. on each handle

185

– easily got rid of, but too much like a boast, a story well worth telling.

Louis was with me.

—See this one? he whispered.

—Yeah.

—Fish knife, said Louis. —See one before?

—No.

—Well now.

He let it drop onto more silver.

—Don't get cocky yet, I said.

—Cocky come natural.

—Rein it in.

—Trying.

—Good man.

We went out the way we came in.

—Bringing the book, Pops?

—I wouldn't fuckin' touch it.

—Fair ee-nuff.

We got him a new car with the cutlery money. I brought the spoons to Cicero; Louis didn't come with me. The fence had a canary in a cage, nothing else, in the window of his store.

—Goes cheap cheap, he said as he looked over the spoons. — All the advertising a good man needs when he does business with people that understand bird.

He put notes on the counter, slowly, one by one.

—Ain't much demand for eating tools, he said as he counted out the cash for me. —Most folks have their own these days.

He stopped counting and pushed the money at me. Just enough to get me back.

—But when they come in silver and you happen to be passing, come in and hear the bird.

Enough for an automobile – I liked the word; it did justice to the thing – and two good dinners. The car was a big black Rickenbacker, with eleven previous owners and several who'd never properly owned it.

—One of these days, O'Pops, we going to get us a car that ain't black.

—That's a thought.

—The fine day coming.

* * *

186

He couldn't get a gig. There was a cold spell in 1928 when the world's greatest musician had no place to play. He could front a band, like no else one could, but he couldn't lead. They wouldn't let him, and he didn't know how. He could give the band his name, make it great and famous, but he'd never be the boss. He commanded the stage, but he couldn't make his own way up there. He needed a manager, but he didn't want one. He didn't want Glaser; he didn't want the dangerous connections. He wanted to cross the line and he wanted to do it himself.

But it was fuckin' chaotic. Even when he was flush, he was two or three days from broke. He was a young horn player, worried about the damage he was doing to his lips, a singer who didn't yet hear what the rest of us did, who didn't trust what it was doing, pushing him further to the front, the only man on stage. He wanted it, and it terrified him. He craved and cringed. There was no such thing as rest. He was trying to ignore the collapse of one marriage, bracing himself for another that he knew was going to be a disaster; he was already running from it. He had an adopted kid I never saw, a line of hangers-on I saw too often. He was running, to get away, to catch up, to grab control of himself and his life and his genius.

But it wasn't happening. He could be who he was, he could play as much and as well as he liked, as long as he was an eejit. Little Louis, Laughing Louie. (He wasn't Satchmo yet; that one was a few years away.)

But he wasn't an eejit.

—Eeee-jit!

And he wasn't going to be one. He was trying to find his own way.

He guested. He was always welcome. He'd turn up – the Metropolitan, the Savoy Ballroom – and exercise the chops. But there wasn't money in it. He sat in with other men's bands, Clarence Jones, Carroll Dickerson, with men who were happy to be managed. He sat among equals, but knew he was better. I could see him shrinking. His one big push so far, his own dance club – just before I properly met him – had been a disaster. The Warwick, just off Forrestville Avenue. He went in deep and expensive, opened with his own band, Earl Hines, Zutty Singleton, on the same night as the Savoy opened for the first time, electric billboard, real peacocks, just two short blocks away.

—Don't know what happened, O'Pops. Made a dollar, dollar and a half apiece. On the good nights.

He ran, defaulted on the lease, and the owners of the Warwick were suing him. He had a bad case of the shorts and the burglary bought him time. And Alpha. And he enjoyed it, the kick – he was a very happy man – the terror, the big silent fuck-you that only we could hear in those libraries and halls.

We'd done three houses on Prairie Avenue. Three Mondays on the trot. Stupid really, but his life needed routine and he insisted on this one.

—They'll be waiting, I told him, on the third Monday.

—Nay, nay. They be waiting next Monday.

He was probably right – it was his city – because we got away with it. We even parked the Rickenbacker right outside. And the next week, the next Monday, we drove – I drove, over ice that had thawed too late in the day, and had refrozen; we hopped and skidded – to Oak Park and I parked under a big tree, in a street where no house lights shone.

—We get ourselves caught, I be swinging from this nice tree.

—Not here, I said. —They're too civilised.

—They get someone else do it.

—Probably. I'll swing with you.

—Shucks.

—Lose the scarf, I told him. —Just in case.

It was silk and very white.

—Prefer to call it a muffler, but you right. Don't make sense, supplying the evidence *and* the noose.

He folded the scarf and put it on the seat behind him.

—Ready when you is, Smoked.

Smaller houses here, but big. Small, easy money. Sleeping and respectable. We stayed there a while, car doors slightly open, letting the cold in, listened for cats and flatfoot leather, looked for house lights, light sleepers and lads like ourselves.

I'd watched these houses. I knew which had kids and dogs. I'd walked right up to them, pretended delivery – an empty box, a good excuse. There were bigger houses, some of your man, Frank Lloyd Wright's; quiet money and a lot more of it. But these were just right. The servants went home every night. And this one was perfect. A little old lady, not that old and not so little, but alone, asleep. In and out, we wouldn't disturb her. We wouldn't be too greedy.

—We'll do the block and then come back, I said. —In case there's someone watching. And we'll keep going and park on the next corner, not here.

188

—Going to snow again, said Louis. —I feel it.

I did too; I'd been feeling it all day. I drove. Around an American block. We saw no one and nothing, except a guy in a dressing gown watching his dog shit on the street parallel to the one we drove back to. I brought the car past our house and parked short of the next corner.

—Let's go.

—With you, Pops.

He went at everything with everything he had; it was all, or nothing at all. He'd become a housebreaker. Mask, gloves – he'd even got himself a gunny sack. The man had style. He was up ahead of me and the sack was under his elbow. He went in the gate, to the side of the house. I was right behind him, keen to catch up. He was onstage now, and it wasn't the right way for work like this. It wasn't the time for a solo.

He was trying to get up on a windowsill.

—Hang on, Zorro.

I grabbed the arse of his trousers. He'd lifted himself to the sill, and now he landed on my shoulder. There was a lot of him but I held on and lowered him quietly to gravel. He grunted mild annoyance but there was nothing real in it.

The Prairie Avenue mansions we'd done before were too big for backyards; all sides shoved their tits at the world. This place had a yard, and good walls hiding it from the neighbours. Bushes, trees, lots of snow-capped foliage. Away from yellow streetlight, and the snow clouds were big and low.

It was cold, freezing. The kitchen window wanted to give but was frozen to its frame. It was my turn to climb onto the sill. I opened my coat, and got up there without slipping; it was covered in ice, lines of the stuff – there must have been a bad gutter right above me. I held the window frame with my left hand, felt the ice grab my fingers, and got into my trousers with my right. I pissed the window loose; I'd enough heat in me to get right around the frame. Louis stood well back. Bottom, top, sides, I melted all ice without wetting my boots or the hand that held me safe. My razor found the catch inside; it hadn't been tightened. I could feel its small weight on the tip of the razor, then gone; the window was open. I lifted, and stepped in, onto the inside sill. I stayed behind the curtain.

I waited; I listened. I held the sill and let myself slip out from under the curtain, to the floor. I could tell by my feet on the tiles

189

– a big kitchen. Dark – no light from the hall, no landing light. I listened. I pulled the curtain back for Louis. I wanted the window shut before the cold ran deeper into the house. He slid in beside me. I got the window shut, the curtain back in place.

And now we could smell it.

—Ummm, said Louis, beside me.

I knew what it was before I could remember.

—Who been eating *my* porridge? said Louis.

—It's not porridge, I said.

—Follow me, Goldilocks, he said.

I knew it now.

Then the voice hit us.

—Two and two?

Louis was past me. The curtain rushed across my face as he went under; I heard the window, felt the cold.

—Don't know. Two and two what?

—Griddle cakes.

The smell.

—Four.

—Correct.

—You were waiting for me.

—I was.

—Where are you?

—Near enough.

I heard Louis's feet break the crusts of drifted snow and, sooner than I'd have expected it, the Rickenbacker coughed, shrieked, and Louis Armstrong was gone.

—Shut the window if you're going to be staying.

I could move; it surprised me.

I clung to the window and let it slide down. I slipped the lock into place.

—You left it loose, I said.

—I did.

The curtains were back in place; I couldn't see anything. I turned. I still couldn't see her. She wasn't moving. I could make out walls and corners but nothing that wasn't lines and shadow.

She spoke.

—Will we have a drop of tea?

—I never touch the fuckin' stuff.

I heard her crying.

—I've been waiting for that, Henry.

190

And I saw her. She was sitting at the table. Facing the window. An audience, waiting.

She rubbed her face, with the outside of her hand.

—Will I turn the light on?

—No, she said.

Both hands were at her face now.

—Are you glad to see me, Henry?

Jesus.

—Yeah.

—Good.

My gut turned.

—What about the griddle cakes?

—I ate them, said Miss O'Shea. —Waiting.

—Sorry I kept you.

—You weren't to know.

She stayed there. I wanted to move. I wanted her to move. She didn't. I didn't.

—How did you know?

—The window.

—What?

—I was looking out the window. And who walked by? And looked in?

—Why didn't you come out?

—I don't know. Coffee?

—Fair enough.

—The tea here is shocking. They've no idea what to do with it.

—I'll take your word for that.

She stood up. She turned away from me. I heard her messing with the percolator.

—Light?

—No. No. I'm grand here. These things are great, altogether.

Water running.

The percolator hit the stove.

—I love watching them bubbling up, she said. —And the smell.

I couldn't.

—What?

—Follow you, when I saw you. I went to the door.

—I came back.

—I know, she said. —I didn't really believe it was you, when you went by. It happened before. A lot. I'd see you and it wasn't you at all. In London. And New York.

191

I still couldn't see her properly.

—Me too.

—So. I hummed and hawed at the door. Then I gave up and went back to the window.

—And I came back.

—You did.

—And it was me.

—It was. With a big box.

—It was empty.

—I knew you were up to something.

The percolator rushed to the finish.

—That was quick.

—It's great, altogether. The electricity.

—They take it for granted over here.

—Indeed, and they take a lot for granted over here.

She was working away; I could smell the coffee now.

—Are you hungry, Henry?

—No, I lied.

—I could do you a bit of a sandwich.

—Thanks.

—Thanks yes or no?

—Yes.

—See, now. I knew you were hungry. The griddle cakes weren't the best.

—Great smell, but.

—Ah, sure.

—Why didn't you open the door?

—Ah, well. I knew you were up to something. And you went around the back. I heard you at the door, and the window. I was in the hall, just out there. Then you came around again. And you tried to look busy. You rang again. You put the box down. You rubbed your hands. You looked in the window. You were up to something alright.

—That was two weeks ago.

—And more.

—I missed you.

—I missed you too.

(—Look for me!

—I will!)

—You found me.

—I did.

—Will I turn on the light?

—No. Here.

I thought she was handing me the coffee; I saw the cup. I held out my hand, and she grabbed my sleeve, my collar. Her pull became a push; the shock left me light. I fell back easily; the table was right under me.

—No, she said.

She grabbed my hair and pulled me to the floor.

—I'm not up to the climb, she said.

She still had my hair.

—Where were you, Henry Smart?

—When?

She slapped me. Hard.

—Where were you?

—All over the fuckin' place.

She was on me. I felt hair on my face.

(—What's your name, so? she asked.

I saw brown eyes and some slivers of hair that had escaped from a bun that shone like a lamp behind her head. There were little brown buttons, in pairs, running the length of her brown dress, like the heads of little brown animals climbing quietly to her neck.

—Henry Smart, I said.

—And the little lad?

—Victor Smart, I said.)

—Where were you?

The answer could wait, the real one. I could see her now, over – on me. The weight the same, her eyes, angry, gorgeous.

—Where were you?

I held her waist. She slapped.

—Answer me!

—Yes, Miss.

—Answer me!

She dropped her weight down on me, pushed. Her hair washed over me, out of the bun; her teeth and tongue.

—Piddling on my clean windows, yeh pup.

—Sorry, Miss.

I tried to grab but she slapped my hands away. She was right over my face now. She filled her mouth with my hair and pulled. She let go and lifted herself. She was gone. I heard cloth pulled and ripped, felt nothing; then there was warm skin on my face.

—Where were you?

Gone again. Hands on my trousers. I tried to help, got slapped for my troubles. She found me, stiff and pinging; she held me there, and left me.

Her voice.

—What if she comes in now?

—Who? Your boss?

—Oh God.

There was daylight waiting behind the curtain by the time we stopped and heard steps on the stairs. And I was squatting in a cupboard by the time the kitchen door was pushed open, the light went on, and I heard the voice.

—I've been waiting, Eileen.

Suddenly – fuck – I knew my wife's name.

It was a cranky voice, cracked by age.

—I'm sorry, Missis Lowe, said Miss O'Shea. —I forgot to set the clock last night.

—Yes, well.

I was in among the brushes, coats. I could smell polish, mouse-shit, bleach. There was a crack between the cupboard doors. I could see a slipper, on the floor outside, a few feet from my toes. And an ankle, white, papery.

—I'll bring it up to you now, said Miss O'Shea. *Eileen.*

—Well, what's the point? said Missis Lowe. —I'm here now.

—I'm sorry.

—Yes. Well.

—It won't happen again.

—Well.

—I don't know what got into me.

All the years I'd avoided it, kept it well away; all the wandering years I'd missed her, I'd never wanted to know. Not fuckin' once.

—Well, Eileen.

And now, I fuckin' knew.

—It does seem a tad unsatisfactory. I *do* employ you to bring me my morning cup of coffee. My one little indulgence.

—I'm sorry, Missis Lowe.

—My one little indulgence. Lord knows, I could spoil myself and nobody would object. I've worked hard all my life and Doctor Lowe, dear, sweet man, worked hard all his life.

—Yes, Missis Lowe.

The noise and smells of coffee-making did nothing to stay the whingeing. The oul' bitch kept at it.

—Put your feet up, they say. But I don't. There's too much suffering in this world. There's too much to do, even for a feeble old woman. But I do allow myself my one little indulgence. One morning cup.

—Go on back up, Missis Lowe. It's early yet.

—Don't be ridiculous, Eileen.

Eileen. It was the old wagon's fault.

—I took you into my house. I was quite happy to do it. Although I've never had the home help live with me before—

The whingeing stopped. Missis Lowe had stopped. She was talking again, almost immediately, but the voice was very different. It was younger, light. She was talking to someone else.

I tried to see. I pushed the door. The crack got bigger; I stopped breathing. Bigger. The slipper, an old ankle, a dressing gown. The foot in the slipper turned, and faced the door. I pushed again. I shifted, an inch, an inch, another.

And I saw her.

My daughter.

Standing at the kitchen door. In cotton pyjamas. My six-year-old daughter. Saoirse. Ten feet from my face. Her toes curled on the black and white tiles. I'd seen her only once before, when she was five months old. (Every movement of her tiny fists and face seemed a new miracle. I looked for me in her, and for other people too. For Victor and Miss O'Shea, for my mother and father. Excitement rippled along her body. She arched her back and I had to open my arms further, to trap her gently.

—Dying to walk, I said.

—Mischief on her mind.)

A serious little face. Annoyed, still half-asleep. Black eyes, little nose and ears. Mad brown hair, like her mother's, the same brown. It had been in the ruined kitchen of Old Missis O'Shea's house, the last and only time I'd known her, just before I did my last killing and left Ireland. There she was. Staring up at Missis Lowe. Concentrating. Half hearing, half asleep.

I heard nothing. Saoirse's mouth opened; she spoke, briefly, but I didn't hear. I saw Missis Lowe now, properly. She was bending down, stroking Saoirse's hair. She wasn't as old as she'd sounded; she hadn't been broken by the yearly child and the hard work in between. She was smiling; I could feel the hair that she was stroking. She held Saoirse's shoulders now, and she brought her past me. I heard a scrape, chair legs on tiles. I saw

195

Miss O'Shea now – *Eileen* – she closed the kitchen door. Her hair was back up in its bun. She looked at my cupboard; she looked above my head. She pushed the door as she passed. I could see nothing.

But I could hear Saoirse.

She wasn't long from home. A little Roscommon girl; there wasn't much of the Yank there yet.

—Thank you, Missis Lowe. But I don't like that stuff at all.

—Saoirse, said her mother, giving out, warning her.

—That's alright, Eileen, said Missis Lowe. —The child knows what she likes.

—Yes, I do, said Saoirse. —And I don't like that stuff.

—She should be thankful for what she gets, I heard Miss O'Shea.

—Non-sense, said Missis Lowe. —This is the land of opportunity, Eileen. It's the truth.

—Yes, Missis Lowe.

—Eggs for our angel.

—Yes, Missis Lowe.

—Over easy, *a Mhamaí*, said Saoirse.

—That's right, said Missis Lowe.

Two and two? said Louis.

I said nothing.

Three days later.

—I knew the answer, Pops, said Louis, —but I wasn't hanging round to tell it. I was out of there, Pops, every way but slow.

I stayed in the cupboard an hour, listening to knives and forks, chairs shifting, silence. Fast feet, slow. Doors slamming. Water running. My heart hammering. I stayed where I was. Until the door swung open and she was looking down at me.

—You're like a little fella in there, Henry.

—Yes, Miss.

—Got to say, O'Pops, I was kind of surprised you weren't right behind me. Actual fact, I was more surprised I wasn't right behind you.

196

—I used to know her, I told him.

—Eileen? I said, as I stood up out of the cupboard.

She helped me; I was stiff – my legs were dead, just coming back to life. She grabbed a chair for me.

—It had to be done, she said.

—Yeah, well.

—It's only a name, she said.

(—His name's Henry, d'you hear me?

I was named.

—His name's Henry! Henry! So you might as well get used to it.

My father stood up, the chair fell back. He came over to the crib. I heard the charging tap tap. He looked down at me. I saw an angry blur, shimmering fury.)

—Used to know her? said Louis.

We were in the Rickenbacker, crawling up State Street. Louis was driving. We'd nothing real to do – I thought – but he wouldn't stay still.

—Used to know? She a spook?

—No, I said. —I hadn't seen her in years.

—Know her well?

—Yeah.

—You didn't jump or holler, she said the two and two. Know her very well?

—Yeah.

—How well?

—I'm married to her.

—Thought so, he said. —Could tell by those big bumps on your face. Now, there's a married man, I said. There's a cat stayed out too late.

—Where are they? I asked her.

—Out for a walk, said Miss O'Shea. —They're great people for walking for the sake of it, the Americans.

—She's lovely, I said.

—Ah now, she said. —She'll have her spoilt. Missis Lowe.

197

—What's the story there?

—She's an ol' rip, so she is. She has me plagued.

—Why don't you tell her to fuck off?

She smiled – for the first time. But there was no fun in it; she was talking to an eejit.

—She lets me keep the lassie with me.

—Oh.

—Oh is right. It hasn't been easy, Henry. Following you all around the place, with herself. There's many not ready to believe me when I tell them I'm married. Even with the ring.

I looked at her hand, the ring.

—You still have it.

—Why wouldn't I? she said. —I'm married.

She stared at me now, stopped arranging things on the table that didn't need arranging. She stared at me, with a hardness I hadn't seen before, or couldn't remember.

—Amn't I?

—Yeah, I said. —You are.

—Well, then.

—Where are we going? I asked Louis.

—Where we *not* going, said Louis. —That the important place. We going everywhere else.

—Where are we not going?

—That place we just now driving past.

The Black Canary. Italian lads standing outside, one to a door. Like most of the other clubs. No different. Not from where I sat.

—Why not?

—Slavery been gone sixty years, he said.

—You're going to have to tell me more.

—They want me to play my cornet there, said Louis.

It was quite a while since his last paying engagement, and we were between robberies. The run from Miss O'Shea had given him the jitters and I'd been too busy to go out on my own.

—What's wrong with that? I asked.

We were past the Black Canary by now, but it had looked like every other club I'd seen him in. It looked exactly like his living.

—For the rest of my life, he said. —They want me for my whole entire life. Ain't doing it.

198

He took a sudden left when the street beside us emptied. It became a U turn, and sent me against his shoulder.

—We're going back, I said.

—See? Knew I made the right move when I em-ployed you.

—Why?

—Why we going back?

—Yeah.

We'd caught up with the flow, crawling south this time.

—Well, he said. —Like a chick.

He took his hands from the wheel and rubbed them.

—See a chick you like, can't take your eyes off of her.

He looked for confirmation.

—Yeah.

—Same with ugly, he said. —Ever notice? I'm not talking chicks here, nay nay. Not necessarily. I mean anything ugly. A scar, a wound, missing leg. Even your bruises there, Smoked. A automobile accident. Or just plain natural born ugly. Anything you don't want to see. You see it, and you can't stop yourself. Telling yourself to stop and get the hell out of that face but you just keep on at that gazing, like that ugly thing was something you wanted more than anything in the world. I making sense, O'Pops?

—Yeah.

We were coming back up to the Black Canary, on its side of the street now. The Italian lads looked bigger, and they were looking at us, at me the passenger, looking back out at them. And one of them was Pink Carmine.

—Well, Smoked, said Louis. —I think this might be one of those ugly things.

She was still staring at me.

—Six years, Henry, she said.

—They flew.

She stared.

—They did not, she said.

She was scaring me. She didn't look like the woman who'd been on top of me half the night.

—You made no effort, Henry, she said.

How could I answer? I'd looked everywhere I went, every day, every new place, all day and night. I'd never not looked. But she was right. I'd never looked back. I'd never stopped and turned.

I said nothing; there was nothing right that I could say.

—You never even wrote a blessed letter.

She was right.

—Have you never heard of the telephone, Henry?

She was right.

—A great invention altogether. Even in Ireland. Or telegrams?

I wished she'd cry now, and it would be over. We'd hug and more than likely ride again; we'd be back on our way, and happy.

But she didn't cry and she wasn't going to.

—I'm sorry, I said.

—Are you now?

I wished she'd hit me, take the steps across the tiles and slap me, punch me right in the head, really give it to me.

—All over England I went. The length and breadth of the blessed place. Months. I left herself with Mammy. Then I found out you were in America.

—How?

—Never you mind now, Henry.

Her face was white; the cheekbones cut through her skin.

—So. What did you do?

—I went home.

She sat down. I stood up. I'd remembered my coat; I took it out, off the cupboard floor where'd she'd flung it after me. I shook it and hung it on the chair. And I sat. I left some distance between us but I kept the table out of our way.

—Yes, she said. —I went home.

—How's your mother?

—She's dead, Henry.

—I'm sorry.

She looked.

—I know. You liked her.

—Yeah.

—I know. Three years ago. Four. She just went in her sleep.

—Oh.

—But I wasn't there, she said. —Saoirse was alone with her. For two days.

—Oh Jesus. She was only, what? Two?

—Two, yes. Two. It was Ivan Reynolds found her.

—Jesus.

—He's grand.

—Grand?

—The fighting's over, Henry; his is, anyway. He's the big politician now, full of himself. But he's grand. And he found her. Thank God. He was visiting Mammy. He's a great man for visiting now that he needs the votes. But I shouldn't be talking like that; he found her and he looked after her, himself and his wife. He'd sit in the kitchen with Mammy and chat away and forget completely that it was him set fire to the kitchen and the rest of the house only a few years before. But Mammy liked him, in spite of everything that went on between himself and myself. And any sort of company is better than no company.

—Where were you? I asked, softly, carefully.

—I was in New York, Henry.

—Oh.

—Yes.

—I was in New York four years ago.

—Yes. I know.

—How?

—You were seen, Henry. You're not the only man on the run. She let me look at her face. I'd have to talk.

—So, did you go back?

—I did. I went back. And I stayed there. For two years, a little less. Mammy was well buried by the time I got there and she had a fine new stone, for herself and Daddy. Ivan did that. He had a young lad keep it clean for when I came home. And Saoirse was in Ivan's house, and getting used to the big stairs and the sweet-cake. So. I took her home and she cried and whinged until she couldn't remember what it was she was missing. And Ivan bought the last bit of land off me and he gave me a fair price for it and I only had to tell him once to mind where he was putting his hands. He's mellowed, has that Ivan. So, then. I came looking for you again and I brought herself with me this time.

—Jesus, Miss. All this time.

—Yes, Henry.

—I'm sorry.

—Well.

She looked at her shoes – soft, black indoor things. And I wondered where her boots were. I even thought of looking in the cupboard.

—All this time, she said. —I've been looking for you. And tell us.

She sat up straight.

—What have you been up to?

The photograph was in front of my eyes; I saw it burn and curl. I watched it fall apart, before the flames could properly eat the bodies and faces, suits and dresses. The smaller pieces floated there, held up in the heat. I saw her face, alone and bodiless. I didn't watch as it left the heat and drifted to the floor.

I told her.

But not everything. I was honest, not stupid. I told her about Fast Olaf's half-sister but I left out the bit about being in her mouth when Johnny No and Mildred came to kill us in Brotman's studio. I left out Mildred as well, and the studio and why I was in it; I only half believed that bit myself. But I told her enough to make fair sense. She could know why I wasn't there when she came back to New York. She could know that there'd been a half-sister. She could know that I'd had to run.

I knew: the half-sister wasn't the problem.

—What was she like?

—Grand, I said.

I got ready for the charge, my fighting woman in my arms.

But she stayed where she was. She sighed. She stared at me.

—I knew you were in trouble, she said, and it took me a while to catch up.

She wanted no more of the half-sister.

—Then what? she said.

I told her.

It wasn't complicated now. I told it all in two minutes. Trains, towns, states – the crops I'd picked, the cities I'd stayed out of, the habit that moving became.

—Until I came here.

She nodded, as if she'd known.

—What made you change your mind?

—What d'you mean?

She lifted her arms and flicked her hands.

—Cities, she said. —This city. Those Italian gangster fellas have the run of the place. It's in the papers every day.

—Well, I said. —I thought if I stopped, then I could start heading back.

—Home?

—Yeah. Home.

—Where's that, Henry?

—Ah, Miss. Eileen.

—Don't call me that.

I was happy not to, but—

—Why not?

—It's not my name.

—Oh.

—I had to give Missis Lowe a name and I didn't want the bother of spelling my own and teaching her to pronounce it properly and all the palaver. And she never would have, anyway. Pronounced it. So, I just said Eileen. It's grand, sure.

—I'm glad.

—Why?

—Eileen's not your name.

—Well, I don't know what that has to do with anything, Henry.

—I've never known your name.

—And that now, Henry, used to be exciting. And now I think, it just makes me very sad. That you never knew my name.

—I went out of my way not to know it, I said. —It wasn't that I didn't care. I stood out in the fuckin' rain so I wouldn't hear it.

—I'll tell you now, so.

—Don't!

She stared at me.

—That's something, I suppose.

She looked away. Out the window I'd come through the night before. At the snow that was back, in fits, and the morning sunshine lighting it. She was beautiful, still beautiful; her profile there was what I'd always loved. The way she stared, examined what she saw. The look of a woman who believed in things. A woman who expected good to come at her. Who, for the time being, didn't have to look at me.

I watched her. She knew it. It stopped snowing and, strangely, became darker.

—Henry.

—What?

She jumped, a tiny jump, surprised at the voice, and surprised that it was mine. She'd been speaking to herself, far away from me. And now she looked, and I knew her. My teacher, my wife, my absolute ride. She looked back at the window.

203

—I'm very angry, Henry.

—I know, I said. —I don't blame you.

—I've been angry, oh, for years now. Years. Especially when I missed you the second time, when I went back to New York, and I knew there was a hussy in it. What's her name, by the way?

—Annie, I said, the first woman's name I could grab. I'd never known the half-sister's name either, but Miss O'Shea didn't need to know that.

—And she was nice?

I told myself not to shrug.

—Yeah.

—Where is she?

—I haven't a clue, I told her. —I haven't seen or heard of her since that time, and that's years ago now.

—Were there others?

—Women?

—Henry.

—Yeah.

I looked straight at her.

—A few.

She was looking at the window.

—But, I said.

She wouldn't look at me.

—It was always you.

—Was it now?

—Yeah.

There was nothing for a while, maybe a full minute, maybe even more. A long, long time. I heard wood settle in the house, and the ice-box was a noisy bastard. I heard wheels on slush, and a branch outside rubbed against another. I listened to her breath, the quick and angry intake. I heard a mouse, mice, under us, somewhere. A clock, somewhere. A whistle. A woman singing, backyards away, throwing her faith at the wind. And I wondered if Dora worked nearby.

She moved a leg; I heard a click. I looked at her not looking at me; I didn't take my eyes from her. Except the once, to see if her boots were in the cupboard. The cupboard doors were partly open. I leaned back, looked in. They weren't.

—What are you looking for?

—Your boots.

204

—My boots.

—Yeah.

—I'm very angry. And not about the others, mind. Although that too. But I know the kind you are.

She slapped her chest.

—There's been no one here, Henry. No one at all. Not one man.

—I wouldn't have minded.

—Fuck off, Henry! Just—

And now it happened. She got up and went for me. I'd been waiting, wanting it and nothing else, but she had me by the hair before I was ready and the chair was gone and her fingernails shot through my hair to the scalp and she was knocking seven makes of shite out of me, kicking, stamping, punching with a fist that came with her wedding ring, stolen from a big house in East Galway, down hard on my head and face; she was dragging me, pulling hair clean from my head and kicking me because the hair had given up. I resisted a bit – I had to. I grabbed an ankle, I slapped a hand aside, and I was thanking Christ her boots weren't on as she stamped down on my bollix, and thanking him too for the quality of Mister Piper's fabric, and I was hoping, hoping she'd soon have enough and she'd get down here on the floor and fuck me, fuck me, fuck and forgive; I felt blood on my face, smelt and tasted, hoped none of it got into the jacket; and she kept at it, at me, digging and stamping, well above, too far above to catch her; and she really was going to kill me and I'd let her do it, and I wouldn't; it wasn't funny any more, it was time to stop and – the room had other voices now, feet, a scream, cold outside air – and I was up – the child, the woman – and I ran at the kitchen door and it was locked and I turned and there was nowhere without pushing through those women, three of them, and I wasn't going to do that. My daughter, my wife, the Missis Lowe one. I wasn't going anywhere.

—Those bruises you got there, Pops, he said.

We were level now, in front of the club and Carmine.

—There might be more on the way, he said.

—You're overdoing it, Louis, I said.

—Ready for that?

—Stop messing. It depends.

Pink Carmine and his pal had clocked the driver. They bent down, waved in, and Louis waved back.

—Depends on what?

We were moving again. A jump, a crawl. They didn't follow. Whatever was happening, now was not the time. And something was happening. Louis knew it and other people knew but the hard guys at the door didn't, yet. And neither did I.

And it annoyed me. So I grabbed the wheel with one hand.

—Depends on if I think another hiding is worth it. And, at the moment, I don't.

I made the car rattle.

—I got a good ride and a dinner after the last one. What have you got to offer?

I let go of the wheel.

—Finished, O'Pops?

—No.

—Sorry, he said. —We stop and talk.

I spoke to the side of his head. He let me talk.

—There was a time, Louis, when a fella, every now and again, a fella would give me a bit of paper and there'd be a name on the bit of paper. And my job was to kill the unfortunate cunt whose name was written on the paper. And I did it, every fuckin' time, no questions asked. Obeying orders. My duty. For my fuckin' country, Louis. I did what I was told. Every time. But I don't do that any more.

—We stop and talk, Henry.

—Yeah.

I put my hands up.

—Caught, I said.

A burglar.

And fair enough. It was why I was there in the first place.

Gasping aside, she looked quite calm. Hair on the floor, blood on her hands – she looked like she'd been doing the cleaning, just a bit put out because there was more to it than she'd expected. But not like a woman who'd been murdering her husband when the boss walked in.

I had one eye working for me. The other was probably gone; there was just a hole full of pain there. I could feel blood travelling over sweat. And my balls were going to take some coming down. But I straightened as much as I could manage, hands up polite and high, and looked at my daughter.

—Howyeh.

—Did Mammy do all that to you?

—Yeah.

—Golly.

—I was robbing the house, I said. —Fair play.

—You're lucky she didn't shoot you, so.

—Saoirse!

—Well, he is. Uncle Ivan said you were a divil for the rifles when yourself and himself were fighting for Ireland.

—Seer-she.

It was the woman, Missis Lowe. She was holding Saoirse's hand, shaking a bit, but too calm for an old lady with a fine man's blood and hair at her toes, mixing with the slush that was sliding off her boots, and her mad servant beside her, blood on her hands and in her eyes, and the fine man himself, half-dead, right in front.

—Do you know this man, Eileen?

—No, I said.

—Yes, said Miss O'Shea.

—I thought the house was empty.

—He's my husband.

—And he came to steal from here?

—I didn't know she was here, I said. —I thought she was in Ireland. Swear to God, missis.

—Eileen?

—It's true.

—My.

Miss O'Shea moved across to Saoirse. She wiped her hands on her apron, saw the blood, and stopped wiping. She looked tired, and edgy, and embarrassed.

—It's your daddy, Saoirse. Say hello.

She stared at me. Huge black eyes examined my face.

—It's not, she said.

—It is.

—It isn't. My daddy died for Ireland. You told me that.

—In case we didn't find him. That was why I told you.

—That's just stupid.

—I didn't know if we'd ever find him. That was why. I didn't want you to be disappointed.

207

I had to say something.

—You told her I was dead so you wouldn't disappoint her?

—Well now, she said. —You weren't around to suggest anything different.

Saoirse hadn't stopped looking at me. The news hadn't changed her face a bit.

—Well, Seer-she, said Missis Lowe. —I believe them. They certainly look like a happily married couple to me.

And that stunned Miss O'Shea. I could see it in the way she went rigid, and in the confusion that rushed across her face. She kept her eyes away from Missis Lowe's.

—You're not like she said, said Saoirse.

To me.

—How come?

—She said you were handsome and you're not.

—I am.

—You're not. Sure, look at you.

—You should have seen me before your ma got her hands on me. You'd have been more impressed.

She tilted her head, planted her cheek on the shoulder of her coat.

—Maybe, she said.

—Listen, love. I know where your mammy comes from. Believe me, there was no opposition.

—That's just stupid, said Saoirse. —That proves nothing. Just boasting.

—Good girl, said Miss O'Shea. —He was always too fond of the mirror.

She was there again, the woman I loved. Suddenly there, as if she'd been hiding. Messing, playing, acting the mad woman. She was up for whatever – up on my crossbar, in charge of the machine-gun. I was delighted, thrilled, ready again for anything.

—And what about you? I said. —Yeh fuckin' cradlesnatcher.

There she was, I could see it, one of my nipples in her mouth, ready to bite down hard, very little stopping her, only her boss and her daughter.

—Yeh pup yeh, she said.

—Off yeh go, granny.

—Now now, said Missis Lowe. —Let us all sit down and—

—No!

It was Miss O'Shea, and music to the ear that wasn't killing me.

208

—Who asked you to stick your oar in? she said, over Saoirse's head, to the poor oul' one.

Saoirse stretched her head back, watching the words as they flew over.

—And where do you think you're going, with your Now Now? You ol' rip.

—She's older than you, *a mhamaí*.

—I know!

—Not that much, I said.

—Well, said Miss O'Shea, across her daughter's head. —Are you going to phone for the police or what? Look at him there, the eejit, dying to have himself arrested.

—Now, Eileen, I don't think—

—Go on, missis, I said. —You'd be doing me a favour.

My hands were still up, and running out of blood. I let them down, slowly.

—He's after taking his hands down, *a mhamaí*. Will he go for his gun now?

—No; don't worry yourself on that score. He'd only do that if our backs were turned.

—That's the way I'd do it as well, said Saoirse.

—Do what, now?

—Shoot people.

—What?

—In the back. It'd be much easier.

And there was silence. Real silence, but for long breaths that tried to take back words and some bits of time.

—You've mice under your floor, missis, I said.

She sighed.

—Unarmed, I hope, she said. —This is turning into quite a day.

—It's snowing again, Missis Lowe, said Saoirse.

—Well. So, it is.

The girl looking out at the snow, her total devotion to it; everything else and everyone gone – it was enough to stop us. We sat at the table and Missis Lowe sorted the coffee and did the talking. Miss O'Shea looked at me as she listened to her boss; she lifted her shoulders and eyes, letting me know that this was a new, different woman we were listening to.

—Many times I wished he'd shout at me. Even once. Or look at me, properly. I wouldn't have minded if he'd shown disgust at my wrinkles and my thin hair and my sagging breasts.

I saw Miss O'Shea blush. And I wanted to laugh. And I looked at Saoirse, making sure – already the daddy – that she wasn't listening to the big people. But she was. She was at the window, concentrating on the snow, her coat and hat still on, her back firmly to us, and listening to every word. My daughter.

—I would have welcomed Mister Lowe's disgust. I would have cherished it.

I looked at Miss O'Shea as she listened to the old woman give us the misery of her happy, silent marriage.

—And the opportunity to shout at him. To watch the reaction on his face. Any reaction at all. To have him look straight at me.

I sat and watched, into the afternoon – without an intermission from your woman; we got it year by year and month by fuckin' month – and I listened to Miss O'Shea's breath and half-words.

—Go 'way.

—I know.

And the snow must have stopped or gone on too long, because Saoirse was sitting beside her now. Then her head was on the table and I thought she'd gone asleep; her hat was off, her hair on top of her eyes. But I saw her eyes through the hair and she was staring at me. I winked but the eyes didn't budge. I wondered was she asleep with her eyes open. But no, she was staring. Making up for lost time, maybe. Trying to make me match the word – father. And then the story had finally stopped and Miss O'Shea stood up, and Missis Lowe, and I must have missed it while I'd been trying to out-stare Saoirse. I was the new lodger.

—Ain't going to do it, Pops.

It was a fight. And Louis Armstrong was going to win.

That was what the running was about. He wasn't running at all. The man was standing firm. He wouldn't work for the mob. He wanted the freedom of his sound. And, all around, they were closing in, ready to cage him. He was the city's biggest draw, and dangerous with it – a genius bigger than any market, a nigger too big for the ghetto. He was profit – he knew it, and the lads wanted him.

—Ain't nothing personal, he said that night. —I like Mister Capone. Nice guy, any time I meet him. But. They *own* the stage, they own the man up on the stage. Own his chops, own his breath. I go into that place, I don't come out.

—Literally? I asked.

I knew the answer but I wanted more. I had to know why I was sitting beside him, why he'd chosen me.

—No, Pops. Not literally. I go home every night, sleep. But they right down here in my stomach. They got me. White folks. I'm a fine, healthy boy – just do what they want me to do. Play the nice things they like. Mister Capone like the sweet songs. And that Carmine.

—OH – TWO BY TWO.

And I do too.

—THEY COME MAR-CHING THROUGH—

THOSE SWEETHEARTS ON – PARAY-DE.

—Let's get off this street, I said. —The fuckers back there are making me restless.

—Fair e-nuff, Mister O'Pops.

And he got us back into the crawl and took us straight till we were alone among the smokestacks of the near-end South Side. The air was red and hard to take, and he talked all the way, clear and straight, told me he was going to own himself or die, told me he was going to be rich or die, rich because he knew how good he was, die because he was never going to be owned.

—Owned and managed, Pops. Mean the same thing to the black man.

And he told me what I was there for.

—You my white skin, O'Pops. You beside me, I manage myself. I can cross the line. Any time I want.

—Why me?

It was hours since I'd spoken.

—Well, he said. —You white.

—That all?

—No no, nay nay. I saw you look.

—What d'you mean?

—At my playing. That night. Saw you look at the notes. You heard.

—Everyone hears.

—No. Not everyone. Not nearly.

He let that rest a while.

—You know, Pops. You know I'm doing things never been done before. I'm that Thomas Edison. I'm Beethoven, O'Pops, but bigger and better. That great Charles Lindbergh. I'm all of those guys and bigger than all of them. And different.

—You're black.

—Yes sir. And I will not be heard unless some white man says the say-so.

We were on Cottage Grove now, moving north, towards downtown.

—But that is not the way it is going to be, said Louis. —Man once told me, before I came up from New Orleans. Man called Slipper. He say, When you get up north, Dipper, be sure and get yourself a white man that'll put his hand on your shoulder and say, This is my nigger. And then can't nobody harm ya.

—And I'm that white man.

—No, Smoked, he said. —That not you.

I was taken aback, and worried again. His smoke – he lit one reefer from another, all night; the ash, the burning wheatstraw paper – it was at my eyes.

—Who am I then, Louis?

—You the white man that puts his hand on that white man's shoulder and say, No, man, this is *my* nigger.

He looked at me.

—You my white man, he said.

—And you're my black man.

—That right, Smoked, he said. —That about the size of it. But not really. Between you me, I'm nobody's black man. That seem fair to you?

—I don't know.

It felt like morning by the time he stopped, his mouth and the car.

—Hambones and cabbage, he said. —How that sound?

—Fuckin' dreadful.

He stopped the car, dead.

—You understand me, Henry?

—I think so.

—I think so too.

7

I made the coffee, braved the cold, shuffled as I worked, and knew that I was being looked at.

I was dancing.

—You've changed, she said, behind me, in the bed.

—How?

I was bullying the coffee-pot. She'd brought a one-ringed stove up to the room.

—You used to stand still.

—What d'you mean?

—You could stand still for hours, she said. —I remember them complaining about you, the lads, making them stand in the water when you were training them. Ivan gave out yards about you, before you knew I was even there. Trying to dry his socks after being out with you.

I put the pot on a tile beside the stove.

—I liked it, she said. —Even before. I'd look out at you in the yard, the school, with your brother. Standing there when the rest of the little lads around you were going mad.

I got back into the bed, with two good cups of coffee.

—And you found that sexy, did you? Two half-starved kids in a school yard.

—It's a long time since you were starved, mister, she said. — You've become a skippy kind of fella.

It was two weeks since I'd broken into the smell of just-eaten griddle cakes. And it hadn't been easy.

She dressed and undressed downstairs in the bathroom.

—You're soft, she said.

She was looking at me but I wasn't looking back.

—How's your coffee?

—As good as it should be, she said.

She was still furious.

—I never thought I'd see the day, she said, —when Henry Smart would go soft. What age are you now, Henry?

I bit the bullet, and gave her the answer she already knew.

—Twenty-seven.

I'd brought home a gramophone. It was on the table now, beside the stove. The gramophone – the *phonograph* – was going to be my explanation. It was a handsome machine, two or three steps up from Piano Annie's, the one I'd smuggled in easy instalments from the Dublin docks. This was serious furniture, with legs, drawers for records, a lid that upped and downed on oiled brass. I'd robbed it from the house five doors to the left.

I'd been away for days with Louis, in the Okeh studio – in the Consolidated Talking Machine Company Building, on Washington Street. The place was still in my feet. I'd taken the stairs here three at a time, the phonograph on my shoulder, all the way to the top. Soft, my arse. My breath still did what I told it to.

But I knew what Miss O'Shea had meant. I was off my guard, sleeping well for the first time in years. Life with Louis was building up to something big and probably dangerous but, so far, it had been good clothes and laughter. Breaking and entering, but none for weeks – Louis was working, guesting for Carroll Dickerson at the Savoy, on the radio every night. I was fat on happiness, not fat at all, just full of it. A father again – for the first time – and full of that too, curls and looks and little words in front of me. I was a family man now, and bringing home good bacon. But Miss O'Shea didn't like it yet, and maybe never would. Time had stood still while she'd spent those years catching me. She was still in Ireland and I was far away.

She kept rolling back to it.

—Why didn't you come home?

She meant Ireland.

—I was going to.

—Well?

—I don't know. I wanted to stop running first. I had to do that. I couldn't run back. And I only stopped running a few months ago.

I had to look at her.

—I had to settle into something first. Stay, you know. Be something, and then go back. I was looking for you, though.

—I'm sure you never stopped looking. When you weren't up to your tricks.

She drank.

—Mrs Smart. I haven't had a chance to be that, Henry.

—No. Sorry.

—They knew, she said.

That kept me still.

—What?

—They knew you were in Chicago.

—Who knew?

—The boys. It was them sent me here.

The boys.

Saoirse was awake; I watched her rise out of the camp-bed.

They knew.

And they'd always known.

And they were waiting.

I was still a dead man.

But, I wasn't.

She slid out of her bed and came across to us.

—Do you go to work? said Saoirse. —Or are you still a robber?

—I go to work, I told her.

—In a big factory?

—No.

—Killing the cows?

—No. I used to do that.

—Policeman.

—No.

—Not a robber.

—No.

—What?

I did the driving, while Louis smoked his way to the right state for recording, in his latest struggle-buggy, a Hupmobile that went from there to there only because it was very fond of Louis. We stopped off at the building where Alpha stayed with her mother. Louis was gone, and quickly back, and angry.

—That woman ain't Lil, he said.

He often said that.

Alpha was a consumer. Louis was the butter and egg man and he didn't get in there without the goods. Her mother stood across

215

the door and Alpha wouldn't see him. He was broke most of the time and Alpha didn't understand or care.

—Drive by Lil's place, O'Pops.

I brought him past the house on 44th. It seemed to calm him. What could have been; what used to be – it seemed to be enough. Maybe he thought there was still a future there, when everything was sorted.

—Time, said Louis.

He was ready for the studio.

I rode shotgun that night, while he recorded *Tight Like This*, in four takes.

—IT TIGHT LIKE THIS, LOUIS.

It was me who supplied the voice of the girl. Earl Hines tried it, Don Redman tried; they all tried, but it was me who found the voice that stopped Louis.

—He the one make me hard.

It annoyed the others; I wasn't a player – but that's me on the record. The 12th of December, 1928.

His lips were killing him. He patted the salve on, but it couldn't smother the pain, or even hide it. He sat in front of a mirror I held for him, and picked at a red sore with a needle.

He sounded far away.

—Got to get them little pieces of dead skin out 'cause they plug up my mouthpiece.

He stood and started again. It hurt to watch, when he put the piece to his mouth, and more when he took it down – the grease clung, blood seeped through. He closed his eyes, wiped flesh and metal clean with his hankie, put the pain back to his lip, once, twice, four times, and played that dirty song like it was the ride of his life. I was there, and that was enough for the men behind the glass. They took Louis's nod. The fourth was the one.

St James Infirmary took six, and the pain was there in the voice – SAW MY BAYY-BEE THERE – even though the singing gave him time to get the horn away from his chops.

—SHE'LL NEVER FIY-ND ANOTHER SWEET MAN LIKE ME.

I hadn't known him long but he'd brought that song through two women, his wife, and the woman who was going to be his wife, even though she'd already finished with him. And then there were other women too. *It tight like this, Louis.*

—Tell us, I asked him during a break, when Wickemeyer was

pushing the piano two inches closer to a microphone. This studio was new, and those inches suddenly mattered. Electricity had come up from the street. Wickemeyer was a calmer man behind his double-glazed window. And the players were too – less stomping and shaking; they kept their eyes on the mikes, made sure they didn't shiver. The walls were strange, detached from the real walls behind them. The recordings, when we heard them, were clearer, better. The piano was there, and all the drums; the banjo was no longer a scratch.

—Did you drop in on Alpha tonight just to get into the mood for that song? I asked him. (—Just hear him play when he's angry, Lil had said.)

He looked at me, shock hanging off him.

—What the song got to do with anything? he said.

—Just a thought.

—Too much of the Irish in you, Pops, he said. —See here. I want her pussy, not sing about not having her pussy. Song's a song, pussy's a pussy. Sing one, wish I could make the other sing.

He exhaled, slowly.

—But maybe you right.

—Nigger jazz.

I rescued the needle.

—What?

—That's what that was, said Miss O'Shea. —I've heard it.

—Did you like it? I asked Saoirse.

—Yes.

—That was Louis Armstrong, I told her.

—The man doing the funny singing?

—That's right. And he played the trumpet as well.

—What was the singing about?

—Nothing really, I said. —He sometimes just does that. There aren't real words.

—It's funny.

—That was called *Basin Street Blues*, I told them.

I turned to Miss O'Shea.

—Did you like it? I asked her.

The answer was everything.

—Oh, yes, she said. —It was grand.

—You didn't like it.

—No, I did. I liked it.

She stood up off the bed and went to the wardrobe. She closed its doors and stretched to grab the handle of the suitcase on the top.

—I'll get it for you.

—You will not.

She slid the case off the wardrobe, grabbed with her other hand just as the case started to fall. She kneeled, and brought the case to the floor.

—Where are we going? said Saoirse.

—Nowhere.

I wanted to tell her now, before she had to go downstairs to work: I was Louis Armstrong's white man. But I couldn't. Her back was to me; she was bending over the case. She sat back on her ankles, and I heard the locks spring open.

—Now.

She took out what I thought was a cardigan.

—What are you doing? said Saoirse.

—Wait and see.

—What's she up to? I asked Saoirse.

—Wait and see.

I didn't have a choice. I couldn't talk to her back. She unwrapped the cardigan; I thought I saw more cloth under it. She put in a hand, and out of the clothes came a record.

—Now.

She held it up, in a purple sleeve.

—What's that?

—That's a silly question.

—What?

—Wait now.

She stood up, and she turned and I saw her face and colour – sex, excitement. She stepped to the phonograph.

—Now.

She lifted my record and handed it to me.

—Thank you, Henry.

She slid her own record from the sleeve, held it to the light, blew its dust at me, and lowered it; her fingers followed all the way.

—Aren't they the great invention?

—Yeah, I said.

—Can I do it? said Saoirse.

—Next time.

—Ah.

—Ah yourself.

And she lowered the needle.

It was Fletcher Henderson's band, but Louis had a dressing room to himself. But he didn't; Louis had nothing to himself. He came down the stairs, surrounded – pulled, pushed and loved. It was Monday night, and the black people were in. I was behind the gang, descending into the steam, the smell of good cooking and working people. Louis's room was right beside the stairs and, two steps shy of the ground, I could see that it was already a squeeze in there.

—Something always sweet about the back of a ofay's head.

I turned.

Dora was one step behind, above me, and I was looking into her eyes.

—Howyeh, Dora.

—How-yah, Henry S.

I looked at her, she looked at me. The bodies came and went around us. I didn't notice Louis's room being emptied.

She came down the last step.

—How you been, Henry S.?

—Grand.

—I heard. You the big news these days.

—I can't help it, I said.

—Running round with Dipper.

She glanced away, at Louis's room, and then I heard. Something hit the door – wooden, something, probably a chair. I turned and had my shoulder on the door before I heard her speak.

—Careful, she said.

Louis was sitting down. His back to the big mirror. Stuffed into a chair with no arms. Crowded by the guys on either side. Stuck there in his shorts and vest. His right hand was up, like a kid in school. There were two of the hard guys, and Louis's hand was being held by one of them, the wrist in one hand, and, in the other, a finger. Pulled back, about to pop. They were teaching Louis a lesson.

The hard guy let go of Louis's wrist and went for the jacket pocket, just as my boot found room between his legs and kicked. He didn't fall or tumble but every part stopped working and stood still. Louis was up and trying to get away, trying to take his clothes out with him. The second guy was bigger than the room. My elbow beat him to it, and he went back against the mirror with his hand still in his pocket. I got myself between the guns and Louis, and he was out – trousers, jacket, coat and shoes – into the corridor, and I grabbed his trumpet and followed. Dora was gone; I saw that as I went after Louis. I tried to run but couldn't. The corridor was too narrow and full. A bullet cracked wood, sent bodies diving and, still, I couldn't run. I heard another; its sting was in my fingers. The bullet had hit the trumpet.

Louis hit the door. He took the thing right off its fuckin' hinges. I was impressed, but it left me without cover. And Louis stopped to get dressed.

—Not now, Louis.

—Not dying without my nice vine on me. It Chicago cold out here.

—For fuck sake.

The alley was empty. They were still inside, unwilling to run into an ambush. We'd see them soon. But Louis was dressed now, and this time I could run.

And Louis was with me. Panting, but right there. I took the corners but I'd no idea where we really were. Into night crowds, and out, alleys and streets. Twice he grabbed my arm and brought me round a corner. I looked and saw the hard men at us, or heard them. They were fit and angry. Frightened. Going home to Al or Pink Carmine, business unfinished. Dead unless they got us. They'd stay the pace; I heard them.

We ran across a crowd.

—Hey! Louis! Her ol' man after you!

Across a street. Wide, still busy. I didn't know it. Through cars and bodies. The light, the music – I didn't know the place. But I felt it.

The water. Under us.

He felt it too. I heard it. A gasp, the sudden pain and pull.

—Oh Pops.

It had us grabbed.

—That's water, I told him. —Keep running.

—Trying, Pops.

—Keep running.

No choice now. We ran above the flow, stuck to its course. It ran us two blocks.

220

—How do we get down there? I asked him.

—Down where?

—To the water.

The river answered for him. It took us off the street, through weeds across a vacant lot. I didn't know it, or the houses that walled it. On to a parallel, quieter street.

—Where are we? I asked him.

—State.

—Really?

—Truly.

—How did that happen?

He didn't answer. He held out a hand and took his trumpet from me. I bent down. I found the gap, a drain, in under the sidewalk. I edged closer to it. I kneeled, got my head in. It was black down there, but I could hear and feel it. Chicago water. And he could feel it too; it was in his face and eyes when I looked up.

—Will you be able to manage? I asked him.

—Manage?

—Get through here?

—Go ahead, Pops. I'll skinny myself.

The hards were coming after us. We couldn't see them but they were on their way. I could hear their shoe leather, angry breath across the lot, just around the corner.

I lay down and my feet found the hole. I pushed backwards. I felt the sidewalk against my back but it didn't stop me. Gut, chest, face – I got them through. I held on with my hands.

—Come on.

Louis was on his knees now, on his stomach. His face was close to mine.

—You're in the way, Pops.

I let go and dropped. I fell through black, and hit the water, tucked in my legs until I knew the depth. My knees hit stone, but the water lifted me; the pain was a memory before I was aware of it. My hat stayed on my head. I was home here. I was home. *Welcome to the Swan River, boys.*

The needle clung to the edge of the record, scratched, stayed on, got in there, past the scratching. The strings and horns – my new-trained ear was rearranging.

And it started.

—MA-CUUSH-LA—
MA-CUUSH-LA—
YOUR SWEE-EET VOICE IS CALL—
INGGGG—

She sat back on her heels, and smiled. Miss O'Shea again. Home, and far from home. She opened her eyes and stared at me.

I looked up, saw a bright hole, night-time bright. I saw Louis's feet.

—Come on, I said. —It's grand.

The light above was sliced, and Louis gasped as he let himself drop. I was out of his way; I heard him land, but didn't see. I turned and felt his wave. I felt him there, standing out of the water, shaking, settling.

Another gasp. Surprise.

—It *is* grand, O'Pops, he whispered, and liked the sound. — O'Pops, O'Pops. Ha ha.

—Told you.

He grabbed my arm.

—That you?

He let go of my arm. I could see him now. He stood to his waist in the fast flowing water, with his hands clasped in front of him, like he was up on the street and the big shots weren't after him. The wounded trumpet was safe inside his coat.

—O'Pops, O'Pops. We should cut some records down here.

It was easy country, American-new, clean-cut tunnels, no falls or juts. It was dark, but flat and reliable, lake water, in no mad hurry. We were in under the prairie.

—Are you right? I said.

—Right, tight, and out for the night.

—Let's go.

—Lead the way. Back there or up here?

—We'll go with the flow.

—'Bout time I started doing that.

I lifted my arms and made short hopping steps, my gut cutting the path. He was right behind me, humming. The terror was still throwing bombs at me but Louis took out his trumpet and started playing. Down there, as we walked under Chicago, Louis played *Basin Street Blues*. The bullet had done no damage.

—They'll hear you, I said.

—But not see. They'll think it the ghost of Louis Armstrong. And maybe they'll be right.

—You're not dead yet.

—Believe you, Pops. Just about.

There was nothing for a while, just us, our breath, our hearts.

—We can't stay down here forever.

—That the Irish in you, Henry. Always the bad news.

—They'll be up there when we go back up.

—That right. But they down here right now?

—No.

—So let me enjoy my swim. Know where we're going?

—No.

—Do they?

—No.

—See, Pops? It's easy. You got to start to thinking like a Negro. We not heading into a whupping. We just got away from one.

She kept my hand pressed to her stomach. I could feel her through my arm. For the first time. The first American time. John McCormack had done it. The Irishman who'd conquered America. *Macushla, Macushla.* The voice that bridged the Atlantic. I couldn't stand him but I'd kept that to myself.

We were happy there. We'd found the people we'd loved and left. We were both home now, both the same. I could smell the sods that had roofed the bunker where we'd lain together the last time, before Saoirse was born, before I'd killed and left. I could put my hand to my head and feel it seven years before, the muck in my hair, the dirt. We were there again. Young, in love. It was good. And it killed me.

She kissed my arm.

—What are you thinking about? she said.

—Nothing much.

—I'll be needing a better answer than that.

—Yes, Miss.

We were older now. I was older and I knew: there was an end, and it was always in sight. And she knew it too, better than I ever would. She thought she'd been there already; she knew she'd see it again.

But not for now, not soon. We were back. Our daughter in the far corner, asleep and miles away. We were under the sods in Roscommon; we were on the road, on the Arseless Horse, pedalling backwards to the start. (—What's your name, so?

—Henry Smart.)

—So? she said.

—So?

—What are you up to?

Her hand was on my gut now. She held skin; she squeezed it. I couldn't tell her.

—Ah, sure, I said.

I was on the run again.

—This and that.

We came up out of the river with the decision. Soaked and giggling, still terrified. Only a streetlight to warm us.

—Maybe I should get a gun, I said.

—No, man, he said. —That not the way.

—I'm kind of a manager, I told her.

—That's a real Henry answer, she said. —And what is it you'd be kind of managing?

—A friend, I said.

—A friend.

—He's a – he plays – he's a musician.

—What's his name, so?

—Louis Armstrong, I said.

—Where's he from?

I was tempted. Roscommon, Dublin. Home.

—Somewhere down south, I said. —New Orleans. I think.

—Does he sing?

—Yeah. And he plays the trumpet.

I pointed at the far corner, at the phonograph.

—That was him, I said. —You liked it. You said.

—Nigger jazz.

—Jazz.

—What does a manager do?

—You liked it.

—Yes, I did.

—I kind of look after him.

—God love him.

But there was fun in it. She was smiling.

—Why does he need looking after?

—Jaysis, I said. —It's a complicated life.

I could see her, listening, in beside me, waiting.

—The same old story, I said. —Exploitation. He has all this, talent. And people want to—

—I know.

—They want to use him. They want to make him—

—But it's only ol' music, she said.

Her hand was there, under the sheet, in mine.

—Isn't it?

We went to the pictures.

Father and daughter. Daddy and his girl. But she didn't call me Dad or Daddy, or anything else. She never ran to me – *I'm ho-ome!* – or let herself be lifted and swung. But she was happy enough to walk beside me. She was happy to talk and listen. She fired the questions at me.

—Why didn't he kill the baddie in the end?

We'd been to see *The Gaucho*, with my pal, Douglas Fairbanks.

—I don't know; he didn't have to.

—They usually do in the end.

—I know.

—So, why didn't he?

—He didn't kill anyone.

—Why did all the ladies in the fillum like him?

—He's good looking.

—No, he's not.

—He used to be. Maybe they remembered.

—How?

—Maybe they liked the way he got up on his horse.

—That's not why ladies like men.

—I don't know; you might be right.

She let me hold her hand; my hand always went to get hers. But I didn't think she held mine. I understood – the little fingers through the glove, the squeeze not given back.

—Why d'you say I Don't Know so much?

—I don't know, I said. —I *don't* know. Most of your questions are hard.

225

—No, they aren't.

—They are.

—Which ones?

—All of them.

—You said Most.

—Fair enough. Why didn't he kill the baddie in the end?

—What's hard about that?

She went for the thin white ice that had been water a few hours before; she let go of my hand. She pushed her toe at the ice.

—Well, I said.

—I know the answer already, she said.

—What?

—It's only a fillum, she said. —It has to end tidy.

—Good answer.

—The goodies win and the baddies don't. And it doesn't matter what happens when it's over. And it's nicer.

—That's right.

—Were the fellas you killed baddies?

—Shhhh!

We weren't the only ones walking home from the pictures, through the cold.

—Well?

—That's a hard question. It *is*.

—Why?

—I don't know.

—Hah, she said. —Got yeh.

I laughed, and held her hand again.

—Mammy says they were, so what's so hard about that?

—Well—

—They were English.

—Did you like the bit where they dragged the house with their horses?

—Weren't they?

—Some of them.

—How many?

I stopped walking.

—I don't know.

—Hah.

—That's the answer. I don't know. I don't know how many were English, or Scottish or Welsh. Or Irish.

—Not Irish, she said.

We were moving again. She pulled me; she walked ahead and held my coat.

—I wish I'd never killed them.

—She said you'd say that.

—Well, I said. —She was right.

—I know, she said. —See? You say, I don't know. But I say, I know.

—Good for you.

—I know.

—Why the fuck did you tell her I killed people? I asked her mother.

—You're far from home, Henry, said Miss O'Shea.

She smiled at me.

—So she'd be proud of you. You were dead.

She kissed my shoulder.

—Fair enough.

I was ready for every skidding wheel, each fast step behind me; I was ready to face them and run. I hung on as long as I could.

—Out of here, O'Pops, he said.

It was still cold, but not savage all the time. Our feet were well into 1929 and the snow was off them. We could walk without looking down, but we had to keep watch everywhere else – front, back, corners, roofs. We did most of our travelling under the ground, when we had to, through pipes made fat by spring. We were wet most of the time, or drying.

—I have to.

I'd said it before. She'd understood then – *I know* – but, now, I saw it cross her face: the hurt. I saw it and decided that it hadn't stayed.

—Where?

She understood. I made up her mind; she knew, she understood. A man on the run, I had to go.

Louis was hiding.

—Where are you going? she said.

—New York.

—I thought you couldn't go back there.

It was the only place to go, the city where Louis could still exist. A black man couldn't go west and Louis couldn't go home; that would have been no escape. New York was the only place where Louis could become Louis.

—They ran you out of that place, she said.

—It's a big place, I said.

I almost believed it, even though I'd walked its length and breadth.

—Harlem, I said.

—City inside the city, O'Pops.

—They won't be looking for me there.

—For how long this time?

—I don't know, I said. —It's not safe here and Louis can't work.

—And, so?

—What?

—Your Louis friend can't work and I'm sorry for his troubles but you don't play the trumpet for him, do you?

—No.

—So?

—It's my job.

—What's your job?

—Looking after him.

—The poor suffering eejit, that he can't look after himself.

—It's complicated.

—I'm sure it is complicated.

—Okay.

—Looking after a black man, instead of your own family.

—When did you ever need looking after?

—I'm tired.

—So am I.

She didn't bother challenging my lie. I was itchy to move even as we sat there, in the kitchen; I was the least tired man on earth. She wasn't trying to nail me down with guilt. She *was* tired; I could see it. And the day was only starting; the coffee was still in the air. It had caught up with her. It was in her face, on her shoulders.

—I won't be long, I said.

She looked at me.

—It was six years the last time, Henry, she said. —More.

—I won't be, I said. —He has to get out of town, for a while.
I'll be back once he's set up in New York. I'll visit. We'll see how
it goes.

—We will.

—I'm not messing, I said. —Ah, look it.

I stood up, and sat down. I wanted to touch her.

—It's my job. I have to travel. I'll be back.

—But they're after you, Henry. You said so. These Italians.

—It's not the same, I said. —It's different here.

—How?

—Time works here, I said.

—Six years is a long time anywhere.

—No. I know. But it's not like home.

I put my hand out. She didn't meet it. I left it there, on the
table.

—It stops, I said. —It's like this. They're after us, especially
Louis – I'm just with him – and they want to get us and kill us,
more than likely. Maybe just hurt Pops—

—Who's that?

—Louis. They'll just want to hurt him cos they want him to
work for them. And they'll kill me cos I'm a pain in the arse.

She said nothing.

—I'm in their way. I'm no use to them, so they'd bump me
off if they got me. So, grand. They're after us. But it stops. They're
out for us, for a while. Then they get on with business. They give
up. There's too much to do. It's a big place, all sorts of money
to make. It's not weakness. But it's not personal. After a while,
they'll lose interest. They've no memory here. It gets in the way
of progress.

—How do you know all that?

—I don't, I said.

And, now, I felt her fingers take my hand.

—But I think I do, I said. —I think I know. I've been here long
enough. It's not like Ireland. They forget here. There's plenty to
do. D'you understand?

—Oh, I do. You like it, don't you?

—Yeah, I said.

—I don't.

—I know.

229

—There are Irish boys here too, Henry. And they have memories. Remember that. '

—Will you wait for me?

—Yes.

I leaned across the table. I got up and stretched across. She grabbed my shoulders and held me there till I was lying on the table and my coffee cup was broken on the floor. She kept my tongue in her mouth; she held it tight. I couldn't move, nearer or away.

She stopped.

—How much does he pay you, this Pops fella?

—Nothing.

—I knew you'd say that.

—All we need is the gas, said Louis.

He was hiding in Lil's house, pretending he'd stay if she'd take him back. It was hard to watch but he'd nowhere else to go. His fiancée, Alpha, wouldn't have him. She hadn't much use for him, not while he wasn't Louis. And he couldn't be Louis till he ran.

—Got a call from New York, O'Pops.

—What is it? she asked.

—What?

—What's all the fuss about?

I liked that kitchen, in the mornings; the two of us. Saoirse was in school, and Missis Lowe kept out of our way, except when she couldn't help it; she'd glide in and expect us to be riding on the table.

The two of us. Every time was the last time. I was waiting for the word.

I shrugged.

—I love it, I told her.

—Why?

—It's not Irish, I said.

She smiled.

—You're gas.

—It's not anything, I said. —It's just itself. New. I like that.

—I know you do.

—I like the speed. And the instruments. I just love it.
—And him?

—They want me there, Pops.
—Who?
—All of them.
—The entire population?
—That right. En-tire. Nice man called Mister Tommy Rockwell told me so. Wired me today.
—Who's he?
—Management type. Wants me to be on Broadway.
Which end of Broadway, I wanted to know. I'd be recognised at the lower end, with or without my sandwich boards. But I didn't say anything.
—A musical, Pops. About a plantation. Guess they'll want me to play Massa.
—What about the Italians there?
—Different Italians.
—Jaysis, Louis.
I rubbed my face, down hard.
—When are we going?
—Now.
He patted a pocket. The money was in there. I found out later, it had come from Lil.

—Well, she said.
I had the suitcase from the top of the wardrobe.
—I'll be back, I said.
—Yes.
—When he's up and running.
She wanted to say something; I could feel it.
But she didn't.
Saoirse was just in from school. She was leaning over a cup of hot chocolate, drinking it slowly with a very small spoon. She washed it herself every time she used it, and hid it somewhere of her own.
—Well, Saoirse, I said.
She looked at me.
—Bye.

She looked back down at the chocolate. I wanted the hug but I wasn't going to get it; I knew I'd no right to it.

I picked up the case.

She took a spoonful and looked at me again. She smiled, and got back to the chocolate.

I put the case back down. I'd stay. I'd fight for her.

But, even as it landed, I was bringing it back up. I was holding it again, going, on my way.

—We'll be here, said Miss O'Shea.

She was looking at the window.

—For now.

PART THREE

8

Harlem was America; it was new every morning. I liked it there. I loved it.

—Who the fuck are you?

All over again.

—I'm with Mister Armstrong.

—That I fucking see. Who are you?

The plantation musical, *Great Day*, never happened. Not for Louis. The producer or director, some clown, sacked, hired and re-sacked all around him, including Louis. He was out the stage door, trumpet under his arm.

—It was shite, Pops.

—It was Broadway, said Louis.

—Fuck Broadway, I said. —Where's your ambition?

—I could've showed him.

—The fuckin' eejit thought you were there to mop the stage.

Broadway was a grimy drag at this time of day, mid-morning. The stink of the night before and the corners the rain never washed, this alley wasn't worth missing. I'd lived in alleys and I missed none of them.

—Come on. It was shite. Believe me.

Back up to Harlem. Up to Louis's future. And away from faces that might have remembered my past. It was safe up there. The city inside the city. I was lost and happy. I'd no rivals or enemies.

Except Tommy Rockwell.

—I'm with Mister Armstrong.

—That I fucking see. Who are you?

Louis had gone to the jacks, on the next landing. We were in Rockwell's office. Staring at each other. Him up, me down. Him sitting, me standing. Between us, his desk. Behind him, the window and some of 42nd Street. Behind me, the door. Behind that, the secretary.

—Mister Rockwell is *busy* just now.

He shouted at the door.

—Mister Rockwell is busy just always.

He looked back at me.

—I know you are with Louie. Why – understand? – *why* are you with fucking Louie?

—So cunts like you don't mess with him.

—Interesting, said Rockwell. —Cunts, eh? Your idea or his?

—His.

—Yare? Good for fucking him. All his?

—Yeah.

—Yare. Bullshit. Listen. I am Louie Armstrong's manager. I am the manager. I am defining my professional relationship with the shine that just went out there to piss in my can. I am the manager. Do you understand what I say?

I didn't answer.

—Do you have a problem with what I am saying now, here, to you?

I took my eyes away from the grime in a corner of the window and I brought them down, no hurry, to Rockwell's. He looked back up at me. The head of a pig but the eyes were relaxed, a powerful charm and hard to hang on to. He was right over the desk – a phone, a couple of theatre programmes, two letters, a penknife – but the eyes were sitting back.

—No, I said. —I don't.

—Interesting, he said. —So? I return to my original question. Which went.

—Who the fuck are you.

—More or less.

—Henry Smart.

—Never heard of yis.

—That doesn't matter.

Now, he sat back.

—I guess. Take a seat.

—No.

He shrugged.

—Fuck you. Don't take a seat. Remember my second question, Smart?

—I think so.

—So?

—Why am I with Mister Armstrong.

—Yare. Why?

—Remember my answer?

—Fuck you.

—I have something to add.

He sat back further. Chair legs left the floor.

—Yare? What's that?

—If you ever say Fuck You to me again, I'll go around there and ram the phone down your fuckin' throat.

—Yare?

—Yeah.

—Hard guy.

—That's it, I said. —I make sure that the dealings are fair. I make sure that Mister Armstrong thinks that the dealings are fair.

—That it?

—That's it.

—How long does it take him to piss?

—As long as he wants.

—He wants, you want?

—He.

—Yare.

It was over, the fight. For now. But he worried me. It was Johnny No again. The cigar, the suit. The office, the style. It was dangerous. The connections were probably there. And we were learning, again, me and Louis: the action was in Harlem but it was controlled from elsewhere, downtown.

Nowhere was safe. Rockwell's office wasn't safe.

—Hey, Smart, you got a name for what you are? he said.

—No.

—No. Kinda like a pimp. I'd say. See, me, I'm the manager. The booking agent. These are jobs. They have names, measure. Percentages. I fucking represent. For fees. I know what I earn and I know why I earn it. But what's with you, Smart?

He opened a drawer and a bottle came out. Good bad stuff, a nice Scotch label on it. Connections again; it was dangerous. But every office had a bottle.

He put it on the desk.

—Rita! In here, baby! With glasses.

He picked up the bottle and went at the cork with his teeth. The fumes were suddenly there, at the eyes before the nostrils.

It was local stuff. I looked for feathers in the bottle.

Louis walked in, right behind Rita and the glasses.

I asked him the question later.

—D'you like white women?

—They're all yours, Fido.

Now, Rockwell poured. Rita had brought two glasses.

—You forget Louie? said Rockwell.

—No, I—

—Louie's your paycheck, sister. Go get a glass.

—Sorry, Mister Rockwell.

—Yare.

—Maybe she forgot me, I said, as she passed.

—No, said Rockwell.

He was right. Her eyes were huge and full of Henry, and Louis was the black guy with me. And Rockwell had probably told her before we'd arrived, bring in two glasses when he called for them.

—Louie, she forgot all about you.

Louis shrugged.

—Bound to happen, 'least once.

They liked each other.

Rita came back, the glass still dripping water. She handed it to Louis.

—Over here, baby.

She brought it to the desk. She was small but she walked big. Her arse cleaned up as she left. She shut the door silently behind her. We heard her at the typewriter.

—Forty words a minute, said Rockwell.

He'd filled the glasses. Small shot glasses. He handed one to Louis. He handed one to me. He looked at Louis.

—Here's to Louie.

He knocked it back, didn't gasp, and filled his glass again.

—Louie Armstrong, he said as he poured. —The one and the only Louie Armstrong.

He didn't want the band. Most of them had followed Louis to New York, in a convoy from Chicago, on gas paid for by Lil. Fred Robinson, Zutty Singleton, Carroll Dickerson. It was actually Dickerson's band, his name. There were no real stars out there yet. Louis was going to be the first.

Rockwell saw that and he didn't want the rest.

—I did not send for your band, he said. —I sent for you.

There was work in Harlem. They wouldn't go hungry; the nightclubs paid two thousand black men every night.

Rockwell was tone deaf. But he'd been a promoter for years and he looked for his tone in the tapping feet of other people. He couldn't hear notes but he could feel a floor when it hopped. And that was what happened whenever he played Louis's records; the feet of his friends and family tapped when that black guy played. He didn't hear the others – Baby Dodds, Fatha Hynes, or Lil – and his kids didn't talk about the others. It was Louis they smiled for – who was he? Where was he? When would they get to see him?

It was what he was good at: Rockwell knew what people were going to want. But the strength came with a weakness: he didn't know *why* they were going to want it. He had the book but he couldn't read.

—You know that one, Louie? he said one time, before a show. —*All Coons Look Alike To Me*?

—Mister Rockwell, I don't believe I do.

He held out the trumpet.

—Want to play it for me?

—I can't, said Rockwell. —It's just, people like it. It's been around for years.

New York was a cosmopolitan place but the black talent went in the back way.

But not tonight. Louis wasn't having it.

We were outside the Audubon Theatre, in the Bronx. We were early. The doormen weren't at the door yet.

—After me, said Louis.

He put his hand to the glass and pushed.

He was doing it his way but, all the time, he was listening to Rockwell. They both wanted the same thing. Stardom for Louis, and the sweet things that were coming with it.

—Stay away from the blues, Louis.

—What's the difference between Rockwell and Joe Glaser? I asked Louis, one night.

—One in New York, the other in Chicago.

—Is that all?

—Mister Rockwell think he manage me soft. Mister Glaser would manage me hard. With me, O'Pops?

239

—No, I said.

—Fair ee-nuff.

—Stay away from the blues, Louis, said Rockwell. —There's plenty of other Negroes doing that stuff. Go for the hits. They'll go up to Harlem to see you but they'll want to hear Tin Pan Alley. My kids are buying the fucking records. All the fucking kids are. It doesn't matter where you are. Your records will go anywhere. It's the future.

Louis listened.

—It's the future.

Rockwell was a bollix and I never saw him read the letters or the programmes on his desk, but he was worth listening to. He walked through it all; he felt the signals. A man of the times.

He sat on the edge of his desk. This was a month after Louis went out to the jacks and let us at it. He thought he knew why I was there. He didn't dismiss me, but he knew my place – he thought. (He was probably right; but I never really knew it.) He made the effort and succeeded: he talked only to the black man. He leaned out to Louis, but I was welcome to listen.

—We can't sell records yesterday, he said. —Only fucking today and tomorrow. Goes without saying, but I have to keep reminding myself. But, the strange fucking thing in all that, Louie – the records have to be familiar. Fresh, but reliable. The past sells, in new fucking pants. With me, Louie?

—Listening.

—So, listen some more.

He stood up. Rockwell was lazy but always restless.

—Ever notice something about kids, Louie? he said. —It came as a shock to me. They don't stay kids. They grow up. We all do, but it's a kick in the fucking head when your own kids do it. You got kids, Smart?

—Yeah.

—Then you know what I'm fucking talking about.

I shrugged.

—The kids we got at the moment here.

He nodded at the office window.

—They're coming up in a different fucking world. They got all they want. Automobiles, money. Phonographs. Fucking phonographs and records. Last year the people of this great nation spent seventy-five million bucks on phonographs and records. Kids do some of the buying. They do most of the fucking buying. Especially

240

the fucking records. And they ain't going to give up just because they hit twenty-five. They're going to keep buying fucking records.

He sat on the desk again.

—They'll want to hear the old songs. They'll pine for the good old days, when their guts and dicks were hard and everything else was fucking soft, but they won't want to admit that. That they've given in, that they're getting old. The kids that are listening to you now, the ones that are going to start listening – and they fucking are, Louie – tomorrow and in 1930 and 1931 and 1930-fucking-2. Somewhere there, while they're listening to you and dancing, they're going to stop being kids and they're going to get some kids of their own. And they'll still want to listen to you. They'll be feeling the fucking blues but they won't want to fucking listen to the blues. You got five screaming kids, you want another one? No, you fucking do not. You're broke, you need reminding? No. The last fucking thing you need. You want to hear the good old days on that phonograph that you're paying for on the fucking instalment plan. But that's not all. You want to hear it like it's new. So you don't feel old fucking listening to it. So it has to be fucking good. Know what's going to sell, Louie? Timeless.

—Timeless?

—Fucking timeless.

He sang.

—WHEN YOU'RE SMILING—

That got me away from the window.

—WHEN YOU'RE SMILING—

Louis looked as upset as I'd ever seen him. Rockwell couldn't hear himself.

—THE WHOLE WORLD—

Rita came through the parting door and walked to his desk. It looked rehearsed, but a good walk always did. She put a letter on the desk, to the right of Rockwell's arse. He grabbed her hand.

—SMILES WITH – YOU-OU-OU— Timeless, Louie. It'll always be fucking that.

He let go of Rita's hand.

—Honey, he said. —What age are you again?

—Twenty-two, Mister Rockwell.

—Do you consider yourself a kid?

—No, Mister Rockwell.

—Married?

—Betrothed.

—Betrothed. Ain't she got style, gentlemen?

We nodded.

—In fucking spades, said Rockwell.

Rita was edging away from the desk but she wasn't unhappy with the attention.

—Got a phonograph, honey?

—Why, yes, Mister Rockwell. You bought it for me.

I watched her back, her neck below that red hair.

—I did?

—Yes, you did.

—Christmas.

—Birthday.

—Good present, either ways.

—Yes, Mister Rockwell; thank you.

—You use it much? You and the betrothed there?

—Yes, I do. *We* don't. It's in my bedroom.

—Taking it with you when you wed?

—Yes, Mister Rockwell.

—Reckon you'll still have use for it?

—Oh, yes, Mister Rockwell.

—You get my point? Rockwell asked Louis, over Rita's shoulder.

—Young lady has a phonograph, said Louis.

But he'd been listening.

She smiled at Louis, a little uncertainly, and at me. And out she went.

—That chippy's your market, Louie, said Rockwell. —Never forget it.

The door swung back into place. All three of us looked at it.

—The average kid, getting older, said Rockwell. —She'll go see you tonight.

He was never finished.

—At the Audubon. She'll go out to the fucking Bronx. That's where she fucking lives, now that I think of it. But she'll go, and she'll love you. And she'll fuck her betrothed to prove it. And they'll get themselves married and move deeper into the fucking Bronx. And the fucking kids will start popping and she'll stop going and maybe even stop fucking, although that's hard to see.

He looked at the door, then back at Louis.

—And then what? he said.

—She'll listen to the nice records.

242

—She'll *buy* the nice fucking records. Just as long as you keep making them new and old. And fucking timeless.

He stood up. He picked up his hat.

—They're the fucking future, Louie Armstrong. Records. And there'll never be enough of them. More and more and fucking more of them. A million Louies in a million homes. The past, the present, and the fucking future.

He put on the derby. It wouldn't quite take to his head. He didn't notice or care.

—A concert? Fine. An earner, maybe. A big earner, maybe too. But done. Finito. A record? A good fucking record? A timeless fucking record? They'll play it all their fucking lives and they'll buy a new one every time they wear it out and their kids will do the same thing, and their fucking kids. They'll hear it on that fucking radio and they'll buy it, so they can play it when the radio don't. They'll be buying the records long after we're dead and fucking buried, Louie. Just as long as they're the fucking goods. I'll leave you with that. See you tonight.

We stood there a minute, then followed. Rita was busy as I passed.

He'd listened, and the music changed.

—OH – TWO BY TWO—
THEY GO MARCHING THROUGH.

—What's going on? I asked Louis.

Louis put salve on his bottom lip; it was savage, raw, like something that was never going to heal. I'd just heard him play and sing. He was sitting in a corner, beside his typewriter.

—What's what goin' on, O'Pops?

—*Sweethearts On Parade?* I asked.

—Ain't what you do, Pops, said Louis. —The way that you do it.

He wiped the mute and watched its shine.

—Still doing my own thing.

And he was.

—I like it.

And he did. He liked the songs that Rockwell wanted him to record. He'd always liked them. The changes came before Rockwell explained them. Louis was there before him.

The mute was new. I hadn't seen him use one before; I hadn't been there when he'd bought it, if he bought it. He wiped it some more.

We were in the Audubon dressing room, under the stage. It was months since we'd been deep inside a club. He was fuelling up on the reefer I'd got him earlier, from a chap called Milton Mezzrow, who called himself the Mezz.

—The Reefer King, the Philosopher, the Mezz, the White Mayor of Harlem, the Link between the Races, the Man about Town, the Man that Hipped the World.

The man was an eejit.

I'd met him in an alley off Seventh Avenue, near the stage entrance to the Lafayette. Connie's Inn was near, and the Bandbox and the Cotton Club, and all the other clubs that mattered.

—How much? I asked Mezzrow.

—For you?

—No.

—For who?

I'd been told to tell him.

—Louis Armstrong.

He grinned.

—For Pops, man, they come cheap. Anything for the man.

—Ain't met him, Louis said now, in the dressing room. —Was told. Jewish boy desperate to be a brother, throw the gage at you for the chance to say he know a black player. Plays a bit himself, was told.

He stopped talking as he took in the smoke, and held. He was quiet now – he was getting quieter – but he grinned when he looked up and saw Zutty Singleton looking in at us. Looking in at Louis. And at me.

—Mister Arm-strong.

—Mister Single-ton.

—This here the place for the music, sir?

—This here that place.

He stepped in. He was older than Louis, and elegant, no effort. The black suit, like Louis's, had seen a lot of nights; it was worn to the wrong type of shininess, but it hung just right. The drumsticks in the breast pockets looked right too. He looked at me.

—Watcha know, Face?

I nodded.

—This here boy Irish? he asked Louis.

—Yes, sir. One of those Irish boys from Ireland.

—From Ireland genuine? Not like most of them Irishes, never been nearer to Ireland than Coney Island?

He was smiling, and he hid his head in his shoulders. He didn't like me.

I left the dressing room. I was tired of being the white boy. It was only starting to seep in: my purpose was my whiteness, and my willingness to walk it beside Louis. It was often a pleasure, but it was none of my doing. It was the age of ballyhoo but I was saying nothing. I knew what I was doing, and I'd known it from the start – *You're the white man puts his hand on that white man's shoulder* – but maybe I wanted my own trumpet.

This was Duke Ellington's gig – *Get out of the way; the Duke's coming* – but Ellington couldn't make the first show; he was stuck in Washington. Rockwell had wanted it that way, or others did – I never knew.

(—You've no stake in the country, man. Never had, never will.

I sat before Jack Dalton, the man who'd recruited me, as he confirmed what had taken me years to know.

—We needed trouble-makers and very soon now we'll have to be rid of them. And that, Henry, is all you are or ever were. A trouble-maker. The best in the business, mind.

I looked at the piece of paper on the desk in front of me. My name on it, my death sentence.)

It was different this time. Louis hadn't fooled me, or promised me anything. He'd sung to me, like Jack had – *The pride of all Gaels, was young Henry Smart* – but the song had been real, not just a couple of words and notes. He'd sung the song from start to end. *Cos Ireland's Gone Black Bottom Crazy Now-ow-ow.* And I had decided to join.

But I hadn't joined anything. I was in because of what I wasn't. I wasn't black, I wasn't a player or an agent or a manager or a shark or a friend of Al Capone's. I wasn't the things that the dangerous white men were. So I was useful – just as long as I wasn't anything. Just Louis Armstrong's white man.

I left them downstairs and strolled the edge of the dance floor, behind pillars and the little potted palm trees that bordered every club dance floor. I was looking for Rockwell. I was looking for Rita. The house band, seven sad men in suits that had seen much more action than Singleton's, were squeezed into the pit and backing a good-looking girl called Letha Hunter as she tore through *Sweet Georgia Brown*. She was giving it her lonely best.

Her face grew more desperate, the mouth got bigger and wouldn't shut. There was no sign yet of Rockwell, and no sign of Rita. It was early, not yet midnight. The tables were full, the floor half empty. They'd all come to hear the Duke Ellington Orchestra but, for one show only, they were going to get Louis Armstrong. The walls were black, paintings of black faces and instruments, but the dancers and diners were all white.

I looked at the boredom and tension, looked for class in the dance, saw none. I hadn't danced in a long time, and I wasn't going to now. The girl up on the stand managed to get to the last notes of *Sweet Georgia Brown*; the boys in the pit had given up before her. And then it happened.

I hadn't seen it. Louis and the other men had come onstage while Letha Hunter did her best. And now, before she gave in to temptation and ran, she was standing in front of the greatest band in the world. And, suddenly, she knew it. And so did everyone else, including the poor fuckers in the pit. Most of them crept out and went home, left their instruments dead on the floor. Only two of the braver ones stayed put to see history. And now I wanted to dance and there was Rita, over there, and there was Letha Hunter, and there was every woman in the house, now and coming in.

—GEE, BUT IT'S TOUGH TO BE BROKE, KID—

It rolled.

—IT'S NOT A JOKE, KID, IT'S A CURSE—

The words came from where she'd had them stored but they were quickly becoming her own.

—I CAN'T GIVE YOU ANYTHING BUT—

LOVE—

The song was hers.

—BAY-BEE—

She wasn't complaining, not with that gang behind her. She was boasting, promising, showing off. Every woman there was, now that there was real music in the house, and real men playing it, the real woman singing it.

—THAT'S THE ONLY THING I'VE PLENTY

OF—

BAY-BEE—

Louis was using the mute. He was riding her slowly, and she knew it. She looked, to watch him, and looked back.

—DREAM A WHILE—

SCHEME A—

WHILE—

She gasped the words, in total control. Fucking the man who was fucking her. Fucking every man in the place – I could feel her breath and fingers; I could feel her tongue on my neck.

—WE'RE SURE TO FIND—

HAPP-I-NESS—

The band crawled on, down on their wicked knees.

—AND I GUESS—

She knew they were there.

—ALL THOSE THINGS YOU'VE ALWAYS—

PINED—

FOR—

Her hands went onto her hips.

—GEE—

And stayed there.

—I'D LIKE TO SEE YOU LOOKING SWE-ELL—

BAY-BEE—

And there was Rita. Done up for the night. Bodies away, behind one of the palm trees. I could only see her head but I knew she was swaying.

—DIAMOND BRACELETS WOOLWORTH DOESN'T SELL—

I made the move.

—BAY-BEE—

I made my way to Rita.

—I CAN'T GIVE YOU ANYTHING—

The way before me was clear.

—BUT—

She knew I was there. She knew –

—LOVE.

And I'd forgotten about the betrothed. He was a big lad, a few inches shy of me. And wide. Stuck in the good suit, because he had to be. The collar was biting his neck, killing the poor cunt slowly. He looked as happy as a strangled man could look, and she liked his hand on her shoulder.

The music stopped and I walked the rest of the way. I nodded to Rita. She nodded back, and nodded at the stand. I looked, and saw Letha Hunter. She was wrapped in the folds of the electric blue hangings. Applause sent ripples across the curtain; her head, face emerged and she stepped forward, the satin still clinging to her shoulders. There were shrieks in the noise, and groans. I looked at Rita. She looked back, and I put that look behind my ear, for later.

Letha Hunter could have stayed. There was no one shoving her off the stand, and Louis had stepped well back. She could have stepped up to the microphone again. There were men there, willing her to do that. But she was bright; she knew to stop just before the right time to stop. In three long minutes, she'd learnt how to play the audience. She stepped back, and let the hangings take her. She disappeared, into the blue satin. (She stayed there, behind the drums, until the night was over. There were boxes and pillars blocking her way to the wings.)

I shook hands with the betrothed – a docker's hand; he worked in the Brooklyn Navy Yard – and I went to the back of the hall. The place was packed now, shaken by Letha Hunter and her invisible band. I stood back, watched, and waited for the band to be seen – not the band, the one and only man.

That song – *but love, bay-bee* – had been doing the rounds for a couple of years, in the clubs, matinées, intermissions, on the radios, all day, all night, and soon in cars, and on the phonographs. Neck and neck with *Makin' Whoopee*, that fuckin' tune was everywhere; it was fuckin' dreadful, and loved. And it would always be loved. Rockwell was right: the song was going to bring millions of men and women with it. They'd cling to it. Unlike the cars, the suits and the radios, that song, those songs, would never be obsolete. A few notes, a line, would always be enough. Rockwell knew – and Louis knew better. Because Louis actually liked the song. He liked the corn; he loved the sentimental. I'd seen his face as he listened to Rudy Vallee and Guy Lombardo. I'd seen him grin when *moon* met *June*. And Louis knew: the songs didn't matter a shite. It was the voice, the trumpet, the fingers, the brain and heart that owned the fingers. It was the man.

And, now, Louis came at the microphone. He ran at it, knees bent.

—Where's the Duke? shouted a red-faced cunt to my right, with his arm around his girl.

I tapped his shoulder.

—Wait.

He saw my eyes, and waited.

Louis came at the microphone, knees bent – did Louis see Groucho, or did Groucho see Louis? – he came at it from an angle, so he'd be seen in profile. It was funnier that way – he'd told me – and set them up for something that they weren't going to get.

The clown was going to kill them.

His face was an inch from the mike. He stopped.

—Good evening, ladies and gentleman.

It was just Louis. Gene Anderson, Fred Robinson, Zutty Singleton, Carroll Dickerson – they were the talented stiffs behind him. It was all there, in front of me. Louis was the man who was changing the world. He was going to smash through walls and play the greatest music ever played.

And he didn't need me.

—My name's Mis-ter Armstrong.

I found Rockwell, and stood myself where I could watch him.

—Stay away from the blues, Louie, Rockwell had warned him, earlier that day.

And there was Louis, playing the blues for a white crowd. *St Louis Blues* – a good song. And Jesus, fuck, it was the wildest, happiest blues ever played. The men up there with him were sweating through their only suits and Louis was flying, charging, stopping – moving back, and at the crowd, like they were new friends he was happy and very surprised to see. And, all the time, playing, eyes gleaming or closed, his body bent over, inches from the wet floor – the sweat became sparks in the air. And he was up now, defiant, catching and throwing the light. One eye open for the high, high notes, watching for their jump from the bell. It was trumpet, and nothing else. It was Louis Armstrong.

I looked at Rockwell. He looked happy; he wasn't hearing the blues. I looked at the waiters. They were trying to deliver food and drinks inside Louis's tempo. Most of them were failing. They'd never had to work at that speed before; there were golden splashes and chicken legs dropping over heads and shoulders.

Louis charged on, and on, the white handkerchief dancing with him. And then it stopped, a clumsy, final break – he pulled the horn from his mouth – and caught the band by surprise. I saw no anger. They were up there in the heat and adoration and they knew: it was the only way they were ever going to get it. They were stunned, gasping for any breath that they could find. They were being pawed from a distance by white folks.

And he was gone again. Same song. *Stay away from the blues, Louie.* And, this time, Louis sang. I looked again at Rockwell.

Louis's message was lost on him, or else had been very happily learnt.

   —SHE PULL THAT MAN 'ROUN'—
   BY HER APE-RON – STRING—

Rockwell was on the floor. He was throwing quarters, low, onto the bandstand, and filling willing hands around him with more. They rolled past Louis's feet, and against his shoes. Two hundred dollars' worth that night; they landed, rolled, and found their way to Louis.

She rubbed her hands in her apron.
   —You like the rest of America? she said.
   —Some of it, I said.
   —I missed anything?
   —Not really, I said.
   —See? she said. —I knew.
   —You're looking well, I told her.
She threw back the words with a flick of her hand.
   —You, she said.
I'd been creeping this way for weeks. I'd wanted to see her, to walk the streets, to catch a bit of what I'd left.

It all seemed different, the Carlmor. The walls, the tables, seating – all gone, all new. But, as I sat at the counter, my arms stopped just where they should have; the same counter. The walls were big yellow, but exactly where I'd left them. There were more tables, more booths, checked cloths instead of oilcloth. The radio was bright new, a polished cabinet, but Rudy Vallee still did the crooning.

It was good to be there.
   —You, she said. —Are different.

There was a stiff sitting three stools up, shovelling his meat-loaf, and a kid and his girl, knee to knee, at one of the tables, eating nothing but the smoke between them, and a man who'd cut himself shaving that morning, playing with sugar on his table-top, making shapes, his coffee dead beside him. I could hear his finger rub across the fabric.
   —It's quiet, I said.
   —Always, she shrugged.
   —What happened?
She shrugged.

—You brought the business to here, she said. —They followed you.

She was messing. I'd come this early afternoon, because it was the quiet between-time, when Hettie kept the shop alone. And because the hard men who owned the Lower East Side rarely came out at this time of day.

I looked out the window, to be sure that I was right.

The usual – it looked and felt like just the usual; nothing and no one lingering out there. This was daylight New York. All changing; nothing different.

I looked back at Hettie. I smiled.

—You, she said. —Are dressed like an African. Why?

That worried me. I hadn't noticed.

I looked again at the window.

Still the shifting same.

I hadn't noticed.

—Am I? I said.

—For sure, said Hettie. —Dressed like an African dresses when he ain't going to work. Sundays.

She wasn't a quiet woman. The stiff at the counter took his head out of the meatloaf and looked at me. He shrugged, and got back down to business.

I looked down at some of myself. I didn't see it.

—How d'you mean? I said.

She laughed.

Harlem was America; it was new every morning. I liked it there. I loved it. But I had to keep forgetting that I was the white man, strolling with the black man; stopping to talk with other black men, entering the barber shop with the black man, bringing my white man's hair in with me.

—See more temple than I used to see, O'Pops, said Louis.

We were sitting side by side.

—Fuck off, Louis.

Saying that to a black man.

He was looking across, at me in the mirror.

—Suits you, Pops.

—Fuck off, Louis.

Hearing the silence in the shop – the Elite Barbershop, on Seventh Avenue. Our hats were brushed back to new, his nails were manicured, while two of the barbers worked on our hair. And deeper in, in the poolroom behind the shop, the sudden, loud clack of the balls, and the absence of comment or curse.

I was tolerated, because I was with the black man.

But that wasn't it. White men weren't rare. Sammy, one of the barbers, was white, and he was working at Louis's head. White families lived in Harlem, and happily, among all the black. Harlem was warm. I was never afraid – the bad men with the gats were white. I could have lived there. (I thought about going back to Chicago, for Miss O'Shea and Saoirse. I even wrote, but I didn't post the letter.) I would have been Henry, not the white man or the Irish man. Henry, or Mister Smart. Henry Smart. I'd have been white but it wouldn't have mattered, much – just now and again. Stay close to the wall on the days when a black man had been shot by a white cop, when a black man was due for execution, on the days when it was bad to be black. Stay in till morning; use your cop-on; have a bit of sense. It was city living. It was what I'd grown up to survive and expect.

But I was with Louis, and that was why I was there. And that made me the white man. The ofay with Louis; Louis Armstrong's white man. I'd been happy being that man, while we were rushing, running, while I found him his water, and let him open his own doors, by walking there beside him.

He stood back and let me pull open the doors, but it didn't work in reverse. I didn't need Louis beside me to do it; it was just a fuckin' door. No one was going to step in my way.

I could have told them: I'm Irish, lads, one of the Empire's niggers, and I *know*.

But they'd have stood back, and maybe nodded.

—That so?

No one was going to ask about my fight for Irish freedom, and the freedom to open our own doors. Being Irish here just made me a cop's cousin, and the men and women here had history of their own they wanted to get away from. So I went ahead and did the expected; I pulled the door and stepped back for Louis. I was Louis Armstrong's white man. That was what I was – not his fault, not mine. I was Louis Armstrong's boy.

Hettie stopped laughing.

—Your tie, she said.

I looked down at it.

—The hat.

I looked at it, on the stool beside me.

—The shirt.

—Ah here.

Not his fault, not mine.

But only if I stopped. Innocence ended now. I had to decide, but I didn't want to. I'd been up to my knees in big history before, but this was a different history. Louis had killed no one, and the music had sent no one off to die. There was no blood on his hands or our shoes. No fault, his or mine.

But only if I stopped.

He didn't need me now, maybe never did. He had Rockwell. (He'd have Glaser.) It was 1929 – March, April, May. The Age was still roaring, and I was doing nothing.

I had to walk away from Louis.

—The jacket, she said.

I'd come downtown, carefully, a block a week, hoping not to be noticed. (I'd walked past Levine's, on Front Street; it was still Levine's, and still dry goods.) The suit was grey, the shirt was white, the collar was white-man tight. The tie was a tie, my boots were boots. And the hat was my pearl-grey fedora. I looked out the window again. Two good hats went by, on top of two men in grey suits.

I'd never seen a black man at the counter in Hettie's, and I'd never seen Hettie outside. Black men came in from the alley, straight into the kitchen, lugging crates and baskets. I'd never seen one in a suit or fedora. *Soil-blacked fingernails inches from my feet. Hanged men, mutilated rebel slaves, trapped forever in water that went nowhere.*

Louis had dressed me, and he'd dressed me white.

—Nothin' too colour, he'd told Mister Piper. —This here some serious white man.

I'd been strict on the shirts. The reds, the yellows, the big blues hadn't come out of their wrappers. A grey, four whites and a light, light blue.

I was wearing one of the whites.

253

—You're talking shite, Hettie, I told her.

—No, she said. —I know. Hungry?

—Yeah.

—See? I know what is.

She turned away and got to work on an American sandwich, one that would need a knife and a fork.

—The walk, she said, over her big shoulder.

—What walk?

—The way you walk. Into here.

—You didn't see me, I reminded her. —Your back was to me, like now.

—I seen, she said.

She turned to me again.

—You walk like an African.

She put the plate before me, and the tools beside the plate.

—Still eat like an Irishman?

—You tell me.

I got dug in.

—Yes, she said. —You are Henry.

I wiped my mouth and chin.

—Grand, I said.

—Say, said the stiff down the counter from me. —Can I have some coffee here?

—Why, yes, said Hettie; she sounded as near American as I'd ever heard her.

She filled his cup and didn't take long coming back.

—So, I said. —I walk like a Negro.

—Yes, she said. —Go, and come back to here.

I got up and walked to the door. I turned, and the stiff was there behind me. He stared, and mumbled as he passed.

—She's old enough to be your mother.

—She is my fuckin' mother, I told him.

I went back across to Hettie. She watched.

—Loose, she said.

She rolled her shoulders, as if they'd been stiff.

—You move loose, she said. —Like an African.

That was fine. I didn't walk like an Irishman. I was getting there, and I hadn't even noticed. The music had gotten right into me and I'd become a walking American.

I sat down again.

I was still worried. My walk might have been too American,

too new, too defiant and bright. I'd have to be careful. I'd spent most of my life trying not to be noticed, and failing.

—D'you see Mildred these days? I asked.

—Some, she said. —Not many times.

—She's okay?

She shrugged.

—Yes.

Mildred had tried to kill me but that seemed like a long time ago, and I wasn't dead.

—Does she look good? I asked.

—Better than her momma, said Hettie.

—Ah now.

—She looks good, Hettie nodded.

She rubbed her cheeks.

—The colour, she said.

—Good.

—She lives clean. Has a child.

—Boy or girl?

—Girl.

—That's good.

She shrugged.

I nodded at the door behind her.

—Did you keep my room for me, Hettie?

—*My* room.

—Is it still there?

—You see the door.

—Is the room still behind it?

—I think so.

—Where's your husband?

—Behind some other door.

—Gone?

She shrugged.

—Sometimes, she said. —Bums ever gone? He's goes, he comes back.

—Can I look inside?

She shrugged.

—Old times' sake? she said.

—I don't believe in it.

—You are too young.

—No, I said.

—Yes.

—I'm like you, Hettie. You don't look back either.

She nodded.

—Sometimes, she said. —I am old. Sometimes the old days are near. And today is not today. I am in a day many years ago.

—You're not old, Hettie.

She flicked the words away.

—Throw that one in the bowl, she said.

She opened the door. I stood up from the counter and followed her.

The room hadn't changed. It was too small for real change, still tiny and fat with hot air. It was late afternoon, and daylight was long gone from the airshaft. It was dark in the room, although very bright behind me. It wasn't just the dark; it was the dirt in the air outside, on the window glass, the smoke and coal gas. Sweat started to run from my head and back.

—See?

—The same.

Her clothes at the end of the bed. An apron, a stocking.

It was good to be—

Home.

She stepped past me, out to the restaurant. I watched her walk – there was nothing slow, nothing stooped or old – to the door. She lifted the sign and turned it, Closed.

I went to the bed. I put my fingers, my hand under the mattress, and felt it. The wallet. And the calfskin belt, the money belt I'd worn around my waist. Both there. The photograph and the money. My fingers, I now knew, had always expected to touch them.

—You found.

Hettie was behind me.

—Yeah.

—And you are going now?

—No.

I looked at her.

—I'll stay a while.

She shrugged, and smiled.

—Up to you.

I left them under the mattress.

—Thanks for minding them for me.

—Too lazy to lift the mattress.

She sat back on the bed. She laughed as it creaked. She let

her shoes drop to the boards. I sat; I lay back. My head found her shoulder.

—Boots.

I sat up, unlaced and took them off. I lay back down again.

He played one night to white men in the Bronx, came back to Harlem and was king by dawn, before he hit the scratcher. Harlem had room for lots of kings. Every instrument had its king, every endeavour and crime. Sex, the con and aviation – barnstormers, wing-walkers, stunters – there were kings and queens of them all in Harlem. There was the Duke, some sheikhs, and a blockful of princes. Dance, hair and literature – they all had their shifting royalty. Morning, early, the milkman was Count of the Moo-Juice. Midday, late into the night, a royal parade, never a commoner in sight. This wasn't Dublin. For the first time in my life, I was ordinary. The only thing going for me was my colour.

I could carry a suit, I had the shoulders – and I knew I was rolling them, now that Hettie had shown me – and the blue eyes that turned push to pull and held up strong women, even as they decided to continue on home.

—Lord! What are they?

Blue eyes were rare in Harlem; eyes like mine were news that no girl wanted to share.

I had to be careful.

—I swear, I'll tear your eyes out if you start making those oogle eyes at my big man.

—What do I care, big bitch?

I cared, but I wasn't the big man they were talking about. It was Zutty Singleton or Carroll Dickerson or Fred Robinson – and Earl Hines was in town, some of Jelly Roll Morton's Red Hot Peppers, and Don Redman came and went, and Johnny St Cyr – and Louis. The big man was, most often, Louis.

Louis was the King. The silver bulbs popped when he walked through doors, and he filled the hush that went before him. The sharp kids had added Louis's white handkerchief to their uniforms. They carried them, mopped brows that didn't need mopping. Louis was everywhere. He let it be known – he told a woman – that his birthday was on the way. The 4th of July.

—Is it really your birthday? I asked him.

—Is now.

—What year?

—Why, 1900, Smoked. Why you have to ask?

Already the man of the century, muscling in on the great nation's birthday. He knew: there was plenty of room.

—1901, he whispered into my ear.

He was sitting beside me, in a hot July room above Lenox Avenue. He'd a dancing girl on one knee and a well-heeled flapper on the other. He was watching them kiss.

—We're the same age, I said.

The girls were his birthday present, from – I didn't know then – a man I'd nearly met before. Outside, the firecrackers bit and hopped.

—Real birthday the 4th of August, he whispered.

He patted the girls.

—Couldn't wait.

The next time I went to the alley off Seventh Avenue Mezzrow knew who I was buying for.

—Uh uh, he said.

—What? I said.

I got set to stand on him.

—I'll deliver it myself, he said.

I shrugged, fine, and walked away. I wasn't going to bring him.

He followed me – I could hear him – right back to Wellman Braud's flat. I left him outside on the steps – the *stoop* – and went up the stone stairway to Louis. He sighed, stood up and went down to get Mezzrow and his merchandise.

I heard them coming back up.

I heard Mezzrow.

—Man, when this tea grabs your glands, you got time on your hands.

I left them to it, but I had to be careful. Louis always wanted me near, especially when he was dealing with a white man. And Mezzrow, God love him, was pale. That was fine. I was only a shut door away. But I was riding Louis's that-day girl, the girl who'd brought herself home with him the night before. That was fine too; Louis didn't mind. Louis had the women he loved, Lil, Alpha, and Louis had the women he liked. And this was one of the women he liked.

I pulled back the curtain and opened the window. There was a good chunk of night above the street. I couldn't see stars but they were up there.

She was sitting up on the bed. She watched me walking back. She smiled, but not sure why. The bed was on castors. I pulled it nearer. Wellman Braud, its owner, was away, touring with Jelly Roll Morton. I kicked a rug out from under one of the wheels, and the bed swam over the boards. I jumped on as it stopped, a foot from the open window.

—My my.

She sat on me.

—Who this for?

She looked out the window.

—My brother.

—He out there?

—Yeah.

She stayed up there. She smiled at me, and at the window.

—He like you?

—Not really.

—Eyes blue?

—I don't know.

—Don't know?

—I never looked.

—Like to meet him.

—Some day.

I put my hands on her waist, and that was that; she fucked for my dead brother and nearly sent me up there to him. She bucked and messed and, while I took back the boss-place and pulled her onto her back, Louis was next door with Mezzrow, talking gage, sampling gage, negotiating and philosophising gage.

I had to be careful.

She was a black woman.

—Blacker the berry, O'Pops.

I could hear Louis and Mezzrow beyond the wall.

—I'll take six of them muggles, Pops.

—Good as did, Pops.

Louis was giving the dealer what he wanted, an audience and a dollar. Mezzrow couldn't believe his luck; I could hear it through the wall. He was sitting with the King, watching him suck in his merchandise. He had the King's dollar and company.

I had to be careful.

The bed was right under the window now. My forehead was on the sill.

It wasn't Louis. He was listening and laughing, looking at

259

Mezzrow trying not to hear. It wasn't Louis I'd have to be careful about.

—How many peoples in this big world, Smoked?

—I don't know. Millions.

—Billions, I say.

—Yeah.

—And listen here, Smoked. Half of them billions is women. And half of billions still billions.

It wasn't Louis.

She got onto her knees and grabbed the sill.

—Introduce me to your brother.

It was the rest. It was the world out there.

—Which window is he at?

A white man fucking a black girl. In Harlem. In an open window. No money changing hands. In an open window, three floors off the street.

I'd have to be careful.

—Are you fuckin' watching!

—Tell him, daddy.

The next time I saw Mezzrow he was dressed like Louis; the Oxford grey double-breasted suit; the big knot in his tie; silk scarf, lisle socks, the hanky. And kids in torn overalls found the odds to buy, or the speed and wit to rob, a white hanky. They were waving the things all over Harlem. Louis was the latest.

Louis knew it.

—What it is, he told me, —is ambition. New York ambition. It's different here. The music isn't as good. It's slick and orchestrated. It's *good*. The Duke is good. But it ain't New Orleans and it ain't even Chicago. It ain't new-born. It's what happens *after*. It's organised. Now—

He stopped for a while. A hand held the word in the air while he inhaled. We were in another dressing room. Connie's Inn, one of Harlem's big ones. Just the two of us – I thought. Louis liked to be on time, in charge, looking at the door as others arrived.

He let go.

—I like that, he said. —The organising. No reason why wild music can't be organised. I like nice strings and the rest of that nice shit. I like that Guy Lombardo. No nicer pipes this side of heaven. But me now, I'm wild. Some of the white types and the black want-to-be-white types call me primitive. Fuck them. I sound

260

wild because I want to sound wild. No reason why the cats giving out the wild music can't be organised.

—The union?

—Fuck the union. We got our own coloured local. Local 802. Know what that is? Black tick in a white dog's back. Fuck the local. See, that's what I like about here. It ain't local. There's ambition here. For the music. Publishing, records. Getting it out there. And white boys tumbling over themselves to get at it. Nice Mister Rockwell, and all of them other nice gents. Trying to get their slice, that don't rightly belong to them. But it's scratch mine, I'll scratch yours. I know that. I'll do my scratching, and take some. I got the back.

He scratched it now.

—Heh, heh. All the best end up here, Smoked. Eventually they do. They roll right in. The best of the good guys and the bad guys, all up for each other. And the nice girls too. They all here or on their way. I play here, in this Connie's, on a corner in Harlem, but I'll get myself heard all over the world. In Africa. In Ireland, O'Pops. Because I'm here, in New York City.

He was talking more than he had in a long time. He was talking to me.

—Know what I want, Smoked? Know what I really want?

—What?

—I want to be known. I want to deserve that.

—Fair enough, I said. —You do deserve it.

—Nice to hear you saying that.

His lungs were full again. He smiled.

—Ireland? I said.

He exhaled.

—Yeah yeah, he said. —Why not?

He was right; I knew he was. He'd get there; he was there already.

—Will you write a song for me, Louis?

—Why, yes, O'Pops. Lay down the specifications.

—It's for a woman.

—Nice. All the best songs. In Ireland?

—Yeah.

—Name on her?

—Annie.

—Nice.

—Piano Annie.

—Ha ha. A friend of yours.

—Yeah.

—Good friend?

—I murdered her husband.

—My my, said Louis. —That as good as it get.

He put his head right back, and laughed.

It's still out there; you've heard it.

—ANN-IE—

SITTING ON HER FAN-NY—

They recorded *Black and Blue* that day as well, and *Sweet Savannah Sue*. The 22nd of July, 1929.

—SHE PLAY THAT NICE PIAN-EE—

JUST FOR ME-EE—

Louis Armstrong and His Orchestra. A few months before, the same men had been called Carroll Dickerson and His Orchestra.

—WHAT A THRILL—

FIT MY BILL—

WALKING UP TO SUMMERHILL—

It's OKeh 40341.

—TO SEE—

ANN-IE—

PIANO ANN-IE—

I told Louis what a fanny was on the other side of the Atlantic.

—Glad you told me, Smoked. Good to know these things in advance.

—HEN-RY –

LIVIN' OFF THE MEM-RY—

And, somewhere between recording and pressing, our names fell off the credit and Rockwell became the composer.

—THINKIN' OF HIS ANN-IE—

HE DANCE DOWN BROADWAY—

It was too late – I was gone – before I knew.

—HE HEAR HER PIAN-EE—

HE THINKIN' OF HER—

FAN-NY—

I listened to the first take and, for the first time since I'd left, I wanted Dublin.

—EVEN THINKIN' OF HIS GRAN-NY—

SAY HELLO TO ANN-IE—

262

It wasn't one of the best. But, eleven years after I'd promised it, I'd sent the letter to Annie.

(—Are you crying, Annie?

—No.

She lives in a mansion of aching hearts. She been singing for me. *She's one of the restless throng.*

—Was that one of the American songs?

—I want to go there, she said. —I could do things there.

She turned to face me.

—I want to own a piano, Henry.

And she turned away again.

—Why don't you go then?

—Because he wants to die for Ireland.

—He?

—I'm married, remember.

—I thought you were talking about me for a minute.

—I don't care whether you die or not.

—Ah, you do.

—No, I don't, she said.

And I believed her.

—Just remember that letter, she said.

—I will, I said. —Don't worry.

—I'm not worried.

—Anyway, Annie, I said. —I'll be back soon.

—No, you won't.

—I will, Annie.

She shrugged my hand off her hip.

—You won't.

—I will, I said. —I swear.

But she was right. I never did see Annie again.)

—THINKIN' OF HIS ANN-IE—

HE DANCE DOWN BROADWAY—

She'd still have her gramophone. It would have been the last thing to go, the last thing she'd have pawned. I'd seen her dust and polish it, and position it near the window, to grab any light that was going. I'd given it to her; I'd stolen it, bit by bit. In the months after Easter Week, the good months before I became a rebel again. Hard work, and home to Annie. Good months measured in gramophone parts. She only played American songs – *climb upon my knee, Sonny Boy.* The months before her dead husband came home from the war and I shot him twice in the head. Not because I wanted Annie, but because I'd been told to.

I was given a piece of paper. His name on it.

(—You know what to do.

—Yes.

—I know you do.)

I put the gun to the back of his head and shot him. Obeying orders. I was a soldier. *Shot as a traitor and a spy*. His name was on a piece of paper, and I'd killed him.

I stood in the studio. Another hot day, and I listened to Louis.

—THINKIN' OF HIS ANN-IE—

She'd know it was me. She'd laugh. She hadn't made it to America, but I had. She'd laugh. *The bastard, the prick*. Her letter from America, sung to her by Louis Armstrong. She'd laugh at the open window. She'd know.

—HE DANCE DOWN BROADWAY—

I decided it then. I was going back. Louis didn't need me. He had Rockwell; he knew how to use him. I was just hanging around.

I wanted to walk through Dublin. And I'd bring America with me. The strut, the size, the sheet nice and clean. I'd bring home the new world; I'd sell it on the streets of Dublin.

—WHAT A THRILL—

FIT MY BILL—

WALKING UP TO SUMMERHILL—

It was there, in the studio, clear as the notes that Louis sent at me – the decision. I was itching, and happy. I'd get back to Chicago first. I could see, feel, the three of us. Leaving, and arriving. I'd left Dublin many times but I'd never arrived. I'd always crept back in, on a stolen bike, in someone else's threads, with someone else's name. A travelling salesman, a happy father, the second son of a big, big farmer. These men and more men, I'd crept into Dublin as all of them. But never as me. Henry Smart had never gone home.

He was now, though. Going home. Henry S. Smart. Henry the Yank.

—SHE PLAY THAT NICE PIAN-EE—

JUST FOR ME-MOI-OH-MEE—

I could see myself with Saoirse; I could feel her hand in mine. I could hear the tram bells, and I could hear the shouts, the accent that she'd know was mine. I could hear our feet, good Yank leather on the cobbles. I'd stroll through Dublin for the first time in my life. No more running away or chasing. I'd stroll through Dublin with my daughter, and my wife.

264

I let myself say it.
—Dublin.
That was it.

—Your house?

She put her finger to the wall above the people in the photograph. Me, Miss, Ivan, Ivan's cousin.

—No, I said. —I never had a house.

—Boo hoo, my Henry.

She dropped her head back to the pillow. Flour stayed there, where she'd been sitting. I blew, but it didn't stray far.

—The wife?

—Yes.

—Pretty.

—Yeah.

—Older than you.

—Yeah.

—Not as old as me.

—Jaysis, no.

She laughed.

—Where is she?

—Chicago.

—Yes? And him?

—Ivan the Terrible.

She laughed again.

—Another.

—Same one, I said.

—No, she said. —Every country has the Ivan. Terrible here, terrible there.

She held the photograph above us for quite a while; her arms never drifted or shook.

—Where is he?

—Ireland.

—And the sad one?

She was pointing to Ivan's cousin.

—I don't know her name.

—Don't remember?

—Never knew.

—You knew.

—No, I didn't.

—Yes, she said. —You knew. You don't remember that you knew.
I leaned across and pointed at Miss O'Shea.
—But I don't even know her name and she's my—
—Yeah, yeah, you tell me all before. I know the story. Miss O
bla bla bla. So.
She put the photograph onto my chest.
—You will go home.
—Yeah.
—You never can go home. No such place.
—I know.
—No, she said.
—Yes, I said. —I know. It won't be the same.
—And you.
—I know.
—You won't be the same.
—I know. If it was the same, I wouldn't be going back.
—And she?
—Which?
—Which. Miss O bla bla. Your wife.
—She wants to go as well.
She said nothing.
—She hates it here.
—She will want it to be the same? There?
—Yeah.
—Bon voyage, my Henry.

He was in Connie's Inn, making it his, giving it the zip that
Ellington gave the Cotton Club.
—JUST BECAUSE MY COLOUR SHADING—
DIFFERENT MAY—
BE—
And, after a shave and sometimes sleep, recording as often as
Rockwell could arrange it.
—THAT WHY THEY CALL ME—
OH BABY—
For Rockwell, for himself.
—I give Mister Rockwell the riff, said Louis. —Watch.
He stood up and walked across the studio floor, and back to
me. The horn was under his arm, a happy man on his way home
from work.

266

—That the riff, Smoked. The walk. That the part that Mister Rockwell interested in. Every song have it.

He walked away.

—That, why, they, call, me. The riff, see? I, can't, give, you, any, thing, but, love, bay, bah, bah, bah, bee. All the same. Some better than others, that true. But back to the point, Pops. The riff is the walk. The distance here to there.

Back he came, across the silent studio floor.

—Up, a, lay-zee, rih, vuh.

He stopped, and lifted a finger.

—Now, see here. You watch me now while I perform the break.

He walked away, brought his arse from side to side, skipped, hopped, gave it the Charlie Chaplin. He turned, came back, knees bent, the trumpet a walking stick, a head on him like the happiest fuckin' eejit in the world. Straight up, and into my face.

—That the break, Smoked. My own things. The nice surprises. They my own.

—THAT WHY THEY CALL ME—

—They go on top of the riff. And that's the jazz. The song don't matter. It the *how* that matter, not the *what*. Mister Rockwell happy. I'm happy. All happy together.

—You're a signifyin' African, Mister Armstrong, said Zutty Singleton, from across the room.

—That right, Mister Singleton. We *all* signifyin' Africans here.

It was the time for me to go.

—THAT WHY THEY CALL ME—

Connie's Inn was one of the hot ones. I shouldn't have been there. The talent was black; the suits were Italian. The actors and actresses, the writers and song men, their rich hangers-on, they gave the place its gloss. Louis would look from the stage and see big faces every night. Pickford, Fairbanks – I sat beside the fucker – Berlin, and Fitzgerald. All there to see and hear him. Durante, Keeler, Gershwin, Marx. He saw money floating in the music, turning and whirling.

But it wasn't the money.

—THAT WHY THEY CALL ME—

He saw deals done, eyes meet; he saw sex promised, taken, the best and the most notorious; he saw them all soak and spark in his music.

In his music.

—THAT WHY—

—THEY—

He moved and they moved with him.

—CALL ME—

Because he told them to.

He closed his eyes and opened one, and knew they loved it, every move and note.

—OH BABY—

The grin, the grimace, knees bent, the eyes.

—THEY CALL ME—

He stood suddenly still, and held a note, and held it. They knew he'd stop. He held, eyes closed – they knew, they knew. He held it. Stop and don't stop, stop and don't – they watched his death. They groaned, they felt themselves. They screamed – stop, Louis stop. He held the note.

—Fuck you!

A roar, one night, of absolute surrender. He held the note, forever.

—Fuck you!

A movie actor, a big face, about to be killed by the talkies. His little lad's roar shot up at Louis.

—Fuck you!

And stop! Louis pulled the thing from his lips and he was charging across the stand.

They watched, they roared.

—THAT WHY—

Bang up to the mike.

—THAT WHAH—

They stood, they roared.

—THEY CALL ME—

Blood met sweat – they saw it.

—THAT WHY—

He wiped his mouth – they saw it.

—THEY CALL ME—

He shook his head; blood hit the air and hit the lights.

—SHINE.

Blood hit a bulb and it exploded.

He'd done it. A minstrel song, a bad song, made glorious, defiant. Three or four, five times a night. Every night, and after. He never stopped.

He bowed and smiled and bowed again and wiped his mouth and turned away – a second to himself; the grin fell off – I saw it. He looked over his shoulder, the teeth, the eyes. Dazed and in control. In big pain and loving every second.

They came up to Harlem for Louis. They came to New York for Louis. They came from Europe and South America, from China and the deepest east. To see for themselves. The latest new. The latest and the newest. And they got more. They knew it, the second his force hit them.

—Oh my God!

—Fuck you!

It would never be the same again.

They felt torn away and raw, skinless, born again. Dropped, broke and bollock naked, into a very foreign world. They gasped, they drowned.

But no, they didn't. The smile, the teeth grabbed and pulled them up. Every time. His gums bled, his lips were swollen, pushed up to the salt-block of agony.

He smiled.

—Thank you, lay-dies and gentlemen.

White ladies and gentlemen.

They felt good.

Sweat rolled over his top lip. He hid the pain behind his white handkerchief.

They loved this black man. They clapped. They loved all black men.

—Now. We going to play for you. One of the old songs. Six months old, and it's called *Dinah. Dinah.* One two three.

It was grand until he stopped. So he didn't. He charged from one song to the next, he charged across the stage, on and off the stage. Out the door, in another.

The great and the good.

Gilbert, Gish, Van Vechten, Ruth.

He played to whites for money, to blacks for nothing, later, in Barron's, Rockland Palace, the Bucket of Blood. (Every place had a Bucket of Blood.)

He charged.

Rent parties, street corners. He took himself everywhere.

I tried to tell him. I was going. I ran after him, and waited for the chance.

Jolson, McCormack, Cunard, and O'Neill.

The great and the good. The bad and the—

—Fuck me.

Dutch Schultz.

I watched the door closing, Schultz's fingers on the handle, closing slowly, Schultz's eyes still there, the door closing, one eye, one bad, bad fuckin' eye – shut.

—Jesus.

I sat down.

—What the matter, Smoked? said Louis.

Schultz had emptied the dressing room and, now that he'd gone, it stayed that way. We were alone.

I saw Louis's handkerchief in front of me. I took it – it was wet – and wiped my brow and face. I held it out for him, giving it back, but he had a new one. He was already wiping his own face.

—You got *me* worried, Smoked.

—It's okay, I said. —I'm fine.

I looked at my legs. They weren't shaking.

—That was Dutch Schultz, I said.

—Certainly was.

—Why's he here? I said.

—Why they all here, Pops? he said.

—To see you.

—Yah yah.

He polished the trumpet with a towel.

—Got it shining like a nice woman's leg.

He put a finger on the lucky bullet mark. He'd be going on again, in a minute. I could hear the gathering feet outside.

—Also, he said. —Why all those types like Mister Schultz come here and hereabouts?

—The women.

—That too, the chippies. But not what I had in mind, Pops. Nay nay.

—What then?

—Mister Schultz is the silent partner. I think that mean he owns the joint.

—Fuck.

—Why fuck?

—I killed some pigeons, Louis.

—All this killing you done, Pops. Some what?

—Pigeons.

—The birds.

—The birds.

—Mister Schultz's pigeons?

270

—Not exactly, I said. —A friend of his.

—Friend.

—Owney Madden.

—That some fucking friend, Smoked. You eat those birds?

—No.

—Then why?

—It's a long story.

—He know?

—Probably. It was a big deal. There was a lot of pigeons. So Madden probably told him, and they'd have been looking for me for a while. But we never met.

—And Mister Madden? Meet him?

—No.

—That good. When did you not meet these nice gents?

I thought it out.

—Four or five years ago, I said.

—Didn't pay you much never-mind just now, said Louis.

That was true.

—Out, Schultz had said when he'd walked in, and the room had emptied, fast. But he hadn't said anything when I stayed put with Louis. I didn't know who he was, just that he was one of the men that mattered; I could see that. I said nothing. He looked at me, but he looked at the mirrors too. Rockwell must have told him I'd be there, Louis's boy. I'd been expected, but unknown. He hadn't nodded to me, or spoken. He'd looked at me, at Louis.

—Great show, Louie, said the tough guy.

—Why, thank you, Pops, said Louis. —Gimme some skin.

He took Schultz's hand and shook it big.

—Enjoy your birthday present? said Schultz.

—Sure did, said Louis. —Took some unwrapping.

They laughed, and Schultz took back his hand. He held his hat, turned it in his fingers. He smiled at Louis, almost shy. There was a kid inside the savage. The smile was bad but the eyes were lit and happy.

—We see your picture in the *Daily News* all the time, Mister Schultz, said Louis.

I knew now who was in the room with us.

—Yeah, said Schultz. —People are starting to bug me for my autograph.

—Got yourself a good pen? said Louis.

271

—Yeah.

—That's all you need.

Schultz squirmed. He wasn't used to nice men. He smiled again, and turned his hat.

A hand outside hit the door.

—Stay out, said Schultz.

He was in charge again, owner and breaker.

—Yeah, well, he said. —Keep it up, yeah.

—Sure will.

Schultz shut the door and I sat down.

—He owns this fuckin' place, I said.

—Now, Smoked, said Louis. —They own all the places. You know that.

—But we got out of Chicago because of the Italians.

—Mister Schultz is not Italian, said Louis. —He's Jewish.

Louis wore a silver Star of David under his shirt. Some family in New Orleans had been good to him, when he was a kid and heading for trouble. *Every night you'll hear her croon, a Russian lullaby.* They'd given him a job or something, and the odds to buy his first cornet. *Just a little plaintive tune, when a baby starts to cry.* Louis had big time for Jews.

He lit up a reefer.

—I'm Jewish too, Smoked, he said. —Mister Schultz know that.

I looked. He was smiling.

—What'll we do? I said.

What would *I* do?

He exhaled.

—We stay put.

No.

—We stay here. We got Mister Rockwell here. He's good; he fits me. We're cutting all those nice records. We got Mister Schultz. He likes me. He likes his music hot. He's the silent partner but don't mean the entertainment have to be. Mister Schultz is proud to have me here.

A running knock on the door.

—One minute, Louis!

—Worried, Smoked?

—No, I said. —Not really.

I was going.

—Anyway, I didn't really kill the pigeons. I was just there.

—At the wrong time.

272

—Yeah.

—Same old story. Happen to me too, though I don't recall pigeons or any shooting.

He went back up for the second show.

I'd finally met one of the big-shots. But he hadn't met me. He hadn't thought me worth meeting – I thought. But I couldn't be sure. I couldn't ever be sure.

It was fine, for now.

But.

I could hear Louis now, killing himself all over again.

—OHHH—

WHEN YOU'RE SMILIN'—

Did Johnny No like jazz?

—WHEN YOU'RE SMI-SMILIN'—

Would he come uptown to see Louis? Would he come with his boss, Lepke, and sit with Schultz and Madden? And would Henry Glick be on the premises when they called?

—THE WHOLE WORLD SMILE WITH—

I was going.

But I wasn't running. I was leaving. I was going home. I'd walk away, smiling, after I'd shaken Louis's hand and said, So long, Louis, see you in Dublin.

The wedding dress, the brooch, the glowing hair, the folds and tears, and – I noticed for the first time – Hettie's floury fingerprints. I saw them eaten, disappear; I smelled them bake.

Then he shot me.

It was her.

It was the hat.

Her back was to me, at the open window, haloed by the sun that baked the wall across the street.

She turned, and I was right. It was Fast Olaf's half-sister and she was still wearing my fuckin' fedora.

She didn't know me; nothing went across her face. I didn't know her. I looked at Rita and smiled.

—Hi.

The first and only time I ever said it.

—Hi, said Rita.

She knew. She saw my eyes lock on hers, my determination not to notice the half-sister. Rita knew I wasn't looking at her.

—Is Rockwell inside? I asked.

I smiled.

—No, said Rita. —Mister Rockwell is not inside.

She smiled.

—Where is he?

—Elsewhere, said Rita.

—One of my favourite places, said the half-sister.

—When'll he be back? I asked.

—I don't recall you making an appointment, said Rita.

She didn't laugh, the half-sister, but I heard her.

—It's Louis business, I said.

It wasn't. I knew where Rockwell was and I knew how long he'd be there.

I parked my arse on Rita's desk, and regretted it, immediately; I was a fuckin' eejit.

I could hear the half-sister laughing.

I'd come up here for a woman and, instead, I'd found two. *Every day, in ev-ery way.* What the fuck was wrong with me? The old Henry would have whooped. Two cranky women – it wouldn't have mattered a fuck.

I stood up.

—Nice hat, said the half-sister.

—And still on his head, said Rita. —They teach you manners where you came from?

I should have left, I should have turned and walked out. It would have worked. They'd have followed me, one of them, both; it didn't matter.

I should have kept walking.

But the half-sister did the walking. Straight past me, her shoulder touched my sleeve, the slightest tug. She stopped at the door, and turned. The sunlight was still clinging to her. She talked to Rita; I was right in front of her.

—Tell Brother Rockwell he knows where to find me.

—Will do.

—Tell him I'll wait one day and one day only.

—Will do.

I was there, right in front of her.

—Been a pleasure, sister, she said, and she'd gone. I could hear her shoes on the stairs.

274

—Who was that? I asked.

—That, said Rita, —was Florence Grattan-McKendrick. Sister Florence Grattan-McKendrick.

—Sister?

—Sister Flow.

—She's not a fuckin' nun.

—That's right, said Rita. —She is not a fucking nun.

Rita was blushing and furious. I could feel her heat. It suited her.

I should have stayed.

—Good luck.

I took the steps four at a time, and made the street in time to see bewildered-looking men coming from the left. (I never got used to the east or west fuckology.) I went that way and the men kept coming at me. The sidewalk was full and flowing; big-boned Yanks came between me and the half-sister. I couldn't see her ahead. The bewildered men kept passing, but fewer of them – I was losing her. I pushed through a herd of scared and sweating out-of-towners. I was sweating myself, stupidly desperate. Rockwell could have told me where to find her. I knew, but I was more and more a drowning man, smaller, and stupid, and something was gone.

Stop.

Something I'd lost, something I'd let go.

I pushed, I shoved. I looked, but no one stepped out of my way.

I needed a gun.

Stop.

That was it. I wanted the old me back. I wanted to be Henry Smart. I wanted a gun and a cause. I wanted to take action, get things done, see them done with a well-aimed stare. I wanted to fuck Florence Grattan-Half-Sister-McKendrick. And Rita. And those fat girls here who wouldn't step back and let the fine man pass. And that woman in the diner window. I wanted them all and, years ago, they'd wanted me. I wanted the old days and a fuckin' gun. A gun and a cause. When women stepped back and admired.

One of the fat girls pushed back.

—Who'ya pushin'?

I hit the glass hard and the woman in the window took my collision like she'd been expecting me. She didn't blink and the small smile didn't shift or quiver. Her pearl-grey hat was on the table.

I found the door and pulled.

I got to the table. She was still looking out the window.

She was still there, the same woman, but she'd changed. She'd added to herself. I had it before I sat down: she was still a doll but she'd become a guy as well. It was the clothes. That wasn't the suit of a moll or a wife with taste and money. She'd added authority to the package. She was the boss these days. It was the hair, the hat – my hat. It was the four or five years; she'd done things with them.

I slid into the bench, in front of her.

—My hat, I said.

—How many heads you got?

I put mine beside hers.

—Sweet, she said.

—So, I said. —Florence.

—Sometimes.

Her face gave nothing.

—How have you been?

—Oh, fine.

She blew her smoke across my shoulder.

—You?

—Fine, I said. —Grand. I got out of town alive that time.

—Knew you'd make it.

There was a waitress now, flat-footed, weepy; it had been a long day.

—Coffee, said the half-sister. —You?

—Yeah.

—Two.

She put her hand on the waitress's as the check was slid across the oilcloth. It wasn't a grab; she held the hand gently and looked at the waitress.

—It will come to pass as you would have it come to pass, said the half-sister.

She let go of the hand but the waitress didn't move.

—You got any of them cream-filled, big cake affairs we're not supposed to eat?

—Yes.

—I'll have a couple of them, said the half-sister.

She tapped the check and it glided back to the waitress. She added the items; her pencil hand was shaking.

—Thank you, she said, and was gone. I watched her move. The day was suddenly young again.

—Still at it, I said.

—It's the thing.

I wanted to hug her; the man she'd fucked for nothing. I sat up. She noticed.

—See? she said. —It works. All I said was, It's the thing. And you're sitting up like a rabbit.

She crushed the cigarette into the ashtray.

—Say what they want to hear, do what they want to see. They love you for it.

She lit a new smoke.

—I been refining it.

—Ev-ery day.

She pulled on the cigarette, and let it go – three rings and, I swear, an arrow.

—Left that one far behind, she said.

The waitress was back, with two mugs.

—I told him to put fresh cream in your cakes.

—Good for you, sister. Right up to your chin.

The waitress scampered off.

The half-sister sat back. She put an elbow on the back-rest behind her, and I saw: she was wearing a waistcoat – a Yank vest – and, under it, braces. Wide Clarence Darrow suspenders, lavender.

—Ev-ery minute, she said. —Every hour and day and ev-ery fucking week. And none of the better and better bullsh.

The waitress was back.

—I'm good enough already. I cannot get any better.

The waitress slid the plate across to the half-sister.

The cakes were like two potatoes, huge and bursting. The cream was too white and piled four inches over the pastry. The half-sister ran a long finger across the cream and brought it to her mouth.

I wasn't the only man watching.

She took her finger from her mouth.

—Delish, she said. —Thank you, sister.

She took her spoon and started shovelling the cream.

—See what I'm up to here?

—You're eating two big cakes.

—Observant. But what I'm really doing, what's that?

I thought about it.

—You still got that kinda cute look when you're thinking, she said.

277

She was already down to the pastry. She'd done it without bending to the plate.

—So, got an answer for me?

—You're delivering some sort of message.

—Everything's a message. Your shoe rubbing my leg there. That's a message I'm choosing to ignore. So, what's the message? Give me the low-down.

She held the back of the spoon in front of her mouth and brought it down to the tip of her tongue.

—You're trying to distract me, I said.

—Not, she said. —Licking the spoon is what I'm doing. But you're right, only it ain't you I'm trying to distract. And succeeding too.

—Another lesson.

She nodded.

Her eyes weren't as big as they used to be. The eyes used to sit back, lie back and drag you with them – fuck me, fuck me. Now they were piercing things, boring right in, needling – fuck you – and still gorgeous.

—So?

—Because you can.

—More.

—You can eat those cakes if you want. They do you no bad. You can put away as much cream as you want and you're still beautiful.

—That cream goes straight to my tits. Right?

—Probably.

—Straight. To. My.

—They see you stuffing your face and looking like that and they say, fuck that. If she can do it, so can I.

She nodded.

—That's right.

—And the poor saps looking at you think that they might even start looking like you if they stuff their faces.

—And they will. The Divine Church of the Here and Now. Your name.

—I remember.

—Yes, you do. I added *divine*. Like it?

—Yeah.

—The Divine Church of the Here and Now. That's little me. The high priestess. You should see me on Sundays.

—I'd like that.

—Get in line. Eat, drink, fuck. God loves it, you know.

—I like the sound of that religion.

—Yes, you do. But I'm not sure, at that. You were never happy. You were always restless.

—So were you.

—But I knew what I was doing.

She sat forward.

—And here. I am.

—The. Slow. Talking. It's part of the package, is it?

—Drives them wild. Like. Sucking. A. Cock.

—I knew that was coming.

—It's still good, though. Isn't it?

—Yeah.

—I've got my own church. Can you believe that?

—Yeah.

—With a big cross on the spire. Electric. Big blue lights. It rotates. You can see for twenty miles.

—Where?

—Los Angeles, she said. —It's the place, you know. And know what? The bird on the big blue cross? He's smiling. Seats two thousand. Radio station, commissary. You can buy your very own little india-rubber me.

—Go 'way.

—Opening a college next year. Spreading the word. More priestesses. But not high. As me. Low. Priestesses.

—Fair. Enough. No priests?

—Nope.

—Why not?

—Did I hurt your feelings?

—No.

—Want to be a priest?

—No.

—Thought all you Irish guys wanted to be priests.

—Not me.

—You still Irish?

—I try not to be.

—Try harder. No, no priests. Know why?

—Why?

—Want to guess?

—I'll skip this one.

—I did think about it. Even found a guy that was kinda the equivalent – like that word?

—Out of your mouth.

—Sweet. The equivalent of me. But guess what?

—He tried to take over.

She smiled.

—The dumb cluck never got that far. See, the problem is. The. Cock.

—What about it?

—Guys can be led by the cock but they cannot, just cannot lead with it. Agree?

I shrugged; I thought about it.

—There's that look again, she said. —Kinda snarly puppy. Works for the other religions. The snarly puppy priest. Don't do this, don't do that and don't do it like this. But in my church there is no place for Don't. And guys don't get it.

—Is it all women?

—You're missing the point. Look.

She picked up some cream-wet pastry and put her head back. She lowered the pastry, and let it go.

—Know why I did that?

—Same as before. The message.

—But there are two messages. The dolls say, she can do it, then I can do it. The guys say, boy oh boy, would I ever like to fuck that doll over there. The dolls want to look like me, the guys want to run their hands over me. I got them by their cocks.

—Do you ride them all every Sunday?

She laughed big.

—I told you. Get in line. But see? You're already there, ain't you? Waiting your turn. Willing to hand over big boodle to jump the line. Right?

I shrugged.

—I understand, she said.

She laughed again.

—Guys like it, she said. —The big laugh. Dolls think it's crude and unladylike. But guys think, fuck ladylike and let me at that mouth. And then the dolls start laughing.

We heard a woman's laugh from the other side of the diner.

—See? Dolls join, to be like little me. Guys join, to fuck little me. And the dolls and the guys end up fucking each other because I tell them it's jim-dandy. It's Sweet Afton but much bigger. Fuck, eat, shit on the rug, do whatsoever you want. Don't put it off. Your cock might not go with you into the afterlife. Or the afterlife might not be all that great. It might not even be there. And here's one I'm working on: *this* might be the afterlife. But I don't know how far I can go with that one. Might work in Los Angeles but I ain't too hot-sure about here. So, anyway, I tell them, my congregation. Spend that dollar, scratch that itch, eat that donut. Because the Lord wants you to. He insists on it.

—Sound man.

—I'll say. He put us here to live it to the hilt. You think the Lord's going to congratulate me if I don't fuck you even though I want to?

—Let's go.

—It's a what-if. Will he congratulate me?

—I don't believe in God.

—Will. He?

—Probably not.

—That's probably right. Want to know if I do want to?

—So, I said. —Your church is in Los Angeles.

—Right. You have to go west to get there but Los Angeles ain't really west.

—Okay.

—It's the place.

—Why here?

—Me?

—Yeah.

—I want to make records.

—Sing?

—No. Talk.

—Sermons.

—Kinda.

—Why can't you do it over there?

—Reasons.

—Let me do it.

—What?

—Do it for you. Make the records.

—I don't think so.

—Go on.

—I don't think—

—Go on.

She looked hard at me.

—That's the daddy I used to know.

He hadn't played the cornet in years. He'd changed over to the trumpet because the cornet looked so small beside other trumpets. The sound was better but the look was the thing that swung it. And the trumpet was never more than a stretch away. He never gave up; he never really rested. He practised during the intermissions. He bent notes; he worked on silences – he forced himself to stop and count. He stood in a corner; I watched him listen.

—I like that, he said.

—What?

—The let-them-wait, he said. —The extra second.

He battled players at clubs and rent parties. He battled men he'd never met. Word went out; there was no keeping up, no matching him. The records proved it, then the radio. He got better, and bigger. And bigger, and more surrounded.

—Louis!

—Pops!

—Hey, Louis!

Rockwell, the hipsters, the hard men, the noises and celebrities, the other players, the women. He sat at his typewriter, alone in a dressing room packed with noise and giddy tension. The Wall Street Crash was weeks-old news but it hadn't been heard yet in Harlem; if heard, it hadn't been felt.

—No coloured man ever jumped out a window cos his pockets went empty on him. Wouldn't be room on the sidewalk.

White money still came uptown, seven nights a week. Diamonds still glittered; there were shoulders worth rubbing. It was business as usual and much of it was done in Louis's dressing room. It was part of the package: come down, say Hi to Louis. He used to keep the dressing room empty for the minutes after a show.

—Rest the pipes, love the lips.

Now, he couldn't do it. His corner was smaller, and still he practised, his back to the gang. Or he wrote, typed his letters, to his sister, to Alpha, Lil, to old friends home in New Orleans. Trumpet, bottle, typewriter, side by side on the card table he brought everywhere. The shoes off, the hanky sometimes across his head, white towel around his neck; he'd tap. I saw it: the performer would drop slowly from his face, and the man was alone. And all I could do was watch.

He'd concentrate on his typing, tap away the desolation, the loneliness; he'd beat it away at the typewriter. Mezzrow's gage was never enough. When the fingers poked his shoulder or pressed, or more diffident fingers were held back and words went over the shoulder instead, Louis pulled the mask back up; it was on before he turned.

—Someone to meet you, Louis.

He was waiting for them, beaming.

—Obliged you come to hear me, Pops.

He didn't have to stand up. A handshake, a laugh. That was the deal. He could turn back then, to the typewriter or the trumpet. He'd put it to his lips, hold it just short of the skin, play it all in his head. It was where he'd go.

I was there, near, most nights. I walked with him, I hailed the cabs; I cut a way through the crowds outside his door – a black man couldn't do that. He still looked for me, still mugged and checked my collar for dirt. But the distance was there now, and we both knew it. But I couldn't say goodbye, and neither could he.

—Stick with me, Smoked.

—Yeah.

And I did.

And I became one of the fingers. I tapped his shoulder.

—Sorry; Louis?

He turned; I saw the face build up.

—Smoked?

He smiled but the eyes were surprised, wary – why was *I* doing this?

—There's someone I'd like you to meet, I said.

It was there, the smile, the face. And he stood up, slowly, like an older man. He grinned, held out the big hand, grinned a bigger one than mine. He pushed out his chest, to give us his room, to bring us in. He did it for me, and I knew I shouldn't have done it – but too late.

—My, oh my, he said.

He held her hand. He looked her up, and slowly down; he did what he could get away with.

—Who are you and where you from?

283

—I'm God's doll on earth, she told him. —And, brother, where I'm from is not the question. It's where I'm going and if you are going there with me.

—They let black gentlemans walk beside white ladies where you going?

She leaned closer to Louis. She whispered; I heard her.

—You walk behind me, Brother Lou-is, you get to watch my ass, all the way to glory.

I was running ahead, impressing myself.

We were still in the diner.

—Sister Flo.

She nodded.

—It's good, I said. —But you should spell it f-l-o-w.

—I already do spell it f-l-o, fucking, w. Have done since 1927 and I thought of it all by myself.

I shrugged.

—We're on the same track.

—Maybe so.

She matched my shrug.

—But I'm way ahead of you.

—I'll catch up, I said.

—I doubt.

She shook her head, slowly, left to right, but stopped on the way back.

—Why?

—I know the business, I told her.

—So does Rockwell.

—I know Rockwell.

—And?

—I know more than Rockwell.

—And this guy Einstein knows more than both of yis – you; I don't say *yis* no more. But I ain't looking to Einstein to make my records. And I still say *ain't*.

—Listen, I said. —Your slow-talk routine.

—It's the thing.

—But you can't do it on record.

—Why not?

—You don't have the time. You've three minutes, a bit more.

—I can say a whole lot of—

284

—Shut up a minute, I said. —The time's not the real problem. There's the silence between the words.

—Guys like it.

—When they're looking at you. Silence doesn't work on records. It's hissing, scratches. There's nothing sexy about it.

She thought about it. She ran a finger across the plate.

—I can make it sexy.

—No.

—Bet I can.

—No.

—So?

—Rockwell hasn't a fuckin' clue. It'd be a fuckin' disaster. Onstage it would be different.

She was listening.

—They'd be looking at you, waiting for the next word. Louis does it all the time.

—Who's Louis?

—Louis Armstrong.

—Oh yare?

—Yeah.

—I've heard of him.

—I'll take you to see him. I'll introduce you. Louis takes the trumpet away from his mouth and he lets the band go on without him. And the crowd goes wild.

—Been there.

—Yeah, but there's a difference. Louis has the band. The silence is full and beautiful. You, alone, the words can be as sexy as you want them but the gaps between them won't be. Not unless you're there. Do you have a phonograph?

—Phonographs.

—You know when you put down the needle? You know the sound. Before the music. That crackle, you know it. That's your silence, missis, and you don't want it.

There was silence now. And it was fine. It was my silence, no hiss, there because I wanted it there. I was ahead of her now.

—So, she said. —Daddy.

—Yeah?

—The Rockwell bird doesn't know this stuff?

—Not at all. Not his field. He's an agent. You don't need an agent.

—Yare.

—You're your own fuckin' agent.

—He is a tad moron-faced at that.

—He's alright.

—Alright ain't the thing. I'm listening to you.

—Atta girl. Sit back.

—Back as far as I can go, daddy.

She'd worked clubs since she was thirteen. She'd been up to Harlem, but she hadn't paid much heed. She knew jazz, the word, but nothing more. She sat while we waited. She took it in and danced when I said she might want to.

She shrugged.

It was a surprise.

—D'you not like dancing?

I'd never been out with her, in the old days. I'd watched her climb out her window but I hadn't followed.

—Ain't here to like, she said.

She had her map; she moved when and where. She shook and kicked and fell back to my arms, but she looked first – she checked. Her beauty drew the gawks, but she was no dancer. And that was grand because neither was I, unless I was dancing with one, like Dora. I was happy to stroll back to our table. I'd seen the kid, the little girl, the struggle to her current brutal dollness. I saw the child on the edge of the school yard, watching the play that would never make much sense.

I knew her.

—Did I ever tell you about my brother, Victor?

—A real-life sob story, daddio.

She was back, herself again. Hard as fuckin' nails, soft as she needed to be; familiar and fuckin' magnificent.

She sat down.

—I ever tell you about my brother and the dumb cluck from the Emerald Isle that might or might not have got him killed?

I sat, got down to her eyes.

—It wasn't me.

—Yare.

She shrugged. The whole place shrugged.

I couldn't help it; Victor was right behind my eyes.

—He was only your half-brother.

She shrugged again. She looked across at me.

—All of him got dead.

She noticed the change, chairs being dragged, short people standing, craning, the ripple across the velvet curtain.

—Here's your hot nigger, I guess.

He shot up to the mike as the curtain was still moving.

—Good evening, ladies and gentlemen. My name's Mister Armstrong. Seeing as we're here, I might blow into this here instrument and see what come out.

It let go of a screech and hauled out the dead. He leaned back and held it, and held, and let it die, and let the silence, not a clink of glass, a squeak, carry through. He held the trumpet at his lips, and a shout came through the crowd, a cry; it ripped the air, and he took its note, and drums and trombone, piano, banjo crashed and rolled and the note rose and swooped and fell behind and raced ahead and he lifted the horn to the air as the last note still jumped across the heads and shoulders, out to late-night Harlem.

She stood and stared. She watched, she listened.

—So, she yelled. —Explain.

—What?

—Him. Me.

—He's the silence on your records.

—Between the words?

—That's it.

—They like him.

—Yeah.

—Too much?

—How d'you mean?

—Wake up, daddio. Whose records? His or mine?

—Yours.

—They like him.

—He'll know what he's to do.

—No room for me up there.

—You won't be up there. I told you.

She kept looking at him.

—That's a performance, I said. —An event. The record's a product. Louis knows that. It's different. He knows.

—He's kinda wild.

She watched him striding, knees bent, to the trombone, inviting the solo, grinning. He stopped on the way, to polish his name on the bass drum.

—It's the show, I said. —The records are different. He knows.
I made sure she heard me.
—It was him that told me.

—I blew a gangster in this very room, she told him quietly, right
into his ear. —Can you believe that?
—Sure can, he said. —He have a name?
—Yes, he did.
—I know him? he asked.
—Might do.
He was checking her out. He knew he'd be seeing more of her.
I hadn't told him, asked him, but he knew.
—Brought a tear to his eye, I'm sure.
—He didn't complain.
—Gentleman.
He was ahead of her from the start. He got her measure real
fast. She'd tried to unsettle him, to hold him by the langer, but
her hand stayed empty. She didn't know how come, but she knew.
And she was angry.
This was Harlem, the black city within the city – surrounded.
And Louis knew it before I did: Harlem was owned and parcelled
by men like the lucky one she'd just been telling him about.
He grinned. He bowed.
She didn't really know it – I don't think she ever did – but she
was talking dirt to the black man because she hated him. Up
close to the man, the sweating black man she'd seen onstage, she
let it slip; she stopped being Sister Flow, all that work and rein-
vention, because she wanted to see him caught; she wanted to
see him dangle. Louis knew that: he'd always known. He'd grown
up with it, and he had the ways to deal with it.
He didn't tell me this. But his look, as he passed me and the
half-sister, back out to the crowd – that look told me all.
I couldn't apologise for something that hadn't happened. He'd
deny it, and I didn't want to hear that.
—He'll do, she said. —'Long as he ain't too primitive.
—He won't be.
—'Long as.
—He won't be.

★   ★   ★

He grinned and slapped my shoulder, winked, and bowed. And pushed me away. I knew, but I couldn't see it clearly yet. He'd done with me.

He held out his hand.

I took it. Felt his warmth, the hardness at the fingertips, years of work and practice. Black kid's hand, grown to confidence, calm, greatness.

He held mine. Hard work, gun oil, leg splinters, frozen handle-bars, the docks, the women, my father, Victor, my life was in that hand. Louis Armstrong held my hand, and I let go.

We both let go. It was a handshake, on a deal. Two friends shaking hands. But I felt it then, before I knew it. The loss. The end. The wave, goodbye. I wanted to grab again, but couldn't. I couldn't bend down, grab his arm, take his hand and clutch it. Pull him to my chest. Forgive me. We'll start again, I'll start again. I'll know. I'll know the next time. I'll never make you be a nigger minstrel.

I let go of Louis's hand and felt it, gone.

—When we do it, Pops?

—Wednesday.

—Bright and not too early?

It was never too early, or too late. Louis's clock was all his own.

—Ten.

—Fair ee-nuff.

He turned and walked away.

He put the horn to his mouth, and spoke around it.

—Me here, then you, and back to me. Then we see.

She was lost, and angry. She'd seen what her mouth could do to serious men. She'd watched it happen, every Sunday. But she was lost in the hollow studio. It was hot, to keep the discs soft, and sweat the size of fingernails ran from Louis's forehead, and hers – she went from dabbing to pulling it off her face with her hand. Hi-Tone Studios was a room high up in a block that was still wet at the corners. The Midtown traffic seeped through, and the half-sister's words fell dead at her feet, beside her sweat. The heavy black cloth surrounded her, killed everything inside it. It was a coffin, hot and nailed, and now there was a black man telling her what to do.

They'd been there for hours, but nothing good was happening.

She kept her accounts, in her monogrammed book, F.G.M., red leather.

—More outs than ins today, she'd told me, after the third stop.

—That's a false way of looking at it, I said. —A hit is a hit.

—Even so, she said.

—Come on, sister. You've got to speculate to accumulate.

—Listen to daddy, she said. —The guy who hides his boodle under that old broad's mattress.

—How did you know that?

—Just know.

She was wrong – my money was close to my gut – but I couldn't remember talking to her about Hettie. Maybe I had when we'd been on the lam together. But how did she know I'd gone back looking for it?

Sherman Booch, the talent boy from OKeh, was reminding us that he was there. His watch twirled slowly on its chain. I turned from his brown and yellow pinstripe but the watch ticked away at the back of my head.

—I want a sermon, Booch had said, in his office, two weeks before, —I'll go to church. But, hey, now I remember. I'm Jewish, so I guess I won't be going.

That was before she'd walked through the OKeh offices.

—Did Jesus die on the cross for your sins? I asked Booch as he watched her step into the elevator.

—Yes, he did, said Booch.

—And he did get up out of the dead three days later?

—Sooner, I'd say, said Booch.

But this wasn't that Booch. This was the son, Sherman Jr.

The half-sister looked at Sherman Jr's watch.

—You in a hurry, brother? she said.

—No, said Sherman Jr.

She terrified him.

—I'm just fine, he said. —It's all part of the creative process.

—I'll say.

—Let's give it another go, I said.

—Ready when he is, she said.

Louis's face gave nothing.

I went back behind the glass. She wouldn't look my way. She smiled at Sherman Jr; I heard him smother a shriek. I hoped to fuck that something would happen, that it would take off, she'd

290

actually listen and know what a thing she had in her hands and how happy she should have been.

I never saw her happy.

But it happened.

Louis mugged for her; the studio was full of his teeth. He stood well back from his mike. He counted down, grabbed her eyes, brought the trumpet to his mouth and gave her three climbing notes. He bent the last one. He clicked his fingers, soundlessly, at her face. This time she watched, and followed.

—Dearly, belove, ed.

He bent another one.

—Oh, dearly, belove-ed.

She watched Louis.

—What does, God, have to, say. About. Love?

Those Dearly Beloved records were the big thing at the end of the decade. They were bought and kissed and smashed.

—Want to, know, the, answer?

They were robbed and swapped for more money than a box of them was worth.

—Want to?

We recorded all four that day in November 1929, and by Christmas the first of them was flying.

—Don't, look, in the, good, book.

Florence Grattan-McKendrick became a big name, hated and secretly loved. Newspaper columns, magazine covers, nickel phonographs – she was everywhere that year-end. Stories tripped up stories. She'd recorded the things in the nip; she had her own harem, a big gaff full of husbands. She was Mata Hari's daughter; she'd brought dead men back to life. Straw Sister Flows were lynched and burnt and cardboard Sisters were hidden under beds.

—Read it, dearly, belove, ed.

Louis was laughing; I could see his eyes.

The notes kept on at her.

—The good book's a, good, book. But.

She was followed and met, everywhere she went. They caught her coming out of her hotel room, going into hospitals, on high roof ledges. Everywhere, she was the most wanted, the sensation, the soul and body of the age. Until she disappeared.

—It's not where, to look.

The Wall Street thing was done and over by the time we went into Hi-Tone. I'd never had money in any kind of a bank and it was months since I'd read a newspaper. Black musicians were always a working night away from eviction. The Twenties were nearly over but everyone I knew still roared and swore and those that didn't wanted to.

—About. Love.

Sister Flow was bang on time. She was the novelty at the end of the party. That first record, *Don't Look in the Good Book,* was perfectly timed.

—He gave you, the. Body.

And no one ever knew.

—He gave you, the. Eyes.

Louis gave it the music.

—He gave you, the. Time and. The place.

He gave it the sex.

—He knew. What. He was. Doing.

She made it through the three long minutes and Louis made a record of it.

—He wants you, to. Look.

The Depression was at the gates by the time the second and other records were sent out.

—Look at, those. Legs.

She watched Louis's fingers.

—He wants you, to.

And she'd suddenly become the soul and the body of a different place. She disappeared and came back but it did her no good.

—Look at, those, hips. He wants you, to.

God was raining locusts, scattering plague all over the land; factories were crumbling, soup kitchen lines were turning corners and the hock shop windows were full of instruments and dusty phonographs and records. They called it punishment, and took it, and waited for deliverance.

Waiting was the thing. Sackcloth was the thing.

—Put your, hands. On those, hips. He wants you, to.

But that was later.

She followed Louis's fingers and no one ever knew. Those records were the final screams of the years they called the Age and then, like her, they disappeared. (Until that young one with the midriff and no surname found them in her granny's attic and took them home and sang on top of them, coughed the words the half-sister didn't use – *take me, take me, baby, baby* – and, seventy years after the half-sister recorded them, sixty years after she died, the half-sister had her second hit, and third, and fourth. New guys and dolls lay back and worked. And, all the time, it was Louis Armstrong who filled their hands and wet their fingers.)

And they didn't know it. In 1929, it wasn't the thing. A black man alone with a white woman, in a studio, yards apart – it just wasn't the thing, anywhere. No one knew; no one was to know. Louis knew the rules. He even disguised himself and his notes; no one ever spotted him on those scandals. He told no one. And the half-sister told no one; it was one of the rules she wasn't interested in breaking. And I told no one.

—Do it and, a. Dore, Him.

Voices of Joy and Uplift. OKVJ 001. *Don't Look in the Good Book.* They couldn't press them fast enough. It was sent out everywhere. Boxed and dropped onto trucks and cars, it went national before engines were kicked to life. Railway porters took them to New Orleans and Memphis, and out west, all cities in between. Her church wasn't big enough any more. Her big blue cross was suddenly undersized, and more blue crosses were plugged in, with silver cross-legged men smiling down from them.

Louis packed up the trumpet. He lowered it, like a baby, into the case.

The trumpet never got mentioned.

He waved and left.

She had a shrug for every answer. I never saw the same one twice. And, for a while, I got my 10 per cent; all her shrugs were varieties of Yes. I told her to go up to the altar in red. I remembered Missis Oblong. (The bed groaned and now I could see her. A head made huge by hair that was plenty for six or seven women, and a red gown that showed off white shoulders, and all of her was massive.

—You're Missis Oblong, I said.

—Am I?

—Yeah.

—Good.) And I remembered Steady and his tin of red paint.

We rented a room downtown, on Houston, a bare old place like a parish hall. The musicians' union owned but didn't use it. They were sitting on it, waiting for the call from the city or realtors. For those in the know, the Depression had already pitched its tent on the island, but the air was still full of the buzz of construction. We drove past the Empire State site, on our way to the hall. It was three, four storeys higher than when I'd last passed, its girders black and climbing up and further up. The union's hall was just minding the spot.

We spent fat money on red drapes and thousands of red roses.

—Like walking into a cunt, she said.

—That's the idea.

—Yare, but I never had to pay for my own puss before.

—It's money well spent.

—You keep saying. Not your money.

—Not my profit either, I said.

—Not your loss, she said. —What's 10 per cent of nothing?

I had two fine girls at the door, to hand out the prayer sheets. The girls wore black suits, trousers, red braces, fedoras. And six more girls for the collection trays. I'd designed the trays myself, a long stick and a tight net of generous mesh; small coins dropped to the floor.

—Good touch, she said.

The altar was big and cardboard.

—Easier to transport, I said.

—Makes sense.

Under the lights, behind the red-draped half-sister, it would look marble and ready for sacrifice.

Midnight was our time and, by ten, the traffic outside was stopped and going nowhere. There were thousands out there, pushing to get nearer the closed doors. They were quietly pouring in from all directions, out of the ground, out of windows. We could hear vendors and cop whistles. She looked out from a window on the second floor.

She was pleased.

—We could have done it without the drapes, she said. —Or your broads in the little-me costumes.

—Think big, I said.

We were shoulder to shoulder. My choice, but she didn't move away.

—You have them here. Now you want to convert them.

—I ain't enough?

—You want them to come back.

—I ain't enough?

—But you'll be up there, in front of the altar.

—Be better on the altar.

—Yeah, but you'd go right through the cardboard.

—Continue.

—So, you're up there and the young ones are down there, near.

—Little me's.

—You said it.

The doors were opened and, seconds later, they were off the hinges and going back over the heads of the thousands. The seats were full, standing room was gone in seconds more. The stairs were packed, to the first floor, and the second. Wood cracked, but they kept quietly coming.

The half-sister moved to a room on the fourth floor. Down in the hall, I nodded and the fine girls started working the collection nets. Hands went to pockets. Folding money came out, went in. I watched. Some of the usual lads did the expected; they helped themselves as the nets went past. I did nothing, said nothing. And the fine girls helped themselves too. I saw them, let it go; I wanted them back, involved, giddy and greedy.

—There she is!

The weak and the faint were passed back over heads, back out to the street. I saw them turn off Houston, on their backs, floating over the crowds that kept coming, crawling at us.

—There she is!

The trays were full, and emptied, filling again before the girls had fully stretched their arms.

—There she is!

The odd shout, the odd eejit, but it was very strangely quiet. The trays kept filling. It worked: they were in a church and stayed respectful. More bodies, more money. More cash would produce her. I leaned against a wall and felt it grumble. The place was being shoved right off the street.

They kept coming. There were no doors now to bar them. The second storey filled, the halls, long empty rooms. Quietly, almost silently, filling the building, patiently, reverently, up the next staircase. Men and women.

I went past, and ahead of them. I walked the banister, no bother, hands ahead of me on the rail. No one complained; no one tried to follow. I was a priest, they saw that. A man in big black. I knew what I was doing.

Permission.

It was bigger than we could have guessed, the pulling power of that record. It was stronger than lit-up crosses, than the churches, the biggest, the highest and widest. The half-sister's record proved it to us that night. And the radio – that was next on our list, and more powerful. Our own radio station, and stations – ours. The airwaves. They'd hear her. She'd float over the nation. Geography wouldn't slow her down. They'd look up and see her. They'd all hear at once. Rockwell understood it, and Louis did. The records and the radio, our salvation army. They'd hear, together, the folks at home, all homes, the folks on the stairs who might not see her: they'd hear.

Permission.

Louis understood it. The man on the radio had no colour. Only sound. They'd love him before they knew or cared. *When You're Smiling*. He'd never hide it; he'd never try to. But he knew: once he got into the studio, he wouldn't and couldn't be stopped. No Jim Crow way up there, no lynch mobs or coloured nights – the air was his.

And hers.

They'd want to see her; they'd need to. The glimpse, the poster. God's doll. The weekly appearance, the wave to her dearly beloved. But she could stay in her rooms and get fat, and build it all from the studio.

Right now, they were a flight away from her; I was trotting up the banister, hands and feet, passing them to get there first. But they weren't searching; there was no rushing or shoving, pushing at doors.

They kept coming.

—There she is!

Heads turned, bodies stopped, until they had to shuffle again, at the gentle demand from the bodies behind them. They already believed, already they followed. They'd be happy with the records and the radio. Tonight, they were just filling the space, waiting, wanting, moving only because they had to, lost until they were told what to do. Not all of them, of course, not every one. The 10 per cent were robbing pockets. But the rest, the big most, were there because they thought they had to be.

It was the deal. We'd advertised. Once and once only. Your one and only chance. It grounded the thing, made it local, near and solid. The drapes, the fine girls in the man-suits, the church hush, the sightings.

They'd have to see her tonight.

The fine girls would be going home rich. Their chests were

getting bigger, beyond belief, swaddled in hundreds of well-used, hidden dollars. And that was another thing: nothing was beyond belief. They were there, smiling, holding out those nets. Just feet away, inches. Real women. God's doll's dolls.

Even I believed that night. My head was racing. I had to see her, quick. I'd only guessed the half of it, the quarter. She'd be more than God's doll. She'd be the God.

Permission.

I ran ahead, tapped her door.

—Come on.

She followed me, for the first and, probably, the only time.

—There she is!

But no one ran. We didn't; they didn't.

I brought her to the roof. I shut the narrow door, and locked it. I heard no hammering or protest. I took her arm and led her. The wind flapped her to hugeness; every light in the city took her red gown. Her hair blew high, but not across her face.

I led her to the ledge; she took some holding. She was Dolly Oblong in that gown, a massive, gorgeous kite. She stepped up onto the ledge. I grabbed the gown before she was lifted. One foot went over the side; I pulled her back. She didn't gasp or stiffen or fall back. She saw them all down there and she knew what was happening.

—There she is!

And this time, she was there. They followed the eyes, the outstretched arm, and saw her. Up above. Arms extended. Floating high above them. Solid in the snapping wind. Shining, frowning and huge.

I was right behind her, keeping her upright. There were pigeons up there, unsettled by the wind, the coming storm; they were in coops on all the roofs along the street. I tried to ignore them. I looked for moving shadows.

She looked and played the part. She raised her arms.

—Fuckin' hell.

I dug my heels in and held her gown. Her stitch-work was giving up.

—What do I say to them?

They were silent, as more and more looked up and saw.

—Keep it short, I said.

A gust – one of my hands lost her. She sailed stiffly over them. No shouts from below, no screaming or cheers. It was expected.

They believed. I leaned out, and grabbed. I wasn't seen – no roars or outrage – I was hidden in her red. And both my feet were there again, safe on the good side of the ledge. I pulled. She straightened, came back towards me.

—Whee, she said, just for me.

—Thou shalt.

—Pardon?

—Say Thou shalt. In a good big voice.

—That all?

—It's enough.

—I agree.

She lifted her arms, and I was ready for her this time. The wind took a hold but I beat it. She let the gown slide slowly down her arms. A good touch, I thought, and wise. She was giving them flesh, and bringing in her sails. My job behind her was suddenly much easier.

They were coming out of the hall below us. I could see it, the slow push, a fat river entering the sea. And they were on the roofs on the other side of the street, a wide street, further away than the people below us. I still couldn't be seen. And so what if I was? They'd still believe. Her high priest, her manly handmaiden, holding her out of the dirt.

She waited.

The gap in the wind.

—Thou. Shalt.

The wind hugged her and shook. And stopped.

She was louder this time.

—Thou, shalt!

And now there was noise, lifted and thrown and joined.

Permission.

—Thou shalt.

—Ah Jesus, no.

It snowed.

—How about that?

She whispered it, her arms still up there, and she slowly brought them down.

—Good old snow.

She was careful this time. She kept her hands at her sides. She held herself over the growing cheer. They saw her breathe it in; they saw her grow. She stood there in the suddenly thick snow, on the edge of the drop, and she soaked up her congregation.

And, as she did, her hands took cloth and the silk gown rose up slowly behind her and right in front of me.

I held on.

The ledge put her arse at my face.

The snow swayed and fluttered.

—Nine per cent.

I kissed her.

—Eight.

I rested my face on her arse.

—That's a seven, you know.

I pressed into her.

—Go home! she shouted. —Six, she whispered.

The smaller percentage still looked handsome. That gang below was only the start. They'd follow her anywhere, and give her the lot. I was buried in arse and silk but I knew: they'd be turning, dispersing, some rushing, others savouring the moment and the snow, building themselves to the bang. They had it now, permission, licence. The good old American thou shalt. And they'd be back, for renewal. And more of them, and more. The records, her word on the home radios. They'd pay for it. Permission. The religion. The way.

One last time, one more per cent, I took her hips and pulled her to me.

—Five.

She grabbed my hair and pulled me even closer.

—Want to push me off for the five?

I'd go over with her. Out there and onto the snow. It would take forever; we'd never land.

But, yes, we would. I wasn't a total sap. She was a big girl and she'd land with a squelch.

—Getting cold, daddio.

She was right. I stood up. She stepped down from the ledge. There was no one down there, a few stragglers, the midnight usual. They'd slipped away, home to their beds and radios and phonographs. They were already there, waiting for the next call. The wind had died. The snow dropped clean. She didn't need my weight.

She swapped hotels every second day. She met poets, painters, men who still had their money. She was always Florence

Grattan-McKendrick. She stayed just long enough. She was there, seen, frightening, long enough – pop, pop – and gone.

—I was attempting to get that Flow woman out of my head, F. Scott Fitzgerald wrote. —Fortunately, I did not succeed.

He'd walked into the sea and told the right people why. It was still there, the story, long after they were both dead.

—There she is!

We went to New Jersey and stood on a new-drained piece of swamp. This would be her first east coast church. She pointed to the site. Walter Winchell – pop, pop, pop – tried on her fedora. He smelled her breath as she took it back. She felt his brow before she lifted the hat.

—He was scared of me.

Hot Nun with the Big Fun. That was what he called her. He recorded their conversation, all the cut and thrust, but she never spoke a word to him. She stared until he turned and ran away.

We rented a Pullman coach – I'd ordered one custom-built, red upholstery and paintwork, *Divine Church of the Here, Now and Nationwide*, but it would take a year to build. There was God's doll, myself, the doll's dolls, a few little brothers, the whole handsome shebang, and we rode to the heart of the nation. We stopped – pop, pop – and made churches out of tiny squares of the vast American field. I broke the sod from the frozen ground; I felt no water under there. She turned the sod with a silver spade. Thou shalt. We brought red to Kansas and Arkansas. We fenced off the sites with red-painted pickets. We tacked on the sign, *Divine Church of the Here and Now # 9 – Here, Now, Soon.* She gazed at the mayor – pop, pop – for two good seconds; she gazed at the governor – pop, pop, pop – for three. She smiled at their wives, what handsome husbands, lucky ladies, thou shalt, thou shalt – they smiled back and smiled at me, and I watched my eyes do their work again.

—You Mister Flow?

—No, missis.

—You're with her.

—I'm Brother Flow.

—Oh. Real brother?

—No.

—Golly.

It was good to be back.

For a while.

We got back on the train – pop, pop, thou shalt – and rolled back to New York. New York, I knew – she knew – was where she'd make it big and lasting. Three days gone, you were forgotten. It was never safe to leave. Musicians came and never left. Politicians came up from Washington to be seen. Writers, painters, impresarios. They had to stay, feed the studios, stations, columns, galleries – the machine, until they were as big as the city.

—Me, she said. —Know who I'll be?

—Who?

—When they look at that Statue of Liberty, I'll be that big broad.

—I'll paint her red for you.

I knew I'd do it.

Thou shalt.

She couldn't stay away from Louis; he was too big to ignore. And that was what got me.

I hadn't seen him since the studio, when he'd packed his horn and waved goodbye. I hadn't waved back; he'd gone by the time I thought of it. I hadn't followed. I'd let him go and I hadn't tracked him down.

She wanted to go.

—Why?

I didn't want to go.

—He's the thing, she said.

—You saw him before and you didn't think that much of him.

—Not the point. He's the bigger thing now. He's going places the jigs haven't been before. He's the nigger that's going to matter. They're saying it.

—Who's saying it?

—Guys that ain't you.

I stared at her.

She stared right back and it was Florence Grattan-McKendrick who did the staring, a WASP, a woman born to stare. I was impressed.

—Worried?

She was the half-one again. I was still impressed.

—No.

—Lie?

—Yeah.

—Yare. I think so. You're worried. But I'm nice. There ain't no men that ain't you. It was you told me, remember?

—I didn't call him a nigger.

—Gee whiz, *O'Pops*. Ethiopian then. If they're going to abolish the slavery thing, he's the boy to be seen with. Maybe convert him. He's a sweetie.

I shouldn't have gone. But I went.

A table at the top, right there at the stand.

And I was seen.

The fuckin' fedora.

I knew it wasn't a photo-scoop she was after. She'd take it – pop, pop – Louis would soon be as big as the city. But that wasn't what it was. And she wasn't there for music. That hadn't changed. She watched but she wasn't hearing; she felt the sweat and excitement, she could see it, white people baying for him, women ready to climb him. I could see it on her face; she could see but she couldn't hear.

—D'you want to dance?

—No.

She fought it back, the scared look. And I knew why she was there.

And I saw him.

He was looking straight at me, putting me together. & Son had put on the pounds since I'd found hooch in one of his da's coffins. It took a while, but I knew him. At the same time he knew me. He still looked like what he was, small fry, smaller now because he was fatter.

I realised: I'd expected this all along, but I'd thought I'd be found by a bigger shot than him. It fuckin' annoyed me.

She saw me looking. She looked, and saw. She knew him too; she must have. But she was good. Nothing went; her face stayed as it had been. It was Florence looking across at him. She looked that way just long enough, a slow second – he, the place, the clientele weren't worth longer – and she looked back up as Louis charged onstage. So did I, but I still saw & Son stand up and move. I saw Louis watching him, and I knew that & Son had gone to a table right behind us.

I looked at Louis. His body bent, eyes shut – chair legs behind me scraped the boards – he was getting ready to hit a high one. He opened one eye – he saw me. I heard metal pulled from leather – Louis looked past me, behind me, at me. He opened his other eye, wide. He knew the story; he knew his white men. I smelt the gun oil – he hit a note I'd never heard. I heard glass smash,

302

ladies screamed. I looked across at the half-sister – Louis held the note; it killed him and he was doing it for me – I stood up, and she stayed. I stood, and turned and Johnny No was looking at me, sitting, no gun, no & Son, just a table or two of the hard lads out and uptown for the night.

I did another stupid thing. I sat back down. Now he knew for sure.

—No, fucking thou shalt not.

Louis opened his eyes – he couldn't hold it longer – he let it go and saw me still there. He pretended it was the heat that made him wipe his face. He looked behind me. He held the horn like a tommy gun as he walked back to the band. He was right. I should have taken my chances. But I couldn't. I couldn't make my mind up. I was stuck, stupid. Louis did the rounds of the other players – I knew none of them – doing the routine – maybe I'd get away with it – pumping them up, giving the wide-eyed look when the trombonist did the trombone, when the drummer patted all the drums. I was still there when he came back to the front mike. He grinned. I'd stick with her, let her brazen it out for both of us. She was Florence and the rest of it, Sister fuckin' Flow, a big enough shield for both of us. I shouldn't have stood, and I should have kept going. But I'd done it, I'd stood and sat back down – here I am, lads, here I am. Stupid, stupid, stupid. I'd stay; I'd hide behind her.

But, suddenly there was another problem, as I looked across at her. She was dressed like me, fedora, boots, Clarence Darrow's braces, me as I was five years before, walking between Johnny No's sandwich boards, taking the business, selling the hooch, stomping in on top of the pigeons. She was dressed like that and I was there, knee to her knee, still dressed like that, she the reminder, me the fact. She was new and I was back.

And there was more.

She was still big enough to hide us. She could do it.

But there was more. I knew, because Louis told me. He was suddenly playing it, *The Wearing of the Green*, at a shocking, urgent pace. *She's the most distressful country that ever yet was seen.* By himself, no band, just him to me. *They're hanging men and women for the wearing of the green.* He opened his eyes, looked over my head. People were puzzled but I knew what he was telling me.

It had become more complicated.

He made another gun of the trumpet, but quickly took it to his lips and now the band was with him. They knew the song, and so did I.

—I'LL BE GLAD WHEN YOU'RE DEAD—

YOU RASCAL YOU—

It wasn't me he was singing to. He was still looking over my head.

They'd found me. This time, I had to turn. I looked at her. She looked straight ahead.

—WHEN YOU'RE LAID SIX FEET DEEP—

NO MORE FRIED CHICKEN WILL YOU EAT—

I got ready to move. I leaned across, to tell her. What? To follow, to lead? To help me?

She got there before me.

—On your own, daddio.

—What?

—Go now, you're on your own.

She smiled slightly as she spoke; her profile was there for them.

—Wait.

She was right. It was all me. If I went now, I was dead. If I stayed, I was dead. She was safe and offering help. My only hope was the half-sister.

Louis played it to a fast end.

—I'LL BE STANDING ON A CORNER HIGH—

WHEN THEY BRING YOUR BODY BY—

He turned from the mike, and back.

—OH YOU DOG—

YOU RASCAL YOU.

And he walked off the stand. The show was over.

She smiled, and whispered.

—One. Two. Little three.

She stood.

I stood, and it wasn't easy. The legs weren't there, but I managed it. I yawned – I fuckin' did – and turned around.

Ned Kellet was looking at me.

—This way, brother, said the half-sister.

He smiled, finger pointing at me – pop. Sitting there among them. He laughed, head back.

I took the trick from her. I looked just long enough. I didn't know him and I didn't see his pointed finger. But I saw him bring the finger to his scar. He hadn't changed. He smiled. I got her chair out of my way.

I followed her. I put a hand in a pocket. The crowd parted for her, and for me. And closed, in front of Kellet's finger. And I could think; I could give it the proper Henry.

Kellet. That was what he'd called himself. (—You're Henry Smart. Aren't you?

I looked at the high cell window.

—Aren't you?

I lay back on the mattress. I closed my eyes.

I opened them.

—I'm Ned Kellet. Don't you recognise me?

I closed my eyes.) He'd been thrown into a cell, beside me. In Dublin Castle. (There was a man on the floor right beside me. Getting up, face down. Coughing and groaning. There was blood coming from his mouth.

—Bastards.

He shook his head. Blood hit my legs and chest.

He was dressed. Trousers, shirt, no collar. Jacket. A cap in the pocket.

He looked and saw me.

—Jesus, he said. —And I was feeling sorry for myself. Look what they did to you.

He was twenty-four or five. His hair was long and wet but I could see a scar running a line across his forehead. It was an old one, part of himself for a long time.

I said nothing. I sat up. I didn't know if I could talk. It was a long time since I'd spoken. I didn't know how long. I'd lost that time. I was starting again.

—Here.

He shook himself out of his jacket and handed it out. Then he came closer and put it around my shoulders, without touching me. He sat back on the floor.

—It's all ahead of me, he said. —Jesus. Hang on, he said. —I know you.

He looked, as if trying to see through lace curtains. He whispered. He looked back at the door first.

—You're Henry Smart. Aren't you?)

The club's tough guys stepped out of her way; they melted and stayed melted as I went through in her wake. (—I'm Ned Kellet. Don't you recognise me?) She was heading for Louis. She made for the door with the star on it. We'd make it; nothing could stop her. But there was only one door, no window, no other escape.

305

The door was shut. The corridor was full; they were hanging on for Louis. And now they saw the famous Sister Flow.

—There she is!

She knocked.

The last time I'd seen her knock on a door, under the El, on Death Avenue, we'd ended up running from Johnny No. And here we were, running from No, and before she'd even knocked. And Kellet was with him this time. How times had fuckin' changed.

—There she is!

She knocked again.

(—I'm right, amn't I? Henry?

I looked at the window. I closed my eyes.

—Henry? In your own time.

I am Henry Smart. I am Henry Smart. I am Henry Smart. I am Henry Smart.

I opened my eyes.

He smiled.

I closed my eyes.

I opened them.

He was gone.)

Louis opened the door. She pushed past him. I followed her. He looked hard at me and shut the door. He'd been alone.

—Trouble, he said.

The word was like a tongue on her skin. She lifted off the floor.

—Not you, ma'am, said Louis.

He was talking to me.

—Probably, I said. —How did you know he was Irish?

—Seen him around, said Louis. —Been visiting.

—Thanks for warning me.

—Hey.

It was the half-sister; she was feeling left out.

—She in trouble? he asked.

—I don't know. I don't think so.

—Hey.

Someone outside knocked.

I'd last seen Kellet in late 1920, maybe 1921. I'd found his name on my cell wall, after he'd gone. *Ned Kellet 14th of December. 1920. Up the Republic.* He'd left his jacket behind; it was on the mattress, and trousers on the floor. And a shirt. I stood up and picked up the jacket. It was my own. Made and bought in

Templemore. I put the clothes on. No shoes, no socks. I was in there because they'd caught me, the night of Bloody Sunday, the 21st of November, 1920. I'd helped kill a man that morning, and they'd caught me among my granny's books that night. They'd beaten me, tortured, starved me, kept me awake for days, weeks, and I'd held on to one name. Fergus Nash.

—Name?

I told them nothing, except Fergus Nash. And then they'd thrown in Kellet. He fished for my name but caught nothing. I gave them nothing, except a name I'd made up four years before.

—My name is Fergus Nash.

They'd moved me from Dublin Castle. Every step, every door, I expected to be shot. A long row of closed cell doors; no sounds came from any. As I neared the end of the passage, I passed an open door and saw Kellet on the floor. An Auxiliary stood over him and drew his foot back to kick him. The Auxiliary behind me pushed me forward. I heard a scream as the door before me opened and I was out in the air and daylight.

They took me to Kilmainham. I was thrown into another cell and I slept.

I woke. It was dark. A slamming door had woken me but I could see nothing. I heard feet outside. I heard keys jangling. I sat up. The door opened, and a man hit the ground hard. The door was closed again, dark. I heard the man breathing through a swollen mouth. I stayed still. The breath rattled. The man groaned. I knew who it was.

Now, someone outside knocked again.

Louis looked at the door and back at me.

—Hey, said the half-sister. —I am here.

Louis turned to her.

—You sure are, Miss Flow. And I know why.

She tried not to look stunned.

—You're here to help our friend, Henry, said Louis. —Right?

She collected her mouth.

—Yare.

(—Help.

I stayed where I was. I heard him crawling. I couldn't see anything but I knew exactly where he was.

—Is there anyone there?

A hand touched my foot. I kicked. He fell back.

—Who's there?

I said nothing. His moving stopped. I waited the hours until the dawn gave enough light.

He looked at me. He sat in the opposite corner.

—Henry, he said.

They'd done more damage to his face. They'd given him another jacket.

—I suppose you know, he said.

I said nothing. I looked across at him.

—They're shooting us this morning.

—Fuck off, I said.

He looked horrified, angry, let down, one by one, exactly one second for each emotion.

—You think I'm a fuckin' spy, don't you?)

I'd been taken away and brought back to an empty cell. I'd escaped, from jail, eventually from Ireland, and I hadn't seen Kellet again. Now, he was on the angry side of Louis's door. I knew it and so did Louis.

—Miss Flow, he said. —Bad men out there.

—I can handle bad men.

Louis nodded. She stared at him. It was clear: she hated him. But he stared right back, and I watched her change.

—Henry is in a hatful of trouble here. And we're going to get him out of it.

She looked at him.

—I know why you came here, said Louis. —But forget about that and let's do right by Henry.

—I'll be alright, I told him.

—Sure you will, he said.

He looked at her. He wasn't smiling.

She shrugged.

—What? she said.

He told her.

She listened.

She took in air and stepped to the door. We were right behind her, in against her back. She unbuttoned her jacket. She opened the door. We heard them gasp, the crowd outside, the good guys and the bad guys.

—There she is!

And she was there. Sister Flow, as big and as bright as they'd said.

—There she is!

308

She was bigger than Louis. That night, she was bigger. I never met her again but I knew that she was pleased. I knew that back. I watched it grow.

She stepped out. We were right there. Another step, and gasps. We were still in the room. She stopped. She lifted her arms. More gasps, and silence.

She spoke.

—Thou.

A scream.

—Shalt!

The cheers grew and rolled. They dropped off the ceiling and walls, made rain of the kitchen steam. She didn't move but there was frantic movement, shuffling and pushing; they were forming a queue – thou shalt! – they were fighting politely to get to the front. She moved one step to the right, and we were right in there, huddled together, me, Louis, the trumpet. She moved and took a wide-armed swerve; her jacket was a cloak – a slow swing to the left and, just like that, she'd trapped them in the corridor, and the rest of it behind us was empty and ours. Louis patted her arse, and we legged it.

Louis hit the exit door.

I was right behind him. I looked, once, one last stupid look. She was damming the corridor, blocking the bad guys, Kellet and Johnny No – I couldn't see them, or anyone else.

Louis had told her she could do it, and she had.

She'd shrugged again, in Louis's room before she'd opened the door. I saw it; she blushed.

—For you, daddio, she said.

I stepped up to her and kissed her on the mouth. Our first kiss, our last.

—Ain't going with you this time, she said.

—I'll be reading all about you, I said.

—Yare.

—You'll be swell, Louis told her.

—Know that, sunshine, she said.

And she'd unbuttoned her jacket.

—Get back there and behave yourselves, she said.

Louis bent down, and straightened up again.

—By the way, he said. —Who was that lucky man you kneeled in front of, in this very room?

—Why, the Dutchman.

—Mister Schultz.

309

—Bingo.

He wasn't smiling.

—He's out there, said Louis. —Mister Schultz.

—Didn't see him.

—He's out there.

—Big deal, she said. —Come on.

We crept in behind her and she stepped up to the door. And now, I looked at her for the last time. She was filling the corridor of Connie's Inn, saving me from the bad guys.

—This is dangerous, I told him.

—Tell it like it is.

—For you.

He shrugged. He thought a while. I drove, but he took us.

—They'll know, I said.

He shrugged.

—Maybe. Maybe not.

He didn't smile.

—Had it planned, he said. —All worked out.

—How?

—Knew something was coming down.

He shifted; he tried to get clear of the wind that came through the car floorboards. He tried to bring his feet and legs up. But it wouldn't work. He gave up, sat properly again. He looked at nothing we passed.

—The way they were grouping.

—The bad men?

—The bad men. Like those nice vultures. They were there, having the time. But there was something about them. They weren't there for the hot music. Like your chippie there, Miss Overflow. Not listening.

We drove through a night. We didn't stop.

—Same guys, every night. Some different, but the same guys. White guys, O'Pops.

Nothing for a minute, more.

—White people ain't real people. No offence.

He wasn't smiling.

We stopped somewhere at dawn and pissed onto grey snow, somewhere in Pennsylvania. He did the deciding in Harrisburg. He pointed the road. I followed.

—Will you go back?

He looked at me.

—Where else?

—They'll want to know where you were.

—Told you. I had it planned. Have me an alibi. This direction we're going in, is not the direction I'm going in. I'm in Philadelphia by now. Woman trouble. Mezz even have a name and an ass for her. They'll understand.

—Sorry, Louis.

He said nothing to that.

—I could get out here, I said. —You could get back in time.

—What about my woman in Philly?

He didn't smile.

—Keep driving.

Nothing, for something long, an hour, more.

—They got a nice boy called Cab Calloway filling in for me.

—Sorry.

—They say he shakes his hair enough to make the ofays smile.

—Sorry.

—Enough of that jive.

—Fair enough, I said. —So why the fuck are you in the car? I've got this far on my own.

—Two answers, he said, but he didn't rush to give them.

American roads went on forever, as long as silence. There was nothing out there. Another night. White paint rings on telegraph poles. The sky pressed down on the roof. Silence out there, and the wind. It was like the Atlantic Ocean; the lights out there, the odd pinprick we saw, meant nothing. I'd crossed the Atlantic, but I'd never felt this scared.

—First, he said, at last. —You didn't get this far alone.

—I know.

Through a town, one long street, a dog, a light swinging green in the wind.

—If I was driving, he said. —You bet there'd be a pole-eesman just about here.

—Feeling sorry for yourself, Louis?

—Fuck you, O'Pops.

The town behind us, the road ahead dead, sleepy straight. I'd never been tired and I wasn't now. I'd do that much; I'd drive the thing all the way. More towns, lights.

—That's the same fuckin' dog we saw hours back, I said.

He didn't look.

—Second, he said. —Friendship.

—What?

—Why I'm here, he said. —It's what you do. It gets called that.

We were starving but he wouldn't let me stop.

—I could bring you out something, I said.

It was what we'd done on the drive from Chicago to New York. I'd go into the diner, store, and bring food out for Louis. Not this time; he wouldn't let me.

—Next time I eat, I sit down, I pick up the menu, I order. The food is brought to me on a plate, and then I eat. Keep driving.

Men stood over shovels, and stared. Men leaned against trucks. Women stopped on sidewalks; they stared and held their children's hands. He looked straight ahead. One last lesson, one final obligation. Friendship's due. He wanted me gone. He was bringing me home. In disgrace, I thought. I wanted to stop the car, jump while the wheels still bit the stones, and run, out into the American dark. But I couldn't. New again – it was still possible; somewhere else. I stopped myself. I'd let him do this. My feet, my arms ached, biting at me to stop and run. But I took the ache and drove it.

I missed Ireland, the corners and smallness, the bumps in the road. Here, the same black dark, the same long street, the same grey faces looking up and staring in at us, at Louis. I didn't know how long ago we'd left. I couldn't tell how far we'd left to go.

—Fuck this.

—Yeah.

He wasn't smiling.

—She wanted to kill me dead.

Dawn hurt.

—How?

It was a quick poke into my left eye, waiting for me on a bend that took us south around a hill, then straightened for as far ahead as I could make myself see. A minute later, the sun was over the hill behind us, cold and blunt, pointing to the road ahead.

—She didn't know how, he said.

—I don't get you, I said.

—What she say to you?

—Nothing, I said. —You mean, with Johnny No and Kellet behind me?

—What she say?

—Nothing, I said. —I just followed her when she got up. I didn't know she was going to your dressing room. It wasn't the way I'd've gone.

—Nothing?

—Yeah, I said. —Nothing.

—Here's what was, he said. —She was going to blast me with that fuckingness she has.

—She did that with everybody.

—Stop being white, he said. —And think.

—You were impressive, Louis. I nearly wanted to ride you myself.

But the smiling days were over. The sun was eating the road ahead, eating shadow, making the road disappear. This was the big one.

—She hated me, he said.

I stared ahead.

—Yeah.

He nodded.

—Yes. You saw.

—Yeah.

—She tell you?

—No, I said. —No, she didn't.

—How d'you know?

—It didn't work on you.

—The Sister Flow stuff?

—Yeah. It annoyed her. It worked on every other man she met.

—That ain't it, he said. —Ain't it all.

The highway was bleached, gone. We saw nothing. We hit nothing.

—I know, I said.

—You know.

—Yeah.

—What you know?

—I think I know what she thought. You stayed out of her spell. You played your trumpet. You made her records work that day. You packed up and went before she could pay you. She's in your debt.

313

I looked. He was staring straight ahead. He knew the road. He spoke.

—She never got to call me Boy.

—That's right.

—She never got to call me Boy.

—I think you're right.

—That's what she came looking for. That chance. Knock me down on my ass. Help me up and call me Boy.

—How would she have done that?

—Second thoughts, said Louis. —That's the one with the happy ending. The other version, the version she was after, she gets me whupped or killed. Lynched.

—How?

—Respecting the white woman bullsh. Laying my black hands on her white hide.

—Are you sure?

A face came out of the white, beside the road, stared in.

—Would that have worked?

He thought about it.

—No, he said. —Not there, in Connie's. Wrong place. I bring in the business, I can fuck their mamas, almost. What I was, Henry, what I *am*, for her. Is unfinished business. She wanted to finish it.

—But she didn't know how to deal with it.

—Right.

—Sorry, Louis.

—Fuck you.

The sun filled the Buick, but gave no heat. It was cold but my fingers worked to keep a grip. They slid, and froze to the wheel. I leaned over and breathed on them.

—And know what? he said.

It was dark again. The headlights made the road. The first time we'd spoken in hours.

—What?

—She might still do it.

—What?

—Get to call me Boy.

Ahead, above the sky. Hours ahead; I saw it.

—When I go back, he said.

314

—Don't let her.

He said nothing. The glow was nearer.

—In a dangerous place.

—What? I said.

—Me, he said. —I'm in a dangerous place.

—I wasn't much good to you, was I?

—You said it, he said.

The glow was lights, a city ahead with shape. We passed silos, we rode over tracks, ran alongside more. We caught, and passed, a train, and trains.

—We did fine, he said. —We took it as far as we could go.

I let it settle. It was the goodbye.

—But I know.

—What?

—Ain't no escaping, he said. —No standing on my own two feet.

—Sorry, Louis.

—You agree?

—I think so.

—Fuckers don't just own the ground. They own my goddam feet.

A street, fenced each side by solid houses, a line of shops, a vacant lot. Factory chimneys, black night again, more chimneys.

—But look on the bright side, Louis, I said. —I'm the one they want to kill.

—Fuck you.

But the streets, the lights, they seemed to warm him.

—Tell you. It was my problem before I met you. It's still my problem. You didn't bring it on. The problem was here, in Chicago. We cut out. Same problem where we went. Bigger problem, maybe bigger prospects. I'm going back. My choice.

—What choice?

He sighed.

—You right, he said. —Some choice. Play, or do not play. No choice. Got to play.

—You're the best.

—I know.

—It's yours. Make the most of it.

He looked at me now.

—I know.

He looked away, and back.

—Why they after you?

—Oh, I said. —I muscled in on their operation, on the Lower East Side. I thought I told you.

—But the Irish gent. Why is he after you?

—We go back, I said. —It's a longish story. D'you want to hear it?

—No.

—It's the real reason they're gunning for me, I said. —I think it is.

He said nothing.

We knew where we were going. He was bringing me right to the door.

—There's more, he said. —Why they're after you.

—What?

—You were in the way. Between me and them.

—Probably.

—They thought that.

—Yeah.

—Should have stayed closer, he said.

—What?

—Been thinking about it, he said. —You should have stayed closer to me.

—Well, I said.

—Might have been different. It would have been clearer. They'd have respected it.

—Well, I said. —When Rockwell got in there.

—Fuck Rockwell. He wasn't you.

—You met other guys like Rockwell, and you'd always walked away from them. Joe Glaser.

—He wanted to manage me. Rockwell didn't.

—He did.

—Wasn't what I was after with Rockwell.

—I know.

Another dawn, the last one. Thick, bright lines crossed the street. Traffic shuffling, pedestrians hunched. Cold light out there; the El beside us broke the air. I shouted.

—It was the records, the bookings. I know that. It's just. I didn't know what I was there for.

He nodded.

—Maybe this the right way.

—I didn't want to be a bodyguard, I said. —I wanted, I don't know, fuckin' more. Then she came along.

316

—And you managed her.

I took my hands off the wheel and slapped it.

—She didn't want to be fuckin' managed either. But it was good for a bit.

—I didn't want to be *managed* by a white man.

—Including me.

He nodded.

—That's fair enough, I said. —I'm finally understanding. But it's a pity.

He nodded.

Nothing for a block or two. We were going back into the sun now.

—Thought I could get away with it, he said. —Thought I just might do it.

—What?

—Be black and not let it matter. Overcome it.

—You did.

—No, man, nay nay. Sick of having to be proud or ashamed. Just want to blow my fucking cornet.

—You do.

—We here.

—I know.

I looked for shape through the glass, for a small running figure. I tried to hear the voice. Was it a school day? I hadn't a clue. I pulled again, and I heard the bell deep inside, in the kitchen. I waited. For a tall woman to take shape beyond the glass, pull open the door, look out. I pulled again. Made out the stairs. Saw the shape. Saw the hesitation, the last step. I knocked, pecked the glass – tap tap. I saw the arm, the hand; I heard the lock.

—Oh.

Missis Lowe stared, then saw.

I knocked on Louis's window. He was back in the driver's seat, his car.

—They're not there, I told him.

—Where?

—Don't know.

—Oh, man. Get in.

She recognised, remembered me. She brought the door more inches towards her; she stepped into the gap.

—Mister Smart.

—Howyeh.

—Why are you here?

I knew.

—Your wife is not – that is, she is no longer here.

—Oh, I said. —Where is she? D'you know?

—I'm afraid not.

—Oh.

—She – well, she left. With the sweet little—

—When?

—Yesterday?

—Yesterday?

—Why, yes. Yesterday morning. They were at the door when I came down.

—You've no idea where they went?

—No.

—Nothing?

—No. I'm afraid – I offered to write her a reference. I was a mite upset. But I did offer. What I wanted, I hoped she'd stay a spell longer. The child. I hoped she'd change her mind. I hoped my reference—

It was creeping up.

—She said she didn't need one.

—Was there anyone waiting for her, or anything?

I could still think, stay calm. It was coming.

—No, she said. —Not that I saw. Nobody. I thought, I presumed she would be joining you in—

—New York.

—Yes.

—No.

—I see. Isn't this – ? A day sooner, Mister Smart.

—I know.

—She didn't know you were coming. Did she?

—No.

I stepped away, stepped down. It was coming. They were out there, anywhere. Any street, any train.

—Thanks. Bye.

—Goodbye. Please, Mister Smart.

—Yeah?

—When, if. When you find them, ask the child to write me.

—I will.

—Thank you.

—Know where you need to go? said Louis.

—No.

—Pops, it's tough.

I nodded.

—Tough as a night in jail.

—What sort of a fuckin' prick was I?

He let me at it. He started the car. He blew on his hands.

I was long enough in this country; it was easy to disappear. She was doing the hiding, and she'd be better at it than I'd been. I'd never find her. What had I fuckin' done?

Louis sighed, and got us out from under the big tree, to the street.

He yelled.

She was right in front of us, on the hood of the Buick. Her face was at the windscreen, staring in at Louis. Missis Lowe. Lost and furious.

She saw me. She looked at Louis, then back at me.

—There was—

I jumped out and helped her down. She wasn't hurt; she didn't seem to be. She stood straight, looked in at Louis. I looked at her face, her hands. She was fine. She looked at Louis. She looked at me. Louis climbed out of the car.

—Are you alright?

—I'm perfectly fine.

She looked at Louis.

—That young man needs his eyes tested.

—Right away, ma'am, said Louis. —Do it this very morning.

She looked at me.

—There was something. Your wife said.

—What?

—When she was checking the child's coat. I went to do it, you understand, to tuck her scarf into the coat. But then I, well – I heard your wife mention a hotel.

—What hotel?

—I cannot recall the name.

—Was it a Chicago hotel?

—I do know that I knew the name. I recall that clearly.

—Any idea?

—I'm—

—Metropole? said Louis.

319

She glared at him. She looked at me.

—I knew the name when I heard it, she said. —But not as a hotel.

—How d'you mean?

—A song, I think.

—A hotel with the same name as a song?

—I think so.

I looked at Louis.

He shrugged. He got back into the car.

—It'll probably come back to you when I've gone, I told her.

I watched to see if she understood.

—That's what often happens, I said.

She nodded. She was cold. I took her elbow. She looked very old and small. I walked her back to the front door.

—When you've forgotten about it, I said.

—What?

—The name of the hotel.

—Oh. Yes.

—Or the song.

—Yes.

—I'll call again tomorrow, I told her. —In case you remember. But I wouldn't.

I could search the stations, streets. I could look forever.

I walked back to the car. I climbed back in. It was colder inside. Louis got her going.

Missis Lowe was in front of the car. He braked.

I got out quickly.

—Macushla.

There was nothing clear, no one I could see yet. No one going in and out. It was a hotel, it had the name, but it wasn't right.

—It's quiet, I said.

—One of those ones, he said. —We been in a few. Go in, you stay in. Been in, you stay out.

—Maybe business is bad.

—Might be. Again?

—Yeah.

He took the corners sharp, as quickly, slowly as he could manage. No skidding, no need for stares or braking. He took me past the hotel again.

We'd be seen this time, if we were being watched. I took it all in, the revolving door, resting still, the guy against the railings at the next building, and the guy at the drugstore on the opposite corner, leaning against the glass. His eyes, under the awning – *Soda, Candies* – under his pork-pie hat, staring across at the door that wasn't turning. The trolley car pushed away, and there was another guy, outside John M. Erickson, *The North Side's Largest Clothing Store*. There were others, and there'd be more.

—Whose hotel is it? I asked Louis.

—Don't know, he said. —This ain't home.

—Strange name.

—Nice tune.

Macushla. In among the Ericksons, and Umenhofers and Aumanns.

—Look at the kids, he said.

Not many of them. Up on the sidewalk.

—None in the gutter, said Louis.

I looked for bare feet. There weren't any.

—Money here.

He took the Macushla corner, right, off the trolley-car tracks. A guy sat on the fireplug, chatting to a cop. Louis crawled as I looked at windows. Lace curtains looked back, all windows shut.

—I have to go in.

He said nothing. He stopped the car. I opened my door, checked first that the running board was safe above the kerb. The street had been recently swept. I was itchy and suddenly exhausted; the street was cleaner than I was.

I could see a slice of the alley that would bring me to the back of the hotel. It was clear. There was a garage on the other side of the alley, on the corner. I heard a radio. I heard a tool hit concrete. I heard work.

—Take the last step, O'Pops. I'm nervous here.

—Okay.

—Could get myself recognised. And I'm supposed to be in Philadelphia.

I got out. The edge was off the cold. Spring was a month away. I bent down. I looked in at him.

—See you, Louis.

—Unlikely.

—Good luck.

He took the hand off the wheel, waved, and went. He didn't

321

look. The only car moving on the street; gone. I knew: I wouldn't see him again.

I didn't wait.

I walked across the alley mouth. It was empty. I looked into the garage. I saw two feet, sticking out from under a Bearcat. I heard the radio. I heard men laugh, a door slam. I saw an Upton Oil Company truck parked outside the garage, down-street from me.

I took the alley.

I strolled, close to the hotel wall. Under windows, fire escapes. *I've a pair of arms to hug and hold, but nobody's using them now.* I walked away from the radio, into darker shadow. I looked behind, I listened as I moved. Another door, another tool, the guy under the Bearcat tapped his boots together. There was no one following, no one over the street.

A door beside the ramp. I checked the knob. It turned; a click. I waited, turned again and let it open. Noise came at me with the heat. I stepped inside, and waited. It was dark. Kitchen sounds. Pots, clanks. An order barked. It was some sort of hallway. Padlocked doors, three of them, to the left. Damp wall to the right. A door in front of me. I waited.

—Where's them eggs?

I waited.

—Wipe its ass before you threw that on the pan?

American accents.

It was a hotel; I could hear that. I could go back out and enter by the revolving door, walk up to the counter, and ask for Miss O'Shea. Who? My wife. Men were at work beyond the door, cooking for the guests.

Something stopped me.

The guys outside. Macushla. The sign, the neon, up new on top of the flaking paint. The door that didn't revolve.

Why was she here, with Saoirse? If she was here. Macushla. It was just a song.

I shut the door behind me, quietly. I walked past the padlocks, quietly.

Work. That was why. She'd had enough of Missis Lowe.

I got to the next door. I held the knob.

And she'd had enough of waiting for me.

I turned it, slowly.

Macushla, macushla. There'd be work amongst her own here. Cousins, maybe. Roscommon people.

The click.

I pushed. The smell before the light. The kitchen. White, silver. Moving figures. Blade in air. Steam. No women. No one looked. I walked further in, kept going, a man with purpose, who knew where he was going.

A waiter, his back, tray going high, in front of me. A coffee-pot, cups, sugar bowl. I followed him, past a butcher's block, around it. Double-doors. He cracked them, shoulder at the centre, saved the tray, held it back. Gone. The doors flapped once, and stopped.

—Turn that goddam steak, goddam it.

—Yessir, yessir.

—Goddam hunkie. We don't burn our meat here in these United States.

—Yessir, yessir.

I took the doors; I pushed them with both hands.

The dining room.

Empty.

—Aha.

Not empty.

Kellet was sitting there, and I wasn't surprised.

The coffee tray in front of him.

—The bold Henry Glick.

He was alone.

My arse. There was no one to see yet, but they were there.

—The train, Henry, said Kellet. —I recommend it. A lot better than the dusty oul' things back home. Will you have a drop?

I didn't answer.

—D'yeh not like the coffee?

I didn't answer.

—Sit down.

I didn't answer.

—Sit down, for fuck sake. We'll have a chat before I kill you. It's the last chance you'll get to rest your feet.

He tapped a chair with his foot as he poured coffee from the silver pot to his cup.

—That's the ticket, he said.

He tasted the coffee and watched me sit.

—She was right.

I said nothing.

—Yep, he said. —She was dead right.

I kept my hands off the arms of the chair.

—She said you'd come through the back door.

He leaned out, put his cup down.

—She said it would never dawn on you to walk in the same way as everyone else. You've put on the pounds, Henry.

I sat back in the chair. There was no more coming or going from the kitchen. The doors from the dining room to the lobby were open.

He was thin. His neck rose out of his shirt, barely touching the sides, and it didn't gather much meat on the way. He was grey-skinned, now that I was looking at him in daylight. The whites of his eyes wouldn't be white again; they were washed red, near pink – surprised eyes in a cynical head. I was looking across at a Fenian hop-head. Or a hop-head who'd pretended to be a Fenian.

I spoke.

—How's the informer business?

—Booming.

He stared back. He wasn't worried that my words might have carried, that Fenian ears behind the drapes or doors might have heard.

He was alone.

—There'll always be work for those daring enough to tell the right men what they want to hear, he said. —That's an informer for you, Mister Glick. He gives good men their licence to murder.

—That's well put.

—I thank you. And, believe it or not now, Henry, but I was never an informer.

—What were you doing in the cell with me?

—I was a spy. There's a difference. I was a plant. I was never *involved*. I was never in. So I couldn't have informed.

—So, what? You're not with the I.R.A.?

—I didn't say that.

I didn't want to talk to him but he'd caught me. I couldn't help myself.

—But you said you weren't involved.

—I wasn't.

I lifted my hand – he didn't react – and pointed at the bulge in his jacket.

—So?

—So, why all this? Why have I come after you? All this way, to bump you off.

—Yeah.

—It's a nixer, he said.

—A fuckin' nixer?

—A fuckin' nixer; exactly. There's the lads who pay me. You know some of them, at home. And then there's the lads who will pay me, once I send you on your way. And you know some of them too. Our Italian friends and some of our Semite friends. I'm doing it as a favour to them and they'll still insist on paying me for it. It's the way they do things over here; you know that yourself. It's a great fuckin' place, isn't it?

He smiled.

—They'd be happy enough to do the job themselves. But, no, I said, I'll take him off your hands. And they're happy with that; they trust me. I wouldn't let them pay me in advance. Do you know how long I've been waiting here for you?

It made sense to keep him talking.

—How long?

—Half an hour.

He grinned, and let go of a snort.

—Money for jam, he said.

—But I'm not dead yet, I said.

Stupid.

—No, he said. —Not yet.

He brought a hand to his jacket, and leaned sideways slightly, to free the cloth under his arse. Then he changed his mind and sat up again.

—You don't carry a piece yourself these days, Henry?

There was no point in bluffing, none that I could figure. I'd stay alive longer if I told the truth.

—No.

—No, he said. —So she said.

I didn't let it sink. I reminded myself of who I was talking to, of when I'd first met him.

I stared at him.

—You've been acting the maggot, Henry. On two fuckin' continents. And where did you think you were going, with your *Glic*?

I shrugged.

—You're confused, Henry. Aren't you?

There was no reason not to admit it. It would keep him talking; he was enjoying himself.

I shrugged again.

—Good man.

He pulled back his sleeve, and looked at his wristwatch.

—We've a few minutes, he said.

He covered the watch.

—Will I start at the beginning?

I was calm again. I didn't feel like a dead man. I wasn't thinking yet. I shrugged.

—That looks like a yes, he said. —So. There I was in Kilmainham. Doing my duty for the Empire. I was no republican, Henry. Did you ever meet a unionist before?

He patted his chest.

—I served. Marched off in 1914. For King and country. And I came home to a different country, and I didn't like it. So, anyway. I was letting myself get thrown from cell to cell. Picked up a bit of information here, a little more there, nothing much from yourself, if I remember right. Anyway, after you hopped over the wall, I was thrown into – I fell gracefully into this one cell. Your friend, Jack Dalton. He was about as talkative as you were. But I'd learnt my lesson. I was as talkative back. I asked nothing and said nothing. The strong man. I must have done a good job, because they fuckin' rescued me. Myself and Dalton, and another flute called Archer – you know him. We all escaped, over the wall. It frightened the shite out of me. On the run with those thicks, trying to stay a step ahead. But I made it up as I went along. Like yourself.

He sat up, and re-crossed his legs.

—And I must have done alright, because they'd have sworn they'd known me since the schooldays with the Brothers by the time we stopped running. And by then I knew that it was all over for King and Empire and the time had come for a change in career. So I just kept on being what they thought I was. Gas, isn't it?

I nodded. I might even have smiled.

—So then we have the Civil War. Jack goes one way, Archer goes the other. I said to myself, no more of the tricks. I'd been against the Republic but I'd changed sides and now I'd go right for it. So, Lieutenant Edwin McKittrick of the Royal Irish Rifles – that was me before I went secret – became a diehard republican. I even shot Jack. And then there was the truce, the war's all over, and they sent me over here.

—For me.

He shook his head.

326

—You're a vain little cunt, Henry. I could see that back then too. We weren't after you. Why the fuck would we have been? You're shite.

It was the line that announced the arrival of the firing squad. I looked at him. I looked around. But no one; we were still alone.

—But we did keep an eye on you.

—You followed me around, all this time?

He grinned, a short one, and stopped.

—I'd love to say Yeah. I'd love to. But, no. There's no point in messing. It'd be more accurate to say we kept an eye out for you. Lots of eyes, actually. Two of which, Henry, have seen plenty of you.

I looked at him.

—She told you, I said.

—She did, yeah.

I didn't believe him; I felt and knew it, a certainty that sat quietly and said nothing.

—But we'd had you marked earlier, in New York, what, six years ago?

I gave a slight nod.

—It was the Glick thing. When we heard the name. Glick, Smart. Very fuckin' clever. More of your fuckin' vanity. Anyway, there was a story about pigeons. Am I right?

I nodded.

—I can't remember. Were they Madden's or Schultz's?

I shrugged.

—One of them, anyway. You killed their pigeons.

—I didn't.

—Yeah, yeah. It doesn't matter. We found out. Madden's a good Irish boy, and he puts a bit of work our way now and again. And he was going to throw you at us, which would have been nice. But that gobshite, Mister fucking No, wanted you for himself. He was very keen. Him and his mott. What was her name?

—Mildred.

No mention of the half-sister.

—That's right. Mildred. So we left him to it. You were off the list. And you got away, of course. You're fuckin' gas. And we lost you. And, to be honest, we didn't give much of a fuck. You were no danger to us. Just a nuisance. A little bit of business it would have been nice to finish, just in case you ever thought about going back to Erin.

327

He stopped, and looked. I shook my head. He shrugged.

—But, anyway, off you went on us. And then you were in Chicago.

He smiled and sat back. The smile stayed.

—She didn't tell you she was still involved, did she? Missis Smart. Did she? After your reunion.

I stared at him. All my shake went to my eyes. I stayed still, and stared. Absolutely still.

He took the gun from his pocket. He pointed it at me.

—What I'd love to do is. I'd love to stop now and shoot you. I'd love to do that. You cunt. She *informed* on you.

I couldn't stop myself.

—Yeah?

—Yeah.

—Is she here?

—Oh, yeah.

—Where?

—Upstairs.

I was out of touch. I didn't recognise the gun. Talk was all I had.

—Why are you telling me this?

—I'm getting it off my chest.

He smiled. I saw his hand shake. Suddenly, and it had nothing to do with what I saw and heard, there was one thing I was sure of. It sat in me, the certainty: it wasn't going to happen.

—You're not alone, are you? I said.

—Of course I'm not.

—Are you not worried your pals will hear you?

—None of them are Irish. They wouldn't have a clue what I'm talking about.

He lifted his hand, brought fingers together, to click them.

—One more question, I said.

—Be my guest. It's a hotel.

—A fuckin' quiet one.

—The question.

—Well, I said.

I sat up and leaned towards him.

—Why?

—Ah now, Jaysis.

—Why are you doing it? Now? I left Dublin eight years ago.

—When did the English invade Ireland? You know yourself.

That's not even a long time. There are men who'll be pleased to know that you're dead and they'll be pleased to know that I was the one that killed you. The diehards are getting very respectable over there, I'm told. They're ready for power. New coats, elections. You're a loose end, Henry. And so am I. But I'm less loose, if you follow me. But, dear old Ireland being dear old Ireland, some of the diehards are getting even harder. They won't be going the respectable way. And they're the ones who've never really trusted me, which is a big reason why I'm over here. I'll tell you, the cloud over my head might not be as black as the one over yours, but it's there. Oh yeah. Doubts. Always been there. But I've a feeling the doubts will blow away when it gets known that I was the one that got rid of you.

He clicked his fingers. And the boys were there. Two at the lobby door, more from the kitchen – I didn't look; probably two more. I heard the door hinges clunk, and clunk again as they settled back. Kellet plus four, maybe three. So what? There was nothing I could do. There'd be more outside. I'd seen them.

—Stand up.

—Why?

It was black, till the pain caught up with me and I was on the floor, and suddenly not. I was in the air, held up, let go, and standing in front of Kellet. My head was hopping – probably a gun butt.

—That's amazing, he said. —I've just seen your eyes fill with blood. Could you feel it yourself?

—I'd other things on my mind.

—Good man, he said. —Joking to the death. The blood just flowed across the whites, like water. It suits you.

He was sweating, now that I was up to him, held tight by the lads who'd come through from the kitchen. I could see the jaundice in his eyes and skin.

—Have you seen your own eyes lately? I said.

He took the step back. I expected the kick.

—Come on.

He turned. He picked his hat up from the floor beside his chair.

—You're not doing it in here? I said.

—God, no. That's not part of the deal. We can't be dragging bodies in and out. This is a business address, Henry. We'll have to put you up against a different wall. Come on.

The shove sent me at him.

—Wrong way.

I turned; he shoved. The doors were held open by someone, two more, inside, and I was in the kitchen, going back the way I'd come in. No one looked, no one stopped working. Life went on, meals for the guests I hadn't seen, sent out on trays to the empty dining room. Back, through two doors to the alley and the cold. Back down towards the street, two men in front, two behind, and Kellet, down the alley. Under laced, dead windows. It was colder again; the sun was well behind the street. No traffic passed, no one stepped across. *Five foot two, eyes of blue.* The radio from the garage. What now? Where? *But oh! what those five feet could do.* I expected a car, the door pushed open, the shove.

A car did pass but didn't stop.

—In.

I stopped.

—The garage.

—Been done before, I said. —Last year. Valentine's Day.

—Good man, said Kellet, behind me. —In you go.

I thought about running. *Has anybody seen my girl?* The corner, the Upton Oil truck around it, maybe still there. I could get to it. I could knock over the men in front of me. *Turned-up nose, turned-down hose.* Or across the street, zigzag, into the department store, through the window the bullets would shatter before me. *Flapper? Yes, sir, one of those.* The two guys in front turned at the entrance and made a wall, coat shoulder to shoulder. I walked into the gloom of the garage. I stopped. I didn't know where to go. *Has anybody seen my girl?* But one of the guys was ahead again. He had a golf bag over his shoulder. Big bag, two golf clubs – there was room in there for other things. Work went on as I was brought through. Metal on metal, somewhere near. *But could she love, could she woo?* I went between two cars. I followed the guy with the heavy golf bag. Another door, steel. Another alley. *Could she, could she, could she coo?* Darker, colder, ice on the ground. No street I could run to. *Has anybody seen my girl?* I heard the door slammed, the bolt pulled across, inside.

I followed the golfer. This alley had corners. He took one, left. I went with him. A rat slipped away. A big bastard, there – gone. There were two men right behind me now, up against my back. The golfer stopped at another metal door. New painted. Dark green. He knocked. Right behind me, close, cigarette breath, sweat. There was no spot I could run to, no room to start running.

The bolt was pulled, the door opened out. We all stepped back. We entered.

A warehouse, or something. Empty, and huge because of that. High, narrow windows in the far wall. They let in good light, and I guessed that there was a wide street behind the wall. There was an arched double-gate, high and wide enough for any vehicle, and I could hear traffic. The place was empty, except for a piece of canvas, folded near my feet, and a couple of broken barrels, on their sides, in the centre of the floor. There were other doors, all shut, and steep wooden stairs to a glass-fronted office, to my left, maybe twice my height above my head. The glass was long-dirty; no face looked down. The place had been cold all winter.

—Home, said Kellet.

I was pushed. I'd been ready but it caught me; a foot took my foot as I went forward. I was on the floor; I landed well. I could smell old alky and the quick stink of the kerosene that had been rubbed on the barrels to mask the profitable stink of the contents. There were other doors, another rat.

—Choose a wall, Henry, said Kellet.

—Lady's choice, I said.

—Make your opponent angry, said Kellet. —Textbook stuff. And bullshit. The bullets will still perforate you. You might as well stand up. To be honest with you, I'm not sure why I put you down there in the first place. Sorry.

—You're alright, I said.

I stood up in time to see the golfer take a shotgun from his bag. I was almost pleased; a golf club would have worried me more. I looked at them all; the blank faces I'd always been right to be scared of. They'd all kill me, not even happily – it wouldn't work them up or down. I was a job today, a very small one.

Bollix to that. I could feel it in me. I wasn't going to be their easy day. I might end up dead, but I was taking people with me. I wasn't going to fuckin' die; come and fuckin' get me. I could feel it in my feet, the certainty – but I hadn't a clue where it came from. There he was, the golfer, and Kellet nodded at the wall behind me. There was no one near to grab. They'd all stepped back, and there were more. There'd been more men in the warehouse, I didn't know how many, but I was grabbed now and held stiff by strong arms, and Kellet stepped over and ran his hands down my coat.

—You really don't have a gun, he said. —For fuck sake, Henry.

—I know.

—Gone soft.

I tried to shrug, but the arms wouldn't let me.

He found my wallet and took it. He flipped it open; he stared at me. He stepped well back, and put his gun in a coat pocket. Then he looked properly at the wallet.

—Ah look.

It was the photograph. His eyes, his hands on it. It made me strong. I felt the fury, I took it and made it flow. He held up the photograph.

—Who's the fat fucker with you?

—Ivan Reynolds.

—The big noise himself.

He laughed.

—He'd pay a few quid for this, I'd say. He wouldn't want to be seen like this, respectable cunt that he is. The best man and all, yeah?

—Yeah.

He laughed again.

—Best man at the soon to be famous Henry Smart's wedding. And it could all come out at the same Henry's funeral. D'you want to know why you're going to be famous, Henry?

He looked at the photograph.

—I'm tempted, he said. —I'm fuckin' tempted. A nice trip home, a visit to Mister Reynolds, at home or in Leinster House. He'd fork out, alright.

He flicked the photo with a fingernail.

—No. I have to stay squeaky. Clothes off, Henry.

—What?

—You heard me.

—Bullets go through cloth.

—Just get your fuckin' clothes off.

—All?

—All. I'll explain as you go.

I nodded. It meant the hands and arms would let me go; it meant more time.

The hands were gone; my weight was mine. I unbuttoned my coat.

—Good man.

The coat was taken before it dropped. I unbuttoned my jacket. Hands took it off my back. I pulled down the Clarence Darrows.

—Can I have them, Henry? said Kellet.

I shrugged.

—A memento.

—Fair enough.

I got down and untied a bootlace. Two pairs of shoes behind me.

—So, I said. —Why am I doing this?

—You'll like it, said Kellet. —You're helping an important man out, with a bit of woman trouble.

I changed knees and untied the second lace. There were seven other men in the warehouse.

—You're her bit on the side.

—Do I know her?

I stood up and pulled off a boot.

—No, he said. —I don't think so.

No one laughed.

—Doesn't seem fair, does it, Henry?

I looked as I pulled off the other boot.

I unbuttoned the trousers.

—Jesus, Henry, if you were always this slow getting the pants off, you'd never have got your reputation.

—It's called foreplay, Ned.

He laughed, and a thick-looking cunt behind him. The shotgun didn't. I could tell: he didn't understand. We weren't talking his language.

—You're calling me Ned now. Suggesting friendship, a shared history. Thinking I'll maybe hesitate, yeah?

—No, I said. —You're a cunt. There's no getting round that.

I stepped out of the trousers.

—Tell me more.

—The important man.

—Italian?

—Probably. He has a wife and children. Loves the lot of them. He has a girlfriend as well. She is beautiful and she's been the girlfriend for quite some time. The gent has had enough of her, beaut and all that she is.

I took off my socks.

—But he is too much of the gentleman to simply ditch her.

If things went wrong and I ended up dead, I wasn't going to be found in my socks.

—And this is where you come in, Henry.

—Do I get to know her?

—No.

I got to work on my drawers. I let them drop.

—There's something missing, I said. —How am I any good to this guy?

—I know, I know, said Kellet. —I'd have thought the same thing myself. That he should catch you in the act. And then he could bump off the pair of you and no one would complain. That's what you're thinking.

—Yeah.

—Me too. And a nice way to go. She's a ride, you should see her. She'd put the horn on a fuckin' corpse.

America was dropping off him, the longer he talked to me.

—But, believe it or not, Henry, actually catching you at it won't be necessary. You were photographed with Mister Madden's piece of fluff five or six years ago.

I nodded.

—Photographs, for fuck sake. I've seen them, you know. Looking much the same as you do now.

He held up my wedding photo.

—They beat this one. You see, you're a danger to decent gangsters. And you've been stuffing the Sister Flow item.

I hadn't, and he didn't know that she was the same woman who'd kept Madden warm back in the days when I was going places.

It was coming up from somewhere: I was still that Henry.

I nodded.

—I have her record, said Kellet. —We all do. Another girl who'd put the horn on a corpse. How do – sorry, how *did* you do it?

—It's not something that can be taught, Ned.

—Pity.

I shrugged.

—But at least I'll live longer than you, said Kellet.

Not with your habits, pal, I thought. But I gave him another shrug.

—Come here, though, I said. —You're not going to shoot this young one as well, are you?

—Won't be necessary. We dump your body at her door, and that's more than enough. She can deny any messing as much as she likes, but our man will be more than justified in breaking the connection. And it'll be noticed how restrained he is in not killing her too. He'll be admired for it. So he can't lose here. And she'll be grand. Back into show business. Another sugar daddy; our man won't mind. She's laughing.

He nodded at the wall.

—You, on the other hand. Move.

I had to ask.

—Why?

—Ah Jesus. Why what?

—The wall.

—There are two clients here, Henry. The maybe-Italian gent just wants to see you dead. My Irish clients, however, want you executed. Go on.

It was up to me; something would have to happen. I stepped, barefoot, to the nearest wall, and I still believed. It would happen. This wasn't the ending at all.

Kellet spoke to my back.

—They'll be looking for the bullet marks in the brick. You remember the way they are. Sticklers for fuckin' formality. It's making a martyr of you, if you ask me. But, orders is orders, so turn around for us there. We can't be shooting you in the back.

I turned.

—Jesus, he said. —You should see your eyes from here.

A line of men in front of me, all with guns out. A door to my left, closed, bolted – no padlock that I could see; maybe outside – the bolt was inside. The office above, empty. Another door, closed – no bolt. The barrels, the stink. The high gates on the other side, behind the line of men. Two smaller doors that I could see, bolt on just one – open. The canvas. The emptiness.

Kellet walked up, right up to me. Here was the chance, but he came right at me and he shot, once, twice – I didn't hear the second shot – right and left of my head; I saw the barrel swing past my face. Brick entered my face and back and arms, hot darts, and he pushed me back against the wall. I couldn't hear.

The wall was cold and sharp against my back. My only hope was to keep pressing until it fell away behind me – but it jabbed and mocked me; it was suddenly hopeless. He could have killed me; he was going to. The barrel was pressed now into my neck, the heat of recent use burning and taunting, daring me to move, cough, blink. And five, six more guns staring at me, ranks of the hard men waiting for their turn. I couldn't move my eyes; I couldn't talk. I couldn't hear. The barrel pressed deeper into my neck, and deeper, inviting me to budge and die. Then it was gone, and I wished it back: it was safer in my neck.

The sound, the world came back. The first thing I heard was the match. Then I smelled it. I couldn't see flame yet, or smoke, but I didn't move my eyes. Then the photograph was up in front of me, three inches from my face, and I saw it burn and curl.

—Can you hear me, Henry?

It broke into weightless black chunks and drifted, up in the rising air, away from me.

—We can't have them finding this. It muddies the picture.

The wedding dress, the brooch, the glowing hair.

—And we have to hide her, said Kellet.

I wasn't looking at him.

—It was her who found you for us, Henry. What d'you think of that?

The creases at the photograph's edges, the tears and folds and flour, the records of the years hidden in a fugitive's wallet, her face. I watched the thin flame turn them all to nothing.

And now I looked at him.

—Get fucked, I said.

Then he shot me.

I fell – a decision; I did it – and the air was full of bullets and feet and brick and cordite and glass and shells and sunlight and shattering glass and running feet. And I was alive and the room was empty, everything gone but the last of the gunshots. I followed the sunlight; two doors were open. And I was still alive and it made no sense and I was delighted with the pain, thrilled, fuckin' agony, and I was still alive. The pain in my shoulder was unbearable, fuckin' wonderful, and there was the blood too, but I thought I could get myself up. I put my weight into the good arm, the right.

And I was kicked.

I looked at brown boots.

—Get up out of that, Henry Smart.

I looked up, and saw brown eyes and some slivers of grey hair, brownish-grey, that had escaped from a bun that shone like a lamp behind—

She kicked me again.

—Get up like I told you. The state of you; you're a disgrace.

She grabbed hair – there wasn't much else to grab – and got me to my feet.

She swept the warehouse, the full circle, with her Parabellum, aiming it at all dangers.

—Get your clothes on.

I looked as she turned past me. Her face was calm and furious, but the eyes were laughing at me. I was bleeding to death and hopping, one-armed, into my drawers. But I managed, and the trousers and the jacket. I stuffed the shirt into a coat pocket and got the coat over the good shoulder. Then the boots. I got the feet in.

—I'll need help with the laces, I told her.

She stopped turning and put the gun into my right hand. Fuck, it was heavy. I aimed it at walls, doors. And she bent down to do my laces.

—What age are you?

—Nearly thirty, I said.

She slapped my shin.

—And you can't tie your own laces?

—I could if you hadn't've fuckin' shot me.

She looked up.

—How'd you know it was me?

—I didn't, I said. —I just said it.

She looked back at the lace.

—It was nothing personal.

She finished one, started the other. The pain was less wonderful now.

—I had to drop you, she said. —Before the other bullets got you.

I nodded.

She stood up and took the gun and I grabbed her collar and pulled her at me.

—You fuckin' shot me!

—And what of it? she said.

She kissed me. I was up at the wall again, the brick digging into the agony.

—You led them to me!

—You did that yourself, sure. I thought you were in New York.

—Oh.

—With your Pops.

She stood away. She looked at me.

—I'd never do that.

She looked away.

337

—I know, I said. —I know that.

She pushed me again. My shoulder hit the wall.

—God, you're the go-boy, Henry Smart. Always getting into trouble.

—Lay off, I said. —Fuckin' lay off. I haven't done anything illegal since I came here.

—You broke into Missis Lowe's.

—Ah, you know what I mean.

—And weed on the window.

—So you fuckin' shot me?

—No, she said. —And less of that language. Come on now before we get into real trouble.

I followed as she went for one of the doors.

—You're enjoying this, aren't you?

—Sure, stop.

—I love you, Miss.

—Go 'way out of that.

She kicked the iron door.

—I love you too.

It swung out, whacked the warehouse wall, and we were out. Air and sun, the pain and the street and Miss and, standing under a butcher's awning across the street, Saoirse. The serious little face, the hand in the air, waving. I tried to wave back.

—I'm going to faint.

—Not here you don't, mister.

But I did.

PART FOUR

9

She finally liked America. She loved it.

—God, it's great, isn't it?

The wind threw us back and stung the faces off us. We held hands and the sides of the boxcar. Saoirse held onto Miss O'Shea's dress. It was flat country we looked at, flatter and bigger than anything they'd seen.

—We're far from home.

—We are, she said. —But, sure.

She smiled, and the wind pulled her head right back.

She began to like the people. These were country people, like herself. They'd never seen cities. They'd no idea how big the land beyond their eyes was; what they saw was more than big. Their grandparents had made the big shove, from the east, from Europe, but they hadn't budged since. (They didn't know that soon enough they'd have to move again.) Miss O'Shea liked them; they looked, and liked her too. They spoke to her and Saoirse, but not to me.

—You're a Dublin guttie, she told me. —They know your clock.

—They never heard of Dublin.

—They still know.

There was no real answer. She was right.

—Fuck them, I said.

—They'd be the same if you came from New York or Chicago, she said. —It's the smell of the city off you. You're the go-boy.

—But you killed men.

—Oh, they'd love that if they knew. One of their own. They'd be proud of me, killing the peelers.

—I give up.

—Grand.

Saoirse listened, watched, and took it in.

—I like the cities, she said.

341

—Good woman.

—I like it here too.

—The best of both worlds.

—What does that mean?

—You're happy everywhere.

—Everywhere isn't both.

—What?

—There's more than both.

I smiled. I put my hand on her shoulder. My own shoulder was still aching.

—I knew what you meant, she said.

—I know.

—I like thinking things out loud.

—So, think about food out loud.

—Oh, don't, said Miss O'Shea. —I'm starving.

We lived for days on air and fingernails. Having a kid came in handy and Saoirse quickly knew this. Big eyes at the back door, little hand on the glass.

—Have you some milk for the mammy's new baby?

Miss O'Shea wrote the lines, after she'd run out of shame.

—I'm just glad my mother isn't alive to see us. Begging.

—She'd have needed fuckin' good eyesight.

We were hiding in a ditch, keeping the eye on Saoirse. Miss O'Shea whacked me, called me an eejit. The ditch was dry and a snake had moved out when we'd moved in, but it felt like home. We were on the run and she was in love again.

And so was I.

We'd jump off at a town – Sandusky, Sioux City – and go looking for bait. A bit of old bread in a bin behind a house, in the early morning; we'd take it around to the front of the house and park it on the step. We'd wait for the smells of breakfast to seep out of the house and give Saoirse the shove to the door. It wasn't needed – she loved the work. She tapped the door and waited, sometimes until kids came charging out for school; she'd be there to stare at them. She'd wait for the mother.

—*Dia dhuit.** Can I have that slice of bread?

She'd point at the crust from the bin. It rarely – big eyes, the little finger – failed. She'd hop back to us with great things in a paper bag soaking up the grease. I often ate the bag.

* Hello; God be with you.

We stuck together. Together, we weren't hoboes. Alone, I was grabbed by the cops and brought to the edge of town, to jail, or down an alley for a hiding. Together, we could stay, not often welcome, but safe. When people saw me, they saw bad news, trouble, theft. They saw us, and they saw themselves – bad luck, hard times, true love. They saw me, the foreigner, the salesman, the city boy with the fancy suspenders. They saw me with Miss O'Shea, and they didn't see me at all.

—'Day to you, ma'am.

—D'you think it'll rain? she'd ask a man who hadn't seen real rain in three years.

—Reckon it might, ma'am.

—Please God.

—You said it, ma'am.

She was having a great time.

—D'you know what? she said, as we landed beside each other on a dirt embankment as hard as history.

We rolled away from the wheels. I held onto Saoirse. She was able to scramble on top of me as I rolled.

—What? I said when we stopped.

—This is our honeymoon, said Miss O'Shea.

She kissed the dirt off my lips.

These people would give us the barn for a night, or a week's good work, a dead man's boots. Hunger was the starter every morning; we'd get up and deal with it together. And the cold of night would push us close together.

—*Oíche mhaith.**

—Good-night, love.

In the first months, in the first year and further.

We listened till we knew she slept; we listened across the sounds of the frogs and other rasping, creaking fuckers that kept it up all night.

—Will you just look at all those stars.

—Fuck all those stars.

—God, you're dreadful. What if they arrived now?

—Here we go. Kellet and his boys?

—God.

—The army of the Free State?

—Oh God.

* Good-night.

343

In the early weeks and months, we were running. We were a man, woman and child on their standing, a small family of diehards. We'd no mountains to hide in and no bike to commandeer and make lethal, but we were back in our good old days. And they *were* fuckin' good. We were happy.

The lad was conceived between Albuquerque and El Paso del Norte, on a bed of coal, on a clear, cold night, while water from a refrigerated truck leaked down onto us and a gang of whistling hoboes entertained Saoirse three boxes back.

Miss O'Shea gasped as the fireman opened the firebox to throw in a shovel-load of our coal. Bright orange light hit the smoke that poured over us and we could suddenly see the flat land, a jack rabbit, the fireman bending, all orange, for a hundred feet all around us. We knew it and we cried.

—What will we call him, Henry?

He was born between Denver and Salt Lake City. In a boxcar that was empty, except for Miss O'Shea, some chaff and the midwife. I was above with Saoirse. My Clarence Darrows held her strapped to the roof. I was trying to get a fire going – not easy on top of a train doing sixty miles an hour – to roast the pigeons I'd caught as they'd pecked at the chaff inside the boxcar. I was excited and scared, and more scared because we couldn't hear a thing from down below. The train roared, the steam whistle screeched, every time we thought we'd heard a new voice. I leaned out and tried to catch the sound. We killed the dangerous time, me and Saoirse.

The midwife was a big-armed girl called Daisy. She'd had three boys and lost all three and she wept all the time I watched her, in the boxcar before she shooed us out on a slow bend. And she was crying when she climbed up to tell us. She crawled off the ladder and stayed on all fours.

She had to roar.

—Boy!

Born to a mother in a boxcar. To an Irishwoman, fierce and lovely and forty-three.

—What'll we call him, Henry?

She was sitting up already. Weak, but ready to fight or run.

I held him, gently. I made an armchair of my hands for him. I sat in a corner and pushed my back well against the walls, to stop the train's shaking. My jacket kept the wind off him.

—Is he my brother now? said Saoirse.

344

—That's right.

I looked at her.

—Is that alright with you?

She thought about it.

—Yes, she said. —I think so.

—Good.

She sat beside me. Her mother – the sweat, the paleness, exhausted eyes – frightened her.

—Will we live in a house now?

—I don't know, I said. —We'll see.

—What will we call him? said Miss O'Shea.

I didn't want the question; I didn't want to answer. I wouldn't hand him the name.

The train was slowing. We heard the whistle. We heard car doors scraped open. We saw men drop from cars, and roll. We saw the Rocky Mountains, huge and close. We saw men run into the weeds.

—I don't know, I said.

—Henry, she said.

—No.

—Victor, she said.

I looked at her.

—No.

She nodded.

The brakes screeched, iron on iron. The baby didn't mind. I watched his face; he roared over the brakes – *What about meeee?* – but got no angrier. The screeching stopped. We heard chains slacken and knock. We heard feet on cinders, billy clubs patting trouser legs. The railroad bulls were waiting for us, the only ones left on the train. Four or five of them, in tight, wet uniforms. Thick-necked cunts, looking robbed and stupid, swinging their weapons.

I jumped first.

—Howyeh, lads.

I turned my back and felt their heat on this cold day, closing in on me.

Saoirse jumped. They stopped. And saw Miss O'Shea.

—Good Lord almighty.

—That child new?

—Baked today, I said. —Where are we?

I helped her down. She resented the need, but pressed herself to my hands.

—You're in Rifle, Colorado.

—That's what we'll call him, I said as her feet found the ground. I could feel the Parabellum under her dress.

—What?

—Rifle, I said.

—We will not, she said.

We strolled right past them. I held Saoirse's hand.

—See yis, lads.

—*Slán libh.**

—Fuckin' hell, I said. —This air is on the fresh side.

We called him Séamus Louis but Rifle was my name for him. And we didn't live in a house. She made sure we didn't.

We were alone when we ran out of Chicago. We'd no idea which way we were headed; we'd just grabbed the first freight train slow enough to catch. There were miles of tracks, dozens of locomotives, dragging endless boxcars. We ran alongside, me and Miss, Saoirse on my back. The bullet was still in my shoulder. But I'd done this before; I'd done it for years. Miss O'Shea was new and her boots weren't built for the loose ground under them.

—Grab the front, I shouted.

She ran, and grabbed, held tight and stiff, and I watched and admired as she lifted herself onto the car. I grabbed one-handed. She leaned out and took a hold of Saoirse, and we landed in a heap, safe from the gaping door. My shoulder hit the boxcar floor; I tried not to scream.

We were alone.

And that was how it was for months, or how it seemed, a year. But then we saw, and began to know that we weren't out there alone. The boxcars filled, men alone, fathers with sons, gangs of kids, girls trying to look like boys, boys trying to be men. There was once – we'd jumped aboard in darkness and slept into a shaking day – we turned on a long curve, and saw them, in boxcars ahead of us and behind, clinging to the roofs, hundreds, maybe thousands of men, travelling with us.

The first time we saw a family standing on the embankment, starting to run, ready to jump and help each other jump, we both gasped, me and Miss. We knew why we were running and now, finally, after months, we knew something else.

—Jesus Christ.

* Goodbye.

The wife was a kid herself. He was a bit older, ten years younger than me, but thinness had made a well-worn man of him; the dust and dirt made him look like slowly running stone. There were two kids, in clothes made of burlap sacks. And their mother's skirt was burlap too. He jumped. I put out my hand. He glared. He sat at the door with his back to us. She ran beside him, and handed him a child. She fell back and grabbed the other. She was fast and angry. He caught the kid. She grabbed his other arm. We sat back, gave them the open door. They ignored it. They sat away, didn't look at the passing country. They didn't talk. The kids didn't squabble or roll. Then I saw it, another child at her breast, grey rags in her grey rags. No bundles, food. No shoes or boots. I was back in Dublin, on the move across America.

We knew now that this was history. This wasn't our story, and I knew that I'd missed my American chance. We knew we wouldn't be hunted, and we knew that there was no point in stopping or speeding up. We'd been passed. It wasn't our story but we were looking at ourselves. I watched the bundle at the breast. I watched our own bundle at Miss O'Shea's breast. I watched the man look at his children. He stared at them, at each one, hard, measuring the effort and luck needed to keep them alive. Desperation held his face. Saoirse found my hand and held it. I squeezed, and smiled at her. We looked out at the dirt.

We followed the weather. *Rise and shine, you sons of bitches.* We learnt where the work was. *Get your ass out and dig them ditches.* We weighed apples, washed dishes. A week, two, a day, an hour. *It ain't near daybreak but it's half past two.* A month, the season – we stayed, and went. *I don't want you but the boss man do.* We walked after the sun – potatoes in Idaho.

—God, they're useless; look it.

Berries and apples in Oregon. We stayed out of the cities.

—That's where they'll be looking, she said.

She didn't want to go back.

—If they're looking, I said.

—You don't have to be looking to be looking.

We stayed alone, apart, until that wasn't possible any more. The boxcars filled, the roadsides; millions were moving, on the tramp. Hoovervilles, the hobo jungles, grew wherever there was water and the chance of a left-alone night. A couple of tents at first, then more, then tin and canvas, slats of wood; they spread along banks and roads, took wasteland, the spaces between use

– thousands of people; they stopped moving, just for now. A night, a week, a breather, a death, birth, arrest, and on. They talked about food, the men and women we joined at the fires. They'd talk about their farms and dust.

—Boys, we was tractored out.

—Dusted out.

—Well, hell, I got kicked out.

They laughed, drily, talked about the banks and landowners. And, as the numbers grew and the fire became fires, they talked about destinations, the jobs waiting and just missed, the routes they'd take and had already taken.

A different day, we were heading west in a full boxcar, a hot day full of cinders and scorching steam. We stopped at a siding, for a freight speeding east. We heard and watched it pass, and the same men clung to the roofs and blinds. Were they coming back or starting? We waved. They waved. We looked at each other and quietly laughed.

They talked about food, about what they'd eaten once and what they'd eat again. The future and past were one – grits, bacon, biscuits, gravy. Only the present got in the way, as we waited for the bits and miserable pieces in the pot to become a stew. We'd bring an onion, our admission, our walk-up to the fire and pot, or hard bread, or an old chicken Miss O'Shea had shot when no one was looking, whatever we could get to buy our arse-room at the fire.

We listened but we kept our mouths well shut.

We watched hundreds of men move on a rumour. They were up and bundled, waiting on the dirt embankment for the steam whistle, ready to cross states because the latest arrival had sat among them with news of a job – pears ready for picking, a pipeline ditch that needed digging. The jungle was quickly deserted, just us left, and empty tin and wood shacks, a broken shaving mirror stuck into a tree trunk, an oul' lad too tired and ancient to go. The next morning we'd wake and the camp would be full again, more moving men, women, kids, fresh off the last freight, following their own rumours, running from the failure of their up-to-now. We tried to cross America alone; we tried to ignore the stories.

We stayed out of California.

—Too many cities and built-up places, she said.

—So what?

—They'll be waiting.

I doubted that, but I was happy. We were a handsome family, and we survived. We kept ourselves clean. *We're in the money, we're in the money.* The dust and sand couldn't hide our glow.

Séamus Louis Smart. He grew as America shrank. Young Rifle O'Glick. He threw back his head and poured the red and grey and the yellow dust into his mouth. And the big belly on him – it looked like starvation, but we knew better. He was eating the place, state by state.

—MACUSHLA, MACUSHLA—

Saoirse sang at the one-street diner doors. And, soon enough, Rifle was with her.

—YOUR S'EET VOIT IT CALLING—

People stopped and smiled and found a penny deep down in worn pockets. They didn't throw; they bent right down and left the pennies at their feet.

The colours went before the money did. The blues, the reds, the yellows dropped off good dresses and hats; people faded into the country. They still stopped – they couldn't help it, even though Rifle kept growing as they watched – but nothing came out with their hands, or the hands stayed in the pockets. They'd nothing left to give.

—CALLING ME SOFT-LEEEE—

And then they didn't stop.

—AGAIN AND A—

GAIN.

They wouldn't search for money that wasn't there, or stoke the terror that it wouldn't be there again. And the diner screen doors pulled away from hinges and fell to the dust, and the dust banked on the sills, and there was no one there to sing to. Whole towns were empty and crumbling. Even the wrecking yards, so busy at the start, full of men crawling under dead cars, searching for parts to bring their own to life – they were still full but dead and owner-less. Until men climbed the wire and built homes there from the parts. Until they, too, moved on.

We'd sit at a boxcar door as the train crawled through some town – the slow warning clang warning no one – and we'd know: there was no point in jumping. There wasn't enough out there. It was all sinking under the dust.

We sang and kept going, and we tried to catch up. We'd land in a town before the lights went finally out. A week, a season. I'd stand on the kerb and, now and again, a man would slow down and lean out his window.

—Drive a tractor?

—Yeah.

—Dollar day, take it, leave it.

—Any work for my family?

—What you got?

—Wife, two kids.

—What age on the young'ns?

—Five and thirteen.

I remember being shocked as I listened to my voice give their ages. So shocked, I didn't see that I was alone again, or hear what the driver said before he took his head back inside and went. But I remember where I was.

Ransom, Kansas.

They came out from behind a dry-goods store, boarded-up, not worth breaking into – Miss O'Shea, Saoirse, the Rifle. They saw my face—

—WE'RE IN THE MONEY, WE'RE IN THE MONEY—

and stopped. I smiled, but they'd seen me.

There'd been the radios at first, through open doors and windows, behind diner counters; and the nickel phonographs, before the windows and the diners closed and stayed closed. *The skies are sunny.* The songs got into the shoulders – *Let's spend it, lend it, send it – rolling along.* Customers shook heads, tapped feet against rails, happy to fork out for a stranger's bread and meatball. My ears hung out for Louis. He was out there – *All aboard for Pittsboig, Harrisboig, oh, all the boigs* – then gone for a while, and back. *Hobo, you can't ride this train.* He'd been to Europe, I read in a barber shop somewhere.

—Not paying you to read, bub.

The cunt wasn't paying me at all. Two hours sweeping for a haircut, that was the deal. Rifle's head was free.

—Known his head was that big, I'd've made you pay cash money. Got yourself a name, sonny?

—Yare.

—Well?

—What?

Pride swept the floor for me.

—What is it?

—Séamus Louis Rifle O'Glick.

350

—What kind o' name is that?

—Better than yours, said Rifle.

That's the boy, I said to myself and I flicked my son's hair away from the other tufts. I chose a lock, bent down and took it. I put in my last good pocket. Rifle caught me at it, and he laughed.

As the times got harder, the songs got cornier. And we loved them.

—WE'RE IN THE MONEY—

We'd nothing and nowhere, but Miss O'Shea saved us before we knew we needed saving. We took to theft; we went right back to crime.

—There's them that can afford to be robbed, she said. —And it's no sin.

—Yes, Miss.

The gun stayed under her dress. The fires at night were full of the deeds of Pretty Boy Floyd and Baby-Face Nelson but they were dead, and they didn't have a family in tow when they shot up the banks and ran. So we stuck to the small-time, the grab-and-leg-it stuff I'd learnt as a kid and could teach to my own.

—Take the first corner you come to, I told Rifle and Saoirse.

—Always.

—Listen to your father.

—But always know where it'll lead you. Do your homework first. The bollix—

—Henry.

—The man running after you knows the town. It's his town, so you make sure that you know it too.

—Better.

—That's right, Saoirse. Better.

—Bollix.

—Good man. And stay out of the towns with no corners.

—Like this one?

—Exactly.

—Maybe we shouldn't be involving them at all, said Miss O'Shea one night, in a barn full of nothing but old smells and mice.

A nice widow had told us we could stay there as long as we wanted, after she'd looked down and seen Rifle staring up at her, then up and seen his daddy.

—Maybe it's not right, said Miss O'Shea.

—I'd agree with you, I said, —if it was five years ago. But there's not much else we can teach them now.

We'd tried, but even the schools were closing down. We'd knocked on a one-room school door on a day soon after Christmas. The dust was frozen in sharp drifts that cracked the soles of our boots; we still had good boots – we always had good boots. We'd decided to stay in Cheapwater for the rest of the winter; we'd keep clean and manage – we had the widow's barn, and the two kids to support us.

—Maybe I'll go for the teaching again, she said, as we waited for the door to open and welcome our children.

We stood there and began to understand the darkness inside, the hollowness of my knock. The school year had ended on the 1st of January, the widow told us; the school wouldn't open again till the fall.

—Sure glad my own young'ns got out before that state of thinking became normal.

There were twenty-five thousand teachers looking for new work. We met some of them, in boxcars, using their leather bags as pillows. *Dishwashers wanted – only college graduates need apply*.

So we gave up thoughts of teaching and staying still; we got stuck into the life of small-time family crime. It was straight-forward and easily remembered. Running away shocked me at first – I used to go much faster. But we were all fit, and hungry enough to want, and brave enough to step over the want and grab. The challenge was in the geography. Disappearing quickly was a doddle in the city, but a much bigger problem in a two-street town that hadn't seen new money in years, where goods were missed before they went. But we managed; clothes off lines, pies off windowsills – women did leave pies out there to cool, until that stopped too – cans off counters, chickens, ducks, piglets where we could find them, potatoes out of the guarded ground, anything that seemed worth the risk. And soon – *we're in the money* – everything seemed worth the risk.

—WE'RE IN THE MONEY—

Then they saw my face. On a street in Ransom. And they stopped singing. Rifle broke away from the women and walked right up to me. He opened his mouth wide.

And he bit me.

I didn't feel it.

—What's wrong? she said.

She had a chicken under her dress, dead but not ready to give up yet. It was shaking away under there.

—I don't know, I said.

—Time, I said, later, as I felt her there, staying awake beside me.

—Time?

—Yeah.

A chicken, but no pot. We'd dug a hole, stuffed the fucker with mud, and built a fire over the hole. It had eventually cooked grand but the smell of stolen chicken had slithered its way all over Ransom and the state of fuckin' Kansas.

—What about time? she said.

—It's flying.

—God almighty.

—What?

—I'm nearly fifty, Henry Smart. Do you hear me whingeing?

—It's not that.

—What then?

—I'm living the way I was when I was a kid. Exactly the way I was when I was a kid. When we – met.

—It's not the same.

—It is the same. It's the same. The exact same.

—You have us.

—I know. But—

—What?

—Nothing. I love you. I'm happy. I love you. And the pair over there. But.

—Victor.

—I had him too.

—And then you didn't.

—He died on me.

I heard her breath.

—It happens when you live like this, I said.

I felt her nod, her hair against my face.

—And know what?

She didn't answer.

—Everyone's living like this. Or else they will be.

Her hair was gone. She was looking at me.

—What do you want to do? she said.

—I don't know, I said. —But we should try to be ready.

—How? For what?

—You've noticed, I said. —You have. The whole place is dying. You've seen it.

—Yes.

—When me and Victor ran into a shop, we always knew there'd be something to rob. Here, though. Christ.

—So, she said. —What'll we do, Henry?

—Go back?

—Back where?

—Chicago?

—Stupid.

—New York.

—Stupid.

—For fuck sake.

—Home, she said.

—Jesus, I don't know.

—Yes, she said. —You do.

—If it's bad here, it'll be worse there.

—Well, she said. —I'm going to sleep. We'll think of something in the morning.

And she did.

She sat up, out of the bedroll. I felt the quick draught.

—Times are bad, she told us. —And we're going to make them better.

And she meant it; her eyes had that look. They were the brightest things in America that day, and the maddest.

—We're going to free this place, Henry, she said, as we hopped the first freight out of town.

I believed her.

She jumped first, landed, and put her hand out. Saoirse didn't need her help; she was a woman now, almost, as tall as her ma, as beautiful. She hopped onto the car in a move that looked effortless and probably was. It was a cold morning, still night-cold; my breath ran ahead of me. I picked up Rifle. He jumped onto the blind behind the boxcar. His foot slid on the frozen engine steam, and now I watched him fall.

I jumped, and I grabbed as I jumped. Never grab the rear end, the hoboes said, but I didn't have a choice. I was swung, and hit the side of the car, hard, but I held on and felt Rifle's hair in my free fist. I had him, before he went under the wheel. I pulled him up and dropped him on the blind, made sure he was safe, and then I was gone – the pain caught up – no grip, between the cars, and I watched the train roll over.

—Look for me!

And days were gone before I knew who I was, and where, and what had happened.

—I will!

They were gone.

10

She was everywhere. But never where I went.

The Hoovervilles were full of her.

—She busted them tractors, every one. Stopped them from breaking up them farms.

At night, across the fires.

—She organised that strike down Abilene. Got the marshals to turn their guns.

I could track her by the stories.

—She took one look at those boys, they turned right round, changed sides.

But I couldn't.

The stories came from all directions; she was everywhere. Men who'd seen men shake her hand. Women who'd seen her walk into the river. Seen bullets melt, seen men kneel down before her.

Our Lady of the Working Man. Our Lady of the Boxcar.

Seen her walk right up to scabs.

—Her little girl beside her.

—Kind of glow off them.

—Glow?

—Word for it.

Our Lady of the Pickers and the Dispossessed. Four million of them roaming, crawling the highways, riding the rails, heading west to be despised. *Negroes and Okies Upstairs.* Ten million, more, out of jobs. Out of farms and businesses. The strikers, squatters. The helpless and the hopeful.

The first story I heard, I knew it was her. Even before Saoirse walked beside her.

—Purty as her mama.

I knew.

Before I heard where she came from.

—Some say she's Irish.

—Heard that said.

—Or Scot.

—Walked right into that bank.

I knew it was her. I said nothing. I sat back. I'd put nothing into the pot. I'd no right to the fire. Just what heat came through the press of men and families who'd earned their right by adding beans or bad meat to the stew.

I waited for the place, the name. I was ready to get up and leave. The second I heard it. I stood up – it got easier – and left, immediately. Abilene. Baring. Junction City. She was long gone, every time, the stories left behind. The same stories.

—She walked right into that bank. All sweet and determined, and the young'n toting the carpet bag.

And I heard them, many times.

—When? I asked, once, twice. Until I understood.

—When what, mister?

—When did this happen?

—Beginning of the hard times.

—Time the black dust started blowing.

—When?

—Time the banks was doing that foreclosing.

She was long gone, running with them.

—This here money's now the property of the Oklahoma Republican Army, she said. The young'n held up the bag. Cousin seed it. Stuffed. Like a hog before it meets the knife. —And it will be given right back to its rightful owners.

She was gone.

—And she marches straight out of there. And folks cheered, right there under the roof of the bank. Hands still holding air.

But I kept looking.

I understood. I knew: they were stories. They came from the people who told them. Desperate men made up their desperadoes. Their outlaws, their rebels and playboys. Men who robbed and got away with it, who fucked impossible women, who'd never been hardened by black wind and dust. Men like themselves, just bigger. Touchable, knowable – cousins, kin, from a town they'd all heard of. Pretty Boy Floyd. Clyde Barrow. Real men, robbing, making fools of the law and lawyers. And they got away with it for a while. I understood. The stories kept these people going. They took some of the heat off their shame, gave them back some self-respect. The

357

teller was part of the story, and so were the listeners, and that was one of their own out there, doing all the winning. The stories were made at the fire. At the fires, fire to fire. Night after night. Boxcar to filling station. Across, up, down, America. Every night, they made up their survival.

She was one of their own. She was their story. And I'd never find her, no more than I'd find Billy the Kid or the Croppy Boy. She was there, in the fire, their comfort, their courage and hope. Their story.

But I kept going. I'd been one of those made-up men. *Oh, he slipped through the night did the bold Henry Smart.* I'd been in stories. I'd killed and loved, and I was real. I kept going. Because I saw her in the stories. She was out there, catching her breath, waiting for me to catch up. I heard her letters at the fires, read by the travellers, but sent to me. The Oklahoma Republican Army, the ambushes, the proclamations. The hints and similarities. It was Miss O'Shea out there, all over there, everywhere, with Saoirse, her apprentice rebel. Freeing America. The stories were full of her. She was telling me to catch up and to hurry. *Look for me!*

And I saw the Wanted posters. On the walls of the sheriffs' and marshals' offices. I laughed the first time – *Dead or Alive* – and the second, and got a kicking for it, twice. *Kathline O'Houlahan.* I saw it, in the corner of a new-black eye, and I burst my shite laughing. They saw me looking at the poster – *aka Dark Rosaleen.*

—What's funny, friend? You know her?

—Yeah.

—Where is she?

—On the ocean green, I said.

They kicked; there was no one to stop them.

Aka Lady O'Shea, O'Toole, O'Bannion, O'Neill. Hair: brown or red or grey. Possibly Irish. Age: 25 to 55. O'Moore, O'Carroll, O'Glick. All the names but no photograph. I laughed as they kicked the day out of me. Her poster was everywhere but I still didn't know her name.

Saoirse was there. *With a young woman. Possibly her daughter. Known as Share O'Shea or Share-Share O'Glick.* They were telling me to hurry. *Hair: red or brown. Possibly Irish. Age: 14 to 25. Aka Freedom Smart.*

I listened out for Rifle. I leaned into the fire, waited for his name; I prayed and let myself burn. He wasn't on the posters. And he wasn't in the stories.

—They have a boy with them?

I tried to sound like one of them.

—Boy?

—Boy.

—No sir.

—Heard mention of no boy.

—Just theyse two gals.

I worried; I died. Where was he? She was keeping him out of trouble; I knew. But Rifle was too big for absence. Why wasn't he there, at the start or the end of at least one story? Holding the horses, handing out dollars. I followed, and listened, for months, a year; I listened, heard nothing. But I wouldn't grieve. I listened. I found a new fire, every night. I tried to get nearer. I met men and women I'd met before; I met them again, and again. I melted and froze, on the same day, in the same year. I got myself arrested; I became a loud vagrant, so they'd drag me in and I'd look for his name on the posters. I spent months in county jails and penitentiaries, there to read the posters. I was a slave, working for nothing on a judge's stoop crops. I was one man on a chain gang. I listened, heard nothing. The stories were fixed: two women blazed the trail. No boy, and no man hobbling up behind them. The leg ached; the silence slowly killed me.

One night, I went on fire. I fell forward. I felt hands pull me, hands beat me. I coughed, I saw. I sat up, I thanked them.

I'd heard.

—You okay?

—I'm grand.

—You smell too much like side-meat, mister. Might be wise to move along.

—Someone got there before us, a man said. —Seems like.

They watched me pour water on the leg.

—I'm grand, I said. —I fell asleep. I was listening.

—Happens a lot of folks listening to Jake there.

I looked at Jake.

—Go on. Please.

—Where I stop?

—You said a kid.

—That's right, said Jake, a thin man who could have been any age, from young to dead. —The kid strolled into the bank, right behind the gals. A boy. And he was singing.

I sang, quietly.

—WE'RE IN THE MONEY—

—That's right, said Jake. —You hear all this before?

—No, I said. —That's my son.

Shamus. Aka Shamus Louie. Hair, brown. Eyes, blue. Age, 6 to 16.
I cried. And a woman, any woman, rocked me till I slept.

He was out there too, barking and alive. Growing up too big to catch, waiting for his daddy. I slept for days. I shaved, I washed deep in a fierce river – the water cut the waste off me. I stole new trousers off a branch behind a farmhouse. I put them on as I ducked the bullets. I put Rifle's hair in one of my brand-new pockets. I followed the stories. I went looking for my family.

—Judge turned round in his chair and there was this boy, about ten years old, right behind him. Hanging onto the chair back, gun pointing straight at the judge's forehead. Good morning, judge, said the boy. That's my mama you been giving out to and I'd be right obliged if you'd apologise.

—Where did it happen?

The interruption annoyed the teller. But he saw my face; I didn't doubt.

—Straightback, Arkansas.

—Thanks.

I stood up and left them to it.

Women liked the leg, and I began to like it. I told them how I came to have it; I sent out letters of my own to my wandering family. I'd sit at the fire; I'd lift the trouser leg, enough to let the light caress the wood. People would shuffle, men would sit back, and give me room at the front of the sitting group. The night made the leg look new, almost flesh. There was a story for them there. Men stared at the leg; women stared at the man who owned it. And I told them how I got it. And, sometimes, a finger would reach out, and a fingertip would kiss the teak. And I began to feel like the fine man I used to be. The story became stories, and the stories went from fire to fire, and from state to state.

Sometimes I told the honest truth.

—I managed to grab the boy. He got into the car but I slipped. I went under the wheel.

—Oh Lord—!

—I didn't feel anything. Not at first, anyway. I heard it, going over. Like a slice.

—No!

360

—Sorry. And I felt it. I felt it ripping. The feeling. The sensation. But not the pain.

—My—!

—Until later.

—Of course.

—Where did this happen, son? asked a man whose wife or daughter had started crying.

There was always a crying woman and, nearly always, an angry man.

—Ransom, Kansas, I said.

—The leg buried there?

—Don't know, I said. —By the time I knew it was missing, it was too late to want it back.

—Does it pain you now?

A woman. Always a woman.

—Ah well, I'd say. —You get on with it, you know.

And, always – always – there were one or two who knew they could deal well with my pain and, sometimes, I'd let them try. We'd meet up on the third snore of the husband or da, away from the tents and tarpaper huts, away from the light of the fire, and I'd let them hold the wood and heal me.

—My, what made these marks on your other leg?

—The ball and chain.

—No end to your trials.

—Who're yeh telling.

And, sometimes, I told them a different truth.

—I was surrounded by the cops, right. All sides. So I had the leg off, like that—

—My Lord!

I'd jump, and stand on one foot.

—And I laid into the fuckers, before they knew what was happening. Skulled the lot of them.

—Where was this at, son?

—Dublin.

—Dublin?

—That's right, I said. —Ireland.

I'd left Dublin with both legs but I wanted them to know, Miss and Saoirse and Rifle, when they heard about the man with the wooden leg who'd beaten his way out of an ambush of fat rozzers, I wanted them to hear it – Dublin, Ireland – and they'd know: I was out there, looking for them.

I'd let them watch me strap the leg back on.

—You come a long ways on one leg, son.

—True.

—Hurt any?

—Now and again.

And they'd know then why I was taking my time.

I wandered, through the seasons, through the dust days and the grasshopper days. I followed the desperate logic of those years, and I told my tales and listened, and I waited to hear the big story. I waited for our stories to meet and become the one. The handsome man, the beautiful woman, the children. The leg, the gun, the happy ending.

I thought it would be soon, and I thought that for a long time. I made up more stories, sent out more and more.

—I ran out of the post office with the leg held high.

—The look on that young one's face, I swear to God, it was worth the leg. And, anyway, I still have the knee and it's grand.

They tried to make me King of the Hoboes, in a jungle outside Macbeth, Idaho. But I turned them down; I stuck to my guns, and hers.

—Up the fuckin' Republic!

I watched that story take off; I could see it fly along the tracks, junction to junction, to her, to them. The man who would not be king. The man who couldn't be someone else. The man who was on his way.

And, sometimes, I held back. I sat at the outside, or stood against a tree, let the limp stay a limp, kept the cloth over the leg. I stopped being my own story for a night or two, and I listened.

—That man crept out from under the caboose. And them Pinkertons was a-waiting for him. Thought they had him this time. They waited for him to stand up and take his beating. The bulls, and the local heavy-foots. And that mean bastard, Lima Slim.

—Heard of him.

—You sure did. They stood there, watching. Watching the blood. Watching the man stand up. Watching where there once was a leg but wasn't one no more. The land where the foot should've beed. The blood pouring out onto that dry land. Paid it such attention and respect, they never saw the leg. Heard the swinging same time they heard the knee hit the side of Lima Slim's head. He was down before they saw. And by then, there was two, three of them bastards lying down beside him, keeping company with the son of a bitch.

362

Your daddy's not a failure, was what the stories said. He's on his way, he's on his way. I knew they'd know when they heard them. They'd understand, and know. They'd know, and understand.

It was tempting to slip the leg off and hop into their centre, the story made flesh, and I did give in, once or twice. But, more often, the loneliness kept me still and quiet, and I listened for more, of them or me, a tale that would hint at where they were, or tell them where I was.

—Tell 'em One-Leg O'Glick's in town and any scab still here come morning is going to be chewing the dust.

I sent out plenty of Irish stories, but I never heard one come back. One-Leg O'Glick had become one of their own, a man wandering the heartland, forced further west. A man of their own ways and accent, a man who would stop their flight.

—He put that leg down in the dust and said, No further.

He'd stop on the road, on the track, the edge of someone else's town; he'd stop, and turn, turn back, and take back the miles and acres they'd lost, the jobs and loved ones, livestock and businesses, graves and homesteads. A man who was winning their fight for them, whose stories would let them retreat in shredded dignity. A man who had stopped being me.

The more I listened, the more I knew, and the less I heard of me.

—One-Leg Hancock, they call him.

One-Leg Hickock, One-Leg Lewis, Hop-along Jethro Dupree.

I stopped telling the stories. I put my ear to the tracks, and listened.

And I heard less and less, and nothing.

Rifle was the first to go. Last in, first out – a character for the times. He'd been in there for two years or more, growing big beside the stories. But then, gone. I listened – nothing. I moved and listened – nothing.

I got myself arrested. It was no big effort. Vagrancy was a crime at the harvest times; the country needed slaves. I picked cotton – I really did; I dragged the cotton bag behind me for three sore months. And, chained, I heard the older versions, from other men who were doing longer time. I hoped that I could trace their movements, and pick out where they'd lost Rifle. But it was her and her girl again, no boy, no son, no mention. And, free again, I crawled the Dustbowl, went back to where the stories had come from, and rooted for my boy. *Every day, in ev-ery way.* I listened. The hard dust got between the wood and stump, made every step and move a red and roaring pain. I listened. I stood on the wood, leaned hard, to keep it raw, to keep me far from sleep. I listened to the old ones left behind, who'd refused to go, living in holes. I listened at the last diners – Will's Eats, Carl's Lunch, Joe and Minnie – to the men who drove the tractors, the mechanics, and Will and Carl and Joe and Minnie.

—Heard tell there was a boy.

I crashed through the screen door. I'd no money but I stood at the counter.

—Heard that too.

—Got himself shot.

—I heard that.

—Drove her clear insane.

—Heard. Believe that's what would happen.

Bing Crosby from the radio. *Ti-pi-ti-pi-tin.* Benny Goodman, or Louis Armstrong.

—Heard different. Heard he coughed hisself to death.

—Heard that too.

Benny Goodman or Louis Armstrong.

—What was his name? I asked.

I wanted to run. I leaned hard on the leg.

—Jimmy Lou-is.

—My name is Henry Smart!

I lay on a rock in the Utah desert, years later – how long, how many? – and I gazed up at the huge black-blue sky, and I found the star. I always found it, I always knew its twinkle and fade – it could never hide or fool me. I'd stare at it, I'd still myself and stare, fix my eyes and refuse to let them stray to any of the other millions of its still and shooting siblings. Siblings, uncles, fathers, sons – all up there, but there was only one that I could ever recognise. I'd stare at that star till I knew I had it. I'd point the leg; I'd stab at it, and yell.

—My name is Henry Smart!

I'd watch it shimmer and fuss.

My voice was hard and triumphant, hard as the rock I was sitting on, cold as the air that was lying on top of me. There was no one else to hear me. My nearest neighbours were as distant as the stars above.

—My name is Henry Smart! The one and only Henry Smart! I'd watch its gases splutter and die.

—My name is Henry Smart!

I'd yell until I could no longer see its shadow against the blueness of the night, until there was nothing out there. I killed my brother every night. I killed the other Henry, the one who'd come before me, who'd taken my name when he died and went to heaven. I killed him, and I watched the space he'd filled. I watched and waited for Rifle. I waited for my little boy to shimmer and fuss; I looked for his rough twinkle.

—Come on!

I watched.

—Come on, Rifle! Come on!

I tried his other names.

—Séamus! Séamus Louis!

I tried them all.

—Rifle! Come on out! Please.

I tried them all.

—I was looking for you! Rifle!

I tried them all. I tried them all.

I tried them all.

His name arrived; we'd heard it spoken.

—Ruzafelt.

We heard relief in the voices, the arguments, and hope. *My fellow Americans*. But elections didn't interest me and Miss O'Shea. Nothing changed, unless we did the changing. We kept running. I fell from the train, and the families at the jungle fires still looked lost and hungry by the time I'd mastered the wood enough to go searching for my own family. The kids I saw in the boxcars and in the headlights that punched the trains' path through the dark, the young lads, the ancient-faced children, theirs were the faces I'd seen all my life, the runaways, the unwanted, damaged and, some of them, dangerous. They'd been riding the rails before Wall Street crashed; no change in the White House was going to mend their lives. The boxcars never emptied; the homeless stayed that way. Boys became sad-faced men as they clung to the roofs and faced west. The wise ones expected nothing.

I was never wise. I kept looking, even when the stories stopped. First Rifle, then Saoirse. She fell out of the stories, no longer

365

rode beside her mammy. *The only thing we have to fear is fear itself.* I listened, I asked – but there was no daughter; there never had been one. Our Lady walked alone.

I held the leg, I held it out before me, but I felt no water. There was none beneath. Roosevelt had done nothing to the dust. I wore the leg and wandered states and waited for the pull. I walked across cracked earth, over fences that divided nothing. I expected, every step. I expected the pain, and needed it. I expected and I prayed. I was Henry Smart and there would be water. I'd find it. I was Henry Smart. I had the power. I was Henry Smart. I leaned out of the racing train, held the leg over the land that blurred and dipped below my face. I waited.

I knew no words, I'd learnt no prayers. But I prayed. There were no corners in the desert but I made them in my head, built corners in my way, and hoped I'd find them when I turned the next one. *Please, please, please.* I prayed across the United States, and back across, and back; across the Mississippi – I heard the wheels grind against the bridge rails; I saw the sparks in the dark; they were stars that I could touch—

—My name is Henry Smart!

And I crossed the Great Divide. I went over it, first time, like a day out in the Wicklow Mountains, one good leg and all. It was early May, but freezing. And I smiled, that first time; I hummed, I fuckin' sang. *On the rocky road to Dubellin, one two three four five.* I knew they'd be smiling, waiting on the other side. *Please, please, please, please.* I walked through mountains and prairies, closed my eyes, saw palm trees when I opened them. I rode the Empire Builder, and smaller trains, and stopped at every junction. *See America First – Travel By Rail.* I woke up clinging to the side of a boxcar; beside me, a kid from Warsaw, frozen, stuck solid to the wall, dead. I jumped; I left him there. He travelled on, alone. I went wherever the new work was. I looked for faces; I stayed, I waited.

I crept back into the cities. I crept back into Chicago. I knew she'd never have gone back alone but I thought, by now, our daughter could have dragged her, to gawk, to live it, to brush against the city walls and glass. I went under the Michigan Avenue Bridge; I walked among the thousands of men and families who lay along the pavement, rolled in coats and *Tribune* blankets. I looked at faces, listened for accents, a cry of recognition. I came and went; I left Chicago twelve or thirteen times.

I stood in Bughouse Square, a week of hot, dry evenings, closed my eyes and waited to hear her shout the truth from a borrowed soapbox. I went out to Oak Park, watched Missis Lowe go, come back, leave the house empty, and fill it, all alone. I watched for attic lights; I gazed in the kitchen window, looked for toys or school books. I saw nothing I wanted, but I thought of Louis Armstrong. Oak Park was surviving the bad times; I saw no men selling apples, and Missis Lowe's coat wasn't too bald. But the South Side was dying, already dead. The music had made the whole mess sparkle, but the music couldn't do that any more – I heard no music. Black business was gone, and it hadn't gone elsewhere. I waited at the trolley but saw no Dora, no Ethel. I walked whole blocks and heard no music. My leg gave out the only beat.

—My name is Henry Smart!
  —My name is Henry Smart!
  —My name is Henry Smart!

I lost the time. I baked and froze, stopped understanding. I saw an old man. In a piece of mirror, cracked, made dull by damp, its jagged edge pushed into a trunk, in an abandoned jungle, somewhere. Anywhere. I saw the man. I made him open his mouth. I made him take a closer look. *My name is Henry Smart.* I looked again. It wasn't me.

The wandering kids went off to war and died. To Europe, the Pacific, North Africa. I didn't know there was a war.

I looked again. It wasn't me.

The hard times turned. The dust stopped messing, became good soil.

I looked again.

It wasn't me.

Dead blue eyes, white dirty beard, teeth shattered, gone; old wounds come back.

It wasn't me.

Frayed suspenders, gone to grey. A filthy grey fedora, sweated through, caked in dust.

It wasn't me.

★   ★   ★

—My name is Henry Smart!

I looked again.

A finger rubbed the glass. Breath burst upon it; the finger rubbed again.

Dead eyes. Washed blue, red veins turned to grey. Old man's bristle; cracked, dry lips – all grey. Dried skin, dirt in the corners of the mouth. I turned away.

He turned away.

—My name is—

He died. He walked into the desert. He walked. He crawled. He lay down in the desert, and he died.

He lay down. He waited. He died.

He waited.

Died.

Warm water. It dried up – warm, old water – evaporated against the inside of my mouth. I felt it, against my mouth, and on my neck. And I could smell it. And I felt the sun, hard on my eyelids, felt it pull my broken skin. My eyes roared where they should have watered; they were dry and baking, white, dead fishes' eyes. I could taste the water now, my tongue expanding, turning, and I could feel something on my lip, something hot and metal. I could smell.

Sweat.

And shadow now, across my eyes. The sun was blocked. I could feel the blade come off my eyelids.

I could smell sweat. A man – people, near me. All around me.

The water was in my throat. I coughed, felt it fight. Felt hands on me, my tongue fill in my mouth. Heard voices. Not words. Mumbling. Men. Their sweat.

I opened my eyes. I tried to. Black shadows – hat brims. Men. Making shade around me. I closed my eyes. Dragged dirt across them as I did.

Metal on my lip again. I closed my mouth – I felt skin break – around the metal. A spout – thicker.

Clean sweat. Clear voices. Polite, patient. Curious.

I coughed.

A hand touched my head.

Soft voices, whispers. Waiting. One big voice. Another. Impressive voices.

My head.

I was alive.

I sucked the water, felt it soak me. Felt the stone beneath me.

I'd died. I knew that. I'd stopped. I knew. There was a point, a time—. I'd stopped. I'd known that I was going. Closing. And I'd stopped knowing.

Now I was alive – burnt, sore, thirsty, hungry. I was alive. I was hungry and fuckin' thirsty.

I was bleached, alive. I was hard. I felt the stone.

The sweat of men who wore clean clothes, who sweated new each day. Who shaved and washed. And perfume. I could smell. Through dust and dirt and blood that blocked my nostrils, I could smell. The perfume.

I wasn't dying.

I was being born.

Hands on my body, on my clothes, pulling, lifting.

Pulling, lifting.

I could talk.

—Get your fuckin' hands off me.

—What did he say?

—Didn't catch it. What did you say?

Then the big voice.

—Give him more water.

I drank. Cooler water. I opened my eyes. Shadows, fewer of them. Had to close my eyes. Hands under my arms. This time, I let them lift. Someone behind me, holding me up, leaning into my back. I opened my eyes again. The sun was behind. I could see legs, feet. A dress, brown boots.

I couldn't lift my head.

Brown boots.

I couldn't lift my head. I wanted to.

A man beside me now. I saw his shirt, heard leather crack. A tall man. I forced my head to see. A new moustache, strong blue eyes.

—What's your name?

—What's your own fuckin' name?

They heard. The man stood. I heard the leather crack again. I heard their laughter.

Another voice, another man.

—Why, that's Henry Fonda.

—Who the fuck is Henry Fonda?

Another quick explosion, laughter. Civilised men.

I grabbed the canteen; the talk had killed me.

—Let him have it.

The big voice. The boss man.

I shook, I rattled, got water to my mouth. I could pull my head back. I could follow the brown boots as I drank. A red dress – it wasn't her – a skirt, a bright white, glaring blouse – it wasn't her – dark and gorgeous skin. It wasn't her.

—Who are you?

More laughter.

—Tell him.

The big voice again.

—That's Linda Darnell.

—Howyeh, Linda.

—Hi.

I could feel the sun again. Men were moving, leaving me alone. I watched Linda go; I could move my neck. A town in front of her, some sort of town, a church, not finished yet – a bell. The desert walked right up to the town. Men now too, going back to work.

I was looking at an old guy. He sat down beside me.

—Heat's a son of a bitch.

The big voice.

—Until you realise there's nothing else.

He was old, carved. His face was huge, and grey. He'd shaved that day; there was a small cut under his mouth. He pushed his cap back. I saw black glasses, thick lenses. I saw the eye patch. Black too.

—I bet that leg of yours has a story to tell, he said.

I said nothing.

—I bet.

This man was important. The men who lingered told me that. They were there for him, hovering. One of them was frightened; I could see that in his feet.

—I know where you come from.

I said nothing.

—Dublin.

I drank from the empty canteen.

—Right?

I took the canteen from my mouth and stopped looking at the sky.

He took it for a nod.

—Yeah, he said. —I know Dublin.

He stood up.

—What age are you?

I spoke.

—What year is it?

—Tell him.

Another voice.

—Why, it's 1946.

—I'm forty-five.

—Yeah, he said. —I knew you weren't as old as you look.

I stopped myself: I didn't touch my face.

—I've been looking for you.

But he wasn't going to kill me.

—You were there, he said. —You saw it. What's your name?

I coughed.

—It'll come back to me.

He wasn't going to kill me.

—You were there, he said again.

I knew what he was talking about.

—You tell me how you got that leg, I'll tell you how I got this eye.

—The leg's recent, I said.

—So's the eye, he said. —What about the rest of you?

I said nothing.

—Yes, he said. —You were there.

His hand now. He touched a scar on my cheek.

—Moore Street, he said.

A chip from a wall – 1916 – as I crawled out of a hail of bullets.

He touched the back of my neck.

—Kilmainham.

371

He was right.

He touched my forehead, the dents left there by nipples.

—You had a good war.

He was right.

—We'll talk, he said.

I heard him move. I heard him creak.

—We'll talk.

—You'll hear them call me Pappy, Coach. Other things.

He spoke quietly. The place was crowded and frantic. He'd given his orders before he came over. Now others were barking, getting them done.

—You call me Jack.

—No, I said. —I knew a Jack.

—One of the bad guys? he said.

I said nothing. He laughed. The place became more frantic.

—Seán, he said. —See your way to calling me that?

I nodded.

—You're the real thing.

—I fuckin' am.

—You fucking are. We'll talk.

I'd walked and crawled into a desert – I remembered – into the desert, deeper, and hotter. I'd pushed myself to the place where it was whitest. No real place at all, I'd thought. My last thought. An oven. I lay down. I waited to be eaten by the heat.

Two hundred yards from a film set. An actor called Fonda went out for a piss and found me.

I'd chosen the right place. Monument Valley – he told me the name – had no real economy or life. It was one of the cruellest places on the planet.

The desert was real, but the town was cut-out.

They were making a film and now I, the dead man, was in it. I was the local colour, an authentic taste of the west. As chiselled and wind-fucked as the rocks and the valley outside. The make-up department kept its distance.

My Darling Clementine. The gunfight at the O.K. Corral. Fonda was Wyatt Earp, and he was taking a break when he walked into the wilderness.

—Your luck was in, the old man told me: Seán. —The real Earp would've shot you. I knew him, you know.

—Who?

—Wyatt Earp.

—Never heard of him.

He looked at me. The patch didn't fool me: he could see with both eyes.

—I believe you, he said. —Remember your name yet?

—No.

—Fine.

He was John Ford.

—I make pictures. I'm from Ireland.

—Never heard of it.

—It'll come back to you, he said. —Same time as your name.

He held my arm.

—We're going to work together. Two fucking rebels.

He held my arm. He squeezed.

—In the meantime, here's what. The limey actor's on the table.

We were in a brand new saloon. The paint was wet, collecting sand. I could smell the varnish.

—The Clantons, the bad guys, are making him do the Shakespeare stuff. It's humiliating. The actor doing the Bard in these surroundings. Drunks, whores, Mexicans. Then Henry and Victor walk in—

He caught my look.

—A different Henry, he said. —Fonda.

He let go of my arm.

—A different Victor. Mature. I knew it was you.

—It's been a long day, he said.

I'd come back from the dead and starred in my first feature film, but I said nothing.

—I like the desert, he said. —But it ain't home.

I said nothing. We sat in rocking chairs, outside the saloon, under a sign that said The Mansion House.

—Miss it?

—What?

—Home.

—Never had one.

—I hear you, he said.

He took something from a pocket.

—I'm a restless son of a bitch myself.

It was a pipe in his hand. He lit it, took his time. I was cold. I liked it. I could smell the tobacco. I liked it.

—Every cowboy's a good actor. I was a cowboy. You ever a cowboy?

—I don't think so.

—Might have been?

I shrugged.

—But we both know what you *were*. And that's what our next picture is going to be about.

—What?

—You.

—Just me?

—You.

—There were others, I said.

—Fuck the others. It's your story. How'd an Irish rebel end up here? That's the real Irish story. We both know that. And that's the story we're going to tell.

He looked across the darkness, straight at me.

—You're the story.

It had been a long fuckin' day.

—Henry Smart, I said.

—That's it, he said.

I looked up at the black-blue sky, at the stars, at all the dead and the wandering.

—My name's Henry Smart!

This time, he said nothing.

I was going. Home? I doubted that. But I was ready to get right up and go there. I'd walk, old man, back from the dead, broken old man, with a leg of cheap wood; I'd walk right out of the desert. I'd walk across America, east, back the way I'd come. I'd walk on the ocean. Back. And I was going to tell my story. I was alive, still fighting.

I was alive. I was forty-five. I was Henry Smart.

To the authors of the following books, thank you:

Laurence Bergreen, *Louis Armstrong: An Extravagant Life*; Louis Armstrong, *Satchmo: My Life in New Orleans* and *Swing That Music*; Thomas Brothers (ed.), *Louis Armstrong – In His Own Words: Selected Writings*; Gary Giddins, *Satchmo*; Joshua Berrett (ed.), *The Louis Armstrong Companion*; Samuel A. Floyd Jr, *The Power of Black Music*; Robert Gottlieb and Robert Kimball, *Reading Lyrics*; Nancy Groce, *New York: Songs of the City*; Rick Kennedy, *Jelly Roll, Bix and Hoagy*; Rick Kennedy and Randy McNutt, *Little Labels, Big Sound*; Nat Shapiro and Nat Henton, *Hear Me Talkin' To Ya: The Classic Story of Jazz as told by the Men Who Made It*; Frederic Ramsey Jr and Charles Edward Smith (eds), *Jazzmen*; Dempsey J. Travis, *An Autobiography of Black Jazz*; Hoagy Carmichael, *The Stardust Road*; Nick Tosches, *Where Dead Voices Gather*; John Hammond, with Irving Townsend, *John Hammond on Record*; Mezz Mezzrow and Bernard Wolfe, *Really the Blues*; Alan Lomax, *Mister Jelly Roll*; Duke Ellington, *Music is My Mistress*; Ethel Waters, with Charles Samuels, *His Eye is on the Sparrow*; Ann Douglas, *Terrible Honesty: Mongrel Manhattan in the 1920s*; Jeff Kisseldoff, *You Must Remember This*; Samuel Fuller, *New York in the 1930s*; Henry Moscow, *The Street Book: An Encyclopedia of Manhattan's Street Names and Their Origins*; Georges Perec, with Robert Bober, *Ellis Island*; E.B. White, *Here is New York* and *Farewell to Model T*; Hasia R. Diner et al (eds), *Remembering the Lower East Side*; Harpo Marx, with Rowland Barber, *Harpo Speaks . . . About New York*; James Weldon Johnson, *Black Manhattan*; Alain Locke (ed.), *The New Negro*; Ric Burns, James Sanders and Lisa Ades, *New York, An Illustrated History*; Maren Stange, *Bronzeville: Black Chicago in Pictures 1941–1948*; Wayne F. Miller, *Chicago's South Side: 1946–1948*; David Garrard Lowe, *Lost Chicago*; Elizabeth McNulty, *Chicago – Then and Now*;

Nelson Algren, *Chicago – City on the Make* and *Never Come Morning*; Studs Terkel, *Chicago, Hard Times, My American Century* and *Talking to Myself: A Memoir of My Times*; Kenan Heise, *Chaos, Creativity and Culture: A Sampling of Chicago in the Twentieth Century*; Allan H. Spear, *Black Chicago: The Making of a Negro Ghetto (1890–1920)*; Herbert Asbury, *Gem of the Prairie* and *The Gangs of New York*; Frederick Lewis Allen, *Only Yesterday: An Informal History of the 1920s*; F. Scott Fitzgerald, *The Crack-Up, with Other Pieces and Stories*; Edward Behr, *Prohibition*; Stanley Walker, *The Night-Club Era*; Henry Allen, *What It Felt Like: Living in the American Century*; Gerald Leinwand, *1927 – High Tide of the 1920s*; Maury Klein, *Rainbow's End: The Crash of 1929*; Claude McKay, *Home to Harlem* and *Banjo*; Jean Toomer, *Cane*; Richard Wright, *Native Son*; Thomas Wolfe, *Look Homeward, Angel*; Carl van Vechten, *Nigger Heaven*; Ring Lardner, *You Know Me Al*; John Dos Passos, *Manhattan Transfer*; Sinclair Lewis, *Main Street*; John Steinbeck, *The Grapes of Wrath*; Upton Sinclair, *The Jungle*; James T. Farrell, *Young Lonigan, The Young Manhood of Studs Lonigan* and *Judgment Day*; Michael Ondaatje, *Coming Through Slaughter*; Woody Guthrie, *Bound for Glory*; Errol Lincoln Uys, *Riding the Rails: Teenagers on the Move During the Great Depression*; Roland Marchand, *Advertising the American Dream*; Gene Fowler (ed.), *Mystic Healers and Medicine Shows*; Peter Huston, *Scams From the Great Beyond*; Emile Coué, *Self Mastery Through Conscious Autosuggestion*; Michael Flanagan, *Stations: An Imagined Journey*; Robert S. Lynd and Helen Merrell Lynd, *Middletown: A Study in Modern American Culture*; William Foote Whyte, *Street Corner Society*; H. L. Mencken, *The American Language* and *Heathen Days (1890–1936)*; Zora Neale Hurston, *The Sanctified Church*; Walker Evans, *Signs*; Judith Keller, *Walker Evans: The Getty Museum Collection*; Lewis W. Hines, *The Empire State Building*; Joseph McBride, *Searching For John Ford*; Garry Wills, *John Wayne's America*; Gerald Peary (ed.), *John Ford Interviews*; James Durney, *Ciontiori: The History of Irish Gangsters in America*; Rich Cohen, *Tough Jews: Fathers, Sons and Gangster Dreams*; Jay A. Gertzman, *Bookleggers and Smuthounds: The Trade in Erotica 1920–1940*; David W. Maurer, *The Big Con: The Story of the Confidence Man*; Emily Thompson, *The Soundscape of Modernity*.

Thanks also to the many people who helped me with information, advice, music and caffeine.